Read the Crusade trilogy:

Crusade

Damned

Vanquished

Also by Nancy Holder and Debbie Viguié

Wicked
Witch & Curse

Wicked 2
Legacy & Spellbound

Resurrection

NANCY HOLDER
& DEBBIE VIGUIÉ

Simon Pulse

NEW YORK   LONDON   TORONTO   SYDNEY   NEW DELHI

SIMON PULSE

An imprint of Simon & Schuster Children's Publishing Division

1230 Avenue of the Americas, New York, NY 10020

First Simon Pulse edition August 2012

Copyright © 2012 by Nancy Holder and Debbie Viguié

All rights reserved, including the right of reproduction in whole or in part in any form.

SIMON PULSE and colophon are registered trademarks of Simon & Schuster, Inc.

For information about special discounts for bulk purchases, please contact Simon & Schuster Special Sales at 1-866-506-1949 or business@simonandschuster.com.

The Simon & Schuster Speakers Bureau can bring authors to your live event. For more information or to book an event contact the Simon & Schuster Speakers Bureau at 1-866-248-3049 or visit our website at www.simonspeakers.com.

Designed by Mike Rosamilia

The text of this book was set in Cochin.

Manufactured in the United States of America

2 4 6 8 10 9 7 5 3 1

Library of Congress Cataloging-in-Publication Data

Holder, Nancy.

Vanquished / by Nancy Holder and Debbie Viguié. — 1st Simon Pulse ed.

p. cm.

Summary: On the brink of the final battle against the Cursed Ones, the Salamancan hunters' internal bickering threatens their cause, and Jenn must try to rally her team while facing her own doubts, especially about her love for Antonio.

[1. Vampires—Fiction. 2. Guerrilla warfare—Fiction. 3. Supernatural—Fiction. 4. Sisters—Fiction. 5. Horror stories.] I. Viguié, Debbie. II. Title.

PZ7.H70326Van 2012

[Fic]—dc23

2012004795

ISBN 978-1-4169-9806-8 (hc)

ISBN 978-1-4169-9807-5 (pbk)

ISBN 978-1-4169-9810-5 (eBook)

For our Crusaders!
—N. H.

To all of the fans who
have joined in our Crusade
—D. V.

ACKNOWLEDGMENTS

Thank you so much to my amazing, creative, wonderful coauthor, Debbie, especially for agreeing with me that we will celebrate the publication of *Vanquished* with a trip to Disneyland. Thank you, Howard Morhaim, for being the fantastic agent and dear friend that you are, and to Alice Speilburg and Kate McKean of Morhaim Literary for everything they do. Thank you as well to our UK agent, Caspian Dennis. Many, many thanks to our editor, Annette Pollert, for your sense of humor, skill, and talent. We're definitely taking you with us to see the Mouse! My gratitude to everyone at Simon Pulse, especially our copyeditor, Karen Sherman. I'm grateful to my friends and family, especially my assistant, Erin Underwood; my daughter, Belle; and my sister, Leslie Ackel, for all that listening and helping and doing. Thanks to all our bloggers, reviewers, and webpals too.

—N. H.

With any book there are always so many people to be thanked. Thank you to my brilliant and talented coauthor, Nancy, or as I like to think of her, my sister-in-arms on this Crusade. Thank you to our magnificent agent, Howard Morhaim, and to Kate McKean and Caspian Dennis. Thank you to Alice Speilburg for helping to keep me sane. Thank you to Annette Pollert for being a wonderful editor and engaging in some of the most hilarious e-mail conversations that have ever existed. Thank you to the fans who have given this series so much support and enthusiasm. Thank you to my husband, Scott, and my parents, Richard and Barbara Reynolds, for supporting me and encouraging me constantly. Thank you to Juliette Cutts and Anthony and all those who came out to see us while we were on tour. I have to also thank my friends, who are eternally patient and forgiving despite the fact that there are sometimes months when I don't have the time to even say hi. So, Ann, Calliope, Teresa, Marissa, and Chrissy, thanks for everything!

—D. V.

BOOK ONE
MÓRRÍGAN

The breeze blew from the turret
As I parted his locks;
With his gentle hand he wounded my neck
And caused all my senses to be suspended.

—St. John of the Cross,
sixteenth-century mystic of Salamanca

CHAPTER ONE

They say that it's always darkest before the dawn. I know it's a cliché that's meant to give people courage when everything seems hopeless, but it's actually true.

My team has spent our nights struggling against the Cursed Ones, counting the seconds until the sun would rise and deliver us from evil, terror, and death. Battling with our last ounces of strength, about to die but holding on for that flash of light as the sun begins to climb the horizon. But there's something else that happens in those moments before daybreak, something far more terrifying than darkness:

Silence.

Silence so terrible, so absolute, it's as if the whole world is holding its breath. It makes you feel incredibly alone, even if there is someone standing beside you.

And right now, that silence is killing me. Everything has fallen apart. My sister is missing. Is Heather alive, dead, alone, with other vampires? No one can say. Skye, our White Witch, was kidnapped by Estefan, her ex, during the last battle with Aurora. Our master, Father Juan, has cast the runes to try to find Heather and Skye, but they've given him no answers. They are silent—as silent as Eriko and all our other dead. We dug their graves in the rubble of our home, the University of Salamanca. We told them good-bye with prayers and tears . . . and their silence broke our hearts.

Even those of us who are here barely speak. Holgar is mourning the death of the werewolf he was once promised to. He had to kill her in the battle. Would I ever be able to do that? Jamie shuts himself away from the rest of us for hours. I know he's working on two guns, one to kill werewolves and one to dust vampires. And our team has one of each. Sade is so traumatized by the massacre that she can barely speak.

Father Juan spends every waking moment on his knees in the chapel, praying in silence for us all. Noah passes the time cleaning weapons and working out.

There's been no word from the outside world,

no way of knowing how my grandmother and mom are doing. There's no whisper of the men with black crosses. No news about anything. Even "Kent," the Voice of the Resistance, is silent here—we don't have a radio, and we're in Spain, which is probably too far away for him to broadcast, anyway.

And Antonio

His silence is the worst for me. When Aurora reawakened his bloodlust, he went on a killing spree back in Las Vegas. He was a monster. A butcher. Skye and Father Juan cast spells to reclaim his goodness, but they can't be sure they worked. Antonio won't even look at me. I know he's afraid of hurting me, or killing me. I want to talk to him, tell him that I know he wouldn't do that.

But maybe I would be lying.

So this cursed silence has fallen between us, and it's worse than the silence around us.

And me? I know my place now. I understand what I have to do, but until Father Juan can point us in a direction, there is nothing to do but wait. In silence.

—from the diary of Jenn Leitner, retrieved from the ruins

The Hell Fire Caves, Outside London
Skye and Estefan

Skye York screamed at the top of her lungs, but she made no sound. Her blond dreadlocks were powdered with vampire ash and soot, and her black petticoats hung in tatters above her knee-high boots. Beneath her bustier, the gargoyle tattoo at the small of her back burned, pouring white-hot fire through her nerve endings. She was nearing her breaking point.

Estefan had been torturing her for what seemed like years, but it couldn't have been that long. She hadn't had anything to eat or drink since he had kidnapped her, and though she was dehydrated, she hadn't died of thirst. Still, though the pain was unbearable, her tears had all dried up.

He had dragged her back into the Hell Fire Caves, chambers of flint and chalk beneath the Dashwood family seat. Sir Francis Dashwood was said to have reigned over the notorious Hell Fire Club in the 1750s, when powerful Dark Witches had conducted unspeakable rituals. The caves remained a trendy partying spot for witches who flirted with the darker side of magick. Skye and Estefan had partied there almost three years ago—before she had known he was a liar and a killer. Now he had her chained to a rock wall in the same spot where he had kissed her one night and asked her if she would move back to Spain with him.

It was ironic, then, that he had dragged her from Spain back to England. Why had he bothered to bring her all the way here from Salamanca? Where was Aurora, the evil vampire he worked for? Had Aurora been staked in the last battle? What about Skye's friends, her teammates? Were they alive or dead? She had tried asking Estefan, but he had just laughed. The worst part was, she wasn't sure he even knew.

He only seemed interested in tormenting her. He rippled shocks of magicks over her skin, burning her without leaving a mark, making her muscles quiver and contract until she shook.

Why doesn't he just kill me?

"Because I love you," Estefan said, stepping from the shadows. There were dark splotches on his tight jeans and black silk shirt. Her blood.

The Spaniard, with his charming accent and macho swagger, had easily enticed an innocent fourteen-year-old Skye. His attributes, which had once seemed dark and mysterious, were just brutal and sadistic now.

Skye wished she had never met him, but then she would never have fled him to Salamanca and the Spanish training school where she had learned to fight vampires. She would never have met her friends or her fighting partner, Holgar.

Holgar. Thoughts of him kept her going. Kind and generous, he was also the strongest person she knew. Now, as her knees buckled and she hung from the iron manacles around her wrists, she let herself fantasize about what he'd do to Estefan when he found her.

"Your friends aren't going to find us," Estefan said.

He had been wandering freely through her mind, torturing it even more cruelly than her body, inserting himself into her thoughts, obscuring her memories, conjuring new ones.

At least, she prayed to the Goddess that these memories weren't real. She wouldn't be able to live with herself. She saw herself here, in this cave, performing Black magick, drinking blood, pledging her loyalty to the Cursed Ones. She knew that Estefan had done all those things. But what had she done? She had been under his spell when she'd gotten the gargoyle tattoo on the small of her back. She actually remembered it, but the memory was detached, as if she were watching herself from a distance.

I'm seeing it through Estefan's eyes, she realized.

"That's right," he chuckled. "You were drunk when you got that tattoo. You told me that love is forever, and you swore to love me always."

Her girlish crush on him hadn't come close to touching such a sacred emotion. What was it Father Juan had said in one of his sermons? *Perfect love casts out fear.* What they'd felt for each other certainly hadn't been love. Looking into Estefan's cold, glittering eyes, she realized he was incapable of understanding, let alone living, that truth.

She squeezed her eyes shut, but she still saw his face in her mind. He laughed at her. He touched her cheek, and she turned her head to bite him, but her teeth just snapped together painfully.

He had been drugging her—she knew that—to keep her from spell casting. Her energy was too depleted to use magick to escape. But the drugs were wearing off. Hope surged through her, and she tried to test the chain around her wrist. She couldn't move.

Horror swept over her as she realized that Estefan had changed his game—he had paralyzed her. And it wasn't only her body that he had in an iron grip. He flashed impressions of everything that had terrified her since she was a little girl. In her mind he showed her images of them kissing, whispering romantic promises to each other, which filled her with shame. Well, two could play at that game.

Skye pictured Holgar. Funny Holgar, howling uncontrollably during the ambush back in Russia and looking so shocked at himself, and then laughing hysterically about it. She loved his sense of humor. More than once it had made the misery of a situation bearable for everyone. Sweet Holgar, who offered his shoulder as a pillow when they were sleeping on the snow-covered ground in the forest. Strong Holgar, carrying her on his back even though he was injured, then protecting her seconds later by ripping out the throats of attacking vampires and werewolves.

She could feel Estefan watching, observing, wondering why she was thinking of Holgar Vibbard. *Good.* The distraction might weaken his spell.

She let herself imagine Holgar as she'd never actually seen him—his face glowing with love. She thought about kissing him, working hard to make it seem like a memory and not just a fantasy. Estefan's startled thoughts flared like lightning as his emotions began to skitter out of control. Jealousy, rage, hate.

She was playing a dangerous game, one that could backfire. Fury provided power to those who used the darker arts. She doubted Estefan was that skilled, though. In place of magickal training, he had relied on his looks and charisma to get much of what he wanted. Skye, on the other hand, had been brought up very strictly in White magick. Estefan might have power, but she had knowledge on her side.

She pushed deeper, showing herself passionately kissing Holgar as they lay in the snow. Holgar sliding his hand up her leg as they pressed against each other outside the University of Salamanca beneath the moonlight, their desire blessed by the silver smile of the Lady Goddess.

Estefan's emotions surged and crashed like stormy waves. And as with the surf that touches the sand, then recedes, she began to slip through his fingers.

Growing hopeful, she pushed harder.

She envisioned making out with Holgar in their Las Vegas hotel. She imagined his hands moving over her, and was surprised at the sudden flash of heat and desire that filled her in response.

She also felt Estefan's wild stabs of jealousy. The threads of his magickal web frayed as his mastery over himself—and her—threatened to snap.

Skye pictured more kissing, more touching.

Estefan gasped. Though she couldn't see his face, she sensed he was caught in the grip of frenzied near madness. The last time they'd been together, she had set him on fire—literally—to escape him. He'd hunted her ever since, to wreak his revenge.

Empowered by his weakness, she let real memories slide through too, memories that were sweet or intimate in their own way. Kindness and tenderness were foreign to Estefan and therefore something the two of them had never shared—and never could. But for her they could be used as wellsprings of White magick—power he didn't possess. And so she let herself think of Holgar tenderly. She remembered when, after one full moon, she had brought him his clothes and let him out of his cage. She'd lifted the tarp that covered his cage to find him still asleep. Naked.

She had quickly turned away, as Holgar whispered—

Noooo! Estefan screamed inside her mind. His control loosened almost completely. And she knew what she had to do next.

She conjured an image of herself entering Holgar's cage, then pulling the tarp back down. She watched Holgar drowse awake as she'd seen him do a dozen times. But then she created a vision of Holgar looking at her with love and joy in his eyes. Holgar reaching for her, and herself reaching for him.

Then Holgar curled himself around her, nuzzling her nose to nose. Sweetly, he cupped her cheek and very slowly and deliberately pushed down the bodice of her blouse just a little. She laughed. They kissed. Kissed harder. The warmth between them heated, then blazed—the greatest gift of the Goddess—as Holgar tore off her clothes and—

Estefan slapped her across the face, and Skye was finally able to scream.

The shrill sound echoed through the caves as Skye grabbed Estefan's wrist. Yanking him toward her, she pulled the power of his Dark magicks and the energy of his consuming jealousy from him and into herself. Taking back what he had cost her—her self-will, and her self-respect—as she grabbed his face.

Estefan grunted.

She screamed again and it boosted her dominion over his power. Anger surged through her, and she used it, growing stronger as he grew weaker. Gritting his teeth, Estefan struggled against her, but purpose and desperation fueled her. Finally she let go, and he fell to the ground with a cry.

"Stay away from me," she hissed. She stared down at him as he sprawled, panting, on the rocky cave floor.

He'll never leave me alone. I should kill him. But I can't. It goes against everything I was raised to believe.

12

The thought made her shiver. Everything she was *raised* to believe. *Did* she believe it was wrong to kill him, even in self-defense?

She wouldn't—couldn't—answer that question now. She had to get away. As she focused on that thought, a burst of energy swelled from within her, shattering the manacles around her wrists.

"No," he rasped.

Skye made a wide berth around him as she stumbled forward. Everything hurt, but she couldn't spare the time or energy to heal herself until she was safe.

Winding her way through the shadowy cave, she staggered out of the darkness and into the bright sunlight. It blinded her, and she tripped, falling to the ground and knocking the air from her lungs.

She scrabbled to her feet as a roar came from behind her. Spinning around, she saw Estefan lurching toward her, his face wild with hatred, his eyes glowing red like a vampire's.

Panicking, Skye threw up her hands. *"Incendio!"*

And just like a vampire, he began to burn, just as he had two years before—the first time she had set him on fire. Near this very spot he had sworn to bind her to the vampires, with or without her consent; she had burned him then, as she burned him now.

Orange flames dancing over his skin like an aura, he screamed, falling back into the opening of the cave. A sob burst out of her. She had harmed Estefan grievously. That was not the way of the Goddess. White Witches were never, ever permitted to hurt another living human being.

I had to do it, she told herself. *My Lady will understand. And besides, I don't think Estefan is completely human.*

He had saved himself before. He wouldn't die. There weren't even any scars from her first attack.

She ran, trying to outrace her own fear. She was in England. She had friends, family. They had to help. They just had to.

How long had Estefan had her? What had happened back at Salamanca? Was Holgar alive? Jenn? Father Juan? She had to find out. But first she needed a place to hide, and food and drink. Estefan's torture had taken a toll on her body. The energy she had extracted from him would only sustain her a few more minutes. She was weaker than she had realized.

Skye fell again and pushed herself back to her feet with a sob. She had to think. Where could she go?

She, like Holgar, would be an outcast to her family. She had run away. She fought vampires. Her family was resolute about doing no harm to any creature, no matter how foul or evil they were. That was why the Yorks, along with most witches, had gone underground when the war started. She imagined she would not be welcome, but there was no choice. She needed to hide.

She had to go home.

Toledo, Spain
The Survivors of Salamanca: Jenn, Antonio, Holgar, Jamie, Father Juan, Noah, and Sade

Seated in a beautifully carved but very uncomfortable monastery chair, Jenn stared at her journal as her frustration simmered. She had asked Father Juan to perform stronger magicks to help them locate Skye, but so far he hadn't come up with anything. Jenn knew how terrified Skye had been of her ex, and she tried not to think about what Estefan Montevideo might be doing to her.

Exhaling and closing her journal, Jenn stood up and headed for the chapel, knowing she'd find Father Juan there. Incense and the smell of candle wax wafted toward her as she pushed open the arched wooden door. A large crucifix hung above the altar, which was strewn with flowers. To the left of the altar, before a large statue of Mary, small votives flickered. The faithful had been asking her for favors, for help.

In the pew closest to the statue Father Juan knelt in prayer—and he wasn't alone. Antonio was beside him, head bowed, eyes closed. Jenn's breath caught in her throat as she stared at Antonio. His dark, curly hair wisped around his ears. His ruby cross earring once again sparkled in his left ear. Antonio had cast it away after Aurora had broken his humanity, returning him to the fiend he had been when

15

he was first converted into a vampire. Jenn had found the earring on the stairs leading to Aurora's penthouse and rescued it. She took it as a good sign that he was able to wear it without it burning his skin. Antonio was the only vampire they knew of who could touch a cross.

Antonio stirred, having heard her or smelled her, or both. He touched Father Juan on the shoulder. After a moment they both crossed themselves, bowed on one knee as they left the pew, and faced her.

Jenn swallowed down all her wanting and grief. Antonio seemed so distant, even when she could reach out and touch him. She folded her arms to keep herself from doing so.

"Jenn?" Father Juan asked softly.

"There's a war to be fought," she said. "And we can't do it if we're hiding here."

A look flashed across Antonio's face. She couldn't tell if it was pride or fear.

Father Juan sighed. "I understand your impatience."

"No," she said carefully, "I don't think you do."

They each raised an eyebrow at her.

"The two of you are used to spending hours, days, praying and meditating. Meanwhile the rest of us are just *waiting*, alone with our own thoughts, and trust me, none of them are happy right now."

"We haven't given up," Antonio said quietly.

"This feels like surrender to me," she retorted. "It's only

a matter of time before Jamie goes off on his own and does something stupid or Sade completely loses it."

"What do you suggest we do?" Father Juan asked.

"Enough with the skirmishes. It does us no good to kill a dozen, a hundred, even a thousand vampire foot soldiers. They can convert more in a heartbeat. We need to eliminate the leadership." She frowned. "We shouldn't have let Greg and the other black crosses stop us from attacking Solomon in Washington when he held that press conference with the president."

"I'm not so convinced Solomon *is* the real power," Father Juan said, glancing at Antonio. "Not after what we saw in Salamanca."

"Even if he's not, he certainly thinks he is," Jenn replied. "And so do most of the civilians out there. If we could take him out—"

"We can't worry about him right now," Antonio broke in. He winced and turned away.

What is up with him? she wondered.

"We think we might have found something," Father Juan said slowly, giving Antonio a concerned glance. "Some*one*."

"What? Who?" Jenn asked.

"My grandsire," Antonio whispered without looking at her. "Lucifer, the father of all this misery."

Antonio was in hell.

He couldn't imagine someplace worse, or a more apt description for what it was he was suffering. Even glancing at Jenn made him yearn to drain her. He still struggled with his bloodlust. It was dangerous for him to be around anyone, even Father Juan.

And Jenn was going through her own changes. Since her knock-down, drag-out fight with Jamie six days earlier, she carried herself differently. She seemed stronger, more aloof.

She's become the leader Father Juan knew she would.

Antonio was so proud of her, even though he mourned the loss of her innocence, which had so charmed him. *She's been through too much to ever go back.*

They all had.

Jenn was right. They needed to act soon—if for no other reason than they couldn't hide where they were much longer. Father Sebastian, the monastery's abbot, had given them sanctuary. But there were three other priests in residence, and Father Sebastian had warned Father Juan that they were loyal to Rome. The Church had outlawed vampire hunters and declared that anyone caught helping them would be excommunicated—cast out from the Catholic community. It was only a matter of time before one of the loyalists figured out who the team was and reported them— and turned in Father Sebastian for aiding them.

Antonio tried to swallow his bitterness. He would never have believed that his beloved Church would turn its back on the hunters they had spent centuries training to fight the Cursed Ones.

The world was upside down.

Holgar had killed a woman he loved.

Jenn, the leader of a vampire-hunting team, was in love with him, a Cursed One.

And he, Antonio de la Cruz, was drowning in guilt and remorse, not only for the lives of the innocents he had so recently snuffed out, but for killing his sire, Sergio Almodóvar, at the last battle against Aurora.

His guilty conscience was proof that he was insane. Killing Sergio before he could harm Jenn's sister—or any human being—had been the right thing to do. Watching Sergio fall into the fiery pit in Salamanca had brought a rush of relief. A burden had lifted once and forever—Sergio loved to kill churchmen, and when Antonio had served in Sergio's court, he had killed seven Catholic faithful for him. Why then was he feeling so sinful? Replaying Sergio's death, torturing himself with it. He hadn't told Father Juan of his torment. He didn't need to give anyone more reason to distrust him.

Especially Jenn.

Ay, mi alma, he thought, crossing himself. My soul.

His soul, named Jenn.

MADRID, SPAIN
AURORA

In the ruins of the palace once inhabited by a Spanish princess, Aurora raged with grief.

Sergio was dead.

In fury she paced back and forth on a cracked black marble floor, hurling an empty bottle of sangria at a stained-glass window of some idiotic saint. The window shattered, revealing the bone-white moon hanging above the ravaged garden.

If anyone was going to kill that bastard, she should have been the one to do it. Not that she was planning to before Antonio de la Cruz had stolen her choice from her.

I hate him. I hate Antonio more than I have ever hated anyone.

She cast a contemptuous gaze at the minion cowering before her, a vampire who had fought the hunters at Salamanca and lived to tell the tale. He was terrified of her, which was good. His knees shook.

He's too weak to be an effective lieutenant. Actually, too weak to be allowed to live.

She reached out with both hands, grabbed his head, and twisted it from his neck. For one second the lieutenant's eyes blinked at her in shock, and then all of him, head and body, transmuted into dust.

That made her feel a little better.

As she wiped her hands on a nearby chaise, she just wished she could do the same to Antonio. And to Estefan. The Dark Witch had gotten his prize, the girl Skye, and fled the battle without a word.

He would pay for deserting her.

But first Aurora would leave Madrid. In a few hours she would be with her sire. When Lucifer called, none dared ignore it. Love and fear mingled within her at the thought of seeing him again. She would have to tell him about Sergio's death, though Lucifer probably already knew. Her dark lord knew everything.

He probably even knows that I captured Antonio and then lost him.

She shuddered at what he might do to her for that blunder. There was nowhere in this world or the next that she could hide from Lucifer, and she would go to him with her head held high.

But first she had once last thing to attend to.

"Come," she commanded.

One of her fledglings entered the room silently. The young girl's arms were full of white satin. She inclined her head to Aurora, who felt her throat actually constrict with unspent emotion.

It was time.

Aurora beckoned the girl forward, and the little thing held out the white gown. It was reminiscent of the style of the Spanish royal court when Aurora had been alive. Aurora had died in 1490, becoming a vampire to escape the Spanish Inquisition.

With a sense of ceremony, Aurora disrobed, and the fledgling helped her don the heavy costume, slipping her arms into the white embroidered sleeves. Experiencing again the confinement of the small, stiff hoops that created the slender bell shape of the skirt, Aurora held herself regally, her posture impeccable.

Then the servant helped her arrange her long, raven-black hair, entwining lilies in it as she piled it on Aurora's head. When she was finished, Aurora fought the urge to glance in the mirror. She was more than five hundred years old, yet it still startled her when she could not see her own reflection.

The dress was beautiful, and she knew that modern society would have assumed she was a bride, and not in deep mourning. The royal court in her time had favored white for funerals. It felt more appropriate to honor Sergio in that way than with the modern black.

"How do I look?" she asked the fledgling.

"Like a beautiful ghost," the girl said with a faint smile.

Better that than a corpse. Or a pile of ash scattering slowly in the breeze.

"*Bueno*, I'm ready," Aurora announced, stepping through bits of brittle colored glass and vampire dust.

The woman walked ahead and opened the door, and Aurora glided out. She descended a circular stone staircase to the main hall, where nearly two dozen of her most loyal followers waited. At her request they too had dressed in white, although they had opted for modern styles of clothing—suits and formal gowns. She didn't begrudge them that.

Leading the way, she left the house and walked slowly toward El Retiro Park. The others fell in step behind her, a funeral cortege, many carrying blood-red roses or lilies, others crystal decanters and simple glass jars filled with blood. Along the route some human passersby stopped to stare. Others fled.

Aurora kept her eyes straight ahead, allowing herself to think more fully about Sergio than she had in years. Memories, both good and hideous, flooded her like a rushing river. Sergio had been magnificent and arrogant, passionate and unpredictable. He had been her one great love. He had also been willful, reckless, cruel, and insensitive. She had hated him as much as she had loved him.

He made me feel so alive.

Sergio had worshipped the dark god Orcus. Orcus no longer possessed active temples or followers. There was nowhere she could go to respect that part of Sergio. So she had chosen instead their favorite trysting spot in the city of Madrid.

Inside the park, the procession wound to the Fountain of the Fallen Angel. Meant to depict Lucifer as he was being cast out of heaven, it had always been their private joke. The sculptor who had fashioned it had given the Fallen Angel the face of a very different Lucifer: their vampiric sire.

Silently, the mourners circled the fountain. Emilio, an aged vampire Aurora and Sergio had both held in esteem, stepped forward, an ebony-and-maroon leather volume in his hand. He opened it and began to read the words he had written for the occasion.

"Immortality—the greatest of gifts—must not be approached with trepidation. Life is not something to be sipped, but to be grasped with both hands and bled for all its worth. This fire—this passion—sustains, nourishes, uplifts, illuminates all. We are blessed, not cursed, to understand, to taste the finest fruits of the universe."

He closed the book. "None knew this more than Sergio Almodóvar. Filled with bloodlust, the finest of killers, he was a vampire who knew how to live. Sergio himself would remind us that though we may have eternity, it can be taken from us in the twinkling of an eye. Every moment must be savored to its last drop of potential in the chance that it is to be our last."

A stricken sigh passed through the assembly. Immortality denied was a terrifying tragedy. Humans were born doomed. Vampires . . . spared.

"We are here to honor his memory and to commit his soul to Orcus," Emilio continued. "God of Light, God Below, look upon your most loyal son with favor."

Around Aurora the others stirred, reflecting on the dark god or goddess they themselves worshipped. Like humans, vampires followed many deities, worshipped in many ways. For some, their underworlds were ruled by beings connected with light and the returning of their souls. For Aurora Abregón, there was only one thing that felt right. She rent her clothes, as her Jewish ancestors had done, ripping the finery with vampiric strength, and she wailed— mourning in the style of the ancient Romans, of Orcus.

Those who had brought flowers ringed them around the

base of the fountain. Those who had brought blood spilled it into the waters—an offering and a remembrance.

I will remember you. I will never forget who did this to you.

As she let out another cry, her heart was truly broken. Aurora would not have killed Sergio, had she had the chance. She knew that she would have forgiven him for every wretched, horrible slight, every cutting insult, every wrong he had committed against her.

She might have tortured him for a few weeks, but she would have declared the slate wiped clean.

Fueled by her passions, Aurora led the procession back to the crumbling palace. But even as she thought of the banquet that was waiting, her misery was so great that she had no hunger. She was too angered by her grief to eat anyone.

"My friends," she said, facing the assembly. "Sergio must be avenged. Swear a blood oath with me that you will kill his assassin—the traitor Antonio de la Cruz." She raised her left hand and sliced a fingernail across her palm. Blood welled up and began to drip as the others followed suit. Under the moonlight the vampires bled.

"He is as good as dead," Emilio said; the others inclined their heads.

And Aurora smiled.

CHAPTER TWO

Salamanca Hunter's Manual:
The Eternal Battle
It may feel as if your struggles against the Cursed
Ones are endless. This is true. The enemy can—
and will—create more of his kind, and all of
them seek your death. So you may question if
your holy calling has meaning, and why you
must press on when fortune favors you so little.
Remember this: The Savior, too, had doubt, and
yet He prevailed when it mattered most. If you
fight without ceasing, dedicating your soul to
the conquering of the foe, you will receive the
ultimate reward—not in this world, but the next.

(translated from the Spanish)

MADRID, SPAIN
HEATHER AND AURORA

I'm starving. I need blood, Heather Leitner thought as she crouched in the overgrown gardens outside Aurora's ruined palace. Her threadbare jeans and shredded sweater were barely distinguishable from her hair and skin. She was coated from head to toe with dirt and dried blood. She looked like an animal—or a nightmare.

She was faint with hunger, and she had trouble remembering how she'd tracked Aurora to Madrid. During the battle in Salamanca, Aurora's vampire army had piled into trucks and vans, and Heather had yanked open the car door of an unsuspecting motorist unlucky enough to be in the vicinity, dragged him out, and taken off after them.

Did I kill the driver? Did I drink his blood?

She was drawing a blank. Or maybe she couldn't face the truth. If she had drunk of him, would she still be this hungry?

She closed her eyes, sick to her soul at the thought. To bite a human being, to drink their blood. It sounded . . .

. . . wonderful.

Clenching her fists, she swayed with weakness as she studied the silhouettes of the Cursed Ones through the stained glass. Which one was Aurora?

"I'll kill you," Heather whispered, feeling her fangs

pressing against her thin, chapped lips. "I swear to God I'll turn you into dust."

If she didn't drink from a living creature, she would lose the fragile hold she had on her sanity. And Heather had to stay sane.

So she could kill Aurora.

Toledo, Spain
The Salamanca Hunters Minus Skye

In the courtyard of the ancient Toledo monastery, Jenn made a double fist and flung herself at Noah. The hardened Israeli soldier dropped to the ground and swept out his leg, grinning at her when, unable to stop her momentum, she tumbled forward and face-planted in the dirt. Then he grunted in surprise as she rolled onto her back, grabbed his ankle, and yanked it toward her chest. He teetered for a moment, then fell on his butt.

"Ha!" she shouted. Before she could gloat any further, Noah straddled her, catching her wrists in one hand as he mimicked slashing her throat with his other.

"How did you do that?" she managed between gulps of air as he sprang to a standing position, then pulled her to her feet.

They were both wearing clean white T-shirts and sweatpants, courtesy of the brothers in the monastery. Their feet were bare. Noah's hair was crazy wild from the tussle, but it only added to his allure. He had freckles across his nose, like her, and his dark eyes were almost as heavily lashed as Antonio's.

Antonio. Jenn drew a slow, steadying breath. She had hoped that sparring with Noah would take the edge off her tension, not add to it. After all, there was no her and Antonio. Before leaving America for Spain, Antonio had shut the door on any hope of their having a relationship. He had told her that he was renewing his vows of poverty, obedience, and chastity to the Catholic Church. He'd been studying to become a priest when Sergio had changed him into a vampire, and Antonio believed that only through prayer and strict observance of his holy orders could he keep from becoming a depraved, soulless Cursed One forever.

"How did I do that? I let you take me," Noah said, as he sidled away from Jenn and took a sip of water from a glass on a wooden tray. He tipped back his head and poured a little of the water over his face. "Then I came in for the kill."

He grinned at her, then grabbed a pack of cinnamon gum from the tray, pulled out two sticks, and handed her one. He was trying to quit smoking because it bothered her, and cinnamon gum was his weapon of choice. It also happened to be her favorite flavor.

"Krav Maga?" Jamie said, coming up behind Jenn. Without the chance to shave his head, he'd let caramel fuzz obscure some of his tattoos. Jamie was a Northern Irish street fighter with tons of anger issues. "We were teaching our tricks to Marc Dupree. Jenn mention him? We got him killed in New Orleans."

Noah stared back at Jamie. "I thought Jenn beat that lippy crap out of you."

Jamie flushed and made a show of adjusting his Adam's apple, which Jenn had dislocated during their fight in the cave. He smiled sourly at her, and she tensed, angry and wary. She should have known Jamie would never really accept her as his leader.

"Talking shite's a bad habit of mine," Jamie said, which was probably the closest he would get to an apology. Still, it meant a lot to hear it, and Jenn relaxed slightly.

Noah chomped his gum. "Habits can be broken."

Jamie ignored his comment. "May as well smoke 'em while I've got 'em. I've got nothing better to do." He pulled a cigarette from behind his ear and fished a lighter out of his jeans pocket. He lit the cigarette. The pungent scent of burning tobacco irritated Jenn's nose as he exhaled, blowing smoke at Noah, taunting him with forbidden fruit; the two had been smoking buddies before Noah quit.

"We *have* something to do," Jenn said. "We're having a meeting about it tonight, after dinner."

Appraising her, Jamie took another drag on his cigarette. "You're one for the mysteries. Why not just tell us now?"

Because it's daytime, and the sunshine makes Antonio tired and sluggish, and I want him at his best when we discuss our next move, she thought.

Without replying, she sauntered out of the courtyard.

"Stones. That girl's grown 'em."

She didn't know if she was meant to hear Jamie, but she smiled grimly to herself. If Jamie had respect for her new-found toughness, it had come at quite a price. Becoming a leader meant changing—a lot. She'd done things she wished she were incapable of doing. And would do them again.

Noah and Antonio were seasoned soldiers—Antonio had fought in World War II, and he carried battlefield scars both inside and out. Noah had been in the Israeli special forces—the Mossad—when the vampire war had broken out. Father Juan had privately counseled Jenn never to ask Noah about his missions.

"You wouldn't want to know," he'd told her.

But as the leader of a vampire hunting team, she knew she should ask. She needed to know what he was capable of. There were darker times ahead, which would require darker deeds.

Then there was Jamie. He wasn't troubled by ethics or morality. For Jamie it was kill or be killed, with no further discussion necessary. Eriko had been the only calming influence on him, and now that she was dead, it seemed that the only way to get Jamie to calm down was to knock him out.

I'd have no problem doing that, she thought, as she rapped softly on the housekeeper's door. She opened it gently and crossed from the simple sitting room to the bathroom. Señora Nevado had offered the use of her bathtub to Sade and Jenn, the only two women on the Salamancan hunting team—until they found Skye. Of course, no one used the word "hunting" anymore. To appease the Cursed Ones, the Catholic Church had ordered all vampire hunters to stand down and, if they weren't Spanish, to go home. Jenn's team was disobeying, and theoretically, Father Juan had been excommunicated. No longer part of the Church and no longer a priest, he wasn't to say Mass or give communion—but he'd done both since. Antonio, himself a very strict Catholic, had assisted Father Juan at Mass and taken communion from the priest's own hand.

To Jenn, the Church's betrayal of vampire hunters was more proof that religion was silly. It was true that crosses and holy water repelled vampires, but so did other religious symbols. Noah used the Star of David. She had a theory that the symbols worked because they were representations not of some god, but of goodness. Jenn believed in goodness, if not in God. She had grown up in a vaguely Christian atmosphere, as her family was originally from Bavaria, a Catholic section of Germany. Antonio had his own opinions, of course: "Deep down, it must be that you really believe, Jenn. In your soul, where it counts." Which could be why crosses worked for her.

The only "counting" she was interested in was how many vampires they had to kill until the world belonged to the human race again.

Jenn took off her workout clothes and stepped into

the shower. She let the hot water sluice over her head. As she toweled off and dressed, she thought she heard familiar voices through the wall. She gathered up her things and darted down the hall. Her grandmother sat facing the entryway, and Jenn's mom was on the sofa with the housekeeper. Gramma Esther saw Jenn first. She rose from her chair and caught Jenn in her arms as Jenn nearly crashed into her.

"Gramma, Mom," Jenn said, as her mother burst into tears and got to her feet. Jenn moved to her and held her. "Mom, we'll find her. We'll find Heather."

"My baby?" her mother gasped, clinging to Jenn. "Oh, God. My baby."

Jenn cast a furtive glance over her mom's shoulder at her grandmother. Did they not know that Heather had been converted—changed into a vampire? Jenn's father had offered Jenn to Aurora to guarantee the safety of the rest of the family. It was a promise Aurora had broken, instead kidnapping Heather to lure Jenn—and Antonio—to New Orleans. Aurora's ultimate target had been Antonio, but first she'd amused herself with Heather.

I'm going to kill you, Aurora, Jenn promised. She trembled, but one steely-calm look from Gramma Esther told her she needed to keep herself under control. Her mother needed her.

Did she cry like this when I ran away from home to join the academy? she wondered. She didn't think so.

"Where did Heather go?" her mom wailed.

"Here is wine," the housekeeper announced. Unnoticed by Jenn, she'd left the room and returned with a bottle of what looked like port and four small glasses. Jenn was eighteen, and in Spain that was an acceptable age to drink, but Jenn hadn't gotten used to it yet. Still, she took the glass Señora Nevado poured for her. Jenn's mother drank hers down quickly, but Gramma Esther barely sipped hers. Instead she looked hard at Jenn, as if trying to convey her a silent message.

"When did you get here?" Jenn asked.

"Just a few minutes ago. *An old friend* offered us a lift," Gramma Esther said meaningfully. "He's moving to Budapest."

Jenn blinked in shock. Did Gramma Esther mean Greg, the leader of the black crosses? He was their contact with the covert government operation dubbed Project Crusade.

A gentle rap came at the door, and Father Juan poked in his head. "Ah, I see that you found Jenn," he said. "Please, Leitner ladies, I have found a place where you will be more comfortable while we talk."

Jenn put her untouched glass on Señora Nevado's tray, murmured *"Gracias,"* and turned to go. The housekeeper gestured for Jenn to hand over her towel and workout clothes. Jenn complied and thanked her again.

The group was silent as they entered the little chapel. Jenn was disappointed not to see Antonio. She felt a deep pang, as if part of her were missing too.

Father Juan gestured for the three to sit in one of the pews. Then he bowed on one knee, crossed himself, and slid into the pew in front of them, half turning to face them. Jenn studied his face as he looked around, ensuring that they were alone.

"I have some things I need to tell you," he said. "I must caution you to keep them to yourselves. Although we are surrounded by my brothers in Christ, we are not necessarily among friends."

"What do you mean?" Jenn's mother asked nervously.

"You are aware that the government of your country is cooperating with the Cursed Ones," he began.

"Yes," Gramma Esther replied. "And so was my son, Jenn's dad."

Jenn clenched her fists in her lap as fresh anger surged through her. Her grandmother said the words so matter-of-factly, as if she were talking about a stranger. Maybe, in her mind, she was.

"He knows that was a mistake," Jenn's mom cut in, looking pale and wan. "And that's why we have to get him out of there."

Gramma Esther made no comment.

"Perhaps you also know that Spain, alone, has refused to surrender." Father Juan's face darkened. "Until now. The hunters have been ordered to disband, and we priests must no longer teach or lead them. I have refused to stop, and for this I have been cast out of the Church."

Esther pursed her lips while Jenn's mother wiped away her tears. "So it's not safe in Spain," Jenn's mother said. "Jenn, how could you bring Heather here?"

Jenn felt dizzy. *Mom doesn't know Heather's been converted,* she thought. Jenn peered under her lashes at Father Juan, who shook his head surreptitiously at her, as if to say, *I'll tell her.*

"You know a few things about us," the priest went on slowly. "You know, for example, that we have among us a vampire who fights for humanity."

"He was at the camp," Jenn's mom said, fidgeting nervously with her fingers. "Something happened to him, didn't it? He had become evil again."

"Antonio is battling his curse, and I think he will win." Father Juan cleared his throat.

He's going to tell them the truth about Heather. He has to. It's not a secret among the hunters, and if he doesn't reveal it, Jamie might, out of pure spite.

"It is true that Heather has gone missing," he said.

Jenn's mother sobbed once, heavily. Jenn squeezed her hand, then put her arm around her mother.

Her grandmother was very still. "Go on. Say what you need to say, Father."

"Aurora, the Cursed One who kidnapped Heather, turned her into a vampire," he said, his voice soft, his words crystal clear.

Jenn's mom stared at him. For a full ten seconds she

was silent. And then a wrenching wail tore out of her — the scream of a mother who had been told her child was dead. Jenn held her with both arms, trying to contain her mom's shock. But her mom pushed her away and got to her feet, still screaming. She flailed her fists at Father Juan, then showered Jenn with punches. She kicked at Jenn's legs, shrieking. Jenn scooted away, protecting her mother from her instinctive response to fight back, but her mother came at her.

"You! You!" she screamed, over and over again.

Gramma Esther tried to grab her daughter-in-law's upper arms, to stop her from pounding Jenn. Jenn slid out of the pew and stood in the aisle, her arms outstretched.

"Mom, we'll get her back. And we'll help her. I promise!" Jenn had to shout to be heard over her mother's screams.

Father Juan joined her in the aisle. "We have to leave," he said into her ear. "The brothers will hear. Tell the others to get ready. We'll depart the second the sun goes down."

She looked over at her mother, who had collapsed in the pew. She was rocking back and forth, shaking her head as she shrieked and cried.

"I should stay with my mom," she said, but as soon as she spoke, she knew she was wrong. She needed to put distance between her mother and herself.

Because she blames me. She thinks I made this happen. Just like Daddy thought when I left for the academy.

Gramma Esther caught her gaze and held it. She

gestured for Jenn to leave the two of them alone. Shaking all over, Jenn obeyed. Tears blinded her as she hurried out of the chapel.

Framed by a stone archway, Antonio was shielded from the dying sun. He remained silent, but his expression—sympathy, pity—spoke volumes.

Oh, why can't you love me? she thought, crumbling inside. Her heart was breaking, for herself, for her mother and grandmother, for Heather.

And for him.

Why do you have to be a vampire and a priest?

Why does it have to be this way?

Antonio retreated into the shadows, becoming almost invisible. As Jenn brushed past him, she cleared her throat and said, "We're leaving as soon as the sun sets."

He didn't reply.

IN A BUNKER BENEATH THE WHITE HOUSE, WASHINGTON, D.C.
SOLOMON AND PRESIDENT KILBURN

The room was octagonal, and ringed with high-definition monitors. Solomon, the leader of the Vampire Nation, strolled beside Jack Kilburn, the president of the United States, pausing before each screen so Kilburn could get the full effect. Solomon had been very busy.

"This beautiful new 'hospital'—he made air quotes—is

in New Mexico," Solomon explained, gesturing to an enormous structure that towered against the brilliant sunshine. "Filled to capacity already. Six hundred beds. People are dropping like flies from 'causes unknown,' and they're begging for help. People are talking about a worldwide epidemic. Which is what we want them to talk about."

President Kilburn tried to smile as his sweat beaded on his brow. Solomon could smell the tantalizing odor of fear. Solomon enjoyed a mini fantasy about ripping into the president's throat and killing him on the spot. Kilburn's price for cooperating with Solomon was eternal life. Solomon had yet to pay it.

Kilburn had yet to earn it. The president was hesitant to get with the program, and Solomon needed someone fully committed to mass extermination.

"And they're dropping like flies from . . . ?" President Kilburn asked.

Solomon smiled patiently. "We sprayed a toxin on the local produce," he said. "Not traceable. Incurable. So the humans come in for help . . . and they don't come out."

Kilburn swallowed hard and nodded. "But we . . . my family . . ."

"Just don't eat any chilies," Solomon said pleasantly.

The monitors revealed more "hospitals" and other camps for humans. Solomon had been building them for months, but was only now informing the president. The camps were being presented as "overflow facilities for our crowded prisons," and of course some of the inmates *were* convicted criminals. But others would be undesirables — rabble-rousers, protestors, and anti-vampire terrorists — who would never face trial. The definition of "undesirable" would be repeatedly expanded until anyone Solomon could not control — human or vampire — found him or herself behind barbed wire.

It would be some time before this bothered the Americans. After the chaos of the war, humans wanted security and order. The majority cheered the removal of low-life scum and troublemakers from their streets. By the time things reached a point where they realized mankind had been reduced to an exotic species, it would be too late for them to do anything about it.

"Now, this camp is located in Malaysia," Solomon said to Kilburn. He frowned. "You seem distracted."

"How's the supersoldier program coming?" Kilburn asked.

Inwardly Solomon seethed. The supersoldier hybrids were disintegrating. He had scientists from all over the world poring over the files Dantalion had e-mailed him before the lab in Russia had exploded, but a critical component must not have come through.

"Come and see," he replied.

Kilburn stood staring at the screens for a few more seconds, then trailed after him. Six armed guards — three human, three vampire — snapped to attention as Solomon and Kilburn entered the dimly lit corridor. As they progressed down the passageway, the guards stationed at other doors saluted them.

At the end of the corridor they paused for retinal and fingerprint scans. Solid steel elevator doors opened. The guard inside saluted as Solomon, Kilburn, and their security detail entered. Then the elevator descended, passing floor after floor, until at last it stopped, seemingly at the bottom of the world.

They walked through a literal maze of corridors, arriving at a steel door guarded by more soldiers in full battle gear. Solomon key-coded the door, and it opened with a vacuumlike *fwom*.

After another series of guarded doors, they finally reached one marked BIOHAZARD. Kilburn stank of terror. Solomon was gleeful.

Six cells, each containing a hybrid, faced them. Solomon led the way to the second cell. A creature, part werewolf, part vampire, part human, and mechanically enhanced, glared at Solomon. Thick, greenish wrists were restrained by handcuffs. Its furry ankles thrashed, clanking the chains that held them. Its long claws tapped against the tile. A thick rope of drool dangled from its mouth. Werewolf teeth gnashed and vampire eyes glowed red.

Kilburn was really losing it, straining to act normal despite his shallow breathing. Maybe he wouldn't have been so frightened if he'd known—as Solomon did—that the hybrid was slowly rotting from the inside out. So were the five other hybrids. The different strands of DNA were unraveling. If Solomon was lucky, these hybrids would last another three or four months—long enough for the team to create replacements—if Solomon still needed to pretend that he was fulfilling his promise to Kilburn. Of course, Solomon planned to create his own army, and he'd make sure his hybrids were bigger, faster, and stronger than the supersoldiers he created for the humans. But right now the project was a failure.

Dantalion, damn you. Did you hold out on me?

Solomon and Dantalion had been partners in the hybrid project. Dantalion had invented the hybridizing process, and there was no vampire scientist more inventive and brilliant than he. Solomon had funded Dantalion's research, so long as it produced results. But those accursed men with their black crosses had invaded Dantalion's lab, and Dantalion had followed procedure, calling for help and rigging the place to blow. Then Solomon had had him killed, rather than chance the black crosses successfully capturing him.

"Amazing," Kilburn said in a strained voice.

Dying, Solomon thought angrily, but he smiled at the president with his long fangs. "It is," he said.

"Kill you," the hybrid ground out in an English accent, grunting as it tried to advance on the two men.

"My God," Kilburn said.

"Used to be the Hunter of London. Those days are over, eh, mate?" Solomon affected a cockney accent.

"Bastard," the hybrid said. "We'll rise . . ."

Solomon snickered. "What do you think you are, a zombie?"

They left soon after that. The president was properly shaken. These humans should never forget that vampires were their superiors in every way.

Exuding confidence, Solomon acted as if he had everything under control until he flew back to his movie studio in Los Angeles. There he unleashed his foul mood on his most recent assistant. First he yelled at her for an hour, then he drank her down.

Afterward he went to see Paul Leitner, the father of Jennifer Leitner, the renegade Hunter. Solomon wanted Jenn gone. But he wanted Antonio de la Cruz, the "good" vampire who ran with her, even more. De la Cruz was a threat, and an error. He needed to be taken out—after Solomon figured out how Antonio could touch crosses and live inside a church.

"There are just so many loose ends," he said to Leitner, whom he kept in a room on the movie lot. Seated on the couch, the man looked back at him with a dazed expression. *Probably descending into madness.* "It's really hard to rule the world, you know?"

Leitner said nothing. Of course he didn't know.

Rolling his eyes, Solomon left Leitner there and went down three flights of stairs into his secret refuge. Like the elevator in Washington, it was reinforced with steel and all kinds of laser-blasting security. It was the darkest room Solomon had ever been in, and it used to refresh him.

Now it was just another source of irritation, as it was where he'd imprisoned a seventeen-year-old fortune-teller from Budapest. Katalin had presented herself willingly, explaining that she had cast the runes and seen that the vampires were going to prevail over mankind. For a while her magicks had proved useful, both alerting him to the treacherous schemes of his underlings and promising him glory and triumph if he made all the right moves. But lately she'd gone dry, and he was beginning to wonder if she'd outlived her usefulness.

She was sitting in a burgundy chair, reading. When she saw him, she put her e-reader down, smoothed her filmy, long-sleeved top over her jeans, and got to her feet. As she walked to him, the bells on her ankle bracelets tinkled.

"Solomon, you're back." He had to restrain himself from slapping her for saying something so stupidly obvious. His nerves were on edge, and if she didn't give him some news this time . . .

"Cast them," he said, gesturing to the ebony box on the table beside the chair.

She folded her arms and looked very sad. "I don't need to. I can feel them. Dark forces, all around you." She rounded her shoulders as if she were afraid he would punish her for giving him bad news.

"You keep saying that. What are these dark forces? Who are they? What can I do to stop them?"

She gave her head a tiny shake. "I don't know."

"Then find out," he said.

She looked down at her hands. "I've tried everything. I've thrown the runes a hundred times."

He could feel the fear rolling off her. She was terrified. For him? Of him?

With the failure of the supersoldiers fresh on his mind, he crossed the room with lightning speed, grabbed her hair, and yanked back her head.

"Then throw them a thousand," he ordered, and sat back to watch.

CHAPTER THREE

And now you see our plans at last
We have come so far so fast
We are the lords of all that breathes
Where once we played the part of thieves
Men will cry and women scream
A hell on earth, a demon's dream
Your children drained, your maidens, too
Years of hiding now are through

TOLEDO, SPAIN
THE SALAMANCA HUNTERS MINUS SKYE;
ESTHER AND LESLIE LEITNER

Holgar sniffed the air and felt his hackles rise. Something was wrong. He had gone to the open-air market in Toledo's main square to take a message to one of Father Juan's contacts and to pick up some groceries for dinner. He had given the note to the fishmonger and then gotten some shrimp.

But as he began to make his way from the white-tented stall, he kept catching the movement of shadows from the corner of his eye. It was broad daylight. It couldn't be Cursed Ones, so who was it?

Holgar tried to look casual, like any other shopper, but knew he stood out. He was very tall, very husky, and very Danish. He had volunteered for the assignment. The chance to get outside had been too good to pass up. He was going mad sitting around in the monastery. But he was beginning to realize that he had been foolish to go. Father Juan should have sent someone who would blend in better.

He turned a couple of corners, trying to get downwind of whatever was following him. The marketplace itself, though, proved a huge distraction. It was difficult to smell anything over the aromas of meat, fruit, and sweat. But still he had to try. A werewolf's sense of smell was his keenest attribute, and one he relied on heavily.

Another flash of movement. He whipped around, but no one stood out in the busy crowd. Then something threw itself at him.

He ducked. Razor-tipped claws sliced the air just above his head. He dropped to the ground and rolled. But when he looked up, the wolf that had swiped at him was nowhere to be seen.

Holgar swore and stood slowly, warily. He was surrounded by noise and stench, and he couldn't track his assailant.

A man walked by. As he passed, Holgar caught the faintest scent of wolf. Holgar jumped to the side, but from the throng a silver knife flashed, slicing open his shirt and jabbing into his side. Holgar howled in pain, then felt all eyes turn toward him. Although the vampires had made themselves known to the world, the werewolves had not. Panic flared. There were at least two assailants after him, but if he continued to draw attention with his werewolf howling, the crowd might decide he was a madman who needed to be apprehended.

He turned and hurried in the direction of the monastery as fast as he dared. Once on the road he began to trot, and to pant in pain. Howling, gasping; *for helvede*—damn it—was he going to change? Holgar had yet to transform except on the full moon. He hadn't been old enough, mature enough to change at will. But the tingling sensation that signaled the change gathered in his wound.

He could feel the other werewolves following him, and now he could smell them too. Three separate scents. He loped, scanning the hillside for a place to make a stand or ambush them.

A bend in the road offered him the only opportunity he was likely to get. Heart racing, he crouched behind an oleander bush and waited.

The man with the knife came first. He was bushy-headed, blond, and muscular, like him. Likely a Dane. Holgar swept the man's feet out from under him, leaped on top of him, and wrenched away his knife. Holgar hissed as the silver cut his palm.

"What do you want?" Holgar yelled at him in Danish.

"To kill you, traitor!" The man struggled to throw him off.

"I'm not a traitor," Holgar said, displaying aggression by lowering his head and baring his teeth. The tingling sensation was suddenly overwhelmed by incredible pain. Silver poisoning?

"You kill your own kind," the man insisted, raising his chin defiantly as he glared into Holgar's blue eyes.

"I defended myself," Holgar said, mind racing. The man wasn't a member of Holgar's pack back in Denmark, so why did he care?

Something slammed hard against Holgar's back, throwing him to the ground. The knife skidded out of his hand, and massive jaws fastened onto his shoulder, missing his throat as he twisted.

Adrenaline racing through his body, Holgar threw off the wolf; then he reached for the knife. His fingers grasped it and he spun around, just in time to plunge it into the heart of the werewolf. The wolf fell on top of him with a scream. A roar of shock escaped Holgar. It was Nils Hansen, someone he'd been friends with since they were cubs.

"Nils," he whispered, "what were you doing?"

Holgar couldn't wait for an answer. The silver was tainting his blood, pushing through his veins and arteries. It wouldn't kill him, but it could incapacitate him, and Jenn had said that they were leaving the monastery that night. He had to get help.

Just inside the monastery's arched walls, Father Juan intercepted Holgar and quickly ushered him into a small room where everyone was already gathered. Antonio sat apart. The vampire lifted his head up as Holgar entered, and Jenn ran to Holgar's side.

"What happened?" Jenn asked.

Holgar grimaced at his bloody shirt, then made a face at Jenn. "Got stabbed. Not badly, though."

"Careful, wolfie. Sucker might think you're dinner," Jamie said.

Holgar had a mind to make Jamie dinner. He shook himself of the thought.

"I was attacked by three werewolves. It was revenge for the wolves I killed in the battle at Salamanca."

"They attacked you in broad daylight?" Jenn asked, as Father Juan pulled the shirt away from the wound so that he could examine it. Holgar sucked in his breath, and Jenn touched his hand in sympathy.

"Motivated," Antonio said.

"Sloppy," Jamie drawled.

"They took advantage of the market crowd. I killed one," Holgar said. "The other two took off."

The new girl, Sade, hugged her arms around herself and started rocking. Holgar wished they wouldn't take her with them. She was too fragile. No good in a fight.

"Let's circle back to that in a minute," Jenn said, looking worried. "We're meeting because Greg and Project Crusade have made a new headquarters for themselves in Budapest."

"They've moved out of the U.S.?" Jamie asked with a raised eyebrow.

"Apparently," Jenn replied, fussing over Holgar. With a pang he thought of Skye. If she'd been there, she'd perform a healing spell, and chide him for putting himself in danger. "I'd leave too. Solomon's putting Americans into camps."

"Concentration camps," Antonio added, and Father Juan nodded.

"As with World War Two," Father Juan said. "Antonio's war."

"It was hell on earth." Antonio's voice lowered. "Hitler tortured those people horribly. Starved them. Gassed them. The Cursed Ones are just as bad. We must stop them." Then he raised his chin. "I fought in that war, but this war is my war now."

"*Por supuesto.*" Father Juan inclined his head in Antonio's direction. "Forgive my words. Sade," he said gently, "there are some bandages and ointment in a black bag in my room. Could you get them for me?"

Sade stopped rocking and hurried out of the room. So maybe she could be helpful after all.

"Solomon's putting people in camps *all over the world*," Jamie countered, sliding his glance at Jenn. "Not just your U.S. of A. In case you haven't noticed."

"I noticed," Jenn said. "I only meant—"

"You don't need to explain," Holgar cut in, irritated with Jamie's nitpicking. "You're our leader."

"Alpha bitch," Jamie retorted, and Holgar growled menacingly. "Just kidding," the Irishman added, even though it was obvious that he wasn't.

"We need to find out what the black crosses are up to," Antonio said. "What they know. What they're doing."

"Exactly what I was thinking. We need to send someone to Budapest," Jenn said.

"I'll go," Holgar volunteered. It seemed like the logical choice. "If I'm gone, the werewolves should follow and leave you alone."

Jenn shook her head. "No. Noah should go. Greg's only seen him once, and that was at night."

"I'll do it," Noah said. "It won't be a problem that he's seen me. This time, he won't."

"Good, because that way we can focus on what *is* a problem," Jenn said, her voice grim.

Jamie lit a cigarette.

Antonio's heart bled for Jenn. He would have given anything to comfort her as a man would comfort the woman he loved. But though Jenn had grown from a naive, self-deprecating girl into a strong woman, he had not changed. He wasn't a man.

As Antonio fretted, Jenn spent the next half hour laying out how they would get Noah to Budapest. They also talked about Holgar's attackers.

Then Jenn brought up Antonio's grandsire: Lucifer, who had sired Sergio. Aurora had called out his name during the battle of Salamanca. Lucifer was truly the Devil, and if they had to go up against him, they would be damned.

Antonio couldn't concentrate. All he could do was stare at the gentle curve of Jenn's lips, the way they shaped each word, and the wisps of her dark auburn hair.

At last the meeting was over. Holgar's eyes were glassy, and Antonio wondered how badly the stab wound was affecting him. They were all to pack, grab a quick nap, and get some food before leaving the monastery that night. All except for Noah, who would be leaving immediately for Hungary.

As the others filed out, Antonio lingered, staring at Jenn. She loved him, despite what he was. Why couldn't that be enough?

It's not a question of enough, he thought. *I have promised myself to someone else. To God.*

"Are you okay?" he asked.

It was a stupid question. Of course she wasn't okay. But he needed to say something, anything.

Jenn gave him a pained smile. He reached out to touch

her cheek, but caught himself. He could see the blood rise to her cheeks, and desire swept through him.

Then he forced himself to turn. He had barely any control over his dark urges. And he had rededicated himself to the priesthood. She was the woman he loved, a child of God in need of saving, a savior who could change the world. But only one thing mattered.

She was forbidden fruit.

EPPING FOREST, ENGLAND
SKYE

Vampires favored cities, where they could find plenty of warm bodies and sheltering buildings. The majority of them shunned the lonely and isolated places of the world. Which was exactly why witches had sought those places out. After her sister's wedding, Skye's entire coven had gone underground to avoid being caught up in the war against the vampires.

Her family had moved deep into the heart of Epping Forest, where they maintained a tiny cottage previously used only for lunar celebrations and private family rituals. Skye knew that was where they would be, unless something had happened to them.

Skye doggedly made her way through the brush, catching sight of a will-o'-the-wisp—a flicker of light. These flickers were said by some to be the burning coal carried by a minion of Satan as he lured the curious to their doom. In Skye's family's faith, the lights were sent by the Goddess to aid the lost.

"Help me now, Lady," Skye murmured, as she reached a familiar stand of oaks.

One of Skye's cousins lived on the outskirts of the forest. The cottage's sloped roof was visible, and Skye followed a trail that was more memory than a physical landmark, until at last she was standing at the front door.

She stared for a moment at the old planks, her heart skipping a beat, as she wondered if she had come to the wrong place. A simple brass handle hung where there'd once been a silver door knocker in the shape of the crescent moon.

She squared her shoulders and forced herself to knock anyway. Regardless of who lived there, she was still badly in need of food and water. She prayed that the occupants would be willing to help.

An ultraviolet porch light clicked on. The light wasn't something she could see, but Skye could feel it. The bulb was a relic from the first years after the Cursed Ones went public. People had rushed to buy them, thinking that the UV would harm vampires as the sun would.

They hadn't worked. No one was really sure what the sun's light did. But the more superstitious had hung on to their lights, swearing that the UV kept vampires at bay.

The door opened just a crack, and a blue eye stared out

at her. Skye tried to smile, hoping that it would somehow compensate for being streaked with blood.

The door slammed shut.

"Please, I need your—," Skye began.

The chain clinked and the door swung open. Skye's twenty-four-year-old cousin Summer anxiously regarded her. Skye moved to throw her arms around her, but Summer tensed and took a step back.

"What are you doing here?" she demanded.

"Blessed be," Skye said, struggling to hide her disappointment at the lack of traditional witchly greeting—of any greeting, for that matter.

"You can't come in," her cousin said, stubbornly setting her jaw.

Skye blinked, fighting to hold back tears. "You can see that I'm hurt."

"From fighting," Summer said. "Am I right?"

Skye looked into her eyes and saw anger there, and fear.

"Escaping," Skye said. "But it wasn't because of—"

"We don't take sides in the conflict, and we don't recognize those who do."

"Then you're lying when you say you're not taking sides," Skye snapped. "Please, just some water—"

Summer slammed the door in her face. Miserable, and worried that she wouldn't be able to make it much farther before she collapsed, Skye took a deep breath and stepped off the porch. She stared into the forest and hoped that her parents would be more understanding, or at least forgiving.

She began to walk. She'd gone only about fifty feet when a sudden sound behind her caused her to turn. Standing there was Summer's husband, Nigel. He held out a glass of water and a brown sack.

"Thank you," she said, tears welling in her eyes. She took the glass of water and drank it down, wishing there were more of it. She handed it back, and Nigel gave her the bag. She opened it and saw a few slices of bread and a chunk of Stilton cheese.

"Thank you," she said again, realizing that he hadn't said a word.

He nodded and turned to go.

"Wait!"

He turned to look at Skye.

"Why are you helping me?" she asked.

"It would be doing you harm not to help you. But there'll be the devil to pay if she finds out," he murmured, then walked away.

Skye's legs trembled. She devoured the food. She was still dehydrated, but she felt a little better after she had finished eating. She folded the bag and slid it into her boot. Witches respected the earth in all ways.

The whole world's gone to hell. My cousin has disowned me, I could die at any moment, and I'm worried about littering, she thought, smiling slightly. *Some things never change.*

Two hours later, as Skye stood staring at her family's cottage, she realized that some things had changed too much. The cottage had once been a simple structure, one large room that they all shared. She could remember many a night choosing her spot on the floor and rolling out her sleeping bag.

Now several new additions completely obscured the original building. Enormous and rambling, it no longer seemed to spring out of the earth, but rather to ride upon its back. The new construction was glass and metal. There was nothing natural or beautiful about it, and it made her sick to see it. The grand old pollarded tree, which had once held a swing, had been cut down to make way for the expansion.

She trudged forward slowly, mindful of the reaction that she had gotten from Summer. When she was almost to the door, it opened, and Melody, her sister, flew out.

"Skye!" she cried, and hugged her.

Skye hugged her back, sobbing with relief at the welcome. When she pulled free at last, she looked at Melody closely. Her sister had a baby bump under her embroidered peasant blouse.

"You're pregnant!" Skye exclaimed.

"Six months. This will be our second," Melody said with a proud grin as she laid a protective hand on her belly.

Second.

The word made Skye feel as if she were falling. She was an aunt and she'd never known it.

"Why didn't you tell me?" she asked before she could stop herself.

Gathering up her loose, caramel-colored curls, Melody made a little face. "Llewellyn takes the whole *underground* thing seriously," she said.

Fear bubbled up in Skye. What else had she missed in the three years she'd been gone? Was everyone all right?

"Everyone's fine," Melody assured her warmly. Melody had always been able to read her like a book. "Come inside and see for yourself."

Skye followed Melody into the cottage. She remembered what Jenn had said after she'd returned home for her grandfather's funeral. She prayed to the Goddess that she would get a warmer reception than Jenn had.

She blinked as she looked around, trying to match her memories to what she was seeing. She saw absolutely no evidence that witches owned the place. Gone were the rows of fragrant dried herbs that had hung from the rafters. The York family charms—White magick sigils hand-painted on the walls, dating from the Middle Ages and even earlier—had been replaced by landscapes of rolling English hills and light-blue wallpaper. Furnished with an oak dinette set, a daybed in blue chintz, and some scattered chairs, the room looked like a pleasant room in a hotel.

A second story had been added, accessed by wooden stairs and a white metal handrail, which was ugly, yet functional. From the sounds above, the rest of the family were about to join them. Skye took a deep, nervous breath.

A playpen in the corner caught her eye. Skye's heart jumped. A toddler a little more than a year old solemnly gazed at her from over the top of the bars. The little one was dressed in brown corduroy pants and a tan shirt decorated with puppies.

"My son," Melody said.

Tears stung Skye's eyes. She had a nephew. She had missed his birth. She didn't even know his name.

Melody's husband, Llewellyn, and Skye's parents descended the stairs. Skye's father, always very handsome, looked old. Both her parents smiled hesitantly at her but didn't move to embrace her.

Skye bit her lip and forced herself not to run to them. "Blessed be," she said, hearing the emotion in her voice.

"Blessed be," the rest intoned.

"Merrily met," Melody added in a whisper.

"How . . . it's good to see all of you."

"It's a surprise to see you," her mother replied faintly.

Skye tried to decipher her tone but couldn't. No one moved. The toddler babbled, and Melody picked him up. Skye got the impression that her sister was trying to avoid the tension in the room.

"I've missed you all," Skye whispered. "I was wounded, and I thought to come home."

"And you've come to your senses?" Skye's mother asked in a tight voice. "You're done with it?"

"And you're sorry?" her father said. He stood unmoving, and she realized that leaving the team was the price for their help.

No. Not their help. Their love.

Skye's heart broke. She wanted to collapse on the floor. She had been through so much—too much—to stand there and face their judgment.

But then she thought of Holgar. He had walked away from his family, his pack, everyone he cared about. He had done it because fighting the Cursed Ones was the right thing to do.

Skye had run to the academy to escape Estefan. Only fourteen, she hadn't wanted to tell her family that she had an evil stalker. With sudden clarity Skye realized that she hadn't told her parents about Estefan not because she believed they couldn't help her, but because deep down she had believed that they *wouldn't*. They would have just hidden her away from him. They never would have trained her how to stand on her own and defend herself.

And staring at their faces now, she knew she had been right to go. In a flash, the guilt she had felt for leaving her family for Salamanca vanished. She had done what she had to do in order to save her life. There was no shame in that.

"I'm injured," she said slowly. "I would appreciate some food and water."

There was a moment of silence that seemed to last an eternity.

"So, you didn't come because of us?" Melody asked. "You came because you're *hungry*? I'm sorry," she added quickly. "That was unkind."

"No, *I'm* sorry," Skye said. They used to be so close. Lying about Estefan, then running away, had changed all that.

Skye looked at her mother. "I can't, not just yet."

"If not now, then when?" her mother asked quietly. There was a challenge in her voice. Skye was the prodigal daughter returned home, but she would only be forgiven if she stayed.

"Mummy, I can't," she whispered.

"Then you should go now," Llewellyn said. "And we'll forget that you were here."

Skye cleared her throat. "Followers of the Goddess take care of strangers. Don't I rate that much?"

"That much," her mother affirmed. She gestured to the dining table. It was a cheesy modern thing made of fake wood, not their old table, the one Yorks had carved their initials in for over a century.

"Sit and eat," her mother said coolly.

Skye knew she needed the strength to travel to rejoin the others; otherwise she would have left. She sat down stiffly and refused to look again at the little boy who was jabbering away in Melody's arms. She had always wanted to be an aunt, but even that was denied her. If her family wasn't going to help her any more than they would a stranger, then she would offer them no more than a stranger would.

Her mother set down an earthenware pitcher and a cup. It was teatime, and Skye smelled steeping lavender and jasmine, her mother's special blend. But no tea was offered, only water. By the time her mother brought Skye two cucumber-and-watercress sandwiches, Skye had drunk all the water. She could feel her injuries begin to repair themselves. She aided them with a whispered spell.

She ate quickly, eager to be gone. When she was done, she stood slowly, aware that this was the last time she was likely to ever see her family.

"Thank you," she said. "Blessed be." She turned to her sister. "Merrily met, and merrily parted."

A tear ran down Melody's cheek. No one else answered as she let herself out the front door.

Toledo, Spain
Father Juan, Father Sebastian, Jenn, Antonio, Jamie, Holgar, Sade, and Esther and Leslie Leitner

"I'm going," Jamie announced. *"Now."*

They were sitting in a little anteroom off the monastery's chapel. They'd been about to leave when Father Sebastian had glided in like a short, skinny angel of the Lord Himself and taken Father Juan off for a chat. Now the priests were back, and two tenser men Jamie had never seen. Which meant . . . more *talking*.

And not fighting.

Talking didn't solve anything. All the plotting and planning in the world hadn't saved Eriko, and it wouldn't save Skye. Staking vampires would, and killing sympathizers would. Blowing up the enemy's stronghold would.

But not talking.

If the hunters of Salamanca were the last best hope of mankind, maybe it was time to restore his Catholic schoolboy faith in miracles.

Although that would be a miracle in itself.

Jamie pulled on his black duster and picked up his duffel, which clanked with weapons. He'd packed his two special guns—the one with silver bullets and the one he was building that would fire wooden ones. Talking was shite, and it was time to take action. With one foot past the threshold, he froze as Father Juan called to him.

"Jamie, one moment, *por favor*," he said, carrying his own small gym bag. Because Father Juan asked politely and—oh, *hell*—because he was Jamie's priest, Jamie huffed loudly and shifted his weight on his hip.

"*Gracias*, my son. Thank you." Father Juan set the bag on the marble floor. "My friends, please listen."

Jamie blew air out of his cheeks. Jenn's ma and that African bint so fond of garlic—Sade—sank down on a red velvet sofa like refugees, the ma's eyes all bloodshot and Sade patting her hand, her own eyes vacant, like a doll's. Holgar had been fixing the zipper on Jenn's grandmother's flak jacket, and he turned to give the two fathers his full attention. Such a nice little werewolf. Give him a pat on the head and get him some goat entrails.

"We've had a message from the Brotherhood of Saint Andrew," Father Sebastian announced. His eyes and cheeks were sunken. Despite the fact that he'd made it clear he was on their side, he gave Jamie the shudders. "They're Romanian. They've heard of you, Antonio, and they admire you deeply. With Father Juan's permission, I told them something of your struggles, and they've offered their help."

The vampire was all ears on *that*.

"They've helped many souls overcome the devil's temptations," Father Sebastian said. "They're located deep in the family seat of the legendary Vlad Tepes—you would know him by his other name, Dracula. They know much about vampiric evil."

"Dracula?" Jenn's mother cried.

"Myth," Jamie assured her impatiently. "Well, the real Dracula was a warrior and he impaled people, but he wasn't a vampire." He pointedly cleared his throat. "But is this the right time for that?"

"Jamie's right," Antonio said, shocking Jamie by agreeing with him. "We have more important things to do."

Yeah. We should stake you and be done with it, Jamie thought.

"But . . . could they make him *not* a vampire?" Jenn asked in a soft voice. Her cheeks were blazing red as coals.

Oh, yeah, she still loves the sucker. American girls — who can understand them?

"No, unfortunately not," Father Sebastian said gently. "As for Dracula being a myth, I wish that were true."

"The lad's *real*? Get on with you," Jamie said, incredulous. "But to get back to the point: We *should* be looking for Skye."

Jamie was a son of the Church, a cradle Catholic, but his obedience only went so far. If Father Juan wanted to hit the road, well and good. But Jamie would be damned if he was going to do anything to help Antonio while Skye was unaccounted for. Jamie's entire reason for going to the bloody academy to learn to fight vampires in the first place was to become the Hunter. He'd trained in hopes of receiving the elixir that bestowed heightened strength. He'd planned to then hightail it back to Northern Ireland to settle a few scores and take care of his own folk.

And if there was anyone among this sorry crew he called his own, with Eriko gone, it was Skye York. English, yeah, but for the love of Mike, why the *hell* wasn't Holgar tearing the world apart to find her? Holgar was Skye's fighting partner.

Because of Antonio, that was bleedin' why. Sodding bastard. It was clear everyone thought he was more important than Skye. And more important than any of the rest of them. But he was a *vampire*, and he would always be a vampire — evil, disgusting, soulless. Damned in every sense of the word.

Antonio had fooled Father Juan with his seminary studies and his prayers, but Jamie knew that sooner or later the Curser would drop the act. And Antonio de la Cruz had finally shown his true fangs. He'd lured everyone to "rescue" him in Las Vegas, where'd he gone on a killing spree and nearly drained a baby at its own christening. *That* was who was getting all the attention. Meanwhile, the warlock stalker who was in league with the very same vampire who had kidnapped Antonio had hold of Skye. And no one was doing shite about it.

Jamie clenched his jaw. Arse-backwards, the lot. If he could take out Antonio with his wood-bullet gun once it was finished, he'd be doing their side a favor.

"Thank you, Father Sebastian," Father Juan said, dismissing the other priest. "I'll give you an answer for the Brotherhood after I've had a chance to talk with my team."

Father Sebastian lowered his head. Then he made the sign of the cross over each person in the room. Father Juan and Antonio crossed themselves as well. It was an abomination, Antonio doing that. Jamie hated him down to the soles of his boots.

Father Juan glanced at Jamie, and Jamie pursed his lips and made a show of obediently crossing himself. *Bloody hell.*

After Father Sebastian left, everyone looked expectantly at Father Juan.

"I've cast the runes," Father Juan said. "And some things have been revealed to me."

Skye, Jamie thought, holding his breath.

"Runes? What's he talking about?" Jenn's mother asked. "What are those? What about Heather?"

"Shh, Leslie," Jenn's gran murmured. "Let him speak."

Father Juan began, "I have prayed about them." He gazed directly at Jenn. "Your leader is right. It's time to take the fight to our enemies. Antonio must go to Romania to protect himself from—let us call it—a relapse."

Jamie opened his mouth to say all the things he was thinking. Father Juan held up a hand for silence. Jamie grudgingly stayed silent.

"And each one of you—of us—must be as strong as we can be. I have been casting magicks since your graduation, and I believe I can create more doses of the Hunter's elixir. Enough for all of you hunters."

"Too right!" Jamie shouted.

When he hadn't received the elixir, he'd nearly packed it in and left. But to have a second crack at it . . . his faith in miracles was restored.

Holgar grunted. "Hunter elixir on top of werewolf strength? That would make me hard to beat."

"The same is true for Antonio," Father Juan said. "Which is why we must be sure of him."

"You said you could only make the one dose," Jenn cautiously reminded the good father. "Because of the ingredients. And all your other supplies were burned up in the fire."

Father Juan nodded at Jenn. "It's true that my things were destroyed. Including the single most important ingredient: the petals of a rose that grew in the garden at Salamanca—a rose called *las Lagrimas de Cristo*, the Tears of Christ. It took two years of cultivating the rosebush to harvest enough petals for one dose. But I've had word that a similar flower grows along the French and Spanish border, in the maquis."

"I was changed into a vampire in the maquis," Antonio said, his voice subdued. "I know the terrain. I should go with you, Father."

"No," Father Juan said. "You need to go to Romania. And I want Jenn to go with you. And as backup, Jamie."

"Holgar can be backup," Jamie insisted. "*I'm* looking for Skye."

"My son," Father Juan began, "let's think this through. We've no way to get in touch with Skye. I tried to reach the Circuit to ask them for news, but they're not responding. We need more information—"

"Damn it to hell!" Jamie shouted. "We need to *track her down*."

"I'll go with you to get the rose," Esther told Father Juan.

"No," Jenn's ma protested, but Esther patted her hand.

"Yes, dear," Esther murmured. "We all have to do our part. You look after Sade."

Yeah, so much for that one helping out. Sade was a freak and a wreck.

Father Juan seemed to catch the old woman's determined expression, and dipped his head. "Thank you, Esther. Accepted."

"Can you . . . can you use this elixir to change Heather back?" Jenn's mom asked, her voice small and agonized. She slid a glance toward Antonio. "Though I suppose you'd have already done that. Unless he *likes* being a vampire."

Antonio frowned, clearly offended. But Jamie thought what she said held some truth. Immortality, superstrength — lots of men would trade their souls for that.

Father Juan looked at the others. "Jamie, you may go look for Skye." He picked up the gym bag and unzipped it, retrieving a rectangular white crystal.

"This scrying stone may alert you when you're closing in on her. The range is approximately twenty miles."

"Finally," Jamie said, grabbing it. He'd been wondering how, with all his magicks, the priest hadn't offered anything in the search for Skye. It was about time.

"Then *I* should be the one—," Holgar began, but Father Juan shook his head.

"There will be werewolves after you, Holgar. You will also go to Romania. You have a better chance of fighting them off with Antonio and Jenn than you would alone, distracted by so personal a mission."

Now it was Holgar's turn to sigh. Jamie reveled in Holgar's defeat.

"When did you make this stone?" Jamie asked. "How long have you planned to give me leave to find her?"

Father Juan's only answer was a philosophical shrug. "There are billions of square miles on the planet, Jamie. That will only work when you're within twenty miles of her."

"It's a start," Jamie insisted.

Father Juan gave Jamie a measured look, then turned to Jenn and Antonio. "You two and I have something to discuss before we part." And then he said to Jenn's grandmother, "Señora Esther, please go into the next room and tell Father Sebastian that we accept the offer of the Brotherhood of Saint Andrew, and that Antonio de la Cruz will travel in the company of Jennifer Leitner and Holgar Vibbard."

"Yes, Juan," Esther said. Jamie liked her. He remembered how well she had run her camp in Montana. She was worth twenty of Jenn any day.

Sade was starting to rock back and forth.

"Who's looking for Heather? Why didn't you make a—a stone for *her*?" Mrs. Leitner cried.

"We'll find her, Mom," Jenn said. "You have to trust Father Juan. And—and me." Her voice was tight and anxious. But she didn't go over to hug her mother. Jamie took note, and filed that information away.

Sade wrapped her arms around Jenn's mother. Tears spilled down her cheeks, and the two held each other.

"Here are new cell phones for all of you," Father Juan continued, dipping into the bag. "I've programmed everyone's numbers, but I want you to take the time to memorize them. I've already given one to Noah."

At Noah's mention, Jenn's cheeks reddened. Jamie's eyes narrowed. Oh, she fancied him, then? Had Antonio figured that out? That would make their trip to Romania all the more interesting. Now Jamie was almost sorry he wasn't going along.

"Now, for other matters," Father Juan said to Jenn and Antonio. "Private ones."

Father Juan led Jenn and Antonio into a side chapel separate from where he had given Jenn's mom the terrible news about Heather. There was one small pew, barely big enough for two people. At the end of the pew, a statue of St. John of the Cross stood elevated above a row of flickering candles. Antonio and Father Juan dipped their fingers into a small silver font attached to the wall, bent their knees, and crossed themselves. Jenn just waited, feeling the odd person out.

"We don't have much time," Father Juan said, "and so I'll be blunt."

Jenn's chest tightened. It seemed that every time they spoke in private, there was more bad news. Reflexively, she began to reach for Antonio's hand, then stopped herself. Those days were over.

But they weren't. Antonio firmly slid his fingers around hers and squeezed. Her throat tightened, and she had to shut her eyes to keep the tears away.

She didn't squeeze back.

She expected Father Juan to start with a prayer, as he usually did. Instead he asked, "What am I going to do with the two of you?"

"Pardon?" she asked.

"*Padre?*" Antonio said.

"You heard me right. You spent two years at the Academia pining for each other, neither admitting your feelings. But I knew, I watched you, and every time I sent up a prayer or cast the runes, the answer was always the same."

Jenn sucked in her breath, terrified of what he would say.

"The two of you belong together." The priest laced his fingers together in demonstration. "Spirit. Mind. Body."

Jenn was shocked. And strangely hopeful. Happy. And then dizzy with fear. Antonio was a vampire, and nearly a priest.

She felt Antonio move beside her, leaning toward Father Juan. He let go of her, and she tried to fold her hands quietly in her lap. Instead she clenched them, determined not to lose her composure.

"But I'm a Cursed One," Antonio murmured. "And I have lost my soul twice. I can't be trusted. Ever."

"But according to the runes, God trusts you," Father Juan said.

"Runes are magick," Antonio protested, "and I'm a Catholic."

"My son, look at the Bible. God doesn't choose the mightiest, the most virtuous to carry out His grand plans. He chooses the weak, the flawed, the outcast. He chooses those who are willing to do as He asks even when it seems impossible."

And this is why I don't believe, Jenn thought. Antonio was right. He couldn't be trusted. He'd turned his back on her. He believed his rampage in Las Vegas was a result of losing focus, and he'd rededicated his body, mind, and soul to the Catholic Church, which had turned *its* back on *him*.

Antonio dipped his head. "But in this case . . ."

"This is no different," Father Juan interrupted him. "We are living in terrible times, and great things will be asked of us all if we are to survive. But the greatest thing God requires of you is faith, and even more than that, love."

Jenn's throat tightened. Father Juan was practically forcing Antonio to declare that he didn't love her as much as he loved his Church. *Please, Father Juan, just shut up.*

Unaware of her turmoil, Father Juan laid a hand on each of their heads. "I know you think it is a fool's errand to go to Romania. But nothing He asks is foolish. Antonio, you need to overcome your vampiric urges. And Jenn, you need to find your faith. Only then can we win this war. Only then will you, too, find the love God wants for you."

Jenn didn't know which task was more impossible, finding faith or being with Antonio. Maybe it was time for her to throw the runes. Because she sure wasn't going to pray for guidance.

"You must find a way, or you will be lost. And the world will be lost too. Now go in peace."

"Peace? That's a joke, right?" Jenn asked, as the priest lifted his hands from their heads.

Beside her, Antonio crossed himself and pressed his lips against his thumb.

CHAPTER FOUR

What is Father Juan trying to tell us? I don't
understand. But I hope . . .
. . . I can't even write it down.
Because it's impossible.
                    —*from the diary of Jenn Leitner,*
                        retrieved from the ruins

EPPING FOREST, ENGLAND
SKYE

Skye had walked these forests since she was a small child, and she'd always had a sense of wonder. Now it felt like some dead, decaying thing. The trees were still green, the animal tracks in the ground fresh, but the vitality, the joy, were gone. And just beneath the surface, evil twisted and turned, growing ever stronger.

They've done this to us, the Cursed Ones, she thought bitterly. *They've slaughtered humanity and poisoned the Earth herself.*

Skye thought of her parents, her sister, and all her kin. *They let it happen.* They should have been the protectors and stewards of this world.

Tears streaked down her cheeks, unchecked. She prayed to the Lady that they might water the earth beneath her feet, returning to it that which was lost.

But they were only tears, not magick.

She balled her hands into fists, as something powerful broke loose within her. *An it harm none, do what thou wilt.* It was the creed of her people. She had clung to it blindly even through the most desperate nights, trying to restrict and regulate her actions accordingly.

But there were things worth fighting for, things worth dying for, and things worth killing for.

And because she had refused to kill anything but vampires, people had died. Their blood was on her hands.

"Never again," she whispered.

The wind caught at her words even as they left her lips. A warning or an affirmation?

"Never again," she said, louder.

She could feel something stirring in the woods.

"Never again!" she shouted as loud as she could. Her nails dug into her palms. She fell to her knees and fed the earth with her blood and her tears. The forest sighed around her, and the ground beneath her seemed to shudder.

"I am a daughter of the Goddess, and I will defend you," she pledged to the Earth. All the fear, the uncertainty, the frustration poured out from her, and she breathed in courage, purpose, and clarity.

Some argued that the code had been transcribed improperly, and that the true words were these: "An it harm none, do what thou *must.*"

She would protect the world. She must.

And when she had shed her last tear, she tumbled down onto the earth and closed her eyes. Mist — or maybe dreams — rose around her, and she could almost see Holgar's face. Almost hear his voice murmuring, *Skye, merrily met.*

Then she realized that someone was talking to her. She opened her eyes. There, standing over her, were her old friends Soleil and Lune, their palms extended toward her. Soleil had grown; she was nearly as tall as Lune now. Both looked much older than when they had last met.

Skye didn't know why, but she felt no surprise at seeing them, just sudden, overwhelming gladness. She rose.

"It's about time," Soleil said softly.

"The Circuit welcomes a sister," Lune murmured.

They raised their left hands — the hand of magick. In each palm was a henna pentagram. Then Skye's sisters in the Art pressed their left palms against each of Skye's bleeding hands and threw their arms around her, and the healing began to take place.

Soleil and Lune wouldn't tell Skye exactly how they had found her, saying only that "a friend" had alerted them that she was in England. They had cast a finder's spell to pinpoint her location. Skye wondered if that friend was Melody, or Summer's husband.

The two gave her a chance to wash up in the bathroom of a pub, then fed her a savory mushroom pie. Lune had brought her a change of clothes; Skye dressed in a pair of brown leggings, an olive pleated miniskirt, and a cream-colored sweater. Everything was a little loose on her, but Skye rather liked Lune's choice of earth tones. Soleil wore jeans and a ruffled yellow blouse, befitting her name, which meant "sun."

Then they drove her to the beautiful castle of Leeds. Part of the castle was built on land, and part extended into a lakelike moat. It was after hours, and all the tourists had left. The three crept to the water's edge, where a small white rowboat waited, and Soleil and Lune guided the boat with magicks onto the water, using no oars to power it. A small, arched gate provided them entrance. They glided in, climbed out, and pulled the boat onto a stone landing.

"So this is the headquarters of the Circuit?" Skye whispered as they went through a small door and up a narrow, circular staircase.

"Just one of many," Lune replied.

"Did you know that a medieval princess, Joan of Navarre, was imprisoned here for using witchcraft? Her magicks have soaked into the stone. Do you feel them?" Soleil asked as they entered a gently illuminated room.

Skye nodded. Deep, powerful vibrations were thrumming through her. A statue of the Virgin Mary crushed a serpent beneath her feet. What had been lost to White magick was that the Lady had taken evil on, and won. The Mother had not stayed neutral, and Skye now believed— no, she *knew*—that in the battle to come, the Goddess would actively fight.

A single candle glowed on a table in front of the three, and she focused on the light. The Circuit was a loose alliance of witches who had decided that going underground was the wrong choice in a world gone mad. Skye had been in and out of contact with them for a while, but she wasn't an actual member. She was a hunter, and they viewed her hunting team as her coven. Skye couldn't help but smile slightly as she wondered what Jamie would have to say about that.

"We'll be back soon," Lune told her, as the two disappeared through a door. A few minutes later they reappeared in long white hooded robes embroidered with silver crescents and golden pentagrams. Lune carried an identical robe in her arms.

"They'll see you now," Lune said. "Put this on."

Together Soleil and Lune helped Skye into the heavy robe. Her friends raised their hoods over their hair; Skye did the same, and followed them slowly across the threshold.

Six or seven hooded women ringed the stone altar, which was covered with pink roses, rose quartz, and five white candles arranged in a pentagram. An illuminated Book of Spells lay open before a statue of Diana, Goddess of the Hunt. Her bow was notched with an arrow; the string was pulled back tightly. Diana had sighted her quarry.

The High Priestess spread her arms in greeting. The woman's papery skin was heavily lined, but her bright blue eyes crackled with energy. She regarded Skye for a moment. A charge skittered down Skye's spine, and she felt as if the other witch were reading her soul.

"Skye of Salamanca, blessed be," the High Priestess said.

"Blessed be," the other witches—including Soleil and Lune—echoed.

"Blessed be," Skye said. "Merrily met."

The High Priestess shook her head. "Not merrily, little one." She waved her hand above the altar. A clutch of carved stones materialized in front of the Book of Spells. "The runes have been cast thirteen times thirteen for the last fortnight."

"What do they foretell?" Skye asked, gazing at them.

A deep sigh echoed throughout the room. It seemed to Skye that, in the flickering flames, the statue of Diana raised her bow slightly, as if to refine her aim.

Then the statue loosed her arrow, and it arced toward the ceiling. A shower of bright white stars burst into flame, then assumed a shape—

The shape of a bat.

Then larger stars appeared, exploded, and formed a larger bat that consumed the smaller.

"The Vampire Nation will fall. And the Vampire Kingdom will rise," said the High Priestess. "Every human death, every vampire victory—these are merely portents for what is to come later. And it will be worse."

"So we have to stop it," Skye said. She looked at the hooded women. "We have to stop it *now!*" Her voice came out as a bellow, and echoed against the stones. The torches flickered. And a low wind wound its way through the room.

She hunched her shoulders, cringing at the way she had just spoken to the High Priestess. She was about to apologize, when the old woman spoke again.

"We have a question," the High Priestess said. "And you are here to help us answer it."

"Me?" Skye said. "How?" But she had a feeling that she already knew the answer.

"We here have worked in secret, behind the scenes. We've seen much, but not all. But you have been on the front line of this war."

"You've been a symbol of inspiration," said one of the other witches.

"Or damnation," said another.

"We've cast spells to strengthen and protect humanity. But we must use our magick to fight shoulder to shoulder with humanity," said a third.

"An thou harm none," a fourth argued.

Skye flared with irritation. "I'm sorry, but this is a war. The only way to win against the vampires is to kill them. There can be no peace."

"A truce," someone said. "A truce with Solomon, and then—"

"Crikey, are you mad?" Skye cried. "The vampires want to destroy us, and we cannot let that happen. You've been working behind the scenes, but the time for that is past."

"Perhaps. Perhaps not," the High Priestess said. "The Cursed Ones wage war against the nonmagickal, not us."

And there it was, the arrogance, the denial, and the fear that allowed people to stand by and do nothing while others were slaughtered. *It doesn't concern me.*

Skye had spoken to Antonio many times about his experiences during World War II. Millions had been murdered because people thought Adolf Hitler could be reasoned with, bargained with. But bombs had fallen on Britain, and still nation upon nation stood by, because *their* countries hadn't been attacked. Let Hitler kill the Jews and the Gypsies; what concern was it to them? And now Skye's people, the witches, were willing to sacrifice nonwitch humanity because they believed that the Cursed Ones wouldn't come after them.

"It won't end with ordinary humans," Skye said. "The vampires fear us and our powers. But that won't stop them from wiping us out too."

"Not everyone believes that," the High Priestess replied.

Raw fury coursed through Skye's veins like blood. "Then believe this. Even if the vampires kill every mundane man, woman, and child, they'll still need to feed. And we, and the werewolves, will be the only ones left. Everyone knows that werewolves fight back, so who do you think they're going to look to for blood?"

The High Priestess nodded. Her face was grim, her lips pursed tightly. "Well said, Sister York. You are young, passionate, and eloquent. You must persuade us all to join this war."

Moments later, blurry images of men and women began to appear in the room, some wearing robes, some ordinary street clothes. They were pale, ghostlike in their transparency.

"Circuit members," the High Priestess explained. "Those who can't be with us in body are traveling here in spirit so that we all might decide on our course of action together."

Around the room, hundreds of astral projections appeared. Witches from every corner of the globe stared at Skye, waiting to hear her argument for war.

Skye's palms began to sweat. The fate of the world hung on what she said next.

DOVER, ENGLAND
ESTEFAN AND HIS COVEN BROTHERS
FROM CADIZ

Estefan's three coven brothers arrived in a thunderstorm. Platinum-colored lightning struck the ground as they stepped from the ferry. Other travelers dodged the rain. But Estefan welcomed the icy downpour. It cooled his super-heated anger and the burns Skye had left like the mark of a slap on his face. He wore a glamour to hide the injuries. As his coven brothers embraced him and kissed his cheek, none of them saw the damage a mere girl—and a White Witch at that—had inflicted on him.

"Hermanos," he said. Brothers. "Thank you for coming." Then he snapped his fingers, and the rains parted in their path.

They walked through the storm, dry as bones. Dark magick—Black magick—sizzled around them, colliding with the lightning and shaking the gray sky like a box of broken mirrors. Estefan's mind kept turning to Skye. It was not long ago that he had imprisoned her in a fun house of her memories. Such joy he'd felt watching her flail in mindless terror like a little sparrow struggling to escape a cage.

And now, days ago, she had *escaped.*

I didn't realize how much she'd grown since she left me, he thought. *How strong she's become.*

His brothers trailing slightly behind him, Estefan allowed

the glamour to drop away completely. He knew what he looked like. His face was purple and white with scars, and his eyes were completely black except for two small circles of crimson at their centers. His eyeteeth lengthened and sharpened like vampire fangs. But when he bit someone, it wasn't the blood he was after. He wasn't even sure what it was he took. A piece of their soul? Their life essence?

He didn't know, but he was fascinated by it. He'd participated in the Hell Fire Caves gatherings, where eager young Cursed Ones, dazzled by magicks, had mingled with witches both White and Dark. The witches had enchanted the blood from the Cursed Ones' veins, and the vampires had drunk it from goblets, savoring the unusual, otherworldly taste of the magick. Then they'd offered it to the witches, too. Estefan had eagerly swallowed the strange sweetness.

After he'd met Skye, he'd taken her with him to the revels. It had required a trance to get her to participate. But one night she'd snapped awake, and she'd set him on fire in an attempt to flee.

She went to Spain, and so did he—leaving with one of his vampire companions to join Aurora's court—not in hopes of becoming a Cursed One but to discover what made them so strong and immortal. He studied mixtures of magick and vampiric blood, but drew no conclusions. He tried to discuss it with Aurora, but she was a bit of a disappointment in that regard. She had no curiosity about what made vampires tick.

However, her lover, Sergio Almodóvar, was another matter. Sergio owned an amazing Book of Spells, compiled by a vampire interested in magick. It included spells of power and transformation — magicks too strong for Estefan to master.

At first.

Aurora had stolen the book from Sergio, not because she wanted it but because she knew it would enrage him. It was a trophy the two of them fought over during their spats, which had apparently been going on for decades if not centuries. So Estefan stayed in Aurora's court, perusing the black-and-maroon leather book whenever possible. He dedicated himself to working these strange new magicks, confused about why, if he had drunk vampire blood, he hadn't been transformed into one. It was his magicks, he decided, that somehow protected him. And made him different enough, he figured, to withstand any magicks that little White bitch leveled at him.

He had never forgotten the agony of the fire she had flung at him that first time in the caves, nor the ridicule of his coven brothers for being dumped by a little fourteen-year-old. And so he worked his magicks.

Then Antonio de la Cruz killed Sergio at the battle of Salamanca, and Skye was there too. The timing was perfect; Estefan had enough power for payback — or so he had thought. Little Skye had surprised him.

He had lost access to Sergio's Book of Spells, but with

his coven brothers back in England, and all the changes he'd gone through to make himself more powerful, more like a Cursed One, he was certain he could track her down.

And make her scream until she died.

LAKE COMO, ITALY
AURORA, LUCIFER, AND DANTALION

Aurora wrapped her furs around herself, not because she was cold, but because ermine contrasted so beautifully with her black hair, and because she had no one to hold on to as she made her grand entrance into the great hall of her sire's villa on Lake Como.

The walls were covered with weapons from eons of warfare, and black velvet drapes were looped back from the magnificent windows overlooking the water. They would be closed soon, to block out the rising sun.

Lucifer rose from a carved chair at the far end of the room and came to her. He was wearing a perfectly tailored white suit in honor of Sergio, and with his mane of white hair and piercing red eyes, he was startlingly attractive. Yes, Sergio had been Aurora's lover, but Lucifer was her morning star. There was no vampire more magnificent. Nor more terrifying.

He took her in his arms and held her. Trembling, she melted against him. He held her more tightly. Panic flared within her. She cleared her throat.

"Please, master," she said in Spanish as she pulled back. "I'll cry bloody tears all over your suit."

He smiled softly at her, then reached his long nails and sliced his suit jacket from the lapel down to the waist. She realized he was rending his garments, as she had done at Sergio's funeral. She felt a fresh ripple of uneasiness. Had Lucifer been present at the ceremony without telling her? Had he had a camera or a scrying stone to spy on her?

Did he know that she had taken Antonio de la Cruz captive in Las Vegas, then lost him? And if he did know, what would he do to her?

"*Ay*, Lucifer," she blurted, dropping into a curtsey out of habit. Back in the fifteenth century, when he had saved her from the Inquisition, women bowed to great lords.

"*Pobrecita*," he said. Poor little one. "Sergio was a prince among us, and you know how much he loved you."

"*Sí.*"

With shaking hands she reached into the cuff of her coat and produced a white silk handkerchief. She daubed her eyes, seeing the flecks of blood, and was about to put it away when Lucifer took it from her and dropped it lazily to the floor.

There was a snorting and a panting, and then a beautiful wolfhound appeared. It caught up the handkerchief and galloped across the floor, bringing it to a figure standing in the shadows. Aurora's blood froze. The hound had belonged to the Russian vampire, Dantalion, who had spent his days trying to genetically engineer the perfect soldier and whose monstrous hybrids she had killed back in Russia for sport. She hadn't realized he was here at the villa . . . and clearly a guest of her sire.

"Aurora," Dantalion said, moving from the darkness.

"Dantalion," she replied, standing tall and proud.

"My condolences on your loss," Dantalion said with a heavy Russian accent. "Sergio was a jewel in the crown of the Vampire Kingdom."

Her throat constricted by fear, Aurora mutely nodded. Dantalion had still been burrowed inside his Russian laboratory when she had captured Antonio on its poisoned grounds. Did Dantalion know that she'd been there for nights before seizing Antonio, picking off Dantalion's beloved experiments for sport? Reducing the ranks of his monstrous hybrids so that when the hunters and the men with black crosses attacked him, his defenses had been severely weakened?

Did he know that she had found his creations so repulsive she hadn't even told Lucifer about them? And now it appeared that Lucifer had not only known about them, but was helping Dantalion fund the supersoldier project.

"We'll cheer you up," Lucifer told her, also speaking in English. He kissed Aurora's cheek, then clapped Dantalion on the shoulder. "Dantalion has been very busy, and he's got wonderful news for us."

"Yes," Dantalion said. "My spy among the hunters has

given me excellent information. We know all the plans of the Salamanca hunters. Where each is going. What their missions are." His pride showed on his face.

She covered her alarm with a cough. "Spy?"

Lucifer beamed at the Russian. "Dantalion used to be partners with Rasputin himself. Do you remember Rasputin? He was a Russian mystic in the nineteenth century."

Aurora nodded stiffly. "He studied mesmerism."

Lucifer nodded. "Which is, of course, one of a vampire's greatest strengths. Hypnotizing our victims helped us keep in the shadows for so long. But it is always a personal thing. We look into the eyes of one person, command them to do our will. Dantalion can do it to many and from a distance." Lucifer waggled his brows. "In fact, he was the one who saved you from Antonio de la Cruz at the battle of Salamanca. He made Antonio imagine that he was burning at the stake. *Magnífico, ¿no?*"

"Oh? Yes. Yes, it is. Thank you, Dantalion," she said, reeling at the implications. Dantalion had seen the battle at Salamanca. Had he told Lucifer that the little Hunter, Eriko, had nearly killed her? And that she, Aurora, had gone to Salamanca to recapture Antonio before Lucifer found out that she'd lost him?

"It was my pleasure," Dantalion said. He sighed dramatically. "I only wish that I could have helped Sergio."

"*Sí,*" Aurora said. "Now, about the spy. Who is it?" She heard how desperate she sounded. "I would love to know," she added in a warm, seductive voice. She needed to know if they had been watching her, reporting on her.

"Someone they'd never suspect," Lucifer replied, chuckling. "But come, Aurora, come and admire what *else* he's accomplished."

Lucifer cupped her cheek. She knew it would be such a simple matter, a trifle, to grab her head and yank it off her neck. She'd killed vampires that way a dozen times, and Lucifer was much stronger than she. If he wanted to kill her, there would be nothing she could do to stop him.

I must charm him, and keep myself dear to him, as I did in the old days. Lucifer had graciously stepped aside when the sparks had flown between Sergio and her. Perhaps it was time to fan those flames once more—between Lucifer and her.

She reached up on tiptoe and kissed Lucifer's mouth, lingering at his fangs. "I can barely wait," she murmured. "Where are these wonderful accomplishments?"

"Why, in the dungeon, of course," Lucifer replied. He cocked his head and stroked Aurora's left fang with his forefinger. *By the gods below, would he break it off?*

She laughed. "Only you would have a dungeon in an Italian villa, my master," she cooed.

"Only I, and all those filthy Popes who reigned during our lifetimes," Lucifer said. His face darkened, and she felt his rage surge through his body. He turned the force of his crimson eyes on her. "They will pay, all those churchmen. And anyone who stands in our way."

"Like Solomon," Dantalion put in.

"I haven't forgotten your vendetta against that one," Lucifer said to Dantalion. "Solomon will beg for mercy." He smiled at Aurora. "And I will show him none."

Aurora made a show of sighing. "I love it when you talk like that."

His smile grew—predatory, calculating, lustful. He raised her hand to his mouth and kissed the back of her hand, allowing his fangs to slice it open, just the top layer.

"I know," he replied. "And I have done—and will do— so many more things that you'll love. Now, come."

Aurora kept her head held high and her fears to herself as the three headed down to the dungeons.

CHAPTER FIVE

Salamanca Hunter's Manual: Emotion
Yours must be the avenging fury of the Lord God.
You can not indulge in the petty hatreds of those
who have not been called to serve as the Hunter.
Anger is a waste of your strength. Stay calm in
the face of insult and adversity. Know that on
the battlefield against the Cursed Ones, your
composure may save your life.

(translated from the Spanish)

LONDON, ENGLAND
JAMIE

Jamie, with his many tattoos and the angry vibe he gave
out all the time, stuck out most places, especially in Spain.
Crossing borders these days meant looking inconspicuous,

which meant wearing a sweater and a knit cap, keeping his eyes on the ground, saying "yes, sir," "no, sir," the whole bloody thing. And carrying nothing that looked even remotely like a weapon that could kill vampires. So he'd had to leave the stakes and crosses and holy water behind. But he'd been able to hide his guns. Only one bloke had found them, and a crisp bill had ensured the guard looked the other way.

Once he had finally made it to London, Jamie found that it was easier to fit in. At least with the fringe crowd. Which was just fine with him. The people he threaded his way through in one of the darker back alleys of London were just his type of pissed-off antigovernment anarchists. He wasn't even the only Irishman.

Tired, wary, he slogged into a small, dark pub and took a seat at the bar. It was midday. He was a good week out from Toledo, and he hadn't slept a wink in going on forty hours. A couple of nifty new spells relayed by Father Juan revealed that Skye had left Spain, and three days ago the Father had called to tell him he'd "seen" her in England. Then nothing, and the stone Father Juan had given him had yet to light up or do whatever it was supposed to do when he was within twenty miles of her.

Which meant she probably wasn't in the city. Which meant she could be anywhere. That was just too much territory to cover without more information. He hoped that a drink would clear his head. Maybe some of the locals could help him figure out where a coven of Dark Witches was likely to be hiding out.

If they even believe in witches. Two thirds of the planet still doesn't believe there are werewolves, and the bloody witches have gone out of their way to hide.

"What's your poison?" the bartender, a man with sallow skin and an enormous mustache, asked him.

"Give me a shot," Jamie said, eyeing the others around him. "Whiskey."

"Seems like you're looking for more than that," the bartender said, his tone suggestive.

"Look, boyo, I'm not—" Jamie turned around and stopped in mid-sentence. Below heavy lids the bartender's eyes were glowing ruby red. And in the mirror behind the bar, Jamie's was the only reflection to be seen. *A dozen other drinkers in this bar, and none of 'em human.*

Jamie leaped off his barstool with a string of swear words. He grabbed the stool and smashed it against the counter. It splintered into a dozen pieces, and he clutched one of them and went to stake the bartender.

But the vampire wasn't there anymore. Jamie twisted and saw that he was at the front door, throwing the dead bolt. Jamie was locked in with the vampires.

I'm going to die. Just like me sister, Maeve. Just like Eriko.

He sucked in his breath and exhaled. He heard himself begin to recite a Hail Mary out loud.

The vampire nearest him snickered. Jamie hurled the

wooden stake in his hand and nailed the monster in the heart.

That's for blasphemy, he thought, as the creature turned to dust.

Two more Cursed Ones rushed him. Jamie dropped to the floor, grabbed each of them by a knee, and flipped them onto their backs. Before they could get up, he had scooped up two more shards of chair. He charged forward and straddled the one on the left and slammed the stake home.

That's for me ma.

He spun and narrowly escaped being bitten by the second one as he lurched to his knees. A quick feint to the left and then he got behind the Curser. Another stake through the heart.

That's for me da.

"Hail Mary, full o' grace, ya sodding suckers!" he shouted. He jumped to his feet just in time to backhand another Cursed One as it came at him. Blood sprayed from the creature's cheek where Jamie cut it open. It struck back, slashing at him with razorlike nails. They cut through his shirt, cut into his chest. He could tell, but he felt no pain. All he felt was . . .

Dust as the monster went up like kindling beneath Jamie's makeshift stake.

That's for Eri.

More Cursers rushed him. His foot slipped on the floor in a pool of blood that he thought might be his, and he crashed down onto one knee. He managed to hold on to his stake, and he jabbed it sharply upward into a Cursed One's chest while he reached for another stake with his free hand.

That's for Maeve.

He hacked and slashed and kept turning, never letting anything get behind him.

That's for Northern Ireland.

Another Curser dead.

That's for the university, the students and teachers all dead.

And another.

That one's for me and the life you bastards stole from me.

And at last he ran out of weapons and still there were more vampires.

The front door suddenly exploded inward, and a hail of arrows came whizzing through. One skimmed his jaw, and he dropped to the ground, pushing a table over to use as cover. There was the roar of angry vampires all around him.

And then there was nothing.

Slowly Jamie sat up to survey the bar. Vampire dust swirled in the air, but nothing else moved. He eased himself up more so that he could get a better look at the door. A slender form filled it, and for a moment he thought it was a young boy. In each hand there was a specially designed crossbow fitted with three bolts each.

Cautiously his rescuer stepped inside, and Jamie saw that it was a girl. She was Skye's age, maybe a year or two younger. She had flaming red hair and enormous green eyes. She was dressed in military-style fatigues, and her hair was pulled back with a black hair elastic.

"I think you got them all. And thanks," he said.

She swiveled toward him with her bows extended. He dropped back down behind the table, afraid she might shoot him by mistake.

"Come out," she ordered in a lilting Irish accent.

He stood slowly, putting his hands where she could see him.

"How many more of you are there?" she asked.

"Just me." He stood and stepped around the table toward her.

"That's as far as you go," she said. "I'll dust you same as the others."

"I'm not a bleeding Curser!"

She dropped one of the crossbows and, swift as lightning, hurled something at him. A glass vial shattered against his shoulder, and water sprayed his face.

"Oi!" he bellowed.

She cocked her head. "That's holy water. You're not burning."

"I told you, not a bloody vampire." He pointed to where the mirror had hung, but noticed that it had been destroyed. Nothing showed through but the moldy wall that had been behind it.

"Well, you smell like one," she observed, lowering her one weapon as she stooped to reclaim the other crossbow.

Jamie stared at her.

"If you're not a fanger, what are you doin' in a bleedin' pub?" she asked, indicating their surroundings.

He lifted his chin and crossed his arms over his heaving chest. "Getting a short, what you think?"

She regarded him with large green eyes. "You're not from around here, are you?"

"Belfast. I haven't been home nor here, either, in a while." He squinted at her. "Why?"

She looked at him as if he were a moron. "Pubs are only for fangers and those what want to *drink* with them."

He closed the distance between them and grabbed her shoulders. "What are you saying?"

She stared down at his hand on her right shoulder, but she didn't move away from him. "Been that way at least a year. Irish, Welsh, Scots, English, we've been driven out of our own pubs by the bloody bastards."

He read the truth in her eyes, and rage flared inside him. "*They took our beer?* And no one fought back?"

"Hard to find any fighters back home," she retorted. "Fangers have killed most of 'em. All that's left are children and old men and cowards."

"Say you're a liar."

"I'm not." She made a face at him. "They took our whiskey, too."

There were no words for what he felt, just a sense of deep anguish. It was a fist to his gut.

He let her go, and she showed her back as she headed outside. He grabbed his bag and followed after.

"So what are you doing here?" she asked as he caught up.

"Looking for a friend of mine that's been taken."

The girl snorted. "Oh, and that's a smart quest. Take my advice. Go back to wherever you been hiding. Your friend is dead. Or worse."

He grabbed her arm and spun her around. "I've not been hiding. I've been fighting. Case you missed it, most of the Cursers in that bar were dead long before *you* got there. And my friend is one of my team and near impossible to kill."

"Team?" She lowered her voice and asked him excitedly, "Are you resistance?"

"Yeah. Hunters."

Her eyes widened for a moment. "Ain't no Hunters around here."

"I told you. Haven't been here in years."

He couldn't read her expression. She looked as if she might hit him, except that a smile was playing along her lips. "Well, it's about bloody time a Hunter showed up. Where were you a year ago when we needed you most?"

"Still in training," he said. It was the truth, but it didn't take the sting out of her words. He had been wrong to stay after graduation. He should have gone straight home to Northern Ireland like he'd planned instead of staying to be part of a bleedin' team.

And if I had, I'd be dead too, he realized with absolute clarity. Yet somehow that didn't make the guilt he was feeling any less. Ireland's sons and daughters had been bleeding, dying for her, and he should have been one of them.

She cocked her head at him. "Hail Mary. Sort of a strange battle cry."

"It worked, didn't it?"

She shrugged.

"I'm Jamie," he said, offering his hand.

"Kate," she replied, shaking with him.

She was the nearest thing to an ally he had here.

"Kate, maybe you have some friends who might be able to help me figure out where my friend is."

She let go of his hand as she shook her head. "I don't have time to deal with your missing persons. I got Cursed Ones to kill." She turned to go.

"Maybe you've heard something on the streets?" he persisted. "She's a witch. She was kidnapped by another witch."

That got her attention. Turning back around, she planted her hands suspiciously on her hips. "What's a good Catholic boy doing hanging out with that lot?" she asked, raising an eyebrow.

"What's a fine Irish lass doing ridding London of vampires instead of the mother country?" he countered. "Why you protecting the English?"

"The enemy of my enemy," she said, "is my friend."

He nodded. "I'll give you that. Now, can you help me?"

"I've heard rumors . . . but it's probably nothing," she said after a moment.

"Tell me anyway."

He lowered his head, and she said under her breath, "People are whispering that witches have returned to Stonehenge."

His stomach did a flip. Could it be a lead? "Stonehenge. Why?"

She hesitated. "Because it's a place of power."

Jamie could tell there was something else. "And?" he prompted.

She looked away. "They say they're stockpiling something, some sort of magic herb that enhances their abilities."

He thought of Father Juan and the promised elixir. "What's it called?"

"I don't know. *I'm* not a bleedin' witch," she snapped at him.

They walked a few more steps in silence. He glanced down at her crossbows.

"So, where are you headed now?" he asked.

"Another pub half a mile from here. Busy day." She looked at him speculatively. "I could use some help."

There it was again. Help a girl from his own people kill Cursed Ones, all he'd ever wanted to do, or go runnin' off on a fool's mission to find someone else's missing fighting partner. He felt the knife twist in his soul.

"You okay?" she asked.

"The whole world's a feckin' disaster and you ask if I'm okay?" he said, fighting back the urge to laugh or cry. Maybe both.

"The ability to care for other people, that's what separates us from them," she retorted, but her voice was gentle. "It's all we've got left."

Cursers couldn't care. He thought about Antonio. The Curser cared for Jenn, and he knew that wasn't a falsehood on the bloody vampire's part. How did he do that?

Jamie shook his head. "I have to find my friend."

She was clearly disappointed. "Well, good luck to you, then."

"I'm sorry, Kate." The words were little more than a whisper.

She raised her chin, all brave. "I'm sure she's . . . important."

The knife twisted deeper. Jamie knew that they needed to part company then, because if they kept walking, they'd make it to the other pub and then he'd help her. And if they survived it, he'd help her with the next and the next.

And Skye would be lost.

And Skye would die alone.

If she hasn't already.

With a terse nod he walked quickly away. Tears stung his eyes, and he swore and kicked an empty beer bottle down the street. It was the most futile gesture in the world, and it only made him feel worse.

And deeply, achingly alone.

Then he thought of what Kate had said about the witches stockpiling some kind of magickal herb. He pulled out his cell. A full minute later he heard Father Juan's voice on the other end of the line. "Have you found her?" the good father asked, voice tense, forgoing any kind of greeting. That kind of blunt abruptness suited Jamie just fine.

"No, but I heard that witches might be stashing some kind of magick plant that gives them a boost. A boost in their magick. Herb."

There was silence on the other end.

"It's at Stonehenge," Jamie added. "Maybe it's like what you use in your elixir."

"I understand. Investigate it."

"I'll get Skye first and she can tell us what it is," he said.

"Maybe she's there," Father Juan said. "You said that *witches* are stockpiling the herb."

"Then she would have contacted us," Jamie argued.

"We're in hiding, and she doesn't have the new cell phone numbers," Father Juan replied reasonably.

"I'll go within twenty miles of the blasted place. And if the scrying stone don't light up, I'm moving on."

"Save the world, Jamie. Focus on the bigger picture. Then you can help Skye."

Jamie huffed. "But—"

"This is not a request." Father Juan's voice was calm

as always. He expected to be obeyed. "Investigate, and call me back."

"Yes, *sir*," Jamie ground out, ending the call. He was furious with himself. Jesus, Mary, and Joseph, why the hell had he called Father Juan? He should have known what the father would say.

He fumed quietly for a moment. Then he reluctantly admitted that since he had no idea where else in England to look for Skye, traveling to a witchy place might be the best chance he had of finding her.

Hocus pocus, he thought dryly.

The Maquis, on the Border Between France and Spain Father Juan and Esther Leitner

"I was too hard on Jamie," Father Juan confessed as he pocketed his phone.

"Maybe not hard enough," Esther observed, her tone dry.

Father Juan smiled faintly. He liked Jenn's grandmother. She was no-nonsense, tough as nails, and at heart incredibly compassionate. He was sure she'd kick his shins in if he pointed that out, though.

"He might have a lead on something I could use for the elixir. Something the witches use to boost their power."

"It'd be nice if it was the Tears of Christ," she said. "Then we could get the hell out of here."

They were deep in the scrubby forest, searching for the rare flower needed for the elixir. The scent of rosemary wafted from the plants at his knees. A week ago they had left Sade and Jenn's mother with Father Sebastian. Neither of them was a known associate of the hunter team. Privately, Father Juan was disappointed over Sade's behavior. She'd been selected to train at the academy, but if there had been a fighting spirit within her, the terror of the fall of Salamanca had extinguished it. Once she recovered from the shock, he prayed she would prove a good fighter.

If all went according to plan, he and Esther would return for her and Leslie Leitner before continuing on to rendezvous with Jenn, Antonio, and Holgar in Romania.

If all of them lived that long.

Father Juan shook his head. He, of all people, did not have the luxury of such negative thoughts. He had to keep it together for everyone else.

"*Sí,*" he said. "I'd like to get the hell out of here too."

At moonrise he had set himself apart for a time to meditate on the presence of the flower. In a trance he had opened a map of the area and dangled a moonstone pendulum above it. The pendulum had pointed to a deep ravine about ten kilometers to their north. But according to Father Sebastian's local informant, those ten kilometers were located in the heart of one of the most dangerous vampire strongholds in the world.

"There are a few hours left until dawn. We should take

turns sleeping, since it'll be safest for us to move when the sun is up," he said to Esther.

She nodded. "I'll take first watch."

"Are you sure you want to continue on?" Juan asked. "This is a perilous undertaking."

"'Perilous.'" She smiled. "Can't be worse than other things I've seen."

He couldn't help but return the smile. These were hard times, and a little sense of humor went a long way.

Esther stationed herself on top of a boulder, armed with crosses, holy water, and an Uzi as weapons. He lay at the base of the outcropping, sleeplessly staring up at the moon. He was worried about Jamie. His hold on him was slipping. And even though Jamie was a pain, he was a pain they couldn't afford to live without. He was vital to the team, even if he did serve as a lightning rod for everyone's anger and frustration.

Which would mean nothing to Father Juan if he couldn't get enough rest and lack of concentration got him killed.

If God will even let me die.

It was a thought he had often, more so of late. He didn't like the direction his thoughts turned in moments of darkness such as these.

He had never liked dark nights.

They were hard on the soul.

Oh, my soul, he thought, *take flight, and repair the world.*

It was a prayer Father Juan had been praying for a very, very long time.

OUTSIDE BUCHAREST, ROMANIA
JENN, HOLGAR, AND ANTONIO

Jenn never liked being alone with her thoughts when she was on patrol. It was her turn, though. She, Holgar, and Antonio had made their way to a safe house on the outskirts of Bucharest that was owned by the Brotherhood of St. Andrew. The crescent moon hung low in the sky, and soon the sun would be up.

Would the enemy succeed in making it possible for vampires to walk in the sunlight? She'd had a dream once where she and Antonio were strolling along a beach in the sunlight, holding hands, kissing.

Her throat tightened, and she willed her tears away. Father Juan had to be wrong. She and Antonio weren't destined to be together. In her mind she saw Noah smiling at her. She remembered the hard muscles of his chest as they sparred . . . and the vein in his neck pulsing from exertion. He was a living, breathing guy with a beating heart. While Antonio . . .

Stop this. Pay attention. You're on patrol.

She scanned the area and moved down an alley. She smelled frying meat. A baby squalled. *"This is the Voice of the Resistance."*

Jenn sucked in her breath and froze in her tracks. It was Kent's voice, speaking in English, and it was coming from a nearby window. She crept softly to it and peered just over the sill. Inside a small room lit only by a candle, two women sat staring intently at something that she realized must be some sort of sophisticated radio.

She ducked back, flattening herself instinctively against the brick wall. Part of her wanted to warn the women, let them know that they could easily be discovered listening to a forbidden broadcast. But she was afraid that if she made a sound, she wouldn't hear what Kent had to say.

"... *more cities have fallen to the vampires. I'm sad to report that in Japan, Kyoto has been the latest casualty. While it is possible that the Kyoto Hunter has escaped the city, we are not holding out much hope.*"

Jenn's breath caught in her throat. The Kyoto Hunter. Wasn't that Eriko's brother, Kenji? Or was this yet another Hunter, who had already filled his shoes? The tears she had held back began to fall as she thought of Eriko, dead at the hands of Aurora. They hadn't contacted her family. They didn't want anyone to know.

"*And tonight I have a message for a special friend. Jenn, if you can hear this, or if someone can reach her: Jenn, follow in Bram's trail and you will find friends waiting to aid you. I wish I could say more. But you know why I can't. And for now this is Kent, praying to make it through one more day and believing that this cursed darkness will pass.*"

Oh, my God. Stunned, Jenn gripped the cement around the bricks as she strained to hear more. White noise followed. Then there was silence. Then she could hear the two women speaking quietly together, in a language she didn't understand.

This was the first time she had heard from Kent since they had been stopped from taking down Solomon by Greg and the black crosses back in America. She was so glad he was still alive . . . and still fighting. It was thrilling to hear her own name on Kent's lips—until she finally processed what he'd said. He had told her to "follow Bram's trail." The only Bram she could think of was Bram Stoker—the author of the novel *Dracula*. *Dracula*, which took place in Transylvania, which was part of Romania. Which was where they were.

A hopeful thrill danced up her spine.

Friends in Romania.

CHAPTER SIX

Mortals, mortals fade away
Vampire lords are here to stay
We'll make you crawl, make you whine
Drink your blood down like it's wine
Who's to blame? you want to ask
Who's the fiend you must unmask?
Gaze upon yourselves and grieve
It is you—your fear, your greed

LEEDS CASTLE
SKYE AND THE CIRCUIT

After pleading her case the best she could, Skye was sent out of the castle while the High Priestess and the other witches debated if they should join Skye in active battle. She walked the hedge maze, marshaling her magickal forces, remembering how on the winter solstice her family would chalk out a labyrinth to walk in the garden behind the cottage. But now that they had hidden all traces of their heritage from the world, had they abandoned creating a labyrinth, too?

Then she remembered that the last time she had walked a maze, Estefan had tormented her with distorted images of the time she'd gotten lost in a fun house as a little girl. She'd told him that story soon after she'd first met him at her sister's handfasting at Stonehenge. She'd been so foolish, lowering her guard, assuming he was going to be her sexy protector, keeping her safe from the Cursed Ones, from everything.

Anger moved inside her, and she began to tremble. Suddenly the maze was a trap; the clouds billowed like smoke around the moon, casting Skye in darkness. She began to run, crashing into a hedgerow as she turned left. Twigs scratched her as she pushed her way back out. She brushed against another as she whipped around to the right. She whirled in a circle, her breath coming fast. She had to get out, get free. Something was coming. Something bad . . . She covered her mouth with both her hands to keep from screaming.

Stop, she commanded herself. You are a child of the Lady. *You are a hunter.*

The hedges rustled as if something was about to burst free of them. Skye murmured a finder's spell, then raised her voice and shouted the words in Latin. The hedges were

made of yew trees, highly magickal, and therefore respon-
sive: The hedge stilled. Then the leafy wall to her left shimmered subtly. She ran along it. The row perpendicular to
that hedge also shimmered, and she turned left when she
reached it. Beyond, more leaves glittered. As a wind picked
up, she followed the magickal light. Slowly it began to dim.
She repeated the spell, feeling the drain on her energy.

Instead of glowing, the hedge in front of her burst into
flame. The heat smacked her face, and as she jumped backward with a cry, the one behind her did the same. Shocked,
she ran; each leafy wall she passed blazed with fiery orange
and scarlet flames.

She uttered spells. *Stop, stop,* she ordered the fire, but
it continued to rage as she charged along the walls, then
took a breath and pushed through one. Her feet slipped on
rocks; there was a stone mound before her, and the black
maw of an entrance. She stumbled inside, where it was cool
and wet. She dashed down slick, uneven stairs as smoke
followed her inside.

Coughing, she whirled in a circle. She was in a cavern.
She heard running water and ran in its direction.

A hole in the roof poured in silvery moonlight. The
clouds must have parted. She darted past figures in hollows
made of stone and shell. Then she stumbled to a stop in
front of a trickling waterfall. Crouched at its base, a repre-
sentation of the Green Man stared up at her. His features
crafted of stone leaves and ivy, he was a symbol of rebirth

and pagan forces, but not a figure her family revered. He was male, while they followed the Lady.

Yet he is here, and so am I, she thought, as she gazed down at his likeness. She stretched out a hand and laid it against his cheek.

"Will you help me?" she asked aloud. "Green Man, will you give me shelter?" No, that was not what she wanted. "Jack of the Green, Herne, Forest Man, will you give me dominion?"

The stone head seemed to dip in agreement. Then, as she watched, its face became Estefan's. Skye jumped back into the shadows. Another face superimposed itself over Estefan's. It was Basilio, one of Estefan's coven brothers from Cádiz. A third face appeared over that one, and then a fourth.

Her blood ran cold. Estefan had called on his coven brothers to help him find her, and they had come.

"Oh, my Goddess," she whispered. Her knees began to buckle.

Then the Green Man's face gazed steadily back at her, and she lifted her head. "I'll kill you if I have to, Estefan," she whispered.

Did she hear Estefan's arrogant chuckle in the splashing water?

"Skye?" Lune called. She held a flashlight, and she, Soleil, and the High Priestess were standing at the mouth of the cavern. Their white, spangled robes were gone, and in their place the women wore normal street clothes.

"Oh! Did you put out the fire?" Skye asked them, rushing toward them.

"Fire?" Soleil asked, frowning.

Skye raced past the trio. The hedge maze stood intact, and the sun had risen.

"We've been looking for you for hours," Lune said. She cocked her head. "Are you all right?"

"I had a terrible vision," Skye confessed. "My ex, he's a Dark Witch, and he's after me. His coven brothers have come from Spain, and they're going to help him find me." Her earlier surge of strength faded, and she felt small and afraid.

"They'll fail," the High Priestess assured her, opening her arms. "You're with us now. We've agreed to induct you as a full member into the Circuit."

"Blessed be," Soleil and Lune said in unison, as Skye moved uncertainly into the High Priestess's embrace.

"As our sister, you're our responsibility," the High Priestess added. "We take care of our own. We'll keep you safe. We have voted not to fight in the light, Skye, but we will protect you from harm."

"No. We need to—," Skye began, but Lune took a step behind the High Priestess and gave Skye a hard look.

"We'll keep you safe," Lune said pointedly.

"Right. Safe," Soleil added, putting her hand on Skye's shoulder. Soleil looked as if she wanted to say more. A lot more. Later, in private.

Skye let the High Priestess think her silence was her consent.

But it was not.

BUCHAREST, ROMANIA
JENN, HOLGAR, AND ANTONIO

As the sun worked its way across the sky, Antonio lay still as death on the floor of their little sitting room beneath a blanket. Seated in a wooden chair beside a small table, Jenn traced the outline of his body with her eyes, catching herself waiting for his chest to rise and fall. It didn't, and it never would. She drank the tea Holgar had made and reminded herself over and over that the Brotherhood of St. Andrew couldn't change Antonio back into a human being. But in quiet moments like these, she could admit to herself that deep down, a part of her was hoping for that fairy-tale ending. She had suffered so much, and Antonio had suffered more. Didn't they deserve a miracle?

Doesn't Heather? she thought, biting her lower lip. Who was looking for her sister? No one. Yes, Father Juan was casting spells and throwing his runes, but he was deep in the forest with Gramma Esther searching for the Tears of Christ. Jamie was looking for Skye, and Noah was infiltrating Greg's lab. There was no one left to spare for Heather.

Because they think she's a lost cause, she thought, and a sob escaped her. *And I—I think so too.*

"No," she murmured. "Please."

Did Antonio stir?

She glanced his way. Her heart skipped a beat as she studied him. She didn't want to look under the blanket. Antonio could function in the daylight if he had to, although it made him very tired. But when he rested, he looked dead: his eyes half-open and unfocused; his lips parted, revealing his fangs. She and he had broken into vampire lairs and staked sleeping vampires together. What did he think when he looked down on them split seconds before he turned them to dust?

"Jenn," Antonio whispered from beneath the blanket.

She blinked and set down her teacup. Remaining where she was, she took a breath.

"Yes?" she said.

"Could you . . . ?" The blanket moved. His hand slid slowly from beneath it, as if it weighed a ton, and he fumbled at the edge, as if trying to pull it off his face. "*Ay,* Jenn."

She touched the cross she wore around her neck; then, flushing, she reached into a bag and pulled out the stake she had whittled from a tree branch after they had landed. Hefting it in her right hand, she lowered her arm to her side as she got up and walked over to him, then cautiously knelt beside him.

She pulled the blanket from his face. His brown eyes — not red — focused on her, and he smiled.

"Are you okay?" she asked.

"I . . ." He looked away. "I had a dream."

She raised her brows. "I thought vampires didn't dream."

He kept his face averted. "I guess sometimes they do." He spoke so softly that she could barely hear him.

"What was it?" She was almost afraid to ask. No, that was wrong. She *was* afraid to ask. It had obviously troubled him. So it probably hadn't been a dream, but a nightmare.

"I dreamed . . ." His voice trailed off again. He turned his head back toward her. "It's so crazy, but I keep thinking that maybe the Brotherhood . . . that they can change me."

Her heart broke a little.

A lot.

"But they can't," she replied. "Father Juan said." Still, she gazed at him and wondered if he knew something she didn't. Maybe he wasn't telling her everything, in case it didn't work.

"I hate what I am," he said. "Cursed. God can't turn His face to mine."

She swallowed down her shock. Antonio always talked about a loving God who accepted all sinners. He spent half his time praying to God, and he helped Father Juan with saying Mass and doing all kinds of religious duties. After all that, was he saying that this same God had rejected him?

"You know Father Juan would hit you if he heard you say that," she managed. "Or make you say a hundred Hail Marys or wash the chapel floor with a toothbrush. Because he doesn't think God hates you." She took a breath. "And on a good day? You don't think that either."

He didn't smile. Glancing at the window, with its faded brown curtains pulled shut against the sun, he pushed himself up on one elbow. His hair was tousled, and he looked like any guy in bed waking up from a nap. She was embarrassed and slightly flustered. She'd never seen any guy wake up beside her except for her teammates—including Antonio—and that was when they were on a mission.

We're on a mission right now, she thought, but the air around them was electric, the way it felt before a thunderstorm. Gazing into his eyes, she tried to remember that not too long ago they had glowed like rubies as he bragged about the people he had slaughtered. But that was after Aurora had tortured and starved him, and Skye's stalker boyfriend had cast spells on him. That had forced him to turn evil.

Was he truly free of their influence now?

"I believe that this curse stands between God and me," Antonio said. "I believe I must work night and day to find His mercy. You know that if I were a man, then I would become a priest. And I could never marry."

Her face went hot. She was mortified. And his words cut her like a knife.

"I'm not old enough to get married," she blurted, dying inside. She was hurt, angry, humiliated. "But why would you want to be a priest if you think God cursed you?"

He cocked his head. "He didn't curse me. Sergio Almodóvar did."

"But if He's God, then . . . I don't get it, Antonio. Why didn't he protect you?"

"Our understanding of Him is so limited," Antonio replied. "But I put my trust in Him, and I pray for answers."

"Answers to what?"

"To questions I don't even know how to ask." He touched her hair, and she closed her eyes at the whisper-light touch, so gentle.

Right now.

He was confusing her, scaring her a little. She opened her eyes and gripped the stake down at her side. His fingertips trailed to her temple and grazed her earlobe. His long lashes glistened — was he crying? — as he closed his eyes and sighed.

"Jenn," he whispered, "when I was a man, I never . . ." He lowered his head slightly. "I was never *with* anyone."

She cleared her throat. "Me, neither," she confessed. "For a Cali girl I'm, ah, behind the times," she added, trying to cut the tension that was building between them.

"This is a coarse age," he said. "Even before the war. Women pressured to parade around half dressed. Men aren't taught to respect women. To treat them as special, and sacred. When I was . . . when I lived in my village, I was taught to stand up if a woman walked into the room. I would carry her parcels. I would open doors."

His shoulders rounded, and for a moment she could see his age in his eyes. He was nearly ninety years old. Older even than Papa Che, the grandfather she had worshipped, and had lost so recently. She'd gone to California to attend Papa Che's funeral, and that was when her father had betrayed her and Heather to the vampires.

"I just wanted to watch out for you, protect you," he said brokenly. When he looked at her, he was young again, and it was almost as if he glowed. It made her catch her breath. It nearly made her cry. She shouldn't love him. It was stupid and hopeless. But she did.

"And you've watched out for me," she said. Her voice broke.

"I will always watch out for you," Antonio murmured. He leaned toward her.

He's going to kiss me. Her heart beat furiously; her body responded. *But we shouldn't. Not now.*

She thought she told him not to, but all she heard was silence. No words spoken, none possible or necessary as Antonio grabbed her hand and kissed it, then cradled it against his chest.

"Ay, mi amor," he whispered. *"Mi luz. Mi alma."* My love. My light. My soul. She understood enough Spanish to understand what he was saying. But she didn't understand *him.*

"Look at me, Jenn. Look at the one who loves you," he murmured, letting go of her hair and lacing his fingers behind her head. Then somehow her head was tipping back, as he bent her backward, and she was staring up into his eyes. His deep, brown eyes with heavy, dark brows, his forehead creased with emotion. His eyes . . .

"Look at me," he said again.

His red eyes.

Oh, no, she thought, but the words slipped away into somewhere, some dream or hope or other place. She tried to look away, but his gaze was locked onto her, and she had to stare into his red, glowing eyes. Her heart was beating so hard she knew it was going to burst. She couldn't break away. He was cold against her skin as he gripped her shoulders, looming over her, *willing* her to arch her back, bare her neck.

Stop. Stop him, she thought, but those words slipped away too. Her heart . . . it hurt. She clenched her fists. Where was the stake? She was no longer holding the stake. Antonio was going to bite her. He was going to take her blood. *Antonio.*

Evil.

His eyes.

His fangs.

STONEHENGE, ENGLAND
JAMIE

THIS SITE IS CLOSED UNTIL FURTHER NOTICE. WE APOLOGIZE FOR THE INCONVENIENCE.

Jamie grunted as he put the motorcycle he had stolen

into idle and stationed his booted foot down on the tarmac. His gaze moved from the large metal sign to Stonehenge itself. The large circle of stones was fenced off with chain-link.

That was the English for you, telling you they were sorry while they inconvenienced you to your grave and back. *We apologize for breaking your country into bits. We apologize for the fact that there was no Irish Hunter to save your people from being ripped apart by werewolves.*

He'd thought to blend in with the tourists in order to have a look round. But there were no tourists to be seen. War had a way of taking the fun out of life.

Along with the bike, Jamie had stolen plenty of food and drink to tide him over until nightfall, when it would be safer for him to *inconvenience* the security fence. But as he scanned the horizon, he saw no evidence that anyone was about.

He wasn't one for waiting when he could be doing something. But his heart squeezed in his chest when he realized that he *was* waiting—for Eriko to tell him what to do. She'd been their leader, their Hunter, until she'd resigned and given the job to Jenn, who'd promptly gotten her killed.

"Eri," he whispered aloud, and it was a vow.

For revenge.

Payback.

Sod it, he was going in now.

Jamie rolled the motorcycle past the sign, right up to the padlock, and turned off the engine. Sliding off, he picked up a stone and tossed it at the chain-link. It landed with a clink and dropped to the ground. He got close beside the fence and listened for a hum. As far as he could tell, it was not electrified, but you never knew.

During his trek, he had "acquired" some more weapons and stashed them in the hard saddlebags—it really was a nice bike—and now he flicked open one of the bags and got out his shiny new Uzi. He wished the gun with the wooden bullets were operational. On the other hand, not many suckers likely to be about in broad daylight.

Yet.

Jamie spat on the ground as bile filled his mouth. Rarely did Jamie O'Leary admit to a fear, much less a sickening fear, but he knew the other side was experimenting with creating vampires that could walk in the sun. If they succeeded, Jamie figured it was all over for the human race. They'd show their true colors then. It wasn't just some humans they hated. It was everybody. Then they'd set those supersoldier hybrids on the folks, save out some humans for breeding and bleeding. And as for the rest . . .

Bloody hell.

He slung the neck strap over his head and sighted back along the road. Aimed the barrel at the padlock. Ricochet might be a problem. Then again . . .

He pressed the trigger and the Uzi blasted to life like God's own staple gun.

. . . it might not.

There was nothing left of the padlock when he stopped. Or of the gate it had been attached to. He stepped through and shortly after flattened himself against one of the stone faces. It rose about ten feet above his head, and he squinted up, looking for cameras. Then he pushed aside short grass with the tip of his boot. He saw no evidence that anyone was doing anything at Stonehenge. And if they were stockpiling herbs, then they were burying them.

No problem.

Jamie sauntered back to the motorcycle, pulled out a shovel with a telescoping handle, set it to rights, and started digging. Breezes filtered through his hair. He hadn't had time to shave his head in an age. Another thing he had to thank this bloody war for.

After he'd made a sizable number of fairly deep holes, he stopped for another cigarette and a sandwich he'd stolen. Kate had been right about London. The Cursers had taken over everything. It was much worse than Spain, or even America. What was Northern Ireland like? Once he'd found Skye, he was going to find that out too.

I'm leaving that lot, he thought, picturing Jenn and her loser companions. *I'll make Skye come with me. They're going to die, and no sense dying with 'em.*

Blisters rose on his hands, and he liked them. He liked hard work. Never one for settin' about on his arse.

But as he took a breather, he surveyed his kingdom of holes and shook his head. It really didn't look as if anyone had been here for a long time. Especially not witches. There was none of their kit—no dried flower petals or candle wax or little bits of incense.

Scowling, he pulled out the scrying stone Father Juan had given him. As always, the smooth-faced rectangular crystal was blank. If it was working, it reconfirmed that Skye was still out of range.

So . . . if once he rescued her, he really did go back to Ireland, did it matter if he found the bloody herb Father Juan was looking for?

"The hell with it," Jamie said, throwing down his shovel. He fell back against one of the towering stones, then slid down to the dirt on his arse. He turned the scrying stone over and over in his hands. He knew Father Juan didn't like him. Maybe he'd given him a chunk of crystal with no magickal properties whatsoever and sent him off to England just to be rid of him.

"Jamie, lad, how can you think that?" he asked himself in a mocking tone. "Father Juan is your priest."

Yeah, and it was a priest that had let werewolves kill his family. Jamie was fairly certain his own grandfather had gunned down the priest in retaliation.

It was the O'Leary way.

"Damn it, Father Juan," Jamie said aloud.

Then, as he looked up at the sky, thick gray clouds bubbled out of nowhere and rushed to cover the sun. The sky turned gunmetal gray. The clouds boiled.

A flash of lightning leaped from the clouds and struck the megalith across from him. The whole thing lit up like a neon sign.

The one he was leaning against began to vibrate and hum. And to grow hot.

"Bloody hell!" he shouted, leaping to his feet.

A new bolt of lightning hit the ground inches from his feet. A jagged fissure burst open, and Jamie darted to the left.

A harsh wind whirled around him, spraying him with dirt. He heard the whine of a motorcycle engine in the distance. He cocked his head. Not just one, then. Not even just two. Many.

And they were coming in his direction.

BUCHAREST, ROMANIA
JENN, HOLGAR, AND ANTONIO

Holgar was in a fury. All he had wanted was a drink of water. And as no humans seemed to be around, he had dropped to the riverbank to lap with his tongue, realizing that it was too polluted at the exact same moment that another werewolf in full wolf form attacked him from behind.

The two tumbled into the water. Still unable to transform at will, Holgar knew he couldn't let the wolf get the upper hand, or he would die. So he flung himself on top of his attacker and held him under the water. The werewolf thrashed, struggling for breath. Finally it stopped struggling, going completely limp. Still Holgar held him down, until he changed back into a human.

Then Holgar lifted his head. The man spewed water and inhaled a deep breath.

"Who sent you?" Holgar demanded.

His answer was greeted by silence. Grimly, he pushed the man's head back below the surface. The man flailed his arms weakly.

Holgar pulled him back up.

"Who—?"

"Lucifer. Save me," the man said in Danish. His blue eyes were bloodshot, his face gray.

Holgar froze. Lucifer was Antonio's grandsire.

"Vampire Kingdom," the man said. His voice was barely above a whisper. "Spare the werewolves."

"For helvede!" Holgar cried as he dropped the man and raced back into the forest separating the river from the safe house where Antonio and Jenn were. In his mind's eye he saw a pack of werewolves and human collaborators breaking down the door, murdering Jenn and staking Antonio. He whined; then he felt himself begin to change. Hair covered his hands; his fingers began to extend.

He threw back his head and howled.

Then everything reversed and he was human again. Just human, running as fast as he could, bursting out of the copse of trees, across a narrow road, into the warren of structures, to their front door.

"Hey!" he shouted, because he shouldn't call out their names. "Hey!"

There was no answer. He tried the latch. It was locked. He pounded once, then threw himself against the door as hard as he could. No good; he tried again. This time it gave.

He burst across the threshold to find Antonio with his fangs sunk into Jenn's neck. She was struggling against him, but he had both her hands in one of his, stretched above her head.

So much blood. Dear God, Jenn —

With a roar he tackled Antonio, and they rolled together away from Jenn. Holgar hit Antonio in the face as hard as he could, then whirled around, scooped up Jenn in his arms, and bolted for the doorway into the sunlight. The blessed sunlight.

His clothes were streaked with blood. It terrified him how much blood there was.

Then he saw two men in dark robes rushing toward him. Each had a cross extended.

"Saint Andrew," one said, in heavily accented English. "What's happened?"

"Antonio is in there; he's gone bad," Holgar said frantically, struggling to convey his meaning in English. "Where can I take her?"

"We have a vehicle."

The man turned and pointed to the opposite end of the

alley, where a dark gray van sat idling. A man behind the wheel gestured to Holgar.

Behind Holgar, Antonio's voice rose in anguish.

"Jenn! What have I done? What have I done?"

"We'll deal with him," the man said to Holgar. "Take care of her."

"It's light out," Holgar reminded him. "If you take him out in the sun—"

The man looked at him with a deadly serious expression. "We know."

BOOK TWO
ANKOU

I remained, lost in oblivion;
My face I reclined on the Beloved.

—St. John of the Cross,
sixteenth-century mystic of Salamanca

CHAPTER SEVEN

*It's true; you can't trust anyone when you're a
hunter. It's the hardest, most terrible truth that can
ever be learned. How do you fight when those who
are supposed to be on your side can turn on you in a
moment? Even those who love you?*

*I wish I had never gone to Salamanca. I wish I
had lived my life in ignorance. But then I could have
ended up just like Brooke. Or Heather. I don't know
which is worse. Death or conversion?*

I'm not sure how much more I can take.

*—from the diary of Jenn Leitner,
retrieved from the ruins*

LAKE COMO, ITALY
HEATHER

She was hungry. Or thirsty. She didn't know what to call it. All she knew was that it burned, hotter than anything she had ever known.

Which was ironic, because her skin was cold as ice.

Which was terrible, because there was nothing she could do to warm it. Not that she felt cold or warmth, not in any real way.

Heather walked across the marble floor, then her toes curled as they sank into a thick circular carpet.

She didn't remember where she'd lost her shoes. It didn't really matter. Her skin was practically impervious to everything now. Even when she'd stepped on some broken glass, her cut had healed the moment she plucked the shard from between her toes. The pain had been nothing, more like the whisper of a touch to let her know that something was different. Wrong.

Everything about her was wrong. And tired. And cold.

And so very hungry.

She thought she might have eaten someone a while back. She wasn't sure. It sort of all blurred together.

A rabbit.

She knew she'd eaten a rabbit at some point.

Bugs Bunny.

Thumper.

White Rabbit.

Brer Rabbit.

Peter Cottontail.

Yes, she had eaten someone named Peter. But he wasn't a rabbit.

She'd give anything right now for a rabbit.

Something moved in the dark, and she dropped behind a couch to the plush white carpet, fluffy like a bunny. She balled her fists into the velvety twists and listened.

She was in a palace. Lucifer owned it. She'd heard others talking about him. They were scared of him.

She'd never believed in the Devil. Now she was a devil. But not for long. Because she was going to kill Aurora and then—

She wouldn't let herself think about "then." Couldn't. All she could think about, all she *must* think about, was Aurora. She mustn't eat until she ripped the woman's throat out and drank of her blood.

Like she drank mine. Drank it all up.

Damn, she was thirsty.

She listened as she heard the voices of two vampires. One had a strong Russian accent. She felt like she should hold her breath so they couldn't hear her.

But she didn't breathe.

Not anymore.

One more reason to kill Aurora.

"We'll be leaving within the hour. Are all the preparations made to transport my *matroyshkas*?"

"Yes, sir. They've been readied for the journey."

"Good. And the other thing?"

"Taken care of."

What other thing?

Her curiosity passed. It wasn't important. All that was important was killing Aurora.

"Good. Lucifer, Aurora, and I leave tonight for Transylvania."

The other vampire started to snicker and then quickly stopped.

"And no one must know of my plans." The Russian's voice was hard, and she knew what was coming next.

"You can trust me," the stupid vampire who hadn't figured it out said.

There was a slight noise and then a gurgling sound. The scent of blood filled the air, and a moment later a body hit the ground with a thud. She could see ash swirl in the air as it disintegrated.

"I can trust you now," the Russian said.

She listened as he walked out of the room. Then Heather scrambled out from behind the couch and ran toward the pile of ash on the floor, but the blood had already turned. She picked up the ashes in her hands, whimpering, tasting it.

The blood was all gone, but she had smelled it.

She started to cry, and blood tears streaked down her

cheeks. She wiped them with her fingers and then sucked the drops from her skin, shaking with desire.

Soon she would have to feed.

Southern France
Father Juan and Esther Leitner

They were in the middle of nowhere. Father Juan pushed his way through the thicket, feeling dozens of branches from the different shrubs catching at his clothes. Behind him Esther trudged, silent, a trooper who didn't complain about the cold or the scratches or the seemingly endless wandering around.

At her insistence he had put aside the clothes that would mark him as a priest and wore camouflage clothes he had packed in a duffel. Although they helped him blend into his surroundings, they itched.

They were fugitives. Outlaws.

Condemned by the Church, hunted by the Cursed Ones. It was hard to draw breath, because it seemed their cause was such a hopeless one.

That's why God makes me live, he thought, trying not to be bitter.

"You're awfully quiet, Padre," Esther said, breaking the silence. "Spending too much time in your own head?"

He chuckled. "Don't we all?"

"A little hard to escape sometimes," she noted drily.

"An old lady like me doesn't want to spend too much time there."

"You're not old," he said, too quickly.

"Uh-huh. Speaking of old, been meaning to talk to you about that."

He felt his skin prickle. Esther Leitner was sharp, with the cunning of a fox and the vision of an eagle. He had often sensed that she was watching him, studying him. It had been so long since any had done that with eyes that truly wanted to know the truth, and it frightened him a little.

"What is it, Esther?" he asked.

"Well, Juan, you strike me as a very old man."

"War makes men old."

"And lies make men older."

Her eyes were locked on him, intense, probing. "I don't know what you mean," he said.

They climbed deeper into the thicket where outlaws and, later, Free French Forces and so many others had hidden. He only hoped the flower they sought had also remained hidden. The entire area was under vampire control. Still, the sun was shining high in the sky, and as thick and tall as the brush was, a Cursed One would be hard-pressed to find cover from the burning of the sun.

"You have the eyes of a very old man," she persisted.

He didn't say anything.

"You look young, but you're not."

That caught him by surprise. He struggled not to give

any sign of his intense discomfort. Esther would make a formidable enemy, and he had the sudden, overwhelming realization that he had underestimated her.

And underutilized her.

She, too, had spent a lifetime hiding her identity. Of course she would look at the world differently, assume others were hiding things as well. Maybe that was all it was. Perhaps he could allay her concerns.

Esther grabbed his arm with enough force to turn him to face her.

Her eyes were hard. "Listen, you want to hide who you are from my granddaughter and all her friends, that's fine. But I need to know who I'm fighting with."

"I promise you we're on the same side," he said.

She pursed her lips. "You know, I did a little research while we were staying at the monastery."

He licked his lips. "Oh?"

"Yeah. I've got my suspicions about who you really are."

He realized that denying it would do him no good. But he was not going to admit it, either.

"You don't want to fess up, fine. But I need to know one thing," she said, squinting at him.

"What?"

"How are you still alive?"

Somewhere to the left a roar split the air.

He spun to face the sound, and Esther aimed her submachine gun.

In the hush she whispered, "What is it?"

He crossed himself. "I don't know."

The tops of the bushes began to shake, and the sounds of breaking branches crackled through the air. The ground beneath his feet began to tremble.

"That can't be good," Esther muttered.

And then they saw it. It was tall, approaching seven feet, and its skin was chalk white except for where it was covered with dingy gray fur. Ragged military clothes hung off its nearly naked body. Its head, shoulders, and chest were bulbous and misshapen, and its overly long arms ended in claws. Its legs were knotted with muscles, and its feet were bare.

"Hybrid!" he shouted, grabbing for his Uzi. He pulled the trigger, but nothing happened. "It's jammed!"

"Got it," Esther said, as she let loose with her own sub-machine gun. The bullets thudded into the thing as it kept coming toward them.

Father Juan thanked the Holy Mother that the monstrosity didn't have super speed. But Esther's bullets weren't slowing it down.

He raised his hands, murmured a spell, and let loose with fireballs that hit the hybrid, one after another, in the face. The creature screamed, sounding all too human, and raised a hand to its eyes.

And then it charged Father Juan and Esther. With a shout Father Juan threw up a protective barrier, and the creature crashed against it so hard that it bounced back and fell on its back.

Esther dashed forward, and he barely had time to drop the barricade before she, too, hit it. She leaped on top of the creature and emptied what had to be most or all of her clip into its skull and chest. The bullets ricocheted off the bony protrusions of its head.

Which meant beheading it would probably be out of the question.

Father Juan raced up beside her. The hybrid was bleeding from several chest wounds. The face was batlike, with an inverted triangle of cartilage and two holes for nostrils. The eyes were dark black, and its mouth was a jagged mess of fangs.

Father Juan conjured a fireball and showed it to the creature. "Are there more of you?"

The hybrid groaned and shook its head, but snapped its jaws at them. Blood and saliva mixed together. And something green and foul-smelling.

"It's sick—infection, gangrene, something," Father Juan said.

"Then it should take this as a kindness," Esther said. She jabbed it in the eye with the barrel of her submachine gun and pulled the trigger.

Blood splattered everywhere, and Juan jumped back with a shout.

Esther nudged the body with a toe as it slowly began to turn to ash.

"Why did you do that?" he demanded, anger flooding him. "We could have taken it hostage, questioned it."

"We did question it. No others around. That's all we needed to know. Anything else wasn't worth the danger of trying to keep him subdued."

"Jenn would have listened to me," he snapped at her.

"Jenn hasn't lived as long as I have," she retorted.

He took a deep breath, struggling to regain his composure. He took one last look at Dantalion's monstrous creation and then turned away, not wanting to watch it decompose any further.

"It might have been able to tell us if the flower we're looking for is anywhere near here. It might have seen it," he said bitterly. It was a foolish wish; he doubted something so small and fragile would have mattered to the creature.

Esther bent down. "Maybe it already did," she said.

He looked sharply at her and saw that she was pulling something off the bottom of the creature's left shoe. A moment later the shoe had turned to ash along with the leg. She stood slowly and showed him what she had found.

A crushed flower petal.

A blood-red rose petal.

"Is this it?" she asked him.

He stared in disbelief. It was a petal of the Tears of Christ.

He looked up at Esther in wonder, and she smiled at him. "You might be older than dirt, Father, but stick with me and maybe I can teach you a thing or two."

He nodded mutely. *She was just lucky,* he thought, but he didn't believe it. He believed that someone—God, or the Lady—had made this happen.

She pointed to the direction from which the creature had come. "I suggest we go that way."

He nodded and then set off, leading the way. She fell into step behind him and a moment later spoke again.

"You never answered my question."

"God keeps me alive. I don't know why. Every time I think it's over . . . it's not." It hurt to talk about it, but there was a sense of relief, too. "When there is great danger to mankind, I'm there. He wants me to help."

"For how long?" she asked.

He shook his head. "I believe that if we win this war, then He will finally let me be at peace." He took a breath. "At least that's my hope."

A few minutes later they found a small clearing, and there, stretching toward the warmth of the sun, a trio—a trinity—of rosebushes glittered in the sun. Deep, blood red, with petals shaped like tears. The Tears of Christ. Tears stinging his eyes, he choked back a sob. He had prayed they would be able to find enough flowers so that he could make the elixir to give his team the extra strength and speed they needed.

And God had answered.

Esther clapped a hand on his shoulder and smiled at him as if reading his mind. "The Lord moves in mysterious ways," she said.

He nodded, not trusting himself to speak.

"Maybe you're one step closer to that rest you're looking forward to."

"From your lips to God's ears," he whispered.

Project Crusade Headquarters, Budapest
Noah

Noah couldn't help but wonder how the rest of the team was faring as he made his way deeper underground through the network of buildings that housed the laboratories and war rooms for the shadow organization that wore the black Jerusalem crosses.

Mostly he was worrying about Jenn. She was so sweet, so vulnerable, and yet she had depths of strength that were astonishing. In so many ways she reminded him of his beloved Chayna.

It was best to put thoughts of both of them from his mind, though, as he strode along the corridors. He was dressed as many others: white shirt, black suit, and black Jerusalem-cross lapel pin. He had learned long before that when infiltrating enemy territory the best way to do it was to walk openly, wearing their uniform, and assume an air of authority and purposefulness. People rarely questioned those who seemed to belong.

Of course, the black-cross guys weren't exactly enemies. They were supposed to all be fighting on the same team. Noah still wished that they hadn't interfered when Jenn and her team had had a chance to kill Solomon. If they wanted to lead the way in the battle to take back the world from the Cursed Ones, that was fine.

But they should actually *lead*.

The time for skulking in shadows was over. The Cursed Ones had come out into the light of day and taken over the planet.

The resistance—in all its forms—needed to learn from that example. Hiding in groups of three and four, clustered together in tiny rooms whispering in the dark, wasn't going to liberate the planet, wasn't going to drive the Cursed Ones back into the shadows.

We are the ones who need to be the light.

He came to a steel door, glanced at it, and then turned down a different corridor. He needed to get behind the door, but biometric scanners guarded it. It was the only place in the entire complex that had scanners, which meant it was the one place he needed most to go.

What are they planning? What are they hiding even from each other?

He kept walking, turning down a few more corridors,

making a mental map of the place in his mind so that he could get out later even if he was being chased.

He thought of everything Jenn and Father Juan had told him about the black crosses—like Dr. Michael Sherman, the scientist who had been developing a weapon to use against the vampires. The one who had been helping the team while Jenn was in Berkeley with her family. Sherman had been converted by a vampire during the battle and then kidnapped by the black-cross commandos who had shown up at the laboratory too.

If they had kept Sherman alive—Noah supposed that was the right word—they'd have to have him locked down someplace. Someplace he couldn't escape.

It took several more hours, but Noah eventually spotted a dark-skinned man leaving the scanner room. Remaining calm and casual, Noah shadowed him to what ended up being a men's room.

As the man stretched his hands beneath the flow of water, Noah knocked him out. Fortunately, the bathroom wasn't far from the locked room, and Noah was able to sling the man's arm over his shoulders and walk the unconscious body down the hall. He didn't see cameras, but he knew better than to assume that meant they weren't there. He'd have minutes if he was lucky, seconds if he wasn't, before his presence was discovered.

He pressed the man's fingertips against the pad next to the door, and it slid open. Once inside, he deposited the man on the floor and stared at a second door. This one had a key-card scanner. He unclipped the badge from the man's pocket and slid it through.

The light turned green, and the door opened soundlessly. Noah stepped inside, trying not to panic when the door closed swiftly behind him.

He was in a laboratory, larger than he would have expected, but still small enough to make him claustrophobic. Everything was gray. No posters on the walls, not even a clock. A small, lone man with pale brown hair, wearing a lab coat, worked at a military-issue metal desk, head bent over a microscope.

The scientist's head shot up, and Noah knew he had heard him. He swiveled slowly and fixed red eyes on Noah.

"You are not one of my handlers," he said.

"No," Noah said cautiously.

The man's hand hovered over a small red button on his desk. "Then you are . . . ?"

Noah decided to go for it. "I'm fighting with Team Salamanca."

The scientist cocked his head. "I met them once. Nice kids." He smiled bitterly. "They couldn't save me from the vampires."

Noah didn't say anything.

The scientist crossed his arms. "So, why are you here?" he challenged.

"The 'kids' need to know what Project Crusade is planning. For tactical reasons."

The vampire raised his brows. "Tactical."

"Yes," Noah said. Then he added, "I'm Mossad. Israeli special forces. I can make you tell me. Even though you're a vampire."

Sherman chuckled. "You catch more flies with honey than vinegar."

"Or in your case, blood."

Sherman made a face. Then he shrugged. "I liked those kids. Except the Irishman. I have no idea why they put up with him. So. We're continuing my work. That's what all this is for." He waved an arm.

"A weapon to kill vampires."

The scientist nodded.

"And you're willingly helping them?" Noah asked, trying to keep the disbelief out of his voice.

"Don't worry. You're not the first to be surprised," Sherman said. "I was a little surprised myself." He smiled as if at some distant memory. "But it really was the only thing to do."

"Why?"

Sherman fixed his glowing red eyes on Noah. Weirdly, although the vampire was small and slight and looked to have been about forty when he was transformed, he reminded Noah of Antonio de la Cruz—who was none of those things.

"Why?" Sherman repeated. He shrugged. "Because all Cursed Ones are evil. We all deserve to die. We're parasites on humanity."

Noah was bemused. "But if you believe that, then—"

"Please." Sherman held up his hand to silence Noah. "I've been through this with my handlers. I'm *not* good. I'm just logical."

Noah nodded respectfully.

"I only hope that when we're gone, humanity can recover. But the vampires have so many in thrall. Under their control, I mean. They've identified so closely with their masters that they've lost themselves. They may fight to save the Cursed Ones." The vampire looked closely at him. "You're a soldier. I think you understand, yes?"

"More than you know," Noah whispered.

Israel, Two Years Earlier
Noah

Noah was fearful and excited all at the same time. It was a momentous day. He and Chayna were finally getting married. He was twenty-two, and she was just eighteen, and her parents had finally agreed to the wedding. The vampires were overrunning humanity; best to spend all the time they had together—except that as an Israeli agent committed to supersecret, violent missions against the vampires and their allies, Noah might not have as much time as other people. Chayna had told him over and over that she was prepared for that. Better one day married to him than a lifetime without him.

As he studied his reflection in the mirror, holding a *kittel*—his ceremonial white robe—in his hands, he remembered tormenting her mercilessly when they were kids. They were four years apart, and in the land of children, four years was a lifetime. They were friends, then best friends. He remembered telling her his dreams of becoming a writer. They'd celebrated when he had won an essay contest at the age of sixteen—with a shy, quick hug. After all, she'd only been twelve.

Filled with love, he wrote about her, about how it seemed that they were destined soul mates, and his first book was published when he was just eighteen. Overnight he became a literary phenomenon—"Israel's warrior heartbreaker" beginning his compulsory military service.

And then he remembered sitting on the couch with her six months later, when the Cursed Ones revealed themselves to the world. Chayna's hand had wrapped around his, squeezing it tight, and she was pale with fear.

He had told her that she was wrong to be afraid. Really, all he had wanted to do was make that look pass from her face. So he wrote—to her, to his country, to his people. His second novel was published after war had been declared, and he stayed in the service. It was not the time to lay down arms. He saw that clearly.

He told her he wanted to join the Mossad. Secret intelligence, assassinations. She cried for days, and her father told her to break it off with him.

"He'll be dead within a year. Six months," her father had said.

But he'd survived. And now they would be married.

"I wish you joy," Yosef said, coming into the room, a huge grin on his face.

"Thank you for being here," Noah replied. "I know you're training."

Yosef shrugged. "I told my master that I had a year to learn how to fight Cursed Ones, but I had only one day to see my best friend married."

"I'm surprised they let you come," Noah said, having heard about the rigor and isolation of the Israeli counter-vampire training facility.

Yosef grinned. "They didn't so much 'let' me. What is it your father always says?"

"Better to ask forgiveness than beg permission," Noah said with a grin.

"So here we are."

Noah nodded. Here they were, and he couldn't be happier.

And then it was time.

During the ceremony, under the chuppah, he knew he was holding his breath until he slipped the plain gold ring on Chayna's finger. For the rest of the day and late into the evening, all Noah could do was grin. *I'm married. We're married.*

Everything else was a blur.

In the hotel room she lit candles and told him to turn

his back while she undressed. He flushed and he heard her laugh, a short, nervous giggle, and he knew that she was as excited, and as nervous, as he was. And then, finally, they fell into each other's arms. And all the waiting in the world had been worth it to make love to his wife.

But something was wrong.

Something was terribly wrong with his wife.

They had been married a week, a week of bliss and parties and prayers for *simcha*—happiness—that Noah would treasure for all of his life. But then on the eighth evening, after all the parties were over, Chayna went to visit her great-aunt, who had taken ill. He wanted to go with her, but he was also feeling unwell, and he was due to go on a mission in two days. She told him to stay home, insisting she would be very careful on the streets of Tel Aviv, where they lived. The vampires had imposed a curfew, but it was hours away. He sat down to write, but he couldn't shake the feeling that something was wrong.

She didn't answer her cell, and he was just about to go looking for her when she drifted over the threshold of their flat, moody and fixated elsewhere. When he tried to kiss her, she wandered past him.

She's upset about her aunt, he reasoned, trailing after her. But when he called her name, she didn't even answer, as if she didn't hear him.

She was standing in the kitchen, staring out the window at the moon. He walked up behind her and kissed her shoulder.

She hissed at him. Startled, he took a step backward. "Chayna?"

"He's calling to me. He wants me to come back to him," she said in a strange, singsong voice. "He's not done."

She turned to gaze at him. The pupils in her normally brilliant green eyes were dilated so much that he couldn't see the green, and her face was slack.

"Chayna? Are you all right?"

"I have to go to him now."

"Who?" he asked. She was acting so strangely.

"We were wrong," she mumbled. "It's so very hard to be one of them. It's the least I can do."

"What?"

She seemed to wake up. Her dilated eyes locked onto him. "I'm a donor," she declared.

"A donor." Chills ran down his spine. He thought his knees might give way.

"Blood donor," she said, voice laced with contempt, as though she thought he was an idiot for asking. "I've been chosen."

No. No, no, no.

"Chayna, while you were out, gone from me, did you meet a Cursed One? Did something *happen*?"

"Yes." She said it as simply as if he had asked her if the stars were shining.

He had heard whispers about people being mesmerized, changing behavior, turning on friends and family who stood in their way. It couldn't be true, could it? But there was his Chayna, standing there, talking about being a *blood donor*?

He cupped her shoulders and bent his knees so he could peer into her eyes. They were so *vacant*. "You've been hypnotized. I'll call Yosef. He'll know —"

And with a scream she threw him off and reached behind herself on the counter. She snatched a knife, lunged at him.

"Get away from me!" she shouted.

He jumped back as the knife sliced across his abdomen. He tried to grab her hand, but she moved like a serpent, twisting and writhing.

"Chayna, please!" he begged, as she stabbed him in the thigh.

She yanked the blade free, and he could feel himself weakening as blood flowed down his leg. He grabbed her hand, twisting, trying to make her let go of the knife.

She kicked and bit at him. He stepped forward, and his foot slipped in a puddle of his own blood. They hit the ground together, her on top, the knife trapped between them. He heard a sudden guttural noise and felt hot blood rushing over his hand.

"Chayna!"

She looked down at him, and blood began to run out of the corner of her mouth and drip onto his cheeks. Her eyes changed slowly, and then she blinked and looked down at him. Love and pain mingled on her face.

"Noah," she breathed. "Noah."

"Chayna!" he shouted.

She whispered something so softly that he couldn't quite make it out.

"What? What?" he asked urgently. "Chayna, what?"

As she went limp, he saw where the blade had buried itself in her chest. Blood was pouring out of her chest, so much. Her eyes went glassy.

She was gone.

He screamed as he gathered her body up in his arms and held her, even as his own blood gushed from his body.

We'll die together. We'll be together.

Something cold touched his arm. He jerked; it was the edge of her Star of David pendant poking out of the pocket of her jeans. The vampire who had mesmerized her must have convinced her to take it off. The Cursed One. The demon had to be made to pay.

Noah staggered to his feet and made it to the sink. He grabbed a towel to staunch the bleeding. His free hand shook as he reached for his phone. He would still call Yosef—to get him into the counter-vampire training facility. And he would destroy the bastard who had done this.

Then he would die, and he and Chayna would be at peace.

CHAPTER EIGHT

Salamanca Hunter's Manual:
Your Role as Hunter
Remember this: You are a destroyer. You are like unto the Archangel Michael, who confronted Satan. You have sworn a solemn vow to kill vampires. Death is what you bring. You are not on this earth to comfort, or heal, or pacify. You are a warrior. Your hand must be steady, and your heart must be stone.

(translated from the Spanish)

STONEHENGE, ENGLAND
JAMIE

"Feckin' hell," Jamie said, as beneath the gray sky and lightning bolts four motorcycle riders zoomed in a row along the near-deserted roadway. The clouds gathered around them like enormous cloaks. Lightning danced and shattered above their helmets.

Jamie was never one to stand down from a fight, but it was four against one, and as they rode closer, a shiver ran down his back. Something was very off about them. Every ounce of self-preservation screamed at him to get the hell out of there. He had the Uzi around his neck, but as sure as they were coming, he sensed the Uzi would be less useful than a rosary. Several of which lay inside the saddlebag.

"Jesus, Mary, and Joseph," Jamie swore.

He raced for his bike, hopped on, started it up. He was used to unfair fights but opposed to suicide missions, so he made a half circle as fast as he could and headed around the chain-link fence enclosing the henge.

Motorcycle engines blared as if in response. He glanced in the mirror.

Seconds ago they'd been hundreds of feet behind him; now they were practically breathing down his neck. Witchcraft. Had to be. Maybe they just wanted to ask him for directions.

The bad jokes were Holgar's department.

And curse it all, he actually wished wolfie were there with him.

He hit the open road. Visibility cut to practically nil, he tamped down his fight-or-flight and tried to find the headspace to strategize. The Uzi was getting in the way of his driving. Maybe in the movies the hero could grab up his submachine gun and mow down the enemy without a spill, but this was real life. Being a down-and-dirty street fighter didn't mean you threw all caution over a cliff and dazzled your enemies with super stunts. It meant you did whatever you needed to *survive*.

The four riders kept solidly behind him. He smelled the fumes of petrol mingling with the ozone of the thunderclouds, which broke open in that moment and poured buckets of rain on him. A bolt of lightning stabbed the earth inches in front of the bike, and he would have thrown himself off if he'd been able to pry his hands from around the handlebars. But he was frozen to the bike, by necessity and fear. They were behind him, too close, and he put the pedal to the metal best he could, narrowly avoiding a lightning bolt on his left.

It wasn't natural lightning. It felt like it was being directed, *thrown* at him. Witches. It had to be.

Another bolt hit to the right, scorching the earth. Another. He dodged each of them, realizing the riders were using them to herd him in the direction they wanted him to go. He didn't have much choice except to comply unless he wanted to get fried.

But he kept going, realizing he was on the road, merging onto the A303. That's what they wanted; they were zooming up behind him, herding him like a sheep. To what end? Who were they? He wasn't about to stop and ask.

But they're witches, he thought. *Maybe they know where Skye is. Maybe she sent them here.*

So they could hurl lightning bolts at him? Another thing street war survivors did was listen to their gut instincts. And his was telling him to get the hell away from these fellas as fast as he could.

He stared down at his fuel gauge. He'd filled up just before arriving at Stonehenge, and he figured he could get forty miles to the gallon, maybe more. That was two hundred miles. A lot could happen between now and empty. Besides, there was an extra gallon in one of the saddlebags. If he could find a way to refuel without getting hit with a lightning bolt, he could be on a ferry to France and still have petrol left to go to a wine tasting.

They stayed behind him for a good thirty miles. Then a flash crackled overhead as he reached the turnoff for the M25. Swearing, Jamie took the exit. The four stayed within view of his mirror.

He kept going. His minders kept pace. Then he felt something warm in the inner breast pocket of his black leather jacket. Bloody hell, what were they doing to him? He grabbed at it through the fabric liner. Then, as his fingers outlined a hard rectangle, he realized it was the scrying stone.

Skye, he thought, catching his breath as his heart leaped with hope.

He didn't believe these bastards were his escorts. Were

they using him to lead them to Skye? The problem with
being part of the underground was that you never knew
who else was part of it too, or who was just really good at
using it to get what they wanted.

He wanted to take the scrying stone out, get a good
look in it, see Skye for himself. His heart pounded with the
reverb of his motorcycle engine. Sweat beaded his forehead,
chilled by the air blasting past him. Twenty miles—she was
within twenty miles of him, and were these bastards going
to stand between the two of them?

Not bloody likely.

He began to scan the roadsides, looking for a place to
make a stand. The rolling hills of England: villages, sheep.
The warmth of the scrying stone was driving him mad.

Then to the right, atop a small hill, he saw the ruins
of what appeared to be an abbey. There was a steeple. He
could leave the road, get over there, throw down the bike,
and climb the steeple. Let the Uzi rip and—

They have lightning bolts, he reminded himself. *And what
are you going to do if you dismount and they set your bike on fire
first? Set you on fire second?*

Raging with frustration, he let the abbey pass. He saw
the canted graves of the old churchyard, and then, past that,
the road sloped downward into a valley. The valley of the
shadow, to his way of thinking. The four would have an
advantage over him as he descended.

I ain't going down into that, he thought.

And then, without thinking, he whipped the bike around, hard, and he did grab the Uzi, like in the movies, and began shooting. The recoil nearly threw him off arse first; blinded with anger and adrenaline and wind, he sprayed the lads as hard as he could.

Lightning bolts answered; then he barely ducked in time as a feckin' fireball whistled straight at him like a bomb. He had no idea how he was staying on the bike. Every time he thought he'd lost control, he managed one more save. Maybe Skye was helping him. Or maybe the sainted Holy Mother herself.

In shock he watched as one of the four tumbled off his bike. *Bullets can kill them.* The other three reacted, two of them slowing, one lobbing another fireball at Jamie. Jamie got off a few more rounds, then wheeled back around and rode for all he was worth. Down into the damned valley, where there were shadows, he began to turn right off the main road but saw nothing but trees pressed closely together; a bit beyond, there was a sturdy-looking stone wall. Not a good place to go.

He had to press his advantage; he went flat out through the valley. Then a lightning bolt slammed down directly in front of him. He swerved left, nearly losing his balance.

The scrying stone moved from warm to hot. It was nearly too hot to bear. He went left, off the road and into some trees. Hotter still. He yelled out a curse and kept going, dodging low-lying branches. *Skye, I'm coming.*

Then a large, flat megalith such as at Stonehenge suddenly appeared about twenty feet in front of him. He prepared to throw himself off the bike when he remembered other times, other barriers, into which Skye had bored magickal holes. They were invisible to the naked eye.

"Is that what you want?" Jamie shouted. "Skye, bloody hell, is this you?"

More likely it was the lads behind him. He had to decide now: throw himself off the bike and risk broken bones — break his neck, maybe — or splatter himself all over the stone —

They're gonna catch up, he thought. Then he closed his eyes, took a deep breath, and drove straight for the block of stone in front of him, gritting his teeth and waiting for his life to flash before his eyes. Nothing was flashing. He was blind with fear. In the next micro instant he would either die or —

Project Crusade Headquarters, Budapest
Noah

Noah knew that he had very little time left before he was discovered talking to Dr. Michael Sherman. He stared at the vampire scientist. "So, tell me about the virus."

"It's a blood virus, a mutated strain of leukemia. When I was human, I was suffering from the disease. Now no more.

But if I'm successful, the new strand will kill me along with the others." Sherman preened as if it were the best news of his life.

Noah was fascinated. Could it be that Antonio wasn't the only vampire with tendencies toward goodness?

As if he had read Noah's mind, the scientist shook his head. "What drives me, what keeps me doing my research and not destroying the humans here, is my hatred for the Cursed Ones and what they have done to me." He nodded. "Revenge, as it turns out, is stronger than blood."

Noah pondered that. "How fast will the virus spread?"

"Very fast. We'll release it into the air, and as the wind carries it . . . those closest will die in seconds."

"Vampires don't breathe," Noah said.

Dr. Sherman smiled, exposing wicked-looking fangs. "They don't have to. Infection will take place at a sub-molecular level. They can try to block it, but we're kicking out potential blocking agents one by one."

"You're creating an antidote?" Noah asked.

The vampire shook his head. "No. That was my condition for working on it, and my handlers agreed."

Noah cocked a brow. "But you'll die too."

Sherman shrugged. "I can't risk it getting into the wrong hands."

Noah thought about Jenn. She would have argued with the man, for the sake of Antonio, but the doctor was right. When it came to something like this, you wanted all your exits closed off.

Nodding, Noah gave the man a salute. "When?" he asked.

"Soon. I know it'll work. I just want to make sure it works perfectly," Sherman said. Then his eyes ticked to a place behind Noah. "But I'm not sure you'll have a chance to tell anyone that help is on the way."

Noah spun and came face-to-face with Greg, the leader of the black crosses. Their paths had crossed the night Greg had forced Team Salamanca at rifle point to stand down from their self-appointed mission to expose Solomon's treachery at his press conference with the president.

"So now you know what we've been trying to create, what we've been protecting," Greg said quietly.

"It's fantastic," Noah said, scanning the space behind Greg. There was no one else with him, at least not inside the room. How many were gathered outside? "We'll win the war."

"Yes. So you have to understand, there are a lot of folks—even in our government—who want us stopped."

"You can count on the support of Team Salamanca," Noah said steadily.

"I believe that's true," Greg said. He smiled, but it didn't reach his eyes, and the hair on the back of Noah's neck raised on end. It wasn't a good smile. Noah himself had given that smile on more than one occasion. He slid his hand into the back of his waistband and let his fingers close around the knife he had concealed there.

"What would you like us to do to help?" Noah asked, stalling for time.

Greg's demeanor didn't change. "Thanks, but the best answer is 'nothing.' We can't risk tipping the vampires off in any way. Jenn and the rest of you provide a great distraction, a place for the Cursed Ones to focus all their energy. We need you all to be able to continue exactly as before."

Noah nodded.

"Which means I can't let you leave this facility," Greg said.

Noah swung his left arm, and Greg blocked it easily, but missed Noah's right arm swinging in low with the knife. Noah felt the knife slide into Greg's flesh, piercing his side, missing the major organs but dropping the man to the ground. Blood pooled everywhere. Noah let go of the knife and leaped over the body, jamming his stolen ID badge through the reader. The door slid open, and he blinked in shock to see no troops waiting for him on the other side.

But from the corridor to his left he heard the sound of running feet. So he took off to the right.

He had to warn the others about what was coming.

If he could make it out alive.

ENGLAND
JAMIE

Jamie's bike went through the block of stone, and suddenly he was in a tunnel, the walls barely visible and no light revealing any end, madly trying to slow down as he burst into victorious laughter. He swore every good curse he knew as he throttled down, aware that he had yet to confirm if friend or foe had created this magickal illusion. The scrying stone was so hot by then that as soon as he stopped the bike and leaped off, he dug in his pocket, grabbed the stone, and tossed it to the ground. Blisters rose instantly on his fingers. He grabbed the Uzi and whirled in a circle, such a mess of adrenaline, terror, and relief that he knew he had no real hope of using it.

"Jamie!" a girl shrieked, and he knew her for Skye.

Then out of the darkness the little witch flew, in a white robe with golden spangles, her dreadlocks gone and her blond hair plaited down her back like a medieval princess. "Don't shoot me!" she shouted.

He had time to lift the Uzi from around his neck as she threw herself into his arms and showered his face with kisses. Kissing for joy wasn't much his thing, but he let her do it, laughing again, and grabbed her and whirled her in a circle.

"How did you find me?" she cried.

Then his street education reasserted itself, and he eased her away. He crouched behind the fallen bike and pointed the weapon in the direction he had come, seeing only blackness.

"I was followed," he said. "Magicians or wizards or witches or something. On motorcycles. Four."

"Oh, Goddess." Her giddiness evaporated, and she crouched down beside him. She began to murmur a spell.

"That better be a fighting spell," he said. "It's your ex, ain't it." It wasn't a question. "I shot one of them. I hope it was him."

She sucked in her breath but went on with her spell casting. Jamie kept his Uzi sighted. "Is there an escape route? Where are we?" The order of his questions didn't matter if she could take the time to answer them.

Murmuring still—sounded like Latin—she tapped him on the shoulder. She had conjured up a little ball of glowing light above her upturned palm. She darted into the blackness, and he had no reasonable choice but to follow her.

She was a damned gazelle as he stumbled along, tired from his ride, legs shaking from all the adrenaline. Everything in him wanted to stand his ground and prepare for an attack. If it was her ex, then from what Jamie knew he was a magick user of the first water, more powerful than Skye. He wondered how she'd escaped him. Or *if* she'd escaped him.

"Skye," he began. She pointed over her shoulder, and he looked.

There was a scraping sound, like the grating of stone on stone, and from either side of the tunnel they were in—he saw now that it had been carved out and reinforced with timber, the whole lot rickety and old—two hulking figures pulled themselves out of the rock: head, shoulders, torso, arms, legs. They were unfinished and lacking in detail, as if they were a child's clay creations. As they stepped out of the rock, they seemed to harden into moving statues. Then they stood side by side, enormous—seven feet, Jamie estimated—their backs to Skye and him.

She said, *"Definite nos!"* and the creatures took a mighty stride forward, toward the opening of the cavern.

"Come on, Jamie," Skye said.

Street fighter that he was, Jamie knew better than to ask questions at the wrong time. Still, he kept firm hold of the Uzi as he trailed after her. Soon the two giants were lost to his field of vision. Then he heard a rumble, low and practically subsonic.

"I've created a wall in front of them," she said.

"And they are?"

"Defenders. I'll explain later."

She scooted along a warren of tunnels, never hesitating as she forked left, then right, then went straight. After a time he heard dripping water. They hurried around to the right, and they were going up a flight of stairs cut into the rock. The little light ball kept glowing merrily away. She ducked into another hole cut in the rock, and he saw a proper little room—a camp bed, a propane stove, and a very elaborate witch's altar presided over by a statue of the Virgin Mary, lavender and white candles, a spray of lavender tied up with a white string, some colorful crystals, and a seashell. She sent the glowing ball to the candles, and they lit up one by one. She looked older. She looked as if she had been through a lot.

She sank to her knees and bowed her head, speaking in a language that wasn't Latin, Spanish, or English, and waved her hands about. Witchy matters. He came up beside her. She reached up, found his hand, and squeezed it. "Are the others okay?"

"Holgar's fine. Gone off with Jenn and Antonio." Then he realized that she probably didn't know about Eriko. He didn't want to tell her. Not now, anyway. "What are Defenders?"

"Like golems. I doubt our 'friends' will get through my wall. I've gotten quite good at them," she said, with a hint of pride. "How did they find you?"

"I don't know. I think finder's spell." He winced. "Father Juan gave me a scrying stone to find *you*, but I dropped it back in that tunnel."

"Oh, dear." Her eyes grew wide. "They may be able to trace us."

"You got backup?" he asked, grimacing as he pictured his lost weapons back in the hard saddlebags of the bike. "Witch mates? I traveled here alone."

"Backup." She took a breath. "Jamie, we're on White magick ground. You know the code."

"'An it harm none,'" he intoned. Then he frowned at her. "Leave off. Those bastards were throwing lightning bolts at me, and *we're* not supposed to harm *them*?"

"L-lightning bolts?" she echoed, looking terrified.

"Yeah. That some signature of his?" he asked. "Your ex, what was his name? Est—"

She covered his mouth with both her hands. "Don't say it. Names have power. He might hear you."

He shifted his weight. "Maybe he's the one I shot."

"I hope so," she blurted; then she paled and looked down at her white robe. The spangles were moons and stars. She looked like people he'd seen etchings of about to be burned at the stake or getting their heads chopped off.

"We have to do something," he said. "If they do break down your wall and overtake those Defender lads, we're in big trouble." He picked up one of her candles and mimicked the sound of gunfire. "Take that, you big mean, bad person! I harm you not with my candle!"

"Show respect," Skye snapped, taking the candle from him.

"Skye?" said a voice. There was a girl in the doorway, also dressed in a white robe. She had dark hair and skin. "Who's this?"

"Farrah, this is Jamie. He's one of the Salamancans. Farrah is one of my—my coven sisters."

"Your Salamancan coven?" Farrah said, looking askance at him, then down at his Uzi. "Why are you here?"

"*Coven?*" Jamie repeated, narrowing his eyes. Skye reddened and kept her gaze averted.

"Skye's with us now," Farrah said, moving protectively toward Skye. "Not you lot."

"What?" Jamie cried.

Skye grimaced. "No one asked me to make a choice."

"It went without saying," Farrah retorted.

"But I belong to both. It was that way before—"

The boom of an explosion shook the earth beneath their feet. Pebbles and chalky dirt sprinkled down from the ceiling. Farrah cried out and grabbed onto Skye. For his part, Jamie checked his Uzi.

"Nice try, witchy, but I think they may be coming through your wall," Jamie said, as a second explosion rocked them. "Come on."

"What's going on?" Farrah asked.

"He was followed," Skye said. "I made a wall—"

Farrah's shock was obvious. *"Followed?* Weren't you going to come and warn the rest of us?"

"He just got here. Farrah, please, get the others. These men are Dark Witches. I set out two Defenders, but they could get past them."

"How did they know about the tunnel?" Farrah demanded. "How did Jamie? Did you reveal it?"

"Hey, leave off. I've seen that trick before," Jamie cut in. "Thought I'd take a chance. I was scrying for her, and—"

"Scrying?" Farrah shook her head in disbelief. "Is there *anything* about our Art that you haven't shared with the Salamancans?"

"She didn't. Our priest did," Jamie snapped, not liking the witch at all. Farrah looked bewildered. "Talk later. Time

to sound the alarm. Assemble your people. We may have a
nasty fight on our hands. These lads were hurling lightning
bolts at me."

Farrah took Skye's arm. "We have to get out of here,
Skye," she said. "Move to safety."

Jamie blinked. "There is no 'safety.' There's fighting."

"Not like this. Not White Witches," Farrah said firmly.
"Skye, let's go."

"You don't know what they're like," Skye told Farrah.
"My ex allied himself with the Cursed Ones. He's done their
magicks. They've changed him."

"All the more reason to leave," Farrah insisted. "Let's *go*."

Skye looked from Farrah to Jamie and back again. It
was clear she was torn. Jamie was incredulous. He was
about to remind her of the vows she took as a hunter—to
hunt, to attack, to destroy. That was their mission. *Not* to
protect. *Not* to defend. But to *fight*—to the death, if necessary. Suicide mission with one, but if only these witches
would take a stand—

"Jamie, I'm with you," Skye told him. "Farrah, *please*,
get the others."

"It's the wrong thing to do!" Farrah cried.

"If it's . . . him, we can't outrun them," Skye shot back.
"Just tell the High Priestess. Tell her. That's all I ask."

Farrah frowned. Then she nodded, obviously coming to
a decision.

"Thank you." Skye took a deep breath and looked at

Jamie. "I can try to create more Defenders. Maybe they can hold the line until my coven sisters reach the cavern."

"Agreed," Jamie said, flashing her a look of approval.

Together they negotiated the warrens and tunnels by way of her little glow light. Another explosion shook the tunnel, and one of the supporting timbers broke free.

The two stone Defenders stood a few yards ahead of them, shifting on their massive feet. Skye's wall before them seemed to wobble and shimmer, and Jamie's hair rose up as if he'd just walked into a field of static electricity.

"They're breaking it down," she said.

"Does that mean they've breached the outer wall?" he asked. Grimly she nodded her head. "Then they've got my weapons and, if they find it, the scrying stone." He raised his Uzi. "Get ready. The only way out for us is through."

"Right," she said, raising her arms. She began to chant.

"Don't hold back," he warned her. "They ain't."

She kept chanting. A wind whistled past him and rushed around the room. He grinned at Skye as the evidence of her power manifested.

The wall jittered. The two Defenders took another giant step forward. Jamie wished he had a rocket launcher. Or twenty.

He could almost see through the wall. See a dark-haired man lying outside the cave, and three others aiming streams of energy at the stone.

"Is that . . . ?" he asked.

"Yes," she murmured, sounding stricken. "But he's not the one lying down. You didn't get him."

Jamie swore under his breath.

The Defenders took another step.

"But Jamie," she said, her voice tight and high. "Jamie, thank you. Thank you for coming to get me."

For getting you killed, more like, he thought. He got ready. Thought of Eri. Clenched his teeth.

"Come on, then, you bloody bastards!" he shouted.

The cold wind howled all around him, like a dervish. He staggered, losing his grip on the Uzi, and the weight of it spun him in a circle. Then he was falling end over end over end, crazily, as the wind howled and screamed around him. He flailed for Skye, crying out for her, but his words were lost in the chaos.

He slammed against a hard stone floor, nearly knocked senseless, and it took precious seconds to catch his breath and survey his surroundings. He was in some sort of chapel. And he was surrounded by women in white decorated robes like Skye's. As one, they were glaring down at him. If looks could kill . . . well, he'd have taken care of Antonio and Holgar years ago.

"Here she is," said a voice. Farrah.

The white robes parted as Skye was escorted like a prisoner by two more white robes, one on her left side with ginger hair, and a blue-black dye job on the other.

The trio stopped and looked down at Jamie. Skye was

freaking out. She reached down a trembling hand to him, but he got to his feet on his own. No sense looking weak. He figured the witches had magickally transported him and Skye from the cave to somewhere else. It would have been a bad fight, them outnumbered and outgunned, but he withheld his gratitude for the moment. He figured he had not been saved because they wanted to save him.

"Blessed be, Jamie O'Leary," said an old lady wearing a white veil over her hair. "We bid you welcome."

"He's *not* welcome," said another woman. "He led evil to our door."

"It wasn't intentional," Jamie said in his own defense, although it kind of was. He looked around. "Where are we?"

"A secure place," the old lady replied. "I am the High Priestess of this coven. You saved our sister. You also tempted her to break her vows."

"You mean to *fight* for her life?" Jamie sniped. "Those lads were coming through, one way or another, and you *do* know they're lackeys of the Cursed Ones, right?"

"We have taken a vow. *All* of us," the High Priestess said. She looked at Skye. "We have agreed to continue to fight by healing our wounded, providing information, and casting spells of protection. But not to directly harm. I know our path can be difficult. But as you can see, we're all safe and no one's been hurt."

"Not this time," Jamie argued. "But they'll keep coming until they get her. Am I right, Skye?"

Before Skye could answer, the old woman held up her hand. "And we will continue to protect her, as we have done. She is our sister."

"She's gonna be your *dead* sister." Jamie felt the rage building inside him. "I had a sister. Werewolves tore her apart while I was forced to stand by and do *nothing*. And I'm not going to twiddle my thumbs while Skye's in danger. And as long as those lads are breathing, she's in danger."

"Your way is not our way," the High Priestess said, and all the white robes nodded their heads in solemn agreement. "And only those who follow the code may remain here."

"I'm sorry," Skye said to him, cheeks scarlet.

Jamie's lips parted in complete, total shock. "So that's it, then? I risk my life to find my teammate and she's gonna stay and play the nun?" He scowled. "Just so you know, Skye, Heather's gone missing, Salamanca has been destroyed, and Eri is *dead*. Your place is with us, and we can't stand to lose anyone else."

As he spoke, he realized with a start that he wouldn't be heading off to Northern Ireland any time soon. His place was with the Salamancans too. He was devastated.

"She's . . . dead?" Skye whispered. "Eriko's dead?"

"Yeah, and she wouldn't—" He clamped his mouth shut. He was going to say that Eriko wouldn't be dead if only Skye had been there. It wasn't in his nature to pull his punches, but there was enough going on at the moment.

"Skye York has given up her warlike ways," said the

178

High Priestess. "She's been welcomed back into the fold of White magick. Her spells and incantations will heal the Earth, and stop the hatred between humanity and the vampires."

"Dream *on*, sister!" Jamie shouted. "Oh, Skye, Skye, you can't believe this drivel!"

"High Priestess," the ginger-haired girl began.

"Be quiet, Soleil," the High Priestess said.

There was a long silence. Then Skye glanced at the girl named Soleil and the dye job, and Jamie realized that the two were holding her up and supporting her, instead of restraining her.

Skye cleared her throat. "I want to believe this 'drivel,'" she said, and the High Priestess nodded encouragingly at her. "But I also know that *he* will stop at nothing until he finds me. And I believe that sometimes you have to take a stand, and that to protect you must attack. And so . . ." She lowered her head and sank to her knees. "I'd better leave with Jamie."

There was a murmur of shock through the coven. The High Priestess's forehead creased, and she pursed her lips.

"Think this through," the High Priestess said. "If you walk out that door, we'll cast you out, and none of us will call you sister ever again."

Skye gasped as if the old bitch had punched her in the stomach. The other witches muttered darkly as his teammate lifted the voluminous robe over her head. Then she

handed it to the High Priestess with two shaky hands, and the old git took it without so much as a by-your-leave. Stared straight ahead like the cold-hearted statue she was.

Soleil and Dye Job made motions as if to remove their robes, but Skye laid a hand on each of them. "Soleil, Lune, this is my path, not yours," she whispered, voice raw with emotion.

Soleil started to cry. Lune shook her head and mouthed the words "no, Skye, please." Farther back in the room, Farrah bit her lower lip and made circular motions with her hands. That got her a dirty look from the witch beside her, and Farrah lowered her hands to her sides with an air of defeat.

"Right, then," Jamie said firmly. "Let's go. There's lots of people waiting to hear that you're found."

The two walked toward the door. Skye was all hangdog, her shoulders round, her head bowed. Whipped she was, by the ones who'd called her sister.

"We ostracize you!" the High Priestess cried. "So mote it be!"

"So mote it be!" the witches cried.

And little Skye cried, too, as her foot stepped over the threshold.

But being ostracized was the least of her worries. Because her bastard ex was still out there. And the Cursers still walked the earth.

And Jamie knew they'd be lucky to survive the coming night.

CHAPTER NINE

And all our plans
You now shall see
The world is ours
The land, the sea
None can stop us
No man, no god
Upon your lives
We now do trod

THE CARPATHIAN MOUNTAINS, EN ROUTE TO THE MONASTERY OF THE BROTHERHOOD OF ST. ANDREW JENN, HOLGAR, AND ANTONIO

"Red wine, drink it," Brother Cristian urged Jenn as he pulled back the blanket they had strung across the back of the panel van to give her privacy. They wanted her to eat red meat and drink red wine to restore her blood. It wasn't that Antonio had taken so much; it was that the tear he had ripped in her neck had made her bleed badly. They had stitched up the wound and covered it with bandages.

"Later, I think," Holgar said.

Brother Cristian sighed and let the blanket drop back into place.

In the four days since Antonio had attacked her, he had refused to see her. Unable to reach Father Juan, the four brothers of St. Andrew had held several long discussions with Jenn and Holgar, trying to get a better understanding of Antonio's current "spiritual condition." Jenn had been in a state of shock, unable to speak, to believe that Antonio could have done what he had done. She lay still and silent. At night Holgar held her, murmuring to her in Danish, promising to keep her safe.

They chained Antonio's wrists and ankles, blindfolded him, and locked him into the back of an old military transport vehicle very like the one they had used in Russia. Jenn thought about telling them that chains couldn't hold a vampire, but she couldn't make herself speak. Her mind slid over fears that the Brotherhood didn't know what they were doing. Or that they might decide he had sunk too far into evil and stake him. Sometimes when she touched her bandages, she wanted them to stake him. Then tears of shame and grief would roll down her face, even though she remained as still and silent as ever.

The vehicle they transported Antonio in was old, struggling as it chugged up the steep mountain passes. The four monks took turns driving. They had to stop often to let the engine cool down. Their journey was torturous. Holgar told her that a monk guarded Antonio night and day, telling rosary beads, praying without ceasing for Antonio to find his way back to them. She didn't ask Holgar if he thought it would happen, and he didn't say.

Then one night, after Holgar had changed her bandage and settled her against his chest, the howls of wolves shattered the cocoon of her sickbed. She jerked, hard, as their shrill cries grew louder, closer, wilder. Holgar held her fast; she felt his heartbeat beneath her cheek, and heard him swear in Danish under his breath. His arms tightened around her until it was almost painful. When she shifted, he loosened them and rested his chin on the crown of her head.

"Lille skat," he said gently, "I have to leave you for a little bit. Just a little while."

There was tension in his voice, and it dawned on her that Holgar hadn't been simply comforting her all this time. He had been guarding her too, and making sure that Antonio couldn't get anywhere near her.

"What do they want?" she asked. They were the first words she had uttered since Antonio had bitten her, and her voice was hoarse and scratchy.

He hesitated.

"Tell me," she insisted. "I'm still your leader." Then she burst into sobs. She cried hard, her body contracting, and Holgar crossed his arms over her chest, cupping each shoulder, allowing the release she had so desperately needed. In her mind she was back in the safe house, alone with Antonio; his eyes were crimson, and he opened his mouth wide, as if daring her to turn away from the sight of his fangs coming at her. Deliberately mesmerizing her, taunting her, and then . . .

"Oh, God," she ground out. "Oh, my God."

"*Ja*, it's good to face it," Holgar said into her ear. "*Ja*, Jenn."

She cried for another minute or so, then forced herself to dam her tears. She wanted to weep and scream forever, but she knew they needed to discuss the crisis at hand. "I'm okay," she said firmly, wiping her face. She molded her hands around his and squeezed them. "Tell me."

"Well, you know there's a price on my head," he said. "And this pack, well, they've come to claim it."

"So it's a werewolf pack," she said. And something clicked back into place inside her. Something worked again. She was being called into action. It was time to do her job — to lead her team, even if it was just a team of two. "How many?"

"I think six," he said. "The alpha and his mate, three males, and one female. The alpha's saying that they know who

I am, and that we're trespassing on his territory." He cocked his head, listening to the howls. "And that there is a vampire named Lucifer who will pay handsomely for my pelt."

"Lucifer," she said, chills running down her spine. Always Lucifer. They had thought Solomon was their biggest problem, but Lucifer was dogging them. Solomon baited Jenn by parading her traitor father, Paul Leitner, on TV and having him beg Jenn to turn herself in for a crime she didn't commit. But it wasn't Jenn whom Solomon wanted. It was Antonio. And Lucifer wanted Antonio. Maybe if they found out that he'd attacked her, they'd lose interest in him.

She hitched a couple of breaths, forcing herself not to lose her composure. Holgar grimaced in response.

"I knew I shouldn't have come," he said, but she heard the mixed emotion in his voice. If he hadn't been there when Antonio had attacked her, she'd probably be dead.

Unless Antonio stopped himself, she thought. *Maybe he would have been able to. Maybe —*

Holgar pulled away the blanket. Jenn slowly sat up by herself and looked at Brother Cristian, who smiled with delight at the sight of her. But his smile faded as Holgar repeated the werewolves' demand. Brother Cristian's eyes widened, and he made the sign of the cross in the air.

"If the driver can slow down the van just enough for me to jump out, then you can put some distance between everybody and the pack," Holgar added.

"Everybody *else*, you mean. Holgar, you can't wolf at will," Jenn insisted. "They'll rip you to shreds."

"They're promising me that if I come out in human form, unarmed, no harm will come to any of you," Holgar translated.

"You're not going out there," she insisted. She turned to Brother Cristian. "Break out the weapons."

The priests had come well provisioned with Uzis. Were-wolves possessed remarkable powers of healing, but it was possible to take one out with a barrage of submachine-gun fire if you could get off enough shots to cut it in half before it took your throat.

"Okay," Brother Cristian said, nodding. He said something to the driver, who picked up a radiophone and spoke into it. Jenn heard the crackle of a response from Antonio's transport vehicle.

Their vans slowed, then rolled to a stop. Neither driver turned off his engine, keeping them idling in case they needed to make a fast getaway.

"Let's go," Jenn said.

"Not you," Holgar insisted. "You're too weak."

She raised her chin a notch and gave him a long, level look. "For now, you and I are fighting partners, Holgar, and I'm not letting you go out there by yourself."

"Noah is your fighting partner," Holgar said. "And that crazy Israeli would kick my ass if I took you outside with me."

"Then prepare to get it kicked," Jenn said, as she crawled to the side of the van where they had stowed their jackets. She got hers and began slipping her arms into the sleeves. The world spun. Her throat hurt. She still hadn't recovered from the loss of blood.

Holgar sighed heavily. "Okay, boss lady, you win. Please hand me my jacket."

"Here," she said, grabbing it up and holding it out to him. When he didn't take it, she looked in his direction.

And that was when he clocked her, his fist against her chin, which *hurt*, and everything fuzzed yellow, and then black.

Holgar caught the unconscious Jenn in his arms. Brother Cristian made the sign of the cross over Holgar. Then the brother pointed to himself and to Jenn, saying, "I am taking care of her."

Holgar gave Jenn one last look as he opened up the van's side door and stepped out, forcing himself to stay as calm as possible. His aggressive instincts had fully engaged, and he was hoping they would push him into transforming. Tonight was only a crescent moon, barely a fingernail slice, nearly as far from the full moon as could be.

Snow tumbled down. The alpha of the werewolf pack stood before him in human form. He wore white snow gear—pants and a parka with a hood lined with rabbit fur. He was tall, with high Slavic cheekbones and crystal blue eyes. His lips were curled in a sneer.

The alpha held up a hand, and the rest of the pack slunk from behind trees and boulders. Six total, as Holgar had counted, wearing magnificent, silvery pelts. So they could all change at will. Impressive. And bad news for Holgar.

They growled and fanned out, flashing their teeth at their common foe. Holgar monitored himself for signs of transformation. To his intense disappointment, he felt nothing.

"Holgar Vibbard, is Marku Barbu," the alpha introduced himself. "And is time for dying." Sneer, sneer.

"Vuy govorite po-russkiy?" Holgar asked him, which meant "Do you speak Russian?" in Russian. The alpha frowned, clearly not comprehending. Holgar had thought it was worth a shot. "Cartoon English for you, then, friend Marku," Holgar said. "Is not time for Holgar dying. Is time for all werewolves killing vampires. Vampires evil. Werewolves good."

The alpha's mouth twisted. "Pack of Marku are making peace with vampire king."

"Lucifer," Holgar said loudly, and the wolves of the pack took a step backward—retreating in submission and fear. "Lucifer is not friend. Is killing Marku."

"I am alpha," Marku declared, throwing back his chest. "Marku say, Holgar Vibbard die."

Without warning, the alpha wolfed. Holgar had never seen such a rapid transformation—muzzle stretching, ears flattening, eyes turning a golden yellow in mere seconds. His clothing exploded off him. Then the werewolf dropped to all fours, his front paws barely touching the snow as he sprang at Holgar.

Holgar threw himself to the side as the werewolf knocked him down. Holgar clenched his jaw so that no scream would escape him, although the pain was terrible. As he tumbled backward into the snow, all he saw was a crescent moon and two glowing eyes.

For helvede, he thought. *I really am going to die.*

Then he heard a blast of Uzi fire and animal whimpering. Someone on his side had shot someone on Marku's side. Beneath the fusillade he shouted out his fury as the alpha dragged him by one wrist, teeth sunk deep through the muscle into bone. Holgar twisted and flailed, trying to grab a rock with his free hand, a tree branch, anything, as he slid through the snow.

All he could hear was the *pop-pop-pop* of Uzis and the outraged howling of the wolf pack. And he heard in their voices just how terrified of Lucifer they were. Although they howled about victory over their enemy and the imminent death of a rival alpha, what they were really singing about was a reprieve from their own death sentences if they brought Lucifer the body of Holgar Vibbard.

As Marku dragged him, Holgar's head slammed against a rock so hard it felt as if his brains were being scrambled. Karma for punching out Jenn, he supposed. Some

werewolves worshipped various wolf gods—the Fenris
Wolf, for one—but Holgar's Danish family was nominally
Lutheran. He sent up a prayer to God and Jesus just in
case they really existed—asking not for admission into
heaven, but for the strength to last long enough for Jenn
and the others to get the hell out of there. He wanted the
deafening roar of the Uzi to recede into the distance.

I actually wish Jamie were here, he thought as his vision
filmed over. He saw two crescent moons and dark smudges
of treetops. *If we had another good fighter on our side—*

His hand caught on to something sharp, and pain stabbed
just as hard. Was Marku going to drag him to death?

Then the air seemed to press down, and he almost saw
something shooting through the air above him. Suddenly
Marku let go of him. Dazed, Holgar managed to raise his
head just in time to see Marku go flying toward the treetops. The alpha's howls were punctuated by yips as the rest
of the pack dodged and pitched in a swirling dervish of fur.
A gout of blood spurted from the neck of a male, and it fell
onto its back, shrieking in agony.

As Holgar watched, Antonio seemed to materialize from
out of nowhere, his eyes glowing like coals, on his knees
bent over the werewolf, long fangs clamped on the werewolf's throat. The werewolf kept struggling. One of the other
wolves leaped at Antonio; Antonio threw his arms around
the one he had attacked and whirled around, using the struggling
werewolf as a weapon to slam into his assailant.

Antonio still wore manacles around his wrists, but his chains had been broken. He threw the limp wolf to the snowy ground and scooped up Holgar, carrying him toward the van. A chorus of howls rose up behind them. Brother Dorin and Brother Cristian had Uzis, one trained on Antonio and one on the werewolf pack. Holgar gave them a dizzy wave to signify that he was all right.

"In, in, in!" Brother Cristian shouted at Antonio as Brother Dorin let loose a hail of sub-machine gun fire over Antonio's head. Werewolf blood was dripping down Antonio's chin.

The panel-van door was open. Jenn was in the middle of climbing out. She saw the blood on Antonio's face and pointed her Uzi at him.

"He's attacked Holgar!" she shrieked.

"Nej, nej," Holgar said, jumping out of Antonio's arms and restraining her. She couldn't get past him—he was superstrong, like Antonio, and she was still weak. "He saved me. That's someone else's blood." He pushed her back into the van. "Stay here."

As the last gleam of bloodlust left Antonio's eyes, he wiped off his chin and turned his head. It was obvious he was trying to hide his face.

"I think I killed the alpha," Antonio announced. "Maybe one other. I'm not sure."

The two brothers of St. Andrew were shooting through the vehicle windows at the werewolves. Holgar heard death cries and fury.

"I'll go back out," Antonio said, and in that instant his eyes turned red and his fangs lengthened. He was once more a terrifying vampire caught in bloodlust.

"No, get in and stay in," Jenn ordered him. She reached over and tapped Brother Cristian on the arm. "We're getting out of here."

"I'll go to the transport," Antonio said.

"*For helvede*, get in," Holgar swore at him. "Brother Cristian, let's go!"

As Antonio climbed in, he kept his face turned away from Jenn. She touched the bandage on her neck. Holgar put his arm around her and stared straight at Antonio.

"One move, Antonio, and you're dust," Holgar said pointedly.

"*Sí. Gracias,*" Antonio replied feelingly.

The two vehicles resumed their journey through the snowy mountain pass, the howls of werewolves trailing after them.

Transylvania, Romania
Aurora, Lucifer, and Dantalion

Dracula's castle.

Home sweet home.

Aurora watched from a windswept, moonlit balcony as Lucifer's minions—human, vampiric, and hybrid—dragged in the beautiful antiques she had picked out for the castle.

There were at least thirty of them, and more hybrids in an outbuilding where Dantalion was setting up his research facility.

Lucifer had purchased Castle Bran — also known as Castle Dracula — from the former royal family of Romania years and years before. Lucifer liked to tease Aurora that the previous inhabitant — Dracula himself — still haunted the narrow passageways of stone and shadow. But Aurora doubted that Lucifer would have allowed Dracula to remain in any form — bat, mist, or wolf, as it was said he could transform. Lucifer wouldn't have permitted the competition.

To keep the Ottomans out of his homeland, Dracula had impaled tens of thousands of his enemies — slid them down on sharpened stakes like skewered meat. Soon Lucifer would wipe out millions. The Vampire Kingdom was about to rise, and if she played her cards right, she would be its queen. She, Lucifer, and Sergio had often played cards together, back in the day. Sergio had loved to cheat. But Lucifer had chided Aurora gently whenever he caught her trying to let her sire win.

"Fight strong, my beauty," he'd instructed her. "Show no mercy."

His beauty. With a sigh she moved from the balcony — the hybrids were so repugnant that she didn't want to look at them.

She kept waiting for news of Antonio de la Cruz. Lucifer and Dantalion wanted to study him, but she was still uncertain if Lucifer knew that she'd had Antonio and lost him. Where the traitor was concerned, she had shown no mercy. She had heaped magicks and torment on him out of pure spite, and after she had lost him, he had killed Sergio.

"I hate you, Antonio. Damn you," Aurora whispered to the soulless heavens. But in her unbeating heart she knew that it was actually a good thing Sergio had died. Now she could concentrate her charms on Lucifer, free of any jealous dramatics.

She turned around and faced the sweet little human minion Lucifer had given her as a maid. The girl had staggered up the spiral staircase behind her, bundled up like a snowman. There was no heat in the castle. All Aurora's personal staff were new; Lucifer had forced her to leave her fledglings behind as well. No minions, no vampires she had made. Not because he didn't trust *her*, he had assured her, but because she and he couldn't trust *them*.

Their plans must remain secret. And if Lucifer and Dantalion were able to infiltrate the Salamancans with a spy, the hunters might have been able to put a spy in Aurora's entourage. That was the reason Lucifer gave her, but it meant that she was all alone. She had a feeling that he'd killed them all—Emilio, who had presided over Sergio's funeral; Louis, her trusty lieutenant, who had told her that Sergio was going to Salamanca to fetch Antonio and take him to Lucifer. Now that she thought about it, it was probably good that Louis was dead. If Lucifer hadn't killed him, she might have had to track him down herself and get rid of him so he couldn't tell Lucifer about Antonio.

Secrets could be so fatal.

"Maria," Aurora said brightly, changing mental tack, "let's go shopping."

The little human blinked nervously and pushed her dark hair away from her face with a mittened hand. "Ah, madame, my name is Flavia, and the stores are closed. B-because it is midnight, madame."

"I didn't mean in a *store*," Aurora said. "And as for your name . . ," Aurora hesitated. What she was planning to do was say, "It *was* Flavia," and then tear off the girl's head. Because correcting one's betters was rude, and because that would have some dramatic flair. But technically, this girl was Lucifer's property. Aurora didn't know how he would feel if she killed Flavia. He'd told her to drink from anyone she wanted. Every human in the castle was a willing donor, and the miracle of the human body was that it replenished its own blood supply. But kill one and it was like stealing food from her sire's table.

"And as for your name," she repeated, "it's lovely." The wind tugged at her hair. "Maybe you need another coat?" she asked Flavia. "It's cold outside."

Castle Bran, Transylvania
Heather

There she is.

Aurora had appeared on a balcony at the back of the castle. Far below, Heather was crouched behind a cistern of slushy ice water.

Heather's fangs pierced her lower lip as she clenched her jaw. Eagerly she licked the blood away. She was hungry. She was impatient. She wanted to kill Aurora and then . . .

. . . and then what?

"Feeding," she promised herself in a mournful whisper. How long did this have to take?

Then her spirits lifted as Aurora announced that she wanted to leave the castle to go "shopping." Out of the castle was good. Maybe there would be a chance to attack her.

"Kill her," Heather murmured.

The dark-haired Spanish vampire was very beautiful. People used to tell Heather she was pretty, and that one day she would blossom into a beauty. She looked down into the water in the cistern to see if that was true.

She had forgotten that she would be unable to see her reflection.

A voice sounded suddenly, loud and nearby.

"It doesn't matter that a few of the hybrids have escaped. We can make all we want." She recognized the voice: Spanish accent, speaking English. Commanding, elegant.

Lucifer.

Thrills of terror washed over Heather. He was even more dangerous than Aurora.

"But, Lucifer, if *they* find them, and realize that they don't last long . . ."

Dantalion. Lucifer's assistant, from what Heather could tell. Nearly just as dangerous.

"What is the problem with that?" Lucifer interrupted Dantalion. "If they think the creatures pose no threat, they're mistaken. It's wonderful if they underestimate us. We can continue to replace the ones that wear out for as long as we need."

They were coming closer. Heather looked left, right, trying to find some way to get out of their way before they spotted her She looked down at her hands. She had forgotten she was covered in filth and dried blood. Everyone in the castle, vampire and human alike, was so *clean*.

"Aurora," Lucifer called out. "What light from yonder window breaks?"

Trapped, Heather thought. *Caught*. Then, panicking, she looked down at the water in the cistern again. Moving with the speed endowed her by vampirism, she looped one leg over the lip of the container, and then the other, and ducked her head beneath the surface. She could stay like that for hours. She wouldn't need to come up for air, ever.

Now Aurora was saying something about a party. As her words carried through the water, they were a bit muffled. But it was clear to Heather that Aurora wasn't going to go out as she had originally planned.

Fury rushed through Heather, and she balled her fists, feeling the water mixing with the layers of grime as her thumb ran over her knuckles, turning the blood and earthen crust to slime. She rubbed her fingers together, then trailed them up her arms. Then remembered that she was hiding, and that if her movements disturbed the surface of the water, she would be revealed.

So she went back to waiting.

And waiting.

Then something dove into the water, grabbed her by the hair, and yanked her straight up. Her eyes filmy, she couldn't see what had hold of her. She flailed as she dangled; then her vampire instincts took over, and she hissed and snapped, grabbing what she saw now was an arm, half rotted and covered with fur.

Without warning she was dropped. She landed on her bare feet and threw herself at her attacker. Her force threw it on its back, and she straddled it, hissing and preparing to rip open its throat.

But it whimpered.

Heather was a Cursed One, which meant that she was evil. She would never show mercy just because someone sounded hurt. That was the time to go in for the kill. But as she paused and stared down at the thing beneath her, curiosity overcame her. It was so *gross*, like a Frankenstein monster sewn together from hacked-off bits of dead human . . . and decomposing werewolf and rotten vampire, complete with glowing eyes.

Then the thing said in a tortured, gravelly voice, "Oh, so lovely."

Panicking all over again, Heather whirled around, fully

expecting to see Aurora—and Dantalion and Lucifer—behind her. But there was no one there.

The monster raised a hand and pointed at her. At Heather. And it said, "Lovely."

THE MONASTERY OF THE BROTHERHOOD OF ST. ANDREW
JENN, HOLGAR, ANTONIO, FATHER JUAN, AND ESTHER

Jenn was in hell. After the werewolf attack, it took only one more day to reach their destination. The monastery of St. Andrew topped a jagged mountain peak of hallowed ground, but rivers of spilled blood had soaked into the stones at the base of the castlelike fortress. Vampires had terrorized Transylvania for centuries. After hearing only a few stories of the massacres that had taken place at the doors of the gloomy, drafty monastery, Jenn was surprised that the snow on the hillsides stayed white.

As soon as they arrived, Brother Cristian and Brother Dorin showed Jenn the special vampire prison cell the monks had built centuries before, when they began their work of "cleansing" vampires of their terrible curse. It was where they wanted to house Antonio. Religious murals of angels smiting demons covered the ceiling of the cell, and on the walls hundreds of crosses were crammed between wooden stakes that pointed inward from all directions.

There were special wheels that could be turned so that the walls shot toward each other with astonishing speed. In the ever-narrowing space, a vampire would be forced to watch as the stakes approached him, then ended his undead life.

Jenn wanted to protest, to say that Antonio didn't belong in such a dangerous place. What if someone accidentally set the wheels in motion?

Even worse, their reassurances of turning vampires to the light were hard to prove. The last vampire they claimed to have made "good" had left the monastery in 1896. According to their records, her name was Elizabet, and she had stopped drinking human blood. She left the monastery in the company of two monks, with the intention of traveling to the sacred grotto of Lourdes, France, where it was said that miraculous cures occurred when one prayed there to the Holy Mother.

"Why would Elizabet go there, if she was no longer cursed?" Jenn asked dubiously.

"She no longer drank human blood, but she was still a Cursed One," Brother Dorin said. "She wanted to ask the Holy Mother to cure her of vampirism altogether." He rarely spoke, and the sound of his voice startled her. It was very hoarse and labored, and she wondered if he'd had some sort of throat injury.

Something similar to her own, perhaps.

Jenn took a deep breath. "And did she get cured?"

The two monks looked at each other, and then at her.

"We don't know. There was a fire, and many of our records were lost."

"Aren't there always fires when it's convenient to have them?" Jenn asked irritably, then let out a heavy sigh. "I'm sorry. It's just . . . he—and I—we were kind of hoping . . ." She trailed off and stared at the cell. *Antonio*, she thought. She didn't know what she had been expecting, but this wasn't it.

"Since the cross does not hold him back, we need to put him in here," Brother Cristian said. "We must think of everyone who lives here."

"God is a merciful Father," Brother Dorin said. "Perhaps if we pray together—"

She swallowed. "The cell is fine. I'll see if any of my people need anything."

"God needs you," Brother Dorin said.

Well, He knows where to find me, Jenn thought, turning away.

After they had escaped from the werewolves, Antonio hadn't spoken a word to her. Inside the van he'd kept his back turned, head bowed, and when she'd started to reach out a hand to him, she'd drawn it back. Holgar had seen her do it, and had nodded sadly. She knew that Holgar had always liked Antonio. They were two men who lived with the knowledge that the supernatural forces within them could turn them into monsters.

Except Antonio's not a man. He's a vampire.

Her back like iron, tears streaming down her face, she left the hellish place.

After Antonio was put in his cell, chanting filled the monastery. Ancient, holy rhythms rose and fell. The monks were begging God to fill their brother Antonio with His grace.

Father Wadim, the head of the brotherhood, conferred with Jenn. He assigned rooms for the group and apologized for the bad heating. He also told Jenn that she would be able to use her cell phone. It took a few tries to reach Father Juan, but finally she heard his calm, Spanish voice. She told him they had arrived safely. She withheld the information about Antonio's attack, telling herself it was because Father Juan had a lot of news to tell her. But the truth was, she didn't want him to know, ever. He would have to, of course. But what if he told the monks to turn the wheels?

Father Juan assured her that Gramma Esther was fine.

"That's great news," Jenn said, struggling to be happy when her own news was so grim.

"And Jamie has found Skye. They're together, but still in England. I'm afraid her ex is proving dangerous and difficult to evade," the priest went on.

"Estefan has found her?" Jenn knew she was terrified of him. She pressed her fingers to her temples and wondered, not for the first time, if Eriko has suffered from so many headaches because of the stress of being the leader.

"So far they've been able to outrun Estefan and his

Spanish coven brothers. Skye's been performing strong spells to blot out their trail, and I've tried to help her," Father Juan said.

"Oh, God," Jenn said, her chest constricting from a breath she now realized she'd been holding mentally for weeks. "What about my mom and Sade?"

"Call them and see," Father Juan said, then relented. "Your mother's fine, if stressed and frightened. Sade is another matter. When you speak to them, tell them to come to you."

"Just the two of them? Alone?" Jenn asked.

"Remember, Jenn, after your father betrayed you to Aurora, your mother joined the resistance. She's been on dangerous recon missions. The news about Heather was a huge blow to her, and I think for a time she felt very helpless. But Sade has not recovered from the shock of the battle at Salamanca. And your mother has had someone to take care of. It's helped her rally."

Jenn swallowed hard. "So . . . no word on Heather?"

"Not through any of my contacts, nor through magick. I'm sorry."

"And Noah?"

Father Juan shook his head. "I've had no word from him. I'll be honest; that worries me."

After all the team members had been contacted, they began to arrive. Jenn's mother and Sade were the first. Anxiously waiting for them in the entryway to the dank, grim chapel, where rows of candles glowed as testament to the many prayers the monks were saying for Antonio's sake, Jenn wore a black turtleneck sweater to hide the wound Antonio had inflicted on her.

"Jenn," her mother said, wrapping her arms around her.

Jenn tried not to feel intense hurt as she felt the stiffness in her mother's embrace. It was obvious that her mom still blamed her for Heather's transformation into a vampire — when it should have been Jenn's father she blamed. As Jenn did.

"Your father was on TV again," Jenn's mom said as Father Wadim brought her some green mint tea. He was very tall, with a stripe of gray hair wrapped around the middle of his head, like Friar Tuck of *Robin Hood*. He was wearing a dark brown robe with a huge cross dangling from a rope belt, and sandals. That was the habit all the monks wore inside the monastery, and Jenn had no idea how they could keep their feet from freezing.

"Welcome," Father Wadim said to Jenn's mother and Sade. Still dressed for the severe weather, Sade stood passively by, watching. The chants rose and fell around them, and Jenn's throat constricted. She wanted her mother to be somewhere else. To be safe. Not to know about a world where holy men prayed to make vampires good.

"Okay, sweetie, let's get you settled in," Jenn's mother said to Sade. She brushed an errant tendril of hair away from Sade's forehead. Sade didn't so much as blink.

Jenn's mom turned to Father Wadim. "If you could show us to our room?"

"I thought maybe you could stay with me, Mom," Jenn said. "And Sade, of course. It's hard to heat the monastery, so we're doubling up. When Gramma, Jamie, and Skye get here—"

"*If,*" her mother corrected her, and she turned her back on Jenn.

Father Juan and Gramma Esther arrived next. Jenn flew into her grandmother's arms. Jenn could tell that Esther sensed that things were not right, but Esther didn't ask, just hugged her back tightly. Wiping away a tear, Jenn turned to face Father Juan.

"I've still had no word from Noah," Father Juan said, his eyes troubled.

She took the words like a body blow. "There's something I have to tell you," Jenn said. Her ears roared with the pounding sound of her pulse. She felt very cold, very frightened, very alone. "It's about Antonio."

His deep-set eyes softened with pity as he took one of her hands in both of his. She was so numb she couldn't feel his skin against hers.

"I already know, Jenn," he said. "Father Wadim met us halfway down the mountain and told me all about it. He described the cell to me. I'm going down now to talk to

Antonio. He doesn't want to see me. He doesn't want to see anyone, but he must."

She took a breath. "Maybe I should go with you."

Father Juan shook his head. "You're the last person on this earth he should see."

I used to be the first, she thought, anguished.

After Father Juan left her, she staggered into the chapel, sat in a pew, and laid her forehead on her hands as she clung to the weathered, dark wood. She cried all the tears she'd kept in for so long. Her eyes pressed against her knuckles, she cried until her stomach hurt and her head throbbed and her back ached. She was aware of people entering the chapel, leaving. Of someone stroking her hair, bending over to kiss the top of her head. She yearned for it to be Antonio, then recoiled from the thought. And then she cried some more.

When she woke, she was in a bedroom on a simple cot with a plain brown blanket pulled up to her chin. Sunlight streamed in through a window. She stared into it, thinking of vampires who might one day walk in daylight. Her throat ached, and she thought of Antonio down in his prison.

She forced herself to get up. She was still wearing her turtleneck sweater and jeans, but the bandage was in place.

In the dining room she found Father Juan talking quietly with Esther and Holgar. The incessant chanting seemed like familiar background noise. Jenn walked in, acknowledging everyone with a nod of her head as she covered a yawn.

"Hello, Jenny," her grandmother said as Jenn kissed her cheek.

"What's going on?" she asked, wondering if Father Juan had been the one to carry her out of the chapel.

"Did you sleep well?" Holgar asked her. So he had tucked her in.

She nodded. "Thanks," she said, and he flashed her a quizzical smile.

"For what?" he asked.

"We've been discussing the elixir," Father Juan interrupted. "The Tears of Christ are essential. I've added cinnamon and cloves to boost strength and suppress pain, and we have everything we need to make the elixir—except that I need more Transit of Venus."

She blinked. "More what?"

"That's exactly what I said," Holgar said. "Except in Danish."

Father Juan acknowledged Holgar's little joke with another gentle smile. Gramma Esther stayed quiet, giving Father Juan her full attention.

"Jamie heard rumors that witches were stockpiling a spell-strengthening herb somewhere in England. I think it might be the Transit. It's a very rare herb, and the secret to its effectiveness is the spell you must cast as you pick it. I don't know if they'll have a chance to acquire any on their way here," Father Juan added. "There was none at Stonehenge."

"Can Skye cast the spell if she does find it?" Jenn asked. "Does she know how?"

"*Sí.* She and I discussed it on the phone," Father Juan replied. "She believes that the Transit, or a close cousin, may also be found deep in these mountains."

"These mountains? Here? No way," Jenn blurted, excited.

"Way. In the territory of the local werewolves," Holgar put in.

"The same pack that attacked you?" Jenn asked, startled.

Holgar shook his head. "Those were Romanian werewolves. These are Transylvanian werewolves."

"Transylvania is part of Romania," Jenn said, confused.

He shook his head. "Not to them it's not."

"Holgar is suggesting that we try to bargain for it," Father Juan said.

Jenn shook her head violently. "Because every other interaction we've had with werewolves has gone so well? Forget it. We can't risk lives. Especially not if there's a chance Jamie and Skye will come through."

Esther cleared her throat and laid a hand on Jenn's arm. "One of the hardest lessons I ever learned was that you can't always wait for your friends to come through."

Holgar nodded. "At least let me try to talk to them, wolf to wolf. I'll take lots of guns." He smiled broadly. "And lots of teeth."

Jenn sucked in a breath. "I'll go with you. And don't

even think about refusing. I'm doing no one any good here. I need to get away, do something, not just sit and think."

Holgar smiled. "Good. I didn't want to go alone anyway."

Gramma Esther half raised a hand. "I'll go."

"No." Father Juan gently pushed her hand back onto the table. "You need to recuperate from our adventure. Jenn, Holgar, the two of you will leave tomorrow morning."

Mutely, Jenn nodded. Then she rose and left the room, heading back to the little bedroom she'd awakened in. She wanted to be alone. No, not alone—she needed someone, someone who could be there for her, who had no other agenda. Someone who might understand just what she was going through.

She opened the door. Sunlight poured through the half-closed curtains, revealing a silhouette on the other side: a man gazing out at the mountains through the glass. Her heart skipped a beat.

"Noah," she whispered.

CHAPTER TEN

When Father Juan gave me this diary, I was going to write
a new Hunter's Manual. Instead I've been pouring out my
soul. I wonder if anyone will ever read it? What will that
mean? That I'm dead? What will the world be like then?
What will my world be like? I can't even think about it. My
hand is shaking so hard I can barely write these words.
                            —from the diary of Jenn Leitner,
                                retrieved from the ruins

THE MONASTERY OF THE BROTHERHOOD
OF ST. ANDREW
JENN, HOLGAR, ANTONIO, FATHER JUAN,
NOAH, AND ESTHER

Jenn blinked in surprise at Noah.

"Jenn," Noah said, pushing away the curtain and coming

toward her as she entered the small room. He was dirty and unshaven, but he looked like home to her. Without thinking, she went to him and put her arms around him. She heard the strong, hard beat of his heart and shut her eyes tightly against the tears that ran down her cheeks.

"You're safe," she said. Her brain told her to ask for a report of his mission, but all she could do was rest against him for a moment, just one moment, and know that he was there.

His lips brushed her hair, and a memory whispered in her mind. Had he been the one to carry her from the chapel last night?

She broke away gently and looked around for a place to sit. All there was was the bed. She sank down on it, gesturing for him to join her. Their noses were practically touching. She could smell his cinnamon gum, and a trembling smile broke across her mouth. To stop herself from kissing him, she cleared her throat.

"Why didn't you call?" she asked.

"Sorry. I wasn't sure of this place," he replied. "Things have happened. I had to do something I already regret." He shifted on the bed, leaning back on his elbows. He looked exhausted. "Goes with the territory," he added. "Regrets."

"We don't have time for riddles," she said, sounding more waspish than she intended, because she felt ashamed for wanting to kiss him when Antonio was in hell. "Fill me in."

He let his head fall back and looked up at the ceiling.

The sunshine etched his profile, and he was solid and real and *there*, and she held on to that as she prepared herself. It was obvious to her that he hadn't come with good news.

He sat back up. "I should do a full debriefing for the team." When she opened her mouth to protest, he added, "But you should hear it first. Alone."

"You're scaring me," she said, all hope flooding from her. He was going to tell her that Project Crusade had failed in its mission, whatever that was; that Greg and the others had been massacred; that they were the last resistance cell in the world.

That all hope was lost.

"Michael Sherman was there," he said.

"I was in the States when the team worked with him," she said. *I was attending Papa Che's funeral. And nothing has gone right since then. Please, let there be good news from Project Crusade. Please.*

Noah nodded at her. "Well, as your teammates said, Sherman's a vampire now. But he's working with the black crosses. He's on humanity's side."

Jenn stared at him in ecstatic disbelief. "So he's good? He stayed good?"

The strangest expression came over Noah's face. "He swears he's evil. He's obsessed with developing something that will rid the world of vampires. Which, for us, is a good thing."

"Why does he want to do that?" She waved her hands. "It doesn't matter. I won't interrupt anymore."

Noah nodded slowly, as if he were choosing his words carefully. "This thing he's making. It's a virus. Airborne. The molecules just have to touch them. And then . . . they are destroyed."

"Whoa." She smiled at him. "*Whoa*. Oh, my God, that's so great! So is it close to being finished? How do we protect Antonio from it? Do they want us to take him to their compound?"

"Jenn." He took both her hands in one of his. Then he locked gazes with her, the expression in his large brown eyes steady, serious. "They're not going to protect Antonio from it."

When she started to jerk away, he held her fast. He put his free hand on her shoulder and held her still. "There's no antidote."

Her face went numb. For a moment the world went dark. She couldn't see him. Couldn't hear anything. She was spinning, falling.

Then she felt him tugging on the neck of her sweater. A hand on her neck. On the bandage.

"What the hell is this?" Noah said in a low, angry voice.

She slapped her hand over his to stop him from pulling away the dressing. She couldn't breathe.

"What do you mean, there's no antidote? *What do you mean?*"

Noah pried her hand off the gauze and lifted it up, revealing the stitched-up wound. To anyone who knew anything about vampires, it was obvious that it was a bite.

"Who did this? Did he do it?"

"Noah, stop!" she said, batting at him. "Tell me about the virus!"

"It doesn't matter that there's no antidote," he said, biting off each word. "Because I'm going to kill Antonio right now."

He whirled on his heel and headed for the door. Jenn gripped his arm; he shook her off. She raced around him, facing him as she flattened her back against the door.

"Noah, calm down. It was an accident," she said, and then her voice broke.

"Move, Jenn, *now*," he said.

"No." She flattened her hands against his chest and pushed him as hard as she could. But he'd been ready for her; he wrapped his hands around her forearms as he stumbled backward, bringing her with him. Then he forced her aside, threw open the door, and stomped into the hallway.

"Don't you do anything!" she screamed, charging after him. "Noah!"

As Jenn ran into the hall, she nearly collided with Noah, who was facing Father Juan. The priest stood in front of the door Noah would have to take to go downstairs. From the other side of the doorway, the monotonous chanting rose and fell.

"There are other doors," Noah said in a low, menacing voice still audible above the prayers for Antonio's soul. "Stand aside."

"I know how you feel," Father Juan replied, holding out his left hand as if Noah were a wild animal he had to calm. His right hand was behind his back. "But he's necessary."

"*Necessary?* After what he did to her? I know you're there, Jenn. Stay clear of me." To Father Juan he said, "Get out of my way."

"I can't, Noah," Father Juan said. "I have cast the runes over and over, and the answer is clear. To win this war, we need Antonio."

Noah laughed harshly. "Father Juan, who's throwing those useless rocks? He's like a son to you."

Father Juan continued as if Noah hadn't spoken. "Antonio is contained. He can't get out. The monks—"

"*Monks,*" Noah jeered. "Don't you get it, Father Juan? This is not some holy war. This is a real war. We have very few soldiers left on our side, and if you leave that monster alive to kill them, we may as well leap out of the tower of this monastery now, because the vampires will win. And I, for one, won't be taken."

"You're talking about Masada," Father Juan said. "The Israelites chose mass suicide rather than be taken by the Romans. And what was *that* but a holy war?"

"Don't twist my words," Noah said.

"Antonio has been chosen to help us," Father Juan insisted.

"And *my* people were chosen, and we were practically annihilated. The Final Solution, didn't Hitler call it?

To round up the Jews and send them to camps, and then to murder them. In poison showers. In ovens. Well, guess what, priest. Our side — the good guys — they've invented a Final Solution too. A virus. It'll wipe out all the vampires. Including that bastard downstairs."

Father Juan turned white. Noah started walking toward him.

Father Juan brought his right hand from behind his back. In it he held a gun, and he pointed it straight at Noah's chest. Jenn covered her mouth with both hands to keep herself from screaming. She jumped backward, not because she was afraid of being shot, but to prevent Noah from taking her hostage. She couldn't believe this was happening. It was as surreal as Antonio's attack on her.

"I'll drop you," Father Juan said.

"I know a dozen ways to disarm you," Noah said.

"*We'll* drop you," Holgar said.

Holgar was standing behind Jenn, and Gramma Esther stood beside him. Both of them were armed with submachine guns, and their weapons were pointed straight at Noah.

And behind them Father Wadim stood in front of at least a dozen monks crowding the passageway, all similarly armed.

Noah huffed and shook his head. "You're insane. All of you."

"Tell me about the virus," Father Juan ordered him. His voice rang out, almost vibrating with strength. To Jenn's ears it didn't quite sound human.

"Dr. Sherman invented it," Jenn said, fighting back tears. Her legs had turned to rubber, but she forced herself to remain upright.

"It'll be airborne," Noah said. He was seething. "There's no cure."

"Was Greg there?" Gramma Esther asked. "Did you talk to him?"

"Yes," Noah replied shortly, and there was something in his voice that sent chills down Jenn's spine.

"Did he mention Antonio? Is there a—what do you say—safe heaven? For him?" Holgar asked.

"Safe haven," Gramma Esther corrected him.

"He didn't mention Antonio. He didn't want any of you to know anything about it. He tried to kill me, to keep the secret."

"Oh, my God," Jenn whispered.

"How did you get away?" Father Wadim asked.

"I'm Mossad," Noah said, as if that were explanation enough.

"You're Salamancan," Jenn corrected him.

"He's not. If he were, he wouldn't try to kill his teammate," Holgar argued.

Jenn thought of Jamie's two guns, the one with silver bullets and the one with wooden ones. How many times had she feared that he would try to kill Holgar and Antonio both?

"Listen to me," Noah barked. "I know you care about Antonio de la Cruz. Jenn, I know you love him. But he's going to die either way. Sherman said the virus would be ready soon."

"No," Jenn choked out, and Noah slowly pivoted and looked straight at her.

"You can't let a monster live, no matter how much it costs you personally." A strange look crossed his face. "I think I know what my wife said to me," he said slowly, half to himself.

"I know about your wife. Chayna," Father Juan said. "I know what happened, Noah."

Noah stiffened, but kept his gaze trained on Jenn.

"She died in your arms," Father Juan said.

"I killed her," Noah said flatly, still looking at Jenn.

Jenn gasped. Holgar reached forward and pulled her back toward himself, farther away from Noah.

"She was mesmerized," Father Juan said.

"And so are all of you," Noah retorted. "You want so badly to be the good guys that you harbor a murdering demon in your midst. You risk everyone's life so that you can pat yourselves on the back." He pointed at Jenn. "You've seen her neck. Tell me, Jenn, did he stop himself from killing you? Or did someone else stop him? Did you put up a fight? I don't think so."

Jenn wanted to say that Antonio had been about to stop himself when Holgar had burst into the room. But she had been barely conscious. She really didn't know what had happened.

I didn't resist. I couldn't. Her cheeks went hot.

"I have my answer," Noah said. He shrugged, and a dozen Uzis pointed straight at him. Holgar brought Jenn against his chest.

"No," she said. "No."

"Noah, we need you, too," Father Juan said. "What else did you find out? What else do you know?"

"Nothing," Noah said. "So now . . . you don't need me."

"Don't be an idiot," Jenn said sharply, trying her hardest to regain command of the situation. But she was barely keeping it together. "You saw me kick Jamie's ass."

Noah smiled. "I saw you kick a lot of ass."

"And you swore to follow me as your leader."

Noah fell silent. Jenn could feel Holgar's heart pounding against the back of her head. She heard him growl very low in his throat. His arm pressed tightly across her collarbone. Loyal Holgar.

"I want you to swear again. And I want you to swear that you won't kill Antonio." His lips parted, and she narrowed her eyes. "Swear it, Noah."

He knit his brows. "All right. Unless —"

"No conditions," she said.

Resigned, Noah dipped his head. "Agreed."

THE MONASTERY OF THE BROTHERHOOD OF ST. ANDREW
ANTONIO AND SADE

Antonio watched.

Back and forth, back and forth, in time to the incessant chanting of monks, hidden away behind a prayer screen.

Back and forth, sitting cross-legged away from Antonio, Sade rocked. It made it just a little more difficult to catch every word of the confrontation upstairs, but Antonio could hear it well enough. Noah wanted to kill him for biting Jenn. A virus was about to be unleashed on all vampires everywhere, including him.

Then it will be over, Antonio thought. *And except for the mop-up, we'll have won.*

Just . . . he wouldn't be there to see it. A tide of emotions surged through him—a mixture of deep fear and sorrow. Although he believed in heaven, he didn't know if he would be welcome there. And like any of the faithful—even like Christ, who had begged to be spared—he was afraid to die. His own priest had told him that the instinct for survival was the strongest driving force of the human animal. God had made it so.

His sorrow at the thought of leaving Jenn was nearly overwhelming. He could feel the ache in his unbeating heart. The thought of never seeing her again—

You told God Himself that you would die for her.

She will be safe from all vampires, including you.

The voice in his head was like someone else's voice. Someone who understood. Someone who would be there, at the end.

And hearing it, Antonio found peace.

"It's a fair trade, Sade, don't you agree?" he said aloud.

Sade just kept rocking.

Silently.

LOS ANGELES, CALIFORNIA
SOLOMON

"So now we come to who opposes you," Katalin told Solomon. "That will be the obstacle in your path to achieving your ambitions."

Solomon sat across the table in Katalin's pretty little hideaway in his private quarters and watched her freeze as she put down the next card in his tarot reading. He glanced down at the image of a winged, horned demon crowned with an inverted pentagram and a naked man and woman chained to a pedestal beneath him.

The Devil. He stared at it for a long time. Disbelieving. Incredulous. Infuriated.

Terrified.

It can't be true. He's not real.

"This card represents someone in your life who holds power over you. And he will harm you unless you find a way to protect yourself," Katalin said in a strained voice.

"You're lying," Solomon said, rising from his chair. He leaned across the chair and lashed out at her with his fingertips. He missed her cheek by centimeters, and that infuriated him even more. He grabbed the table and threw it across the room. It shattered against the wall, muffling her cry as she leaped to her feet and ran in the opposite direction. "Someone put you up to this. What is this, a joke?"

"Solomon, I'm not. I swear to you I'm not." In her fear she began to babble. "It's your card. You cut the deck yourself. Please, I would never lie to you."

He left Katalin's room without another word, went into his private office, and shut the door. Then he sank down into a chair.

"It was just a card," he said aloud. "He's just a myth."

The Devil. And who was the Devil but Lucifer, vampire king of shadows? The vampire said to have defeated Dracula. The vampire other vampires feared. Just a myth.

He wouldn't have been so shaken if he hadn't been pushing Katalin so hard for information. Crystal balls, pendulums, rune stones—he'd had her run through them all. And each had given him a tiny piece of the identity of his most dangerous opponent: One said that he was ageless; one proclaimed him "above the mountains." It went on and on until the last puzzle piece: that damned tarot card.

The Devil. Lucifer was the Devil incarnate.

Solomon shook. He hung his hands between his knees and lowered his head, fighting for composure. Maybe someone had put Katalin up to giving him that answer. To distract him. To scare him. But who could get to her? He kept her under lock and key.

"It's a lie," he whispered.

His phone rang, and he was so startled that he nearly

fell out of the chair. He fished in the pocket of his jeans and held it up. He brightened. It was one of his spies, deeply embedded at the new headquarters of Project Crusade, in Budapest. A human, code-named David Book.

"Yes," Solomon said.

"I can't talk long," David whispered into the phone.

"Then get to the point," Solomon snapped. "Do you have something?"

"*They* have something." David took a deep breath. "It's a virus, Solomon. It's going to make vampires extinct."

Solomon laughed, but it was a hollow, frightened sound. After the tarot card, it was hard to believe what David was saying. But David was his most trusted spy, of all his spies. And he had a lot of them.

"There's no such thing," Solomon said. "Nothing on earth that can do that."

"There will be. It's the ultimate weapon, and there's no protection against it. *None*, Solomon."

Solomon silently cleared his throat. His hand trembled.

"Prove it. Send me a picture, anything."

The line went dead.

Solomon stared at it, disbelieving. Then he speed-dialed Jack Kilburn, the president of the United States, on their ultrasecret private line. No one else had the number, and Kilburn always answered, day or night. Kilburn might know something about this.

Sure enough, after one ring the connection was made.

"Jack," he said jovially, hiding his consternation, "listen. I just heard—"

"This is Alberto Sanchez, President Kilburn's chief of staff," an unfamiliar voice informed him. "President Kilburn is unavailable at this time."

Solomon was speechless. No one except the president had *ever* answered this phone.

"Do you know who I am?" Solomon asked in a friendly, conversational way. The leader of the Vampire Nation didn't lose his cool when talking to lackeys.

"Yes, Solomon, I do," said Sanchez, in a voice completely devoid of deference.

"What's happened to Kilburn? Has he been assassinated?" Solomon asked. His mind was racing. He didn't understand what was happening.

"The president is in a meeting. If you would care to leave a message—"

Solomon jerked as if he'd been slapped. Without another word he hung up. He began to shake, sick to his soul. This couldn't be happening. The president was severing their relationship. It had to be true, then. The humans had a weapon. And the president knew it. *If only I had converted him, he would be stopping the use of that weapon right now. I should have done it. Then there would be vampires the black crosses would have to spare. Good vampires.*

He jerked. Good vampires. There *was* a good vampire

they had to spare—the one everybody wanted to get their hands on. Maybe even Lucifer.

Antonio de la Cruz. They had probably already provided him with the antidote. He probably had it with him.

And Solomon knew where Antonio was.

TRANSYLVANIA, ROMANIA
HOLGAR AND JENN

Jenn lingered at the door that led downstairs to Antonio's cell. It was the same door Noah had tried to pass through less than twenty-four hours before. She took a deep breath and reached for the latch.

"No," said a voice behind her.

It was her grandmother. She was dressed much like Jenn, in jeans, boots, and a heavy coat. For a second, Jenn thought Gramma Esther was coming with them to parley with the Transylvanian werewolf pack. But it was so chilly inside the monastery that everyone—except the monks—was bundled up.

"I want to say good-bye," Jenn said. "Just in case."

Gramma Esther shook her head. "You need to keep your head in the game. Good-byes can really mess you up. Trust me, I know. Charles and I had to say good-bye so many times, to so many people. After a while we stopped, because it was just too painful." A fleeting, somewhat bitter smile flashed over her mouth, then was gone.

"Don't let Noah hurt him," Jenn said. "Please, Gramma."

"I'm here, Jenn," her grandmother said. "I'll do what's right."

Jenn took a breath. She didn't know exactly what her grandmother meant.

"You need to walk through a different door," Gramma Esther said. "The *front* door. And you need to leave all this behind and concentrate on your mission."

"Ready, Jenn?" Holgar asked, coming up behind her. He was wearing a parka with a fur-lined hood. When in human form, werewolves felt the cold. He handed her an Uzi and her Salamancan jacket.

"Your parka's by the door," he told her. "Let's go."

Jenn gave her grandmother one last look, and Gramma Esther nodded.

Please, protect him, Jenn thought, slipping one arm into a sleeve.

And then she walked through a different door.

Jenn and Holgar took one of the monks' SUVs—not a snowmobile, because the weather had turned bitter. They also needed protection in case their meeting with the werewolf pack didn't go as hoped. The snow came down hard, and it was difficult for them to find the little warming hut that the monks had suggested might serve as a place to overnight.

Neither slept. Jenn tried to call the monastery to check

226

on Antonio, but the snow impeded her cell reception. In the morning Holgar drove, and soon they had penetrated deep into a thick forest of frozen white trees, cutting the high beams of the truck. Then the howls began, and Jenn looked out the window. Flashes of light-colored shapes darted through the trees, and the howls grew louder, louder still. She glanced at Holgar.

"No, I'm not sure this is the right thing to do," he said, as if she'd asked the question aloud. "But it's nice to know you have faith in me. To come along for my ride." He quirked a grin at her. "I can tell what you're thinking. I can read your body language."

"It must be nice to be a werewolf," she said, smiling faintly back at him.

"The best."

The path they carved took them up a steep mountainside, but the tires held. As they angled upward, the light-colored shapes slowed, then gathered on the rise before Jenn and Holgar. Wolves, staring down at them with golden, glowing eyes. Their howls nearly shattered the windshield, and Jenn reflexively gripped the armrest.

"That's my cue," Holgar said, setting the emergency brake but leaving the motor running.

"Our cue," Jenn said, grabbing her Uzi.

"*Nej*, stay here," Holgar protested as he looped the strap of his submachine gun over his head.

"Not a chance."

Jenn's gloved hands were ready to fire off a barrage of ammunition; her snow boots crunched on the snow as she walked toward the wolves. Werewolves, facing her. Six crouched, showing their teeth. Behind them, sitting tall and proud, two more glared steadily at her and Holgar. One was pure black; the larger one was completely white. The alpha pair, she guessed.

Her heartbeat picked up, her body's natural reaction to danger. The first time she had seen a pack like this, the werewolves had been attacking the students and teachers at the Salamancan hunters' academy. One of them had killed Taamir, the only other survivor from Noah's combined Jewish and Muslim fighting band. And in the fracas Holgar had killed the werewolf he'd once been engaged to.

The second time she'd seen a pack, Antonio had saved his traveling companions from them. He had been *good*.

Or maybe he was just guarding his food supply, a little voice whispered in her head.

A gust of wind smeared ice crystals against her eyes. She raised a glove and wiped them away. Immediately the black wolf lifted its forepaw, as if in greeting.

Holgar said something that sounded Russian. The werewolves shifted very slightly, as if in response. Then the white wolf threw back its head and howled. All the wolves followed its example, including Holgar. Though he was still in human form, the most amazing sound burst from his mouth. It echoed off the mountains, firm and strong. It was beautiful, but it was so loud that Jenn wanted to cover her ears with her hands. Instead she let her head drop backward, and she howled too.

Holgar slid her a glance and grinned as the wolves stopped. Then he took Jenn's hand.

The white wolf whined, and then the black. The others carefully watched, like bodyguards.

"They want to talk to me alone," Holgar said, letting go of her hand.

"I should go. I'm the alpha," Jenn argued.

"They know you're my leader, but they also know you're not a werewolf," Holgar told her. "They're not used to mixing much with mundane humans. And besides, male werewolves are in charge. There's an alpha pair, but the female's the little woman."

"Do you think you can . . . ," she began, wanting to ask him if he would be able to morph into a wolf at will if the need arose. But she also didn't want the pack to know that so far he couldn't make it happen. So she let the question trail off.

"Wait in the truck. Behind the wheel. With your Uzi," he added meaningfully.

She wanted to argue. Instead she nodded and walked backward, not turning away from the pack. She watched them as cautiously as they watched her.

From the safety of the cab she tracked Holgar as he walked up to the row of wolves, then stepped through a space between two of them. More golden eyes glowed from the stands of frozen trees. She bit her cheek and touched her Uzi on the passenger seat as the vehicle exhaust billowed around her like clouds. How big *was* the pack?

Holgar reached the alpha pair. The black and white wolves turned and headed up the rise, then disappeared among trees and boulders there. Holgar lifted his arm and waved it back and forth for Jenn's benefit. Though he couldn't see her, she waved back.

Four of the remaining six wolves raised their forepaws again. Then they slowly began to advance on Jenn's vehicle.

"Nice wolfies," she muttered.

As soon as the stately pair of alphas passed into the ice forest, they transformed into a man and woman in fighting trim. They were clothed, which astonished Holgar. In his pack you had to dress and undress to keep from ruining your clothes.

The woman's long black hair cascaded down her shoulders, reminding Holgar of Aurora. The man's white hair cupped his jawline.

"We can speak in Russian," the man said. "Put down your weapon."

Reluctantly, Holgar obeyed. Unless he could transform, he was now completely defenseless against this fighting pair.

"I am Radu. This is Viorica," the man informed him coldly.

The woman slid Radu an irritated look, as if she didn't

like him speaking for her. Then she said to Holgar, "What do you want?"

"You know who we are," Holgar stated boldly. "We're the hunters from Salamanca, and—"

"And you took down some of our cousins," Radu interrupted, narrowing his eyes, venom glowing in them. "That pack you fought on your way here runs with us."

"They ran with Lucifer," Viorica said meaningfully. "We were not close."

"*Both* our packs run with Lucifer," Radu snapped, not looking at her. Dismissing her. These two were nearly at war with each other.

Radu raised his chin in a challenge to Holgar. "As you are a lone wolf, I invite you to apply for pack entry. I'll select a young wolf to test you in battle."

"You know I'm on the other side," Holgar replied. "Against Lucifer."

"The losing side," Radu shot back.

"*Nej.*" Holgar shook his head and took a couple steps to the left, trying to keep the smell of his fear downwind. "We're looking for an herb we need. We want permission to search for it on your territory."

"Our territory is Lucifer's territory," Radu said, and Holgar smelled *his* fear. And then Holgar scented Viorica's anger, directed not at him but at her mate. She didn't want this alliance with Lucifer.

Good. Maybe he could use that.

"What's the herb for?" Viorica asked Holgar.

"It doesn't matter," Radu bit off. "We won't give it to him."

"And now we can't tell Lucifer what the Salamancans are up to," she ground out, clearly furious with him.

Radu's face purpled. Both he and Holgar knew Viorica was right. Radu had played his hand badly.

Holgar decided to push back a little. "There have always been vampires in Transylvania, *ja*? And they have always treated you like slaves."

"Watch what you say!" Radu shouted. His temper was flaring. Holgar could read shame and humiliation. A werewolf alpha should be subservient to no other creature, living or dead.

Both alpha wolves transformed in an instant, Radu large and white; while she was smaller, Viorica's flanks gleamed with muscle as she growled low in her throat.

I have to change now, Holgar thought. He tried to force it. His blood began to pump harder. Adrenaline surged through his body. His jaw and fingertips began to tingle.

Come on, come on, he told himself.

Viorica growled again, golden eyes filling his field of vision. Working overtime not to panic, Holgar channeled all his energy into releasing his wolf nature. Nothing.

"We should bow to no other being," Holgar said in Russian, trying to stir his own emotions. To call out his wild side. *"Ever."*

Viorica growled and slowly advanced, sleek and deadly. Radu did the same.

They're going to kill me, he thought. An image of Skye filled his mind, then vanished. No. He wouldn't let them take him. He wasn't done with this war.

He feinted an approach of his own, then dove to the right and grabbed up his Uzi. He was about to start firing when Viorica hurled herself at Radu, toppled him, and ripped out his throat.

Blood splattered the snow as Radu's howl became a scream. Then he went limp, returning to human form. Viorica's muzzle dripped as she flattened his body into the white, howling in victory.

The other werewolves came running. Still in werewolf form, Viorica stared at Holgar. He took a deep breath. He'd been unable to transform, and by her body language he sensed her great disappointment.

As the werewolves joined them, Viorica changed back to human form. She was fully dressed, and blood smeared her mouth.

She walked up to Holgar and brushed her lips across his cheek, marking him with the blood of his rival. She tipped back her head and looked into his eyes.

"I'll help you change," she murmured, for his ears only. "If you'll help us change."

"You killed your mate," Holgar said, thinking of his childhood love, Kirstinne, whom he had killed in battle.

"Radu was Lucifer's lapdog," she said. "*I* am not." She raised her voice and spoke in a different human language to the approaching werewolves, who were changing into human form. Some were bending over Radu and looking over at Viorica. She'd hidden how large the pack was from Holgar and Jenn. He counted over twenty. Wails of grief and fury echoed through the forest.

"I am telling them that we are joining with you," she said. "That we will combine our packs—hunters and the werewolves of Transylvania. We've dreamed of throwing off the yoke of vampire rule for generations. In fact, we've been planning our rebellion for some time. I just took advantage of the moment."

Thank God you did, Holgar thought.

"You'll help us find our herb?" Holgar asked her.

She licked more of her dead mate's blood off her lips. "That and more," she promised. "Much more."

She spoke again to her pack. The werewolves in human form smiled at him and began to clap him on the back, shake his hand, and embrace him. Holgar threw back his head and began to howl. They joined him, werewolf howls blazing through the night like fireworks.

CHAPTER ELEVEN

Salamanca Hunter's Manual: Allies
It is a sad truth that human beings are weak.
Though many will swear to help you in time of
need, most of those will turn away if the threat from
the adversary is too great. Though they promise to
hide you and keep your secrets, they will shout
them to the hilltops if the darkness comes for them.
Choose your allies with great care, and never fully
trust them. Or you will die.

(translated from the Spanish)

TRANSYLVANIA
HOLGAR AND JENN

As Holgar and Jenn followed Viorica and her pack toward
their village, Jenn tried to process everything that had

happened. They would spend the night with the pack, and tomorrow they'd search together for the Transit of Venus.

"So, about Viorica," she said leadingly, as Holgar wiped blood from his cheek.

"What a black widow," he replied, making a face. "You know, when my pack decided to ally with the vampires, I left. But Viorica plotted, and bided her time."

"If you'd stayed, you wouldn't be here now, with us," she reminded him. "You'd have attacked us at Salamanca with Aurora."

"And since Aurora would have had *me*, she would have won," he bragged. Then his humor faded. "Except . . . she did win, pretty much, *ja*?"

"The battle, but not the war," Jenn said.

Holgar nodded emphatically. "Not the war."

Holgar's cell phone rang.

"I have phone reception," he said, surprised. He answered it. "Father Juan," he said, nodding at Jenn. "*Ja*, things have gone well here. They're going to help us." Then, as he listened, his expression changed to bewilderment. "*Ja*. Yes. We'll leave right away."

He hung up, still looking stunned.

"What is it?" Jenn asked, her stomach twisting. She thought of Antonio in the cell. "Is it —"

"It's not Antonio," he said. He hesitated a beat, and then he said, "Someone wants to meet with you tomorrow night.

Father Juan and Noah will be there too. He gave me the rendezvous point."

"Who? Who wants to meet me?" Jenn asked.

Holgar gave his head a little shake, as if he still couldn't quite believe what he had just heard.

"Solomon," he replied.

CASTLE BRAN, TRANSYLVANIA
HEATHER

Heather had made herself a secret little nest in an abandoned shed behind the castle. And the creature who had pulled her from the cistern protectively guarded her.

She was beautiful. The realization came as something of a shock. There was bitterness in that she could not see her reflection for herself, but she saw the admiration mirrored in the eyes of her pet monster. And with the realization that the creature found her beautiful came another one.

She had a plan beyond her killing of Aurora.

She wanted to be like Aurora.

Aurora was beautiful and sophisticated and so many things Heather had never thought herself to be. Heather had been watching the vampire queen since Berkeley, since Aurora took her prisoner. Humans and vampires alike both feared and adored Aurora. They rushed to do her bidding. And often the only reward they received for their troubles was a snapped neck.

But it didn't matter. There were always more to take
their place.

Aurora had wealth and luxuries Heather had never
even dreamed of.

But now Heather wanted them too. And for what
Aurora had done to her, she deserved them.

As she stalked Aurora, hoping to get her alone in the
castle, Heather turned her eyes on Lucifer as well.

A shiver went up her spine every time she thought
of him. He was magnificent and terrible. Glorious and
depraved. He was the soul of evil.

She'd always heard that evil was beautiful, enticing.
She had never believed it until now. Maybe it took the eyes
of a vampire to see the truth. But evil was beautiful, pure of
purpose, elegant in focus.

And Heather wanted him with everything that was
in her. The thought made her tremble with a kind of mad
desire. Aurora was afraid of him. Heather could smell her
fear when Lucifer approached, even when their bodies were
intertwining.

He was monstrous and dangerous and everything
Aurora believed him to be. But Heather wasn't afraid of
him. What was there to fear? As a human she'd feared the
Cursed Ones, feared losing her family. She had been right
to be afraid, but her terror had not kept those things at bay.
The existence she lived was a nightmare. Final Death would
simply be a release.

But to spend a night in his arms? Heather thought that might be the only taste of paradise she would ever have. A snatch of a poem she'd been made to memorize what seemed a thousand years ago came back to her.

> *. . . Here at least*
> *We shall be free; th'Almighty hath not built*
> *Here for his envy, will not drive us hence·*
> *Here we may reign secure, and in my choyce*
> *To reign is worth ambition though in Hell:*
> *Better to reign in Hell, than serve in Heav'n.*

Paradise Lost by Milton. In her old life she and Tiffany used to make fun of it. "Where is hence? I'm going to drive to hence for my vacay. Wanna come?"

Now she understood it. Not all could have heaven, and she knew she was one of those. So be it. She would gladly embrace Lucifer in this hell they lived in.

And that was when she realized she'd been going about her plan all wrong. She'd been trying to catch Aurora alone so that she could kill her without being caught.

But that wasn't what Heather wanted.

She wanted to kill Aurora where all the world could see, especially their glorious dark lord.

Transylvania
Jenn, Holgar, Noah, Father Juan, and Solomon

Although Holgar had originally planned for him and Jenn to spend the night with the pack in a compound in the forest, the werewolves understood when they told them they had to go. Viorica had even promised to find the Transit of Venus that they needed. So much luck in one day was hard to believe.

Jenn looked tired, but determined, strong. On her guard, but ready to do what must be done.

Noah and Father Juan greeted them; then, by tacit agreement, they parted company, concealing themselves in the trees, armed with stakes, crosses, Stars of David, holy water, revolvers, and machine guns.

Holgar couldn't figure out why Solomon wanted to meet. Every instinct in him screamed that this was some sort of trap. They were meeting sixty miles away from the monastery—too far for those Uzi-loving monks to serve as backup. It felt as if the Salamancans were sitting ducks about to be tagged so they could lead the birders to their nest. He should have asked Viorica for pack support. It would have been a good test of their new alliance, and, frankly, the Salamancans could have used the help.

The sound of a helicopter filled the night air, and Holgar bared his teeth. It was time. The streamlined chopper came into view a minute later, lights brilliant as it descended. Holgar slipped out of the ring of light into the darkness, where he could better see without being as quickly seen. He crouched low to the ground, still wishing he could change at will if things went badly.

He could smell the fear coming off his teammates. Even Noah. Holgar had warned them that the vampires would be able to smell it too, and they had repositioned themselves so that Solomon would have to exit the helicopter upwind of them.

It was a small thing, but to creatures like werewolves and vampires, scenting fear on an enemy gave them a surge of energy, a boost. Denying it to Solomon would keep him that much more on edge. And they needed every edge they could muster. This was the president of the Vampire Nation.

The chopper touched down. The rotors were still whirling as Solomon emerged and, with an exaggerated show, took off the sunglasses that were an affectation. Holgar felt a rumbling of hatred deep in his chest.

Solomon approached Jenn, who stood a few feet in front of Holgar's hiding place. Holgar clenched his jaw and positioned his Uzi. He sighted down it. Jenn was standing to the right of his firing line, as they had discussed. But it would still be far too dangerous to let loose.

He knew Father Juan's job was to monitor the helicopter. Like Holgar, Noah would be concentrating on Solomon. Holgar wished Father Juan had brought along

Esther Leitner and Father Wadim. The four of them were spread too thin for such a dangerous rendezvous as this.

"So, Ms. Leitner, we meet at last," Solomon said, his voice slick and polished.

"So it would seem," Jenn said. Holgar smiled. She sounded cool, detached, and in control. Good. This was the Jenn who had nearly killed Jamie. This was an alpha to respect—and fear.

"I believe we have a mutual enemy," Solomon said, clearing his throat delicately. "Lucifer." Solomon emphasized the name as though expecting it to cause consternation.

Instead Jenn shrugged. "So?"

Uncertainty flickered across Solomon's face for a moment. It was quickly replaced again by the suave, sickening smile that he trotted out to charm millions on television.

"I don't know how much you know about him, Jennifer, but he's legend, even among *us*. He won't be easy to kill for anyone."

"Hmm," Jenn said, sounding unimpressed.

Solomon smelled worried. "Maybe you're not getting this. If you thought *I* was bad—and we both know just how bad I am—wait until Lucifer makes a move. He won't hesitate to wipe out all of humanity and us, too, to rule this world. No one is safe."

If he wipes out all of humanity, what will he eat? Holgar mused, glad to see that Jenn was still holding her ground.

Shoulders back, head held high, she was a warrior. His admiration for his alpha surged.

"Why are you here?" Jenn asked.

Solomon's grin changed, more real, less artificial. "Okay, you're not big on the buildup. I admire that, so I'll be equally blunt. We can help each other."

"How?" Jenn asked, curiosity and skepticism heavy in her voice. Holgar leaned forward, wanting to know how, too.

"An alliance," Solomon said, as if his answer should have been obvious. "We band together to destroy Lucifer and send him straight to hell where he belongs."

Holgar was so amazed that he nearly burst into laughter, his default mode when life got too weird. It was a good week for truces, wasn't it? First the Transylvanian werewolves and now Solomon.

"And then what? You alone rule the vampires, the world?" Jenn asked.

Solomon slowly shook his head and his grin faded. "No. In exchange for your help in ridding us all of this tyrant, I and the remaining vampires will fade back into the shadows from which we came. I had hoped we could all live together in peace, but . . ." He shrugged his shoulders. "Who knows. Maybe we'll try again in a couple more centuries."

He must not know about the virus, Holgar thought. *Or maybe he's stalling us while he sends his guys into Dr. Sherman's lab.*

"And if I say that I don't believe you?" Jenn asked.

Good, Jenn, Holgar thought.

"I'd say that I don't blame you after everything you've been through," Solomon said, daring to sound sympathetic. "But I have a gift for you, a gesture of my good faith."

He raised his hand, and the side door of the helicopter opened. A lone figure stepped out on shaky legs. Holgar blinked in shock as he recognized Jenn's father from TV, sitting beside Solomon, imploring Jenn to come to him. The bastard who had betrayed her to Aurora and gotten Heather converted.

Jenn sucked in her breath. Holgar heard her nearly soundless hiss of anger and hatred—almost vampirelike. Fury rolled off her.

"He's been through a lot," Solomon observed, as Paul Leitner staggered toward them. "But I saved him from Aurora. Don't be too hard on him. After all, in the end all we have is family," Solomon said, sounding sad and wise.

Her father lurched forward a few more steps, and Father Juan broke from his position to intercept him. Leitner was human. Holgar could smell him. But Jenn's father was still a traitor.

Holgar clawed at the ground reflexively.

"Jenn?" Leitner said, voice quavering.

Solomon gave a short dip of his head. "Please, think over my offer. You have everything to gain." His face darkened. "But with Lucifer still alive, you have everything to lose." He glanced at Father Juan, then changed his line of vision to where Noah waited in the darkness.

"Okay. I'll think about it," Jenn said.

"Don't think long," Solomon said. "We're the last, best hope for both our peoples. Your priest has my phone number," Solomon said.

The vampire got into the helicopter, and it flew away, plunging them all back into darkness. Holgar looked down and realized with shock that the fingers he had dug into the earth were no longer human, but wolf pads and claws instead.

Jenn was reeling. There was too much to take in: Solomon's offer, the unknown status of Project Crusade, and not least of all her father standing in front of her, tears streaming down his face. He looked old, and small, and helpless.

And she hated him.

"He's human," Father Juan confirmed.

"*Ja,*" Holgar added, his voice deeper and more gravelly than Jenn had ever heard it. She turned to glance at him and saw him straightening slowly, hands clenched at his side, and his eyes . . .

She blinked in surprise. They were glowing wolf-yellow, reflecting the light from the moon.

Noah placed a hand on her shoulder, pulling her back to the moment. "Are you okay?" he asked.

She shrugged his hand off. She needed space, needed

to breathe. "Fine," she said, more tersely than she'd meant to.

As if she were in a movie, she saw her father reaching out a hand toward her. She couldn't deal with it, couldn't deal with him. A week before, a day, an hour, she knew in her heart she would have killed him for what he'd done to her family, to *his* family.

Now everything was so complicated.

"We need to get back to home base," she said. "Let's move out."

THE MONASTERY OF THE BROTHERHOOD OF ST. ANDREW
ANTONIO AND ESTHER

In the cell bristling with stakes, Antonio spent every moment hating himself. The thought that he had bitten Jenn still made him shudder, but with a terrible mixture of remorse and longing, regret and desire. He wanted more of her blood. He wanted it the way a drowning man wanted air.

The monks of the Brotherhood of St. Andrew had told him they could help. They came to pray and chant, but he felt no different. They were wrong. Just as Father Juan had been, and Jenn. *They should never have trusted me.* But then again, if what he had heard about the virus was true, it would all soon be over.

The tumblers of a lock clicked in the distance, and,

moments later, footsteps echoed against the stone floor. One of the monks coming to check on him, no doubt. He didn't even raise his head.

"You're a sorry excuse for a man, vampire or not."

He jerked his head up in surprise and saw Jenn's grandmother, Esther, standing and staring at him, arms folded across her chest, eyes critical.

"Excuse me?" he asked, so shocked to see her there that he could barely process what she'd said.

"You heard me. Sorry excuse for a living creature."

He felt his lips twist in a snarl. "You don't understand."

"Then enlighten me," she said, raising an eyebrow.

"You should back away from the bars," he warned her. "You're standing too close. I might . . ."

"What? Bite me? Kill me? Bore me to death with your sad tale about how you just wish you could be good?"

"What is wrong with you?" he asked, wondering, just for a moment, if the woman had lost her mind. Grief could do crazy things to people.

"That's what I want to know about you," she said with a snort.

He stood, slowly, and wrapped his hands around the bars of his cage. "I'm a vampire," he said, pulling back his lips to reveal his fangs.

She shrugged. "So what?"

He felt as though she had just slapped him. He shook his head. "I don't understand your attitude."

"And I don't understand yours." She frowned at him. "You love my granddaughter, right?"

"With all my heart," he admitted, though the words tore at him.

"Love's stronger than hate, or fear, or anything. Except maybe faith. And from what I hear, you've got plenty of that." She cocked her head. "At least, you say you do."

"I have faith," he insisted. "I *do*."

"Prove it," she said, not even flinching.

Without hesitating, he placed his hand against a cross tacked on the wall of his cell. After a moment he showed her the skin, unburned.

"I'm not talking about parlor tricks or magick or superstition," she said, shaking her head at him. "I'm talking about real faith. And real love. Either you have them or you don't."

He stared at her. No one had challenged him like this in a very long time.

"Last time I read the Bible, it said that if you have faith the size of a mustard seed, you can move mountains," she continued.

Antonio nodded. "I know the passage."

She looked at him full on, challenging. "So if you have faith, you can overcome the evil urges in your heart."

He lowered his head.

"And Antonio? Mustard seeds grow in the dark."

"I want to believe that you're right," he whispered.

Esther exhaled, exasperated. She looked as if she wanted to strangle him.

"Then do it. Don't want to believe—believe. Or maybe that's your problem. You just don't have the will."

"I do, *señora*," he insisted, but he couldn't look at her. He wondered what she saw. A monster that had attacked her granddaughter?

A silence fell between them. He heard her sigh.

"When it all comes right down to it, what a man has is his will," she said. "If his will is weak, so is the man. If it's strong, the same applies."

He thought of the scriptures—*not my will, but Thy will*. But that spoke of freely handing over his will to God. He had spent his lifetime trying to understand the will of God.

But there are some things about His will that I do know. He wants me to be good, and moral, and decent.

"Antonio," Esther Leitner continued, "the history books are filled with stories of men with iron will who have done great or terrible things. Look at Churchill. Look at Hitler. Two men from your youth on opposite sides of a war. Two men with iron will. When things seemed bleakest, one of them took his own life. Hitler. In the end, his will was weaker."

"That's one way of looking at it," he said.

"His cause was also evil. It's harder to maintain that."

"Why are you here?" he asked, raising his head to meet her gaze, desperately trying to make sense of everything she was saying.

She looked at him for a long minute without speaking, and he began to wonder if she was ever going to again, or if she would just stare at him as if she could read his very soul.

"I'm sure Jenn's told you all about her grandfather and me. Well, I was never a revolutionary, not at heart."

"But—"

She held up a hand to silence him. "What I was was a woman in love with a revolutionary. And because I loved Charles, I stood by him through thick and thin, through years of running and hiding and everything else." Her eyes took on a faraway look. Then she smiled faintly and directed her attention back to him.

"Now, this might surprise you, but my dad didn't exactly approve of Charles. In fact Papa disapproved with everything he had in him. Two men couldn't have been less alike. But in the end he saw how much I loved Charles, and how Charles looked after me the best he could."

The conversation had taken a more comfortable turn. Antonio was from a time when the approval of fathers mattered in the affairs of the heart. "Then he changed his mind?"

"We *earned* his approval, and kept earning it day after day." She looked misty again, and Antonio thought of the countless widows who had attended the masses at the chapel in Madrid, when he was preparing to take his vows. The grief. The desolation. Esther Leitner's happy memories made her burden lighter.

"I'm happy that you were able to make a life with the man you loved, but I don't understand what this has to do with me," he said.

"Before Jenn came here, she never had a real boyfriend, so she never knew what it was like to have her heart broken."

He bowed his head again, shame filling him.

"Now, a grandmother doesn't want to see some guy rip her granddaughter's heart out of her chest and stomp it into little pieces. Problem with you is that's a figurative danger *and* a literal one."

"I know," he whispered.

"In case you haven't noticed, Jenn's father isn't exactly around to object to you. So the burden falls on me."

"To object to me," he said. Of course she did; she must. He objected to himself. Why, then, did it hurt?

"Yes. Deeply."

They stared at each other for a moment. He heard the beating of her heart, sure and steady.

"But I'm going to give you a chance," she said.

He blinked, surprise mingling with something else — elation? Fear? He wasn't sure.

She reached out and flicked her wrist. There was the sound of metal grating on metal, and then suddenly she swung the cage door open. Reflexively, he sucked in a breath.

"Now be a man. Prove to me that you deserve her."

Esther moved back, and Antonio took a hesitant step forward. Her words had cut him deep, stinging, burning, shaming. Could it really be as easy as she made it seem? Was it just a matter of faith and love and will? He squeezed his eyes shut and felt blood tears seeping from them. There was an ache in his heart that was lifting, twisting.

Had he imposed this prison, this hell upon himself? Upon both of them? He wanted to tell Esther that he would try to be the man she was asking him to be. But he knew that trying wasn't enough. He couldn't *try* any longer.

He opened his eyes and looked at her. "I will," he vowed.

She nodded, and then turned and walked toward the door of the cold, dark room. He hesitated for a moment.

"Are you coming, then?" she asked without looking back.

"Yes," he said, marveling at the strength, the resolve in his own voice. *God help me to be the man I need to be and not the vampire I fear that I am,* he prayed.

They climbed the stairs and eventually came out into the passageway near the chapel.

Antonio heard Esther swear soft and low.

"What is it?" he asked, for her ears alone.

"Looks like I was wrong about one thing."

Fear gripped him tight. "What?" he asked, moving to see around her.

"Jenn's father *is* here."

Dover, England
Skye and Jamie

Running and hiding, running and hiding. It had become like a sick little game Skye and Jamie were playing. Hide-and-go-seek and Estefan was the seeker. *Come out, come out, wherever you are,* she could hear him in her mind, though there were times she thought she might just be imagining it.

That would be a relief, to only have imaginary voices in her head instead of real ones.

She shook her head, tired of running, tired of the games. But what else was there? She glanced uneasily at Jamie as she set up wards around the room. They were in the tiny attic of an ancient inn. It was dangerous to rest where other people were, but neither of them could spend another night half-asleep on the freezing ground.

As soon as they got upstairs, Jamie fell headlong on the bed and passed out. No one could fake those snores.

She wrinkled her nose, tempted for a moment to do a spell to mute the sound, but she surrendered the idea with a sigh. It was dangerous to cast unnecessary magick. Anytime she conjured anything other than a protective ward, she suspected it served as a beacon drawing Estefan right to her. She wasn't sure how he was managing to see it, but then there was a lot about his magick and what he had become that she didn't comprehend.

She shuddered at the thought of it.

How had Estefan become so evil? Or had he always been that way, and she, being so young and so love-struck, had never seen it?

She finished her wards and winced at the burning sensation in her left shoulder as she lowered her arm. During the fray in the cave, one of Estefan's lightning bolts had singed her, and she hadn't dared to use magick to speed the healing.

She hated Estefan for that and for so much, much more. She shoved Jamie over slightly, and he flipped onto his side but didn't wake up. She eased herself down onto the mattress beside him, being careful of her injured shoulder. Jamie's bag of weapons was on the other side of him. It made her nervous knowing that there was a gun within such easy reach.

Especially since it fired silver bullets.

She took a deep, steadying breath. After leaving the Circuit, they had doubled back to the cave and retrieved Jamie's weapons. They hadn't found the scrying stone, but regrettably, they had found the gun with the silver bullets. She had watched with intense interest, though, when Jamie had worked on the gun that would fire wooden bullets and explained how it worked.

It was almost perfected.

And she hoped and prayed that vampires couldn't outrun bullets like they did everything else. She and Jamie needed an edge, and as much as she disliked the gun meant for werewolves, she couldn't help but be very, very excited about *this* gun.

Jamie was still snoring as she struggled to clear her mind so she could go to sleep. Somewhere, out there in the night, Estefan was still coming after them. It was ironic — she was running from the guy who had spent years chasing her, with the guy whom she had spent years chasing.

And she didn't want either of them anymore.

She wasn't sure when or how it had happened, but her heart had set itself on Holgar. Funny Holgar, loyal Holgar, good Holgar. She'd always been drawn to the bad boys, but it was the best and noblest man she'd ever met that she had fallen truly in love with. It had happened so gradually she hadn't even realized it — until that moment when Estefan had been torturing her and she'd been trying to take back her mind with thoughts of Holgar.

She was in love with a werewolf. If her family had still been speaking to her, she was sure they'd be shocked. There was probably something in their code that forbade such a love.

It didn't matter. She'd turned her back on them and now on the Circuit as well. She knew she should feel guilty about it, but she just couldn't bring herself to.

She squeezed her eyes shut and saw Holgar in her mind. What would he say when they saw each other again? What would she say? Would she have the courage to tell him how she felt?

She hoped so, but she worried she'd never get the chance to make that decision.

She drifted off to sleep and dreamed of Holgar, of staring into his eyes as she told him she loved him. And then the scene changed and she felt as if she were watching from afar as Holgar charged across a silvery landscape, leading a pack of werewolves. Or was he running from them?

She couldn't tell, but in front of Holgar there was a line of monsters, hybrids like from Russia, and vampires. Oh, Goddess, there were so many!

Holgar crashed into them, bowling several over. Then Skye lost him, couldn't see him for the thrashing bodies. And then, finally, he appeared again. But her relief turned to horror as she watched a tall vampire who seemed to blaze like the sun rip out Holgar's throat.

"No!" she screamed, waking and sitting up. Her heart was pounding, and she felt dizzy and somewhat disembodied. Her cheeks were flushed, and she felt as if her entire body were on fire.

Cursing, Jamie leaped out of bed and landed in the middle of the floor, eyes wild, a gun in one hand and a stake in the other. "What?"

And in that moment Skye knew two things for certain. What she had just seen in her dream was a glimpse of the future—Holgar dying at Lucifer's hands.

And Estefan had arrived at the inn.

They had run out of time.

CHAPTER TWELVE

Predator, prey, the oldest game
Somehow it always ends the same
Prey a tangled mass of legs and head
The predator's fangs shining red
You'd do well to know your place
You can not change name or face
For real hunters always thrive
And the hunted ne'er survive

DOVER, ENGLAND
SKYE AND JAMIE

The room around Skye and Jamie erupted in flames. Beneath her feet Skye could hear the startled screams of the other patrons of the inn as fire engulfed the entire building in one blinding moment.

"Where are they?" Jamie roared, his voice barely audible over the crack and whoosh of the flames.

They were trapped with no way out. Once more Estefan was calling the shots, herding them in the direction he wanted to go.

And this time he was killing innocent people. People Skye realized she couldn't save.

She grabbed hold of Jamie's arm and yanked him toward the window. Before they reached it, she lifted her other hand and exploded the glass outward. She shoved Jamie halfway through it.

"We can't jump. It's four stories down!" he shouted.

An explosion rocked the ground, and she could feel the floorboards starting to give way beneath them. Heat and smoke rushed up toward them both.

"No choice!" she screamed. She hit him low, hard enough to throw him off balance and to send him toppling through the window with a shout of terror.

She sent a spell chasing after him, which slowed him and cushioned his fall right as he hit the ground. His weapons bag clattered down beside him. She hoisted herself up into the window frame just as tongues of fire began to lick at her hair. With a scream she hurled herself out.

She didn't have enough time to properly cast the spell before she hit the ground with a bone-jarring thud. She tried to pull herself to her feet and realized that some of her ribs were broken.

And there was the taste of blood in her mouth. She prayed it was from a bitten cheek and not a punctured lung.

Jamie scooped down and picked her up and then ran with her into the darkness. She tried to cast spells to protect those they left behind, but she couldn't focus. Her magicks were being blocked.

Then, in her mind, she could hear Estefan laughing. But even over that horrendous sound there was a worse one, the screams of the dying as they burned to death in the old inn. She screamed, too, sharing their pain, their desperation, because she was powerless to help them.

And still Jamie ran, his arm wrapped around her broken ribs, making the pain unbearable. A root shot up from the ground and tripped Jamie. Skye went airborne and slammed into a tree with a thud before sliding down the trunk to the ground.

Fresh blood blurred her vision, and she whimpered in pain and fear.

Come out, come out, wherever you are, Estefan's voice taunted.

"Skye!"

She turned at the strangled cry from Jamie. He was sprawled on the ground, hands wrapped around his leg. Bones were jutting out through holes in his pants. The same root that had tripped him now snaked up and over him.

Magick.

The root encircled one of the broken bones extending

from Jamie's shattered leg and yanked it suddenly downward.

She wouldn't have believed that the shriek of pain that followed could have come from a human if she hadn't been watching Jamie.

She lifted her hand and whispered a spell, wheezing as she did so. She could taste blood in the back of her throat. Punctured lung.

Panic flooded her, but she forced herself to finish the spell. The root released its hold on Jamie's leg bone and dropped to the ground, once more a harmless object.

One, two . . . She heard Estefan's voice in her head.

Why was Estefan counting? She dragged herself across the ground toward Jamie. She needed to heal his leg.

Three. Four.

If she could just help him, then he could escape. At least one of them would.

She sobbed in agony as she touched his leg and felt her own bones shattering as she took the injury and made it hers while mending his.

Five. Six.

Her chest contracted even more with the extra pain and trauma of Jamie's injury. She was amazed that he had lived through the attack; Estefan had nearly crushed him. How had he endured?

Her bones began to knit, but so very, very slowly. She wanted to scream, but now she was having problems just drawing breath. The cries from the inn had stopped, which probably meant that all there were dead. Despair poured through her, and she gasped at the very real psychic pain overlaying the agony of Jamie's wounds.

Seven.

The bone fragments fused, but she didn't have time to repair the muscle or nerve damage. She wouldn't be able to move.

To escape.

"Go!" she shouted to Jamie.

Jamie pushed himself to his feet, his leg nearly collapsing when he tried to put weight on it. He remained upright, though, swaying slightly as he tried to catch his balance.

"C'mon, then, Skye," he slurred, staggering forward as he tried to bend down and extend a hand toward her. He sucked in his breath through his teeth, still in pain. "Bugger. Skye, up."

Eight.

"Go!" she repeated. "I can't hold him. Get out of range."

"I bloody well won't leave you," he ground out.

"Get free," she ordered him. "Then I'll come."

Nine.

"No, I won't—"

She was out of time.

Furious with him for not listening, wild to save him, Skye summoned magickal forces and flung them at Jamie. He stumbled backward, blinked, and opened his mouth, probably to argue some more. She managed another push, her body shrieking at her to get back to the healing.

"Go!" she screamed at him.

"Bloody hell," Jamie swore.

He stared down at her, picked up his bag, and hobbled toward the darkest part of the woods. She gave him one last push.

She was alone.

Ten.

Skye tried to heal her lung, but she couldn't think. There were words that had to be said. They were right there, on the tip of her tongue. She opened her mouth.

Ready or not, here I come.

And all her words left her.

The Monastery of the Brotherhood of St. Andrew
Jenn, Holgar, Noah, Antonio, Father Juan, Jenn's Family, and Sade

The welcome party for Solomon arrived back at the monastery, having driven the entire way in silence. Jenn sat up front with Father Juan, who drove, while Holgar and Noah flanked her father in the backseat. The ice forest retreated from the bright beams of the vehicle, or so it seemed to Father Juan. Jenn sat ramrod straight, like a statue, and he had yet to see her so much as blink her eyes.

He was still mulling over what Solomon had said. With the vampire, they could never take anything he said as gospel, as he could always be counted on to look out for his own skin. That was what had led Solomon to make the offer in the first place. Which meant Solomon was running scared.

Of what, though? The resistance fighters around the world amounted to no more than buzzing flies where the Cursed Ones were concerned, and Solomon had been so dismissive of Project Crusade. That could have been an act. Maybe Solomon did know about the virus, and that was what had terrified him so badly he'd run for shelter with his enemies.

Or maybe he'd been telling the truth about being afraid of Lucifer.

Either way, they had a big decision in front of them — one they most certainly could not discuss when there was a possible spy in their midst. Father Juan glanced in the rearview mirror at Paul Leitner. Despite all the years Father Juan had trained hunters, he didn't know how to tell if someone was under a vampire's sway. He didn't know if there was a certain look or any telltale mannerisms to those who knew what they were looking for. When he'd watched Antonio mesmerize Heather, she hadn't seemed any different to him — just quieter.

He'd have to take Paul to Antonio. And he'd probably have to remind Antonio that murder was a mortal sin. This man had hurt Jenn beyond the telling—just as Antonio had, in his own way.

Wearily, Father Juan rubbed his forehead. Leitner was a complication none of them needed, but, as Spaniards liked to say, it was what it was. At least Jenn hadn't killed him on sight. Father Juan would have to be grateful for the small miracles for now, and take them where he could find them.

When they finally entered the monastery, Father Juan was tempted to breathe a sigh of relief, although nothing was over and they weren't safe, not truly. His age was sitting on him heavily, and he could feel all the years as though they were piled on top of him like one blanket after another.

He was ready to be done with it all, and he hoped that God would see things his way soon.

Vaguely he registered that the ever-present chanting seemed to have stopped. He had no time to wonder about the significance of that. His mind was racing as he rehearsed how to tell Esther and Leslie Leitner about Paul. A dozen steps into the building, though, he realized two things: The cat was well and truly out of the bag, as Esther stared at them with shock. And to add to Father Juan's anxiety, Antonio was free and peering around Esther to see what it was that had caused her consternation.

The stress was all too much. He wanted to cry.

And then he saw Holgar. The tall Dane's mouth twitched; then he burst out with a hearty guffaw, followed by rolling, full-hearted laughter. Tears ran down Holgar's cheeks.

And Father Juan couldn't stop himself from joining in. As Holgar doubled over, Father Juan laughed so hard that his sides ached, and he sank down right onto the icy stone floor, to the amazement of all of the monks, who had converged on their location from seemingly every-where.

Half of them were staring at the priest making a spec-tacle of himself, while the other half crossed themselves as they took note of the vampire at large among them. Antonio was staring down at Father Juan in amazement.

He heard Paul Leitner ask, "What's going on?"

And although it was the most natural question in the world, Father Juan had no easy response. In fact he had no answers at all. All he could do was laugh helplessly. Holgar joined him on the floor, tongue lolling out, blue eyes shining with the ridiculousness of their situation.

Jenn was gazing thunderstruck at Antonio, ignor-ing everyone else in the room. Wiping tears from his eyes, Father Juan heard pounding feet and looked up as Jenn's mother arrived. Of course. Because that was the only way things were going to get more ludicrous.

Leslie Leitner screamed, but with excitement or fear or anger or shock he didn't know, and at the moment he couldn't care. He and Holgar just kept laughing. And then

Holgar began uncontrollably howling, and Jenn's father turned white as a ghost.

And it was that much funnier.

Noah eyed the priest and the werewolf, wondering if the two of them had finally gone mad. Well, if so, at least they had each other, which was more than most who went mad could say. Then he turned his full attention on Antonio, his blood pressure skyrocketing at the sight of the vampire who had attacked Jenn—free and uncaged, unfettered.

But after the initial surprise of the group's arrival, Antonio only had eyes for Jenn. And Jenn was just as mesmerized by him.

Noah slid a stake out from the quiver on his hip, ready to use it at a moment's notice. He had sworn to Jenn that he wouldn't kill Antonio, but all bets were off if the vampire decided to go on a rampage. Still, Noah was torn between watching him and watching Paul Leitner, who was numbly staring at his wife, mother, and daughter in turn.

And then Paul Leitner did the wrong thing. He opened his mouth and asked, "Where's Heather?"

Quick as a cat, Jenn turned on him with death in her eyes. Had her grandmother not leaped forward and grabbed her by the shoulders, Noah had no doubt that Jenn would have killed her father then and there.

And she wouldn't have been wrong to do so.

If Leitner was compromised, then the longer he was

alive, the greater the danger for the rest of them. He should be interrogated, forced to tell anything and everything he knew about Solomon. And then killed. Noah gritted his teeth, wishing for a moment that his new hunting team had the discipline of his old one, or of the Mossad.

But for all their emotional baggage and crazy, messed-up sentimentality, Noah had to give them one thing: In all their time together, they'd only lost one of their team, while he was the only survivor of his. So they must be doing something right.

Then Jenn's mom fainted dead away, which stopped the incessant screaming, so that was a bonus. Jenn caught her and gently draped her in a chair. Noah felt for the woman. He imagined that she had never expected to see her husband alive again, and after what he'd done to her daughters, she probably had never wanted to. But there was still a bond there, one that only death could break. Better for her, too, if they killed him quick.

Noah would have no problem making that happen. No problem at all.

Jenn was relieved when her mother finally stopped screaming. She couldn't think with that sound rattling around in her brain, crowding out all her sane thoughts.

Or was it Antonio's warm brown eyes that were making her brain feel like mush? He stood, shoulders hunched, uncertainty on his face, behind Gramma Esther. Had her grandmother let him out? Had he mesmerized her like he'd mesmerized Jenn herself the day he'd bitten her?

She hazarded a glance at her grandmother and saw that the other's eyes were clear, quickening with thought as they took in the scene around her. She looked like a woman who was fully aware and fully in control.

I wonder what I looked like when I was under his sway.

Jenn took a step forward, then another, having to skirt Father Juan's legs to do so. He and Holgar were still laughing themselves sick on the floor.

Antonio gazed at her, but stayed behind her grandmother as if she were a human shield. Which one of them was her grandmother protecting from the other?

"Antonio?" His name came out as a whisper.

He dipped his head. "*Sí*, Jenn." That voice. His voice. She swallowed hard against the tide of emotion inside her. Except for a few words during the battle with the werewolves, they hadn't spoken since the attack.

"Are you . . . okay?" It sounded lame, and she didn't even know what "okay" meant anymore. *Are you going to murder us?* How did you ask that?

"I will be," he said firmly. He looked at her father, and Jenn thought she saw red glowing in his eyes. To her shame she wished Antonio would lose control and attack him.

"We had a little heart-to-heart," Gramma Esther said. She looked at Jenn's father, and at Jenn. She crossed to Jenn and bent down in front of her. She pushed ringlets of

Jenn's hair away from her forehead. "Now, how about you fill us in on what happened to you?"

Jenn opened her mouth and then closed it, having no idea how to begin. In the background, Holgar and Father Juan kept laughing.

An hour later Jenn stood in the dining room, staring at everyone else gathered there. Jenn's mom had come to, but the monks had given her something to calm her nerves, and she had gone back to Jenn's old room. Sade hadn't left the room she shared with Jenn and her mom when Jenn and the others had returned, and now she fussed over Jenn's mom as she tucked her in bed.

Noah insisted on handcuffing Jenn's father's wrists; then he escorted him to a previously unoccupied room and made sure that monks were stationed to watch him. Jenn was incredibly grateful to Noah for taking charge of their prisoner, because there was no way she could trust herself to deal with her father even on that rudimentary level.

"Where's Heather?" he'd asked. The question still rang in her ears. A thousand wicked retorts had come to mind, but none of them was so painful as the truth. *We don't know.*

Father Juan and Holgar had both regained their composure and were sitting quietly, soberly, at the table where they took their meals. Antonio and Gramma Esther sat across from them. Jenn took a place next to Holgar, where she could study Antonio. Noah sat down next to her when he returned from "securing" her father. Noah was chewing his cinnamon gum. When he offered her a stick, she took it. Antonio watched them together. He watched everything.

They quickly filled Esther and Antonio in on Solomon's offer, as well as his goodwill return of Jenn's father. The two listened carefully to everything before the general discussion began.

And after it had gone on for three hours, they were still no closer to knowing what to do about it. Finally Father Juan stood up with a yawn. "We're all exhausted. Might I suggest that we get some sleep and come at this again in a few hours?"

"Good idea," Jenn agreed. She was so tired she kept fuzzing out and missing parts of the debate.

Everyone had agreed that if Solomon sided with Lucifer, their cause was hopeless. But his offer of an alliance could easily be a ruse, and he might already be in league with the other vampire—helping him gather intel, or trying to soften them up for the later attack.

But if Solomon was telling the truth, he could be a valuable asset, if not a totally trustworthy one.

It seemed like an impossible situation. Jenn hoped that sleep would make things clearer. At least for her.

The others began to disperse, but Antonio stood, looking a bit lost. After a moment she understood. Unlike the rest of them, he had no room to go to. He'd spent his time in the cage downstairs. Gramma Esther must have arrived at the same realization, because she put a hand on Antonio's arm.

"Why don't you sleep in the hall outside Jenn's room, guard her against any intrusions while she gets some rest?"

The suggestion surprised Jenn, but Antonio looked so grateful it was almost comical. Then the seriousness of the situation penetrated. Her neck ached where he had bitten her, and she resisted the urge to rub it.

Jenn nodded her assent and headed for her room, Antonio trailing behind her at a respectful distance. Gramma Esther must have her reasons for trusting Antonio, or else she wouldn't have suggested that he guard Jenn while she slept.

Jenn didn't trust Antonio, but she trusted Gramma Esther. For now that would be enough.

Alone in his room Father Juan quickly realized that even though he was bone weary, sleep was not going to come. Frustrated, he sat up and debated his limited options. He wasn't in the mood to speak with anyone, even to be around anyone, which pretty much meant he was trapped in his room.

He sighed. At least he could find something useful to do. From a small velvet sack beside his bed he pulled out his runes — rectangular black stones inscribed in gold with arcane symbols — and began to cast them, seeking answers.

An hour later he was still getting answers he didn't like.

Much as he didn't want to admit it, the runes had never lied to him.

Battle was coming, and it was true that forces from without would sorely test his warriors. But the forces within were just as important, and those he could do very little about.

The stones told him that there was a darkness in Jenn's soul that was blinding her on her path. Unless it could be lifted, all would be lost. He thought of the look on her face when she had first seen her father step off the helicopter. There had been murderous rage there. And she had ignored Paul Leitner since—or had seemed to.

Her inability to forgive him would hinder her in every aspect of her life, but most particularly in being able to trust Antonio and lead the others with a clear head. That was dangerous for all of them. But forgiveness did not always come easily, and in this case, her father had done nothing to truly earn it. He was repentant, of that much Juan was certain, but that wasn't going to be enough.

He sighed and gathered up the stones. They clinked together as he put them back in the bag. He set it by his bedside and tried again to go to sleep.

Sometimes Esther thought she might be the only sane one on the funny farm. She had gotten some sleep, but mostly she had worried about Jenn and Antonio. She had stopped herself from going to check on them, though. It was a test, and Antonio needed to pass it without someone watching over his shoulder. It was also a risk, but most things worthwhile were.

She was also struggling with her anger toward her son. She knew she needed to go to him, talk to him. But she didn't have the words yet, not like she'd had with Antonio.

Antonio was a good man fighting against the darkness inside of him.

Paul was a coward.

And she had no words of comfort for a coward.

Was it because of the life Charles and I gave him? Life on the run, always one step away from getting caught? Picking up in the middle of the night, making him memorize the details of a new false identity, forcing him to abandon his friends? She remembered one night in the car, speeding out of town, when he had sobbed hysterically, finally confessing that he'd been hiding a puppy under his bed. They couldn't go back for it. Esther had called a local no-kill shelter and told them to pick up the little dog.

Antonio's been handed a worse deal, she thought. *At least he's trying. My son caved at the first sign of a threat. He didn't just leave a puppy behind. He handed my two granddaughters to the Cursed Ones.*

Wearily, she finally rose. It was almost evening. She found the others gathered again in the dining room. Her relief at seeing Jenn and Antonio was short-lived as she realized that everyone was hovering around a computer.

"This should be it," Noah said, and sat back.

A static sound filled the room, like a radio station not quite tuned in right. Finally it cleared up, and she could hear it crystal clear.

"*. . . of the Resistance with word of the latest tragedy in this war.*" The man's voice was shaking. Esther hugged herself and listened hard. Something was horribly, horribly wrong.

"*Last night just outside Milwaukee, humans imprisoned inside a concentration camp were massacred by vampires loyal to Solomon.*"

Everyone shifted in their chairs and looked at each other. When Jenn met Esther's eyes, Esther saw her own fear mirrored there. But when Antonio looked up at her, she saw the full understanding and horror of a man who had lived through World War II.

"*More cities have been overrun by the Cursed Ones. America, when will you wake up? When will you see what is happening to your sons and daughters?*" The man's voice was pleading. Esther could feel his pain, and her eyes burned with unshed tears.

"*But there is hope.*"

Esther saw as everyone around the computer actually leaned forward, as though that would help them hear about the hope he offered.

"*There are those who are still fighting. They have not given up. They are your heroes. There are fighters all over the world. And one group has done more than all the rest to strike back at the vampires who have been terrorizing your families and destroying your homes. Team Salamanca, we salute you and we pray you Godspeed.*"

A look of surprise rippled across each face. Esther smiled grimly. These young people didn't truly realize how special or how important they were, not just as a symbol but also as a fighting force to be reckoned with.

That was something she could help with. That was something she could teach them. And suddenly she knew why she was there instead of with her own group back in Montana. Her people were all seasoned fighters and could carry on without her. But here she was needed.

"This is Kent, the Voice of the Resistance, wishing you all a better future."

And the voice was gone. Looking around, she could see the impact it had had on each of them. Hearing that one voice crying out in the wilderness did give them some hope, strength, resolve. She wondered if Kent, whoever he really was, realized that he was vital.

The clatter of pots and pans echoed down the halls, and she was brought back sharply to the present. The smells of food wafted from the kitchen. It was time for dinner.

The brown-robed brothers of the monastery appeared in ones and twos, casting side glances at Antonio. Their nigh-incessant chanting had ended, and now there was only silence from them. Father Wadim had explained that their order observed the vigil of contemplation when they were "home," in the monastery. They had raised their voices in chanting so that Antonio could hear them, and know that he wasn't alone.

Jenn's mom arrived, supported by Sade. And last, escorted by two monks, Paul appeared in his handcuffs. Esther looked at the cuffs and felt another rush of shame. This was her *son*.

Paul saw Jenn's mom and headed straight for her, a determined look in his eyes. Jenn's mom hadn't yet noticed him. Esther took a deep breath. This was going to go badly.

When Paul was four feet away from Leslie, Sade looked up, and the two stared at each other. Both sets of eyes widened.

"You!" they both cried simultaneously, loudly enough to be heard by all.

All other sound ceased instantly as attention focused on them. Leslie jerked and looked up at her husband.

But his gaze remained riveted on Sade. And hers on him.

"Hail, my lord Dantalion," Paul said, in an eerie singsong. Esther shivered at the bizarre, unworldly sound of his voice—and of his words.

"Dantalion," Sade echoed in that same voice. "May he feast on us forever."

CHAPTER THIRTEEN

I can't believe how much I hate my father. It's a part of me I've never seen before, and it's freaking me out. I want to say I'm ashamed of it, or that I'm trying to stop it, but I'm not. It's freeing, but I feel like a prisoner. I feel powerful, yet terribly weak. And the weird thing is, I hate myself for hating him like this—but I also love it. I love it, and I never want to stop. It's like a magick spell, or a curse. Is this how the cursed part of Antonio feels? Because if it is . . . how can he be good? Because I don't think I'm good anymore. I think I'm dark, and twisted. And unlovable.

—From the diary of Jenn Leitner,
retrieved from the ruins

The Monastery of the Brotherhood of St. Andrew
Father Juan, Jenn, Father Wadim, Antonio, Esther, Solomon, Paul Leitner, and Sade

Father Wadim's breath billowed as he led the way down frigid stone stairs to the lower depths of the monastery, deeper even than Antonio's vampire cell. In addition to Father Wadim and Father Juan, Jenn was accompanying the prisoners.

The steps had been swept clean, and monks were still getting rid of cobwebs and dust at the bottom of the staircase. The abbot had explained that the Brotherhood of St. Andrew had no wish to behave vindictively toward any soul "afflicted with darkness." Jenn wondered what he would think of her if he knew how much darkness seemed to have filled her.

"Dantalion, Dantalion, I am here." Her father's whispers echoed off the walls.

"May he feast upon us," Sade added fervently.

They couldn't help it. They didn't know, she thought, but her anger only grew. Barely able to contain her rage, she balled her fists and bit down hard on her lower lip.

No one was sure how Sade and Jenn's father had recognized each other as Dantalion's minions. Not even Antonio understood exactly how the mesmerism worked—if Dantalion made them check in with him on occasion, or if he could see directly through their eyes. Jenn thought back to the Battle of Salamanca, when Dantalion had been able to convince Antonio that he had been set on fire. Had he watched the fighting through Antonio's eyes?

Now they knew that Sade had been the spy in their midst, revealing whatever she knew to Dantalion and, through him, Jenn assumed, to Solomon. Had Sade known she was? Is that why she had come to the academy in the first place? Jenn figured that Aurora and her sire had planted spies in Solomon's camp as well. Secrets and mis- trust ran everywhere.

Jamie will be disappointed that the spy wasn't one of the origi- nal Salamancans, Jenn thought. Maybe it was small-minded and unfair of her, but she'd put up with Jamie's sour atti- tude for a long, long time. Even though she was worried about Skye and him, she found that with him gone she was no longer bracing herself for some kind of snarky retort every time she said two words aloud. Just thinking about dealing with him again made her tired . . . and so very, very angry. It was as if her hatred of her father were spilling into every other part of her life.

All this personal stuff . . . it's too much on top of everything else. I don't know how to deal with it.

"Jenn?" Antonio asked softly. She remembered his hand around hers, squeezing it in comfort.

She didn't remember his fangs on her throat.

I've been mesmerized too, she reminded herself. *I know how impossible it is to fight against it.*

"Jenn?" Father Juan said, and she jerked herself back

to attention. She looked into the cell—a small square that had been cut into the rock. There was a cot, a small desk, and in a sort of antechamber what appeared to be a portable toilet and washbasin. Her heart clutched. Her father was their prisoner. He had betrayed her in return for safety, and what had happened to him instead? He had become a complete and total victim, a puppet, a dupe.

"Please, Mr. Leitner," Father Juan said gently, "go inside."

Ducking his head, Jenn's father turned to obey, then turned back and grabbed Jenn's hand. She caught her breath. Father Juan stood poised to intervene.

Her father blinked at her in deliberate rhythm. Morse code. When Solomon had paraded him on TV, he'd tapped his leg, sending out a secret message to Jenn. *Don't come. I love you,* he'd said. But Jenn didn't know Morse code, and she didn't know what he was saying now.

Somewhere inside his mind, her father struggled to *be* a father.

Twin tears streamed down her cheeks as she jerked her hand out of his grasp. She wouldn't forgive him, ever. She couldn't.

"God bless and protect you," Father Juan said, making the sign of the cross. Jenn's father hissed.

"Your god has lost this war," he said. "Lucifer will cleanse the world of him and all who follow him."

Jenn's lips parted as she traded shocked looks with Father Juan. *Lucifer? Dantalion is in league with him?*

Betraying no further emotion, she stepped back as Father Juan guided her father into the cell and closed the heavy metal door with a clang. A tiny rectangle was cut into it, and through it Jenn watched as her father sat down on the cot.

"Jenn," he whispered brokenly.

I hate you, she insisted.

She and Father Juan moved away from the door just as Father Wadim approached. Antonio and Holgar followed him. Noah had remained behind to guard Sade.

Holgar took up position beside her father's door. Neither Holgar nor Noah would reveal their presence to their prisoners. Food and other personal business would be attended to by monks.

Once they were upstairs, Jenn whipped out her cell phone as she, Father Wadim, Antonio, and Father Juan took seats at the dining table, Antonio facing the doorway, scanning anxiously, as if for more intruders. The three of them looked as thrown as she felt.

"What's Solomon's number?" she asked Father Juan.

"I'll punch it in," he said, taking the phone from her.

Jenn watched him. "That double-crossing vam—"

"Señora?" Antonio said, half rising. "Are you all right?"

As Jenn's grandmother paused on the threshold, she looked haggard. She shrugged and walked slowly into the room, as if the wind had been knocked out of her sails.

"It's Leslie," she said. "She's having a rough time of it.

She'd taken to mothering Sade, and now, with Sade locked up . . ." She ran a hand across the side of her mouth and let her hand drop to her side. "And then, seeing Paul like that. Leslie had been pushing hard for a rescue mission, ever since we realized he was communicating by tapping during those broadcasts. Then he finally shows up, and he's in thrall to a vampire we thought was dead."

"Plus, there is the heartbreak of Heather," Antonio said.

The heartbreak. Well put. This war is destroying my family, Jenn thought. Her throat tightened, as if she were choking on more rage, more fury.

"Yes, our Heather," Esther agreed. She shook her head. "I wish Charles were here." She sighed and looked at the others. "And I'm guessing from the looks on your faces that there's even more bad news."

"The call has connected," Father Juan announced.

"Hold on," Jenn said to her grandmother, as Father Juan handed the phone to her.

"Jennifer, have you missed me?" Solomon said pleasantly.

Jenn made sure he was on speaker, although the sound wouldn't carry very far. "Why don't you put this on speaker so your friends Dantalion and Lucifer can hear what I've got to say?" she said sourly.

"Dantalion? What are you talking about?" Solomon asked on the other end of the phone.

"What's going on?" Esther murmured to Antonio. Antonio

remained silent. Since Antonio had been in the room when Paul Leitner and Sade had revealed each other to be spies, Solomon probably already knew he was at the monastery. But as with the others, it had been agreed that Antonio should stay off the radar.

Father Juan gave Esther a grim half smile. "We're not sure."

"Jennifer?" Solomon said anxiously. "Dantalion? What are you talking about?" Jenn quickly filled him in.

"Lucifer? Dantalion is with *Lucifer*?" Solomon repeated. Either he was a very good actor or he had been truly caught off guard, just as they had been.

"My father's been Dantalion's spy while he's been with you," Jenn told him. "He's been telling us all your secrets," she lied. But she could have kicked herself. It had just occurred to her that they should have seen if Antonio could demesmerize her father and Sade both. They could still do that. Or maybe it would be dangerous. She was sure of so little.

"Dantalion's alive. And he's with Lucifer," Solomon said again, as if he just couldn't get over it.

"What about Milwaukee? What happened there?" Jenn demanded, changing the subject.

"That was done by rogue vigilantes, without my permission," Solomon said. "I swear I had nothing to do with it."

"That's what you said when the president's daughter was converted on national TV," Jenn said.

"Do you think I would authorize an attack at the same time I'm trying to make peace with you?" he asked, sounding wounded.

"You tell me," Jenn shot back. "In fact, I want you to tell me everything you've done. And are doing. All of it. Or I'll come and get you myself, Solomon. I'll drive a stake through your lying, evil heart. I swear it." The rage inside her roared like a wild animal. She wanted to break something.

Kill someone . . .

"*You?* You aren't . . . ," Solomon began in a patronizing tone; then he cleared his throat as if thinking the better of what he'd been about to say. "Okay, okay, Jennifer. Here it all is."

And he told her about his supersoldiers, and how he'd double-crossed Dantalion in Russia, and that he had a spy at Project Crusade who had told him about the virus. Antonio, Father Juan, Father Wadim, and Gramma Esther listened intently. It dawned on Jenn that she was the youngest person in the room, but she was the one in the leadership position. A little fillip of panic tickled the base of her spine.

I was chosen, she reminded herself. *I can do this.*

"So I came to you because I need allies. My vampires will fight with you against Lucifer," Solomon concluded. "In return, I want the antidote."

The antidote that they didn't have. She decided to test him. Mentally crossing her fingers for luck, she said, "Oh, come on. Your spy at Project Crusade must have some hidden away for you."

"I think something happened to him," he said. "The line went dead while he was briefing me."

Jenn wondered if Noah had had anything to do with that. She'd have to ask him.

"What about your best friend, the president?" she prodded. "Can't he get it for you?"

There was a pause. "You don't have it either, do you," the vampire said.

Jenn's heart skipped a beat. "I didn't say that."

"What about the president?" Father Juan said loudly. "Doesn't he want his ally to survive? Or is humanity turning its back on the charming vampire from California?"

"You don't want to piss me off, priest," Solomon hissed through the phone. "You really don't. If I come at you from one side, and Lucifer attacks from the other . . ."

Father Juan smiled thinly. "Then you'll deplete your troops before you face each other."

Solomon went silent. Antonio and Father Wadim gave Father Juan a nod. Priest power.

"We're very busy here," Jenn said. "So let's get to the point. If you want to join forces to fight Lucifer, prove it."

Solomon chuckled. "I have to say, Jennifer. You're twice the man your father is."

"Maybe what we'll do is wait you both out and let you die from the virus," Jenn said.

"Oh, if only it were that simple," Solomon said. "You have to know I have *massive* numbers of my followers on their way right now to blow up Project Crusade."

She looked at the others in the room. If Solomon had an inside man, then he knew where Project Crusade was.

"But if they fail," Jenn said.

"The virus will only inconvenience me, Jennifer. Some of my supersoldiers have no vampire parts in them. The virus won't affect them. And of course we have escape routes. We haven't survived on this planet for centuries without our own safe-houses."

She glanced over at Antonio, who shrugged and shook his head, signifying he didn't know if that was true.

"Think about it. We don't have to breathe. We don't need air. So if this is an airborne virus . . ." Solomon chuckled.

"Then why do you want the antidote?" Jenn persisted.

"I haven't lived this long by narrowing my options."

Antonio raised his chin. "Lucifer," he said aloud.

So much for keeping off the radar, Jenn thought, confused why Antonio had spoken up.

"Antonio, *amigo*, hi," Solomon said, but his voice shook. "You know, it occurred to me to offer you to Lucifer as a way into his good graces."

"He has no good graces. He doesn't need you," Antonio said. "You're going to be fighting on two fronts—stopping the virus, surviving Lucifer. Our side doesn't have to worry about the virus. You're running scared. But *we've* decided to stand and fight."

"Fine." Solomon sounded defeated. "Fine."

Antonio nodded at Jenn, who took back over. "So send us fighters," she said. "A lot of them. Vampires, supersoldiers, and humans loyal to you. Send them right away, Solomon."

She hung up.

"Greg will make sure the virus gets out," Gramma Esther said. "Even if the black crosses have to blow the whole lab sky-high themselves to stop Solomon."

"And Lucifer." Antonio frowned. "Forgive me for jumping in during the call," he said to Jenn. "But I know what Lucifer means to vampires."

"Is he as scary as a virus that will kill every vampire on earth?" Esther asked him.

Antonio nodded once. "Scarier," he said.

The room fell silent for a moment.

"Then it's more important than ever that we create more elixir, so we can fight him," Father Juan announced. "You said that the werewolves gave us permission to search for the Transit of Venus on their territory?"

"Yes," Jenn said. "Father Juan, take Holgar and go. Go quickly."

She turned away to hide her terror, and her resolve: Once she drank the elixir, maybe she could save Antonio. Or maybe after he drank it, he would be immune.

Let something save him, she thought.

But it was not a prayer.

Jenn Leitner did not pray.

Transylvania
Holgar and Father Juan

It was nearly dark when Holgar and Father Juan reached the territory of Viorica's werewolf pack. As the two climbed out of their SUV, howls filled the sky. As if in response, snowflakes began to drift down.

Then a black wolf appeared at the top of the rise above them. It was a female, and Father Juan bowed.

"Viorica," he said.

The wolf chuffed in response, and looked expectantly at Holgar, who took a breath and held it. He sniffed the air and growled deep in his chest.

The snow drifted down.

"For helvede," Holgar swore. "Nothing."

He had confessed to Father Juan on the way there that he had begun to change when Solomon's helicopter had landed and Paul Leitner had appeared. And that Viorica wanted him to.

Father Juan hadn't asked if Holgar intended to do anything and everything that Viorica wished of him. They didn't have time for werewolf-pack politics. He didn't know that much about werewolves, but in his mind's eye he imagined

males fighting for dominance, blood on the snow, injuries —
and more distraction. The team couldn't afford distractions.

The sleek black wolf slunk toward them. Her eyes
glowed, and she purred. Then, as Father Juan looked on,
she transformed into a fully clothed human woman. She
was wearing white snow gear: parka, pants, and fur boots.

"Holgar," she said, then spoke to him in what sounded
to Father Juan like Russian.

He didn't know what she said, but Holgar threw back
his head and howled. Viorica joined him after a moment.

And other wolves — werewolves — appeared on the rise,
observing. Their breath spun clouds in the icy air. One male
wolf, silvery and huge, bared his teeth. The one beside him
moved her head, a gesture of warning.

As Father Juan ticked his attention back to Holgar, he
saw that Holgar's ears had extended, flattened. Holgar's
jaw was longer, and tufts of gray wolf hair extended over
his white-blond human hair. The woman murmured to him,
then growled and pawed at him. She was making it clear
that she wanted him. Then she took off one of Holgar's
snow mittens and examined his hand. The fingers had elon-
gated, and fur rippled over the knuckles, but it was still a
human hand. She turned it over and ran her tongue down
the center of it.

Holgar howled again. Father Juan heard the frustration in it, and possibly the defeat.

And Father Juan closed his eyes and prayed.

AD 1591, Ubeda, Spain
St. John of the Cross

St. John of the Cross lay on a pallet in a plain and simple room in December 1591, and everyone had given him up for dead. He held his beads, and made a prayer:

The soul takes flight, to repair the world. Oh, my soul, make good out of this long journey, so that I will achieve my true purpose and end my days in bliss.

Prayers are like magick, moving through the ethers of time and space. Like finds like, need finds need.

Fate finds destiny.

A prayer found the vampire Antonio de la Cruz. In 1942.

A prayer found Jenn Leitner when the vampire war broke out.

And in the snowfall in the mountains of Transylvania, Father Juan's prayer found the mystical essence of St. Edmund, the patron saint of wolves, who had himself prayed many times for the protection of all species of canines, including those enchanted by moonblood.

The strands of their prayerful selves wrapped around each other, and Father Juan reeled, feeling himself changed as he prayed for Holgar. He tingled, and then he burned, and he knew that when the prayer was over, he would be different forever.

But such a thing had happened to Father Juan over and over again. For had not God Himself said, "Behold, I make all things new"?

TRANSYLVANIA
FATHER JUAN AND HOLGAR

Whatever needs to happen, let it happen, Father Juan prayed.

He had prayed many times for the will of God to manifest through himself. It was God's grace, and no special quality of his own, that made it possible. But it was not a thing to be undertaken lightly—because it did change him, and it was a changed Father Juan who would make the next prayer for the next battle. And so down through time had his prayers changed his essence and the world's, until he was no longer sure where he ended and Mother Earth began.

Amen.

And of course one so blessed, so deeply blessed, knew that the Earth was as alive and as real as God—and so Father Juan worshipped Her, in Her incarnation of the Goddess.

So mote it be.

When he opened his eyes, a black wolf and a large silver one loped toward the waiting pack. Howls stretched toward the stars, toward heaven and the moon.

"Arrouuoo."

The silver wolf looked over his shoulder at Father Juan, and howled.

"Arrouuoo."

The pack answered Holgar, as the black wolf pranced around him.

Then the pack disappeared over the rise. Tired but happy, Father Juan started working his way through the snow in the same direction.

"Arrouuoo."

And the howls became a chant that in Father Juan's mind became a prayer for another: *Antonio.*

And so little by little the world changed, because those who prayed changed.

A man who had prayed on his deathbed in 1591 wished for his soul to take flight, to repair the world.

Across the moon a bat flew, small and fierce and beautiful. Father Juan crossed himself, and prayed to God for strength.

DOVER, ENGLAND
JAMIE AND SKYE

"Bloody hell!" Jamie shouted from the snowy forest, planting his feet as winds blew hard at his duster, buffeting him like a kite. Through the waving tree branches, lightning illuminated the burning inn as the roof and timbers collapsed, crushing everything inside. Jamie swore, and swore again.

Surrounded by flickering ebony shadows, a man appeared in front of the inn. He strode toward the forest in a blurred, slow motion. Magick. Flames danced over him, then extinguished, then danced again. His eyes burned like coals.

Vampire, Jamie thought; then, *Estefan.*

"Skye!" he screamed. "Jesus, Mary, and Joseph! Get the hell out!"

Jamie tried to step forward, but the wind knocked him down and sent him tumbling. Digging his hands into the dirt, he latched on to a root and held tight as the wind blasted at him. He saw the man walking, then saw nothing; then the man closer, and always his burning eyes.

Jamie hurt everywhere. He didn't care. He smelled the stench of the dead in the fire.

The man seemed to move in unison with a heartbeat that thrummed through the ground. The root Jamie clutched pulsed like an artery.

Lightning burst in all directions from Estefan, crackling and smacking into trees. They sizzled and exploded, one after another, to the heartbeat rhythm. Crashing, bursting apart.

Estefan kept coming. He was staring with his burning eyes at something on the ground, and his smile cracked open his face. Teeth shot out in all directions like double, triple sets of fangs. Smoke poured from around his head and shoulders.

"No, you don't, you soddin' bastard," Jamie cried, struggling to get up. Estefan had hold of something. An arm.

Skye's arm.

"Are you seeing this?" he shouted into the night. "You witches, you standing over a cauldron in your safe little hidey-hole? Cacklin' away because you're not hurting a fly?"

Estefan's mouth opened wide, fangs gleaming.

"You going to let this happen?"

"No," said a familiar voice behind him.

"No," said another.

Then something was wrapped around him, and the wind let go of him. It was one of the witches' white cloaks with spangles. Flanking him were Skye's friend Dye Job, in a white sweater and jeans, and Soleil, wearing a cloak same as his. They raised their hands and began to shout against the wind. He didn't know the language, and he wasn't about to stand there while Estefan pulled up Skye like a marionette. Her head lolled back, and the Dark Witch leered at her white neck.

Jamie broke into a run, vaguely aware that behind him there were more than two girls chanting. Voices roared over the rush, lots of them. More witches: Skye's mates, come to the rescue.

He ran harder, approaching the hideous tableau of Estefan bending over Skye like a pantomime villain, about to bite her. Jamie let out a good Belfast yell and doubled his fists. Estefan glanced up, his eyes crimson and evil, and Jamie let out another yell because he was pretty sure he wasn't coming back from this fray, not this one.

But as long as Skye did, that was all that mattered.

Then Estefan's two mates from their last encounter appeared on either side of the warlock and tossed something

Jamie's way—huge, spinning fireballs. Jamie dove toward the ground as something shot over his head from behind and smacked into the fireball on his left. A golden stream of sparklers from his right hurtled toward the remaining fireball. They collided with an enormous explosion that shook snow from the trees.

The witches were taking up arms, then. Or else defending Jamie so he could dismember Estefan himself. Digging in his elbows, he crawled toward Estefan, who had paused to watch.

"*God*, if I could rip you apart from here, I bloody would," Jamie ground out.

Estefan smiled straight at him, as if he could hear him—

And then, suddenly, blood streamed from Estefan's mouth, as if he were vomiting it. Thick, red, clotted. It spewed from his eyes, and his nose, and even his ears.

Estefan began to shout like a man on fire. Blood poured down his chest and back; Jamie had no idea exactly how it was happening, but he didn't care. *Too right, witchies*, he thought, as he pushed himself to his feet, raced forward, and threw himself at Estefan.

Arms and legs tangled as Jamie and Estefan fell to the ground, rolling over and over. Jamie was soaked in Estefan's blood. All he heard was the roaring of his own voice as he damned Estefan to hell and back again. Then he rose up on his knees and pummeled whatever part of Estefan he made contact with.

Estefan flopped on his back, completely limp, and Jamie took advantage. Hitting, kicking, pounding, until hands were wrapping around his arms and dragging him away. The witch girls, at least three on each side, all in their robes except the one. As they moved him, he tried to kick Estefan. He tried to kick anything.

There was no wind. Estefan's two henchmen lay inert on the ground as well, surrounded by dark pools that Jamie guessed were blood.

"Skye," he yelled, struggling to get free of the witches.

"Oh, Jamie," Skye cried, stumbling toward him. She was holding her side. "Jamie."

He broke free of the girls and threw his arms around her. She winced and he caught her up, holding her in his blood-coated arms. He was as red as the dead men on the ground, and everywhere Skye's body came in contact with his, she was soaked in blood as well.

Turning to face the others, he was shocked to see at least twenty of them, most in robes, and most holding each other and crying. They were staring at him and pointing at Estefan, and sobbing.

"Sisters, my sisters," Skye said. "Jamie, please put me down."

"Never. Never in a million years, Skye," he said, and tears streamed down his face. "Skye, if I had lost you, I would have . . ." He trailed off. He didn't know what he would have done.

As he set her down, he collapsed onto his knees and put his arms around her waist. He rested there, completely and totally undone.

"I love you," he said. "Oh, dear God, Skye, you have to know it. And if you'd gone . . ."

He saw Eriko lying dead. He felt the roughness of the rocks he had piled to make her grave. And he said good-bye to her.

"Jamie," Skye said, shushing him as she put her hands on his head. "I—I . . . you're my brother in all things. And that's how I love you, too."

He froze as the meaning of her words penetrated the tidal wave of his emotions. "I'm not too late. I didn't tell you too late," he said desperately.

She hesitated. And then she said, "Holgar."

No. Jamie's world stopped.

"Skye, what are we to do?" Soleil wailed, as the witches gathered around the two of them. "We've broken the code. What we *did* to them! We didn't have to do that. But we *did.*"

No.

"We were vicious," said another.

"Murderous," a third moaned.

No.

"Sisters. Warriors," Skye said, embracing each of them, one after the other. Estefan's blood blotted their spangly robes. "You were *powerful.* That's what we need, to win this fight."

She looked over her shoulder at the bereft Irishman. "Jamie, you'll come back with us."

They kept crying, and Skye comforted them, painting a rosy picture of what it would be like to die in battle with a vampire ripping out your throat. A vampire, or a treacherous werewolf.

Holgar. Jamie let his own near-animalistic rage rush through his body. He shook from the adrenaline surge caused by the battle. She couldn't love that monster. Couldn't.

No.

No.

No.

He felt the same way he had when Father Patrick had held him back and he'd watched the werewolves rip his little sister, Maeve, apart. Fangs and claws slashing, her screaming—

No.

Then Jamie got hold of himself. Shaking, he exhaled slowly. Street fighters didn't live long if they gave in entirely to their anger. He began to strategize.

Wolf had once left a deer head in Jamie's bed.

Fine, then. Jamie would leave something for the wolf: a silver bullet, deep in his *head.* Marked with an *H.* And another in the heart for good measure.

Yes.

Once the battle was done.

The Monastery of the Brotherhood of St. Andrew
Father Juan

Father Juan knelt in the gloomy chapel of the monastery and gave thanks for the heaps of Transit of Venus beside him. The leaves of the herb glowed like moonstone. By the light of the Goddess the werewolves had found a large patch of it, and they had transformed into human form to harvest it for Father Juan.

Afterward, when Holgar had slid behind the wheel of their SUV, Viorica had raised her slender arm in farewell. He'd rolled down the window, and she'd said something in Russian. He had replied very softly under his breath. Softly, and tenderly.

In the chapel Father Juan's cell phone rang. Crossing himself, he answered it. When he heard Bishop Diego's voice on the other end, he couldn't help but smile.

"How's it going, old friend?" he asked by way of greeting.

"Better, I think, than for you," Diego said, sounding skeptical.

"Any luck on turning the tide in Rome in our favor?"

"I'm afraid not. But courage, Juan. There are many here who would help if they were only shown the way."

"Isn't that what I sent you there for, to show the way?" Juan teased gently.

"*Sí,* and I'd rather you had sent yourself."

Juan laughed, and it felt so good.

Then Diego's tone grew more somber. "Tell me, old friend, is it true you're trying to gather the ingredients to make the Hunter elixir?"

Juan sobered quickly. "Yes. I want to make enough for all of them."

"Do you have a priest assisting you?" Diego asked, more somber still.

"No," he admitted.

"Father, you mustn't," Diego cried, reverting, as was his habit when he was stressed, to a deferential tone toward Juan.

Father Juan smiled gently, grateful that he had such a friend. "I must. Don't be sorry, my old friend. All things end some time."

"Not *all* things, in my experience," Diego said pointedly. "But they should."

"An argument for another time," Diego said. "Now let me pray."

SOMEWHERE IN THE UNITED STATES
KENT WALLACE

In his sleeping bag in the abandoned Pizza Hut, Kent woke with a shout. Sweat was pouring down his body, and he was shaking. The imagery of the dream faded, but not its meaning. He pressed his hands to his eyes. It was time.

Years of watching, waiting, guiding, praying had come to an end. All the players were on the board, all the pieces in motion. It was now or never. It was time to gather all the allies together from the corners of the world.

Time to take the fight to the Cursed Ones.

He nodded to himself and got up.

Time to let everyone know just what time it was.

BOOK THREE
ERESHKIGAL

All ceased and I abandoned myself,
Leaving my cares forgotten among the lilies.

—St. John of the Cross,
sixteenth-century mystic of Salamanca

CHAPTER FOURTEEN

Salamanca Hunter's Manual: Your Vows
The calling to become the Hunter of Salamanca is like any other summons to serve God. To be free from earthly distractions, to walk alone, and to place your sacred duty above all other concerns. You are married to destruction.

(translated from the Spanish)

THE MONASTERY OF THE BROTHERHOOD OF ST. ANDREW
ANTONIO, JENN, FATHER JUAN, AND ESTHER

There was a soft knock on the door of the little bedroom Jenn had made her sanctuary, and Jenn rose to open it. Her grandmother stood there, a wry smile twisting her features.

"What is it?" Jenn asked, dread settling in the pit of her stomach.

"Father Juan wants to see you in the chapel."

"Oh," Jenn said, searching her grandmother's face for a clue as to what it might be about.

If Esther knew, though, she was good at hiding it. Jenn followed her out into the hallway.

"You've been spending a lot of time with him," Jenn said, instantly regretting it. It sounded like an accusation when she'd just meant it to be a general comment.

Esther nodded. "He's a fascinating man. I've been enjoying our talks."

"How fascinating?" Jenn asked. She told herself she wanted to know more about Father Juan—not that she was concerned about her grandmother spending so much time with him.

Esther chuckled as though at some private joke. "More than he'll admit."

Jenn waited, but her grandmother didn't say any more. When they reached the door of the chapel, Gramma Esther gave her a quick wink and then turned and walked away.

Jenn watched her for a moment, then went inside. It was very dark except for rows of lighted candles in glass holders in front of a statue of a sad-looking monk. Jenn guessed it was St. Andrew.

Father Juan was waiting at the front of the chapel. He wore a gold stole over his shoulders, and he was standing in front of the altar, talking to someone in the first pew. With a start she saw that it was Antonio.

Father Juan glanced up and saw her. He beckoned to her to come sit on the bench beside Antonio. She hesitated, then walked forward.

Antonio gave her a weak smile that showed no fang. His dark brown eyes were warm and natural-looking, so she allowed herself to relax ever so slightly. She still remained on guard, though. *Mesmerize me once, shame on you; mesmerize me twice . . .*, she thought.

Father Juan stared at her, and she ducked her eyes, wondering if he could see her doubts and fears in them.

"Now that you're both here, there's something we should discuss."

She felt Antonio shift uncomfortably next to her, and she flushed. *He couldn't possibly want to discuss what happened, could he?* There was no way Jenn wanted to dissect the attack or its aftermath. Maybe Father Juan just wanted to talk about Solomon, Dantalion, and Lucifer with them in private. But why? Surely there was nothing he had to say that couldn't be said in front of the others?

Father Juan cleared his throat, and she hunched her shoulders as though bracing for a physical blow instead of a lecture. In many ways she'd prefer it.

"Antonio de la Cruz, you are my brother in Christ and my spiritual son. The Church gave you sanctuary in Salamanca, where your namesake, Saint John of the

Cross, studied as well," Father Juan began. He cocked his head. "And what would you say is the most important thing Saint John had to say to us?"

Antonio did not hesitate. "'Nothing is obtained from God except by love.'" His voice was hushed.

"The exact words of the saint himself. You learned your lessons well." Father Juan patted Antonio's cheek. "But have you made those lessons your own?"

Antonio cleared his throat. "I believe that I have, Father."

Father Juan put his hands on their shoulders. "I bid you both kneel."

Antonio pulled down the prayer bench, then knelt on both knees. Feeling awkward, Jenn knelt beside him. Where her shoulder brushed his, she felt the chill of his skin. It was cold in the chapel, and Antonio had no body heat.

"This is another thing Saint John said." Father Juan placed his hands on top of their heads. "'Where there is no love, put love and you will draw out love.'"

"What are you doing, Father?" Antonio asked, his voice still hushed.

"In the tradition of the Church, we believe that the purpose of the sacrament of marriage is to create new life — whether that be of children, or the new lives of the united couple through the expression of mutual love and support. But there are those who, for various reasons, cannot be together in this way."

Us, Jenn thought, and she closed her eyes as tears

spilled. She wanted to die of embarrassment. Antonio had made it clear that they couldn't be together in *any* way, first by his words, then by his actions.

The scar on her neck still hurt, though the wound had finally healed. "Phantom pain," that was what one of the brothers had called it.

Father Juan removed his hands from the crowns of their heads. Jenn kept her eyes closed as she listened to his voice.

"Ever since you came to the Academia, Jenn, I have cast the runes in order to know the best path for you, and for Antonio. And the answer is always that you must be together. Your power, combined, is what will save us."

She shut her eyes more tightly, aware that beside her, Antonio shifted his weight.

"I can't, Father. I've given myself to God," Antonio said.

"And what is God but love?" Father Juan replied.

"But . . . I'm a vampire."

Jenn heard the self-loathing in his voice. And despite her own turmoil, she opened her eyes and placed a supportive hand on Antonio's. His chest rose.

"You're the only vampire capable of such devotion. Such love," Father Juan said. "But you're holding back."

"Out of love," Antonio whispered. He turned to Jenn, and his eyes welled with real tears. "Because . . . I love."

Antonio, Antonio, Jenn thought, nearly overcome with the force of her emotion. *I love you.*

"Out of *fear*. Because you *fear*," Father Juan corrected him. "And this terrible fear prevents you from loving Jenn as fully as God wants for you. And for her."

Jenn caught her breath. *What is he trying to say?*

"You must free yourself to love her as much as you possibly can. But you've created such obstacles to giving yourself."

"Because I'm a Cursed One," Antonio said.

"And what would you say to another Cursed One who sought to love God? If he came to you on bent knees, head bowed, humbled and broken-hearted?" Father Juan prompted.

"None of us is deserving of the love of God," Antonio replied. "But He loves us anyway."

Father Juan was silent for a moment. Then he said, "Before I was a priest, I served the Goddess. And Her teaching is this: that we are lovable, and She is completely in love with us. Two paths, perhaps? Or is it that you haven't understood the teachings of our Mother Church?"

"*Ay,*" Antonio murmured, crossing himself with his free hand.

"Do you dare to see yourself as worthy of Holy Love?" Father Juan demanded. "Do you have that much courage?"

Antonio kept his head bowed, but she could feel him trembling beside her.

"And Jenn," Father Juan said.

She jumped when Father Juan said her name.

"You have a shadow in your heart as well," Father Juan said. "Yours is also hatred."

She looked at him in surprise. He was standing in front of the candles, and the gauzy yellow light seemed to give him a halo and to make him seem timeless, ageless.

"Of course I hate the vampires," she said. "Don't ask me not to."

"I'm speaking of something else. Someone else," Father Juan said. His expression was so patient, and kind. "The man who betrayed you. Your father."

Jenn's mouth dropped open. "He gave me to Aurora. Heather's a vampire because of him!"

"I'm not talking about his sins. I'm talking about you. Your hatred of him *is* a shadow in your heart. And while the shadow is there, love cannot grow."

Jenn felt even more anger rushing in, over her. Filling her to overflowing. "But what he *did*—he betrayed me, nearly got me killed."

"Can't the same be said of Antonio?" Father Juan asked.

Jenn reeled as though he had just slapped her.

"And yet you don't hate him," Father Juan said.

"It wasn't his fault."

"Yes, it was," Antonio said roughly.

She turned to look at him, her heart beginning to beat faster. She could tell by the way his lips pursed that he could hear. Suddenly his eyes flashed red, but before she could jerk away, they were back to brown.

311

"I wasn't strong enough," he explained. "I couldn't overcome my fear and my evil and my lust. I was weak. And for that I am truly sorry."

Jenn swallowed hard.

Father Juan gestured to her hand on top of Antonio's. "I believe that God has put you two together for a very specific reason. Jenn, you're as broken as Antonio. You've lost the warmth that brought you to me, to learn how to save your fellow man. You've shut down. You need a full heart to be a good warrior."

"No," she began, but Antonio stopped her with a finger pressed against her lips. Then he drew back, and averted his face.

Dumbfounded, Jenn stared at him—the blue-black curls, the ruby cross in his ear. Her heart pounded. She felt confused, breathless.

"I hear it," Antonio whispered. "I hear you *wanting*. That's your heart. That's life. That's being alive."

"You must turn wanting into giving, both of you," Father Juan said. "Listen to me, Antonio, you are not a Cursed One. No one who is loved is cursed."

"*Ay, Padre,*" Antonio murmured. "How can that be?"

"My children," Father Juan said, "these times weigh heavily on all of us. Your hearts are longing and your souls are yearning. But you won't be able to love until each of you steps out of the shadow and walks in the sun cast by the beloved. That is the way to give love. And giving love is the greatest act of faith there is. Do you believe me?"

Antonio dipped his head. "I have faith, Father. But belief . . ." He tipped back his head and gazed into the darkness of the chapel ceiling. "I'm working on that."

And I don't have faith, Jenn thought miserably. *I've tried to, but I don't.*

"Jenn, my poor child," Father Juan said, "I can almost read your thoughts. Tell me, what can you place your faith in? Think of something that you can believe in. Search. Hard."

She was silent. Empty.

Antonio spoke softly. "Remember when you used to call yourself just Jenn? You thought you didn't belong on the team. You didn't understand why I . . ." His voice broke. "Why I loved you."

She swallowed down horrible grief as she nodded. Antonio reached over and took a tendril of her hair between his fingertips and stared at it.

"I . . . I have faith in you, Antonio," she blurted. "I have faith that you're trying to be the man you want to be."

Cautiously, yet deliberately, Antonio put his arms around her. They were strong . . . and cold.

"Then you love me in the same way that God loves me."

"No," Father Juan said. "God is sure of you. As each of you must become sure of yourself. And then the gift of your love will give us victory over the Vampire Kingdom. That's what the runes have been trying to tell me. I understand that now."

Father Juan turned and gazed at the statue of St. Andrew. "Here beginneth the lesson."

Dover, England
Sky, Jamie, Lune, Soleil, and the Coven

We look like a freakin' parade, Jamie thought as he glanced back at the line of witches following him and Skye.

Well, mostly Skye.

He glanced at her again. Her face was hard, jaw set: one determined witch. She'd have to be. The motley assortment trailing behind them was doing so because of her force of will. It remained to be seen how many of them would actually fight when it came down to it. Would be an interesting thing to see if they did, though. That'd take the Cursers down a notch or two.

He touched his gun with the wooden bullets, which he had tucked into his waistband. He'd run his final test that morning. It worked. After months of blood, sweat, and tears, it finally worked. He had that and the one with silver bullets as well. His granda would be right proud of the work he'd done on her.

He'd risked a call that morning to Father Juan. Sounded like the whole bleedin' war was about to be centered in Transylvania. It was fitting when he thought about it. There was a kind of poetry to it, if you liked that kind of thing. Himself, he preferred less drama, less irony, and more killin'.

He felt the weight of the gun on his waist. *Steady, old girl, you'll get your chance soon enough.*

Skye walked quietly beside Jamie, far too busy wrestling with her own demons to even try and begin to take on his as well. He kept fidgeting with a gun holster, and unzipping the leather satchel over his shoulder and glancing inside. She had relived the fight with Estefan a thousand times. She kept picturing his face as he died, and it sickened her every time.

She had broken every vow she had ever made. She was a killer, not just of vampires but also now of witches. *Or whatever Estefan was in the end,* she thought with a shudder.

Lune and Soleil marched right behind her. Once her best mates, now they were more like her lieutenants. *And that makes me what, a general?* She had a sudden fleeting taste of what it must have been like to be Eriko, or now Jenn. She hated it. She didn't want to lead. Many of the witches walking behind her would die in the coming battle.

Maybe all of them.

Maybe even her.

And yet all she could do was relive the guilt of killing Estefan over and over again. Even though he had deserved it. Even though he had given them—*her*—no other choice.

It was me. I made him bleed like that, she thought, though every other witch present had said that they had done the same thing.

She sighed. Holgar wouldn't take it as hard as she was taking it. He had killed before, and it didn't seem to bother him. Maybe it was because he was a werewolf. Maybe it was just that he wasn't a witch who had taken vows to harm none.

"What you thinking, witchy?" Jamie interrupted her thoughts.

She glanced at him. "I was wondering how Holgar is faring," she said after a minute.

Jamie cocked his head. "Truth? I'm not sure you know the full story on Holgar. Him killing his girl, y'know."

"Girl?" Skye asked cautiously, heart stuttering for a moment.

"Yeah. Werewolf at the battle at Salamanca," Jamie said. You know, his fiancée. She stayed with his old pack, and they made a treaty with Aurora. She fought us, and he had to kill her."

Fiancée. Skye's head spun. Holgar had killed the woman he loved in that fight. She hadn't know that. And she hadn't been there for him afterward. She'd heard him speak often of a girl he had known back home, who had refused to see that joining with the vampires was wrong. Skye had had no idea they had actually been engaged.

Tears burned her eyes.

The war destroyed everyone and everything that was good and decent and beautiful. That had to end. And if it meant she had to march into hell at the head of the coven trailing behind her, so be it.

She could rain fire as well as the next witch.

She blinked at the sudden ferocity of her thoughts. The idea of killing to protect or avenge Holgar seemed so much easier than killing to protect herself. She sighed. It was more proof of how Holgar had stolen her heart and made it his.

"You're doing this because you're jealous," she said. "Trying to drop this on me when you know it'll shatter me. It's beneath you, Jamie."

He ducked his head. "It is that," he agreed. "I'm sorry, Skye. Then again, it seems like there's not a one of us hasn't been buggered by this whole bleedin' mess."

In her heart Skye agreed. The war had made monsters of them all. Look at Jamie, trying to diminish Holgar in her heart. But she couldn't deny that she was shaken by what he'd told her. She couldn't picture Holgar killing the girl he'd planned to marry.

They walked a while longer in silence. They passed the landing for the commercial ferry that took passengers to France. A large fishing boat idled in a protected cove — their boat. It was time to say good-bye to England. When they landed in France, they'd catch a train.

Skye stiffened a moment later, though, when she realized that there were at least a dozen young people clustered near the landing, dressed in warm coats and jackets, watching them.

Her senses went on high alert. Gordon, the witch who had arranged the meeting at the landing, had assured them that the dock would be deserted, their passage secret. Had something gone wrong?

The sun was still high in the sky, so the people couldn't be vampires. They could be minions, though, or mutated monsters. She swallowed hard. Or even werewolves or more Dark witches like Estefan.

"Feckin' hell, what's this? A going-away party?" Jamie asked softly.

Skye shook her head. She called softly over her shoulder to Lune and Soleil. "Keep your eyes out for trouble."

They didn't answer, but she sensed a warming on her shoulders, as if phantom hands had touched her there. Her coven sisters understood. Reassured, she continued to stride forward, senses alert.

Beside her, Jamie eased a gun out of his satchel. It was the one that fired silver bullets. So he shared her fear that it could be werewolves waiting for them. Though the silver would drop a human or a witch just as fast as a regular bullet.

They came closer, and she saw one ginger-haired girl standing slightly apart, crossbows slung over her back and a quiver of bolts, like Robin Hood.

The girl turned, and Jamie raced forward with a shout.

Alarmed, Skye stared after him for a moment before running to catch up. What had he seen that had set him off? Her heart pounded, and she willed her mind to be calm. If there was magick to be done, better to do it when she had full control of herself.

A dozen paces from the girl, Jamie stopped short, and Skye nearly slammed into him. Gordon was standing a little ways from the girl. It was clear the two had been talking before Jamie and she had shown up.

"Kate! What the feckin' hell are you doing here?" Jamie demanded.

The girl crossed her arms defiantly. "It's still a free country. It's the cities you have to watch out for."

"Thought you didn't consort with witches," Jamie snorted, nodding toward Gordon. Gordon gave a little wave.

The girl shrugged. "They were good enough for you. Plus I figured the enemy of my enemy—"

"I heard you the first time you said that," he said, cutting her off with a grin. "Come here."

The two embraced in a quick hug, and Jamie practically beamed at her. The girl was younger than he was, and Skye couldn't help but think that she was about the age Jamie's little sister would have been had she not been torn apart by werewolves.

The rest of Skye's coven was arriving, though, and she still had no answers.

"Umm, hello?" Skye said, quickly moving from bewildered to irritated.

Jamie made a face. "Sorry. Skye, this is Kate, a lass from the old country who can kick bleedin' Curser arse all day long. Kate, this is Skye, my mate I was tellin' you 'bout."

"You found her? Alive and not converted?" Kate said.

"See for yourself," Jamie said, his grin growing bigger.

Kate gave Skye a once-over. "Nice."

"So, what are you doing here?" Skye asked, cutting straight to the point. There would be time enough later to hear how the two of them had met, and from the enthusiastic greeting she figured that was one story she didn't want to miss.

"Yeah, Kate?" Jamie echoed.

Gordon took that as his cue to join the conversation. He smiled. "I knew Kate and her friends from an incident a few months back. I reached out to them and told them that if they wanted to help kick the vampires back into the shadows, they should meet some friends of mine."

"So here we are," Kate said.

"What, raiding pubs become too tame for you?" Jamie asked, smile faltering slightly.

"Let's just say I'm ready to go where I can do the most damage," Kate said. "As are my mates here. Irish all, except Jason, who's a Scot. Oh, and Max, who's a bloody Englishman, but we poured so much Guinness down his throat after a brilliant bar rout that he's *almost* an Irishman."

"Never," Jamie retorted with a grin. "Takes more than beer in your blood to take the English out of you."

"Takes the vampires stomping on us all," Kate replied, "to make you forget where the lad who's got your back is from."

"Well said, then," Jamie replied, his smile fading.

Skye's throat constricted. The ragged group reminded her of the ones they had fought beside in New Orleans, the ones who had died when Team Salamanca had left.

"Kate, you should know that we're on a suicide run here," Jamie said, all trace of mirth evaporated.

"Sounds like our kind of fight. Besides, Jamie, who else is gonna cover your arse when you've run out of weapons?"

Skye bit back a snarky comment. It was good that they recruited more help. They needed to be more than just Team Salamanca if they were going to have a prayer of winning. And, she realized as she glanced behind her, she'd already brought an army of her own.

I have the witches. Jamie has the street fighters.

Poetic.

Skye nodded to herself. She liked poetic.

"The more the merrier," Skye said, holding out her hand. Kate took it. "We can do introductions after we get underway."

"Yeah, sooner I'm out of England the happier I am," Jamie said.

Skye couldn't help but laugh. The whole world had

gone to hell, and Jamie still hated England. Maybe it was true that the more things changed, the more they stayed the same.

Castle Bran, Transylvania
Aurora and Lucifer

With the sun soon to rise, Aurora used the excuse to retire to her private rooms. Lucifer and Dantalion had been discussing philosophy, which bored her to tears. Worse, though, they had moved on to discussing Antonio de la Cruz and speculating on what it was that made him different from other vampires.

When Aurora had first heard Antonio's name on Lucifer's lips, she'd frozen, terrified that he knew she'd briefly had Antonio in her grasp only to lose him. It was one of the many fears that she lived with, but it was the one that burned brightest. She should have brought him immediately to her master. Or killed him.

It was her fault that Antonio was free and Sergio was dead.

And if Lucifer found out, she'd end up the same way.

So she'd excused herself and retreated to her boudoir, where she paced for nearly an hour before forcing herself to go to bed. By the time the first rays of light stabbed at the blessed darkness, she was asleep.

And she was dreaming.

She found herself standing in a cell in Spain, staring at herself, vulnerable, human, awaiting trial by the Inquisition for being a Jew.

The same terror she had felt in that cell gripped her even as she watched the horrors she had once endured.

And then, in the dream, Lucifer came to her.

She shook as she watched. He spoke to her, told her what the Inquisition had planned for her. And she watched even as she remembered.

He pulled her against his chest, wrapping himself around her, muffling her screams. He was as cold as the grave. His icy hand came over her mouth, and his other hand held her by the back of the head. She beat her fists against his chest.

He cut off her air supply, and she stopped hitting him, instead fighting wildly for air. The world dissolved into dots and blurs; her eyes rolled back, and she slumped into his arms. He loosened his hold slightly; and she began to suck air into her lungs, smelling him—the world—oranges, and roses, and pine trees. His arms were sinewy, his chest broad and muscular.

"Listen to me, Aurora Abregón," he whispered. There were more words, but she barely heard, barely understood, her fear was so great.

Gasping, Aurora let out a heavy sob. She shook her head and burst into tears. He covered her mouth with his hand again, and her body spasmed. Weakened as she was, she had no strength left to fight him.

"I can end your torment," he said, "in one of two ways. If you wish to live, nod your head. If you wish to die, do nothing."

Too exhausted to move, she lay still. He sighed and lowered his lips to her neck. A searing chill moved through her skin and crept into her blood. It burned. She didn't know what he was doing, but she whimpered.

"Do you wish to live?" he whispered.

Aurora nodded.

And as she watched and dreamed, she remembered the most important thing of all.

She had no memory of choosing to live.

She had nodded. She remembered nodding. But had it been her body spasming for air, her will to survive subverting her mind? Could Lucifer have been moving her head himself?

Aurora began to scream inside her dream. Because she didn't know. She didn't know if she had chosen. Or if he had chosen. Or if she had even known that she was choosing.

But she knew that she had never known what the choice truly was.

"He did this to me!" she screamed.

Silently.

And then she woke up, panting, gasping. She no longer needed the air, but her remembered self had needed it so desperately that she could almost feel her lungs burning.

She swung her feet over the edge of the bed, but didn't get up. She sat there, staring into the darkened room, remembering that night so long ago.

The night he had freed her.

When in truth he had enslaved her.

Rage and hatred and fear coursed through her. But in the end the fear won. He had thought her a fighter, but in his presence she was too afraid to fight. So she manipulated, schemed, seduced.

Her dark and glorious lord was far darker than she had let herself remember.

"And what were you thinking so hard about just now?" Lucifer asked suddenly from beside her.

She stiffened. She had never even heard him enter the room. She lowered her eyes, terrified that he might read the truth in their depths.

"I was thinking of you, and how overpowering my love for you is."

"Ah."

She licked her lips and continued. "Deeper than an ocean, higher than a mountain," she babbled, and what was worse, it sounded like some horrific song lyric. She hoped it wasn't. That would just be the most degrading thing ever.

More degrading than being locked in that cell, forced to choose?

She shook her head sharply, trying to dislodge the voice that seemed to mock her.

"What?" he asked.

"Words escape me to tell you how much I love you," she said, fighting to hide the tremor in her voice.

He placed a finger underneath her chin. "And what will you do, my darling, to prove this great love?"

Aurora felt the icy hand of fear on her even as she forced herself to smile up at him. Only one answer sprang to mind, and she went with it. "Why, bring you the traitor Antonio, of course."

CHAPTER FIFTEEN

Blood on neck, blood on hands
Bloody wounds across the lands
The scars we leave will never heal
The tortured pain you'll always feel
And count your blessings yet you must
We could have left you ashes and dust
For life itself is the cruelest game
And played by us, ne'er twice the same

TRANSYLVANIA
JENN, ANTONIO, HOLGAR, NOAH, FATHER JUAN, AND ESTHER

"The natives are restless," Jenn tried to joke, as wolf howls echoed through the monastery dining room. They'd been keeping it up since sunset. Her teeth were on edge. It was a couple of nights until the full moon, but apparently Viorica's werewolf pack was getting a head start.

Holgar was listening, head cocked to the side. He was sitting with them all at dinner, even though he had already eaten; he was a werewolf, and raw meat was still gross regardless of the country you ate it in. Antonio, too, sat at the table. He was drinking something from a goblet, and Jenn tried not to think too hard about it. If it was blood, she didn't want to know.

They hadn't had a chance to speak privately about what Father Juan had said to them. She blushed just remembering it. The priest was right. There was darkness in her. She could feel it. But how could there not be?

She sighed. It was too much of a headache for the moment. All she wanted was to have one evening of peace. With her mom refusing to come out of her room and her father and Sade locked up, she had high hopes that she would get just that.

The howling stopped, which really got Holgar's attention, Jenn noted. He straightened, his pupils dilating slightly.

A single cry pierced the night. It was sad and terrible, and it sent a chill down her spine. She could see why mankind had always feared wolves, even when they didn't believe in werewolves. There was something eerie about their cries.

What was it Dracula would say? *Listen to them, the children of the night. What music they make!*

And then, as she watched, Holgar bared his teeth.

"What is it?" she whispered.

"It's a wolf from Viorica's pack. Says he needs to see me. Something is wrong."

He rose abruptly from the table as Jenn's heart flew into her throat. "She couldn't be . . ." She couldn't bring herself to say the word "dead." Not when they'd finally found an ally who had agreed to help them fight Lucifer. Not when they'd finally caught a break.

From Holgar's grim expression she could tell he was worried about the exact same thing.

"I'll find out."

"You shouldn't go alone," Jenn said.

"I'll go with him," Antonio said, rising quickly. "If there's a problem, I can help."

"*Ja,*" Holgar said approvingly.

"We could all go," Jenn offered.

Holgar shook his head. "A show of force like that could be seen as hostile. If something has changed, Antonio will have my hide."

"Your back," Antonio corrected softly.

"That too," Holgar said without cracking a smile.

"Okay, but be careful," Jenn said, pushing back her plate. She wasn't hungry anymore.

"If we're not back in an hour, come get us," Antonio said, locking eyes with her.

She nodded, hoping it wouldn't come to that.

* * *

It was cold outside, and Holgar wore a jacket. Antonio walked beside him without even bothering to roll down the sleeves of his shirt. Holgar envied him that. Werewolves were impervious to cold only when in wolf form.

Well, maybe not impervious, but certainly far better equipped to deal with it.

"You're shivering," Antonio noted.

"Because it's freezing," Holgar said, wanting to make a joke, but not sure the other was ready for such things. Antonio seemed on edge. And rightly so. The wolf who had been calling to him was nervous too.

Holgar hoped nothing had happened to Viorica. They needed her. He needed her. She'd promised to help him learn how to change more easily. Her Transylvanian pack actually coached their young in how to change at will instead of waiting for it to happen, as they did in his Danish pack. And just how did she do it without shredding her clothes? He had to know.

Holgar and Antonio were a couple hundred yards from the monastery when the werewolf approached, still in wolf form. Holgar scowled. They could still understand each other, but it was rude, particularly when Antonio could not.

"What's wrong?" Holgar asked.

The wolf danced from one foot to the other.

Why is he stalling? Holgar wondered.

Suddenly the wind shifted, and Holgar could smell the wolf's fear and hatred. And there was something —

"Run!" he shouted to Antonio, turning back toward the

monastery. A moment later something ripped through him, and he fell to the snow as he heard the report of a rifle.

A second shot rang out, this one sounding completely different from the first, and Antonio hit the snow beside him. A tranquilizer dart was protruding from the vampire's neck.

They tranqued him. They tranqued him and they shot me.

And then his insides began to burn, and fire traced its way along his veins.

They shot me with silver.

Something was wrong; Noah could feel it. Holgar and Antonio should have been back already. At the very least they should have heard more howling, but there hadn't been any since the pair had left.

Jenn's fear was there in her eyes for all the world to see, and Father Juan wouldn't stop pacing.

Noah stood. "I'm going out there," he said.

It was the signal everyone seemed to have been waiting for, and they all exploded into action. He didn't bother to tell them to stay put. It would do no good. So a minute later he, Jenn, and Father Juan strode outside.

Esther was stationed just inside the monastery doors with half a dozen monks, all armed, all prepared for an assault.

Because that was what it felt like was happening. It felt like they were under siege.

Fortunately, it wasn't snowing, so the tracks the two had left were crisp and clear. Noah followed them at a jog, keeping eyes and ears focused for any attacks that might come from the side.

Jenn kept pace with him while Father Juan followed behind, covering them with a stake in one hand and a gun in the other.

The farther they went, the more Noah's skin crawled. Then, finally, he saw a dark shape in the snow. He pointed to it, and Jenn took off at a dead run. Lighter than he, she didn't sink as far into the snow with every step.

He swept his Uzi from side to side, trying to see where danger would be coming from. Father Juan caught up to him, and together they approached Jenn, who had fallen to her knees beside a body in the snow.

Noah looked down.

Holgar.

His chest looked like hamburger, and there was so much blood in the snow.

Too much blood.

"He's dead!" Jenn screamed.

CASTLE BRAN
AURORA, ANTONIO, LUCIFER, AND DANTALION

Aurora had kept her promise to her dark lord. She had brought him the traitor Antonio, proving her love, her devotion to him. Why then did she feel more nervous than before?

The werewolves who had helped her, those still loyal to Lucifer, laid the unconscious vampire on the floor and then departed quickly. She'd shot Antonio with enough tranquilizers to keep him out for two nights at least. The last thing she'd wanted was for him to awake on the journey and escape.

Or get himself killed in the process.

As for the werewolf, she had shot it through the heart with a silver bullet. It turned out you *could* keep a good man down. You just had to have the right weaponry.

"I'm so proud of you," Lucifer congratulated Aurora, his eyes glowing like embers as he stared at Antonio's inert form.

"Thank you," she whispered, smiling up at him with what she hoped were doting eyes.

"So, the enigma. We can see it at last for ourselves," Dantalion said as he entered the room.

Aurora fought the urge to bare her fangs at him. She hated him and was infuriated that he hadn't died in Russia like he was supposed to. But as long as Lucifer favored him, there was nothing she could do.

Dantalion was crafty. She had yet to figure out a way to discredit him with her sire. She was sure that he knew she hated him and returned it in full measure. Which meant she needed to watch her back as well.

"Do you think it's his blood?" Dantalion asked.

"We'll find out," Lucifer replied. "Bleed him, study it."

"And if it's not his blood?" Aurora asked, trying to calm her fear. After all, hadn't she already experimented with bleeding him? Of course, she had been more interested in his psyche than his physiology.

"Then we'll carve him up inch by inch until we figure out exactly what makes Sergio's little priest tick," Lucifer said, his voice dripping with menace.

Aurora shivered as she studied the unconscious Spanish vampire. She had sworn to kill Antonio de la Cruz. She wanted him dead. But somehow the thought of what Dantalion and Lucifer had in mind sent her into a near-mindless panic. They were butchers, both of them. Antonio deserved everything they did to him, and more. Just . . . what if they ever did anything like that to *her*?

She'd have to find a way to get rid of Dantalion soon. Maybe then she could rest easier. With the Russian vampire out of the picture, it would be just her and Lucifer . . . and the memory of whatever they had done to Antonio.

It's not that I pity him, she insisted. But she found herself thinking of the Inquisition, and how they had tortured her entire family, making them confess that they observed Jewish customs, to save their souls for Christ. But the Church hadn't cared about their immortal souls. The greedy bishops had wanted their lands.

Everyone in her family burned alive, even her little sister.

I've done worse, she thought. *And taken pride in it. Antonio killed Sergio, my love. I should save my worst tortures for him.*

She'd already tortured him with the finesse of centuries of cruelty. She had driven him back to the fold of evil, only to lose him. And to hear from Dantalion via his spy, the little hunting student Sade, that Antonio had undertaken some kind of pilgrimage to Romania to make sure he remained "good." Didn't it seem that fate decreed a reunion?

Despite torture and torment, something inside Antonio de la Cruz reached its arms toward heaven. Sergio had attacked him and changed him into a vampire while he'd been trying to save someone else. Aurora had been changed into a vampire while trying to save herself. Was that the difference?

I don't care. It doesn't matter, she thought. But ever since her dream, somehow, it did matter.

Transylvania, on the Grounds of the Monastery
Jenn, Noah, Holgar, and Father Juan

Jenn heard no sound as she knelt over Holgar's body. Maybe she was screaming, maybe the others were shouting orders at each other to cover her and Holgar while they searched for the shooter—she heard nothing. Shock was like a live wire that made her tremble and jerk. Holgar was the best of them. He couldn't be dead.

Her hands fluttered uselessly over the bloody mess that

had once been flesh and bone. He had been shredded to pieces.

Returning to her side, Noah flicked on a flashlight. A glint of something shiny in the snow caught her eye. She picked it up. It was a small shotgun pellet. No wonder he looked like he had been riddled with bullets. She held it up to the flashlight and heard Father Juan suck in his breath, and his words pierced her silence:

"It's silver."

Silver. Silver killed werewolves. That was why Holgar wasn't sitting up and complaining to her about how much the pellets had stung. Whoever had done this had done so on purpose. They had come hunting a werewolf.

But what of a vampire?

She didn't see Antonio anywhere. Was it possible he was tracking down Holgar's killer? Or had he, too, been killed, his ashes scattered on the winds so that she could never find them, never know for sure?

She heard Noah talking, something about the number of tracks in the snow, but she couldn't focus on what he was saying.

She lowered her forehead and pressed it against Holgar's. She wanted to cry, but there were no tears left. And the loss was too great. She could hear Father Juan and Noah resume their search of the area, trying to understand what had happened.

And then, as her fingertips held Holgar's head, she felt something stir beneath them.

She blinked, then held her breath, focusing all her energy on what it was she had felt.

There, beneath her fingertips, was the tiniest pulse in the vein in his temple.

"He's alive!" she shouted.

TRANSYLVANIA
SKYE, JAMIE, KATE, SOLEIL, LUNE, JENN, FATHER JUAN, HOLGAR, VIORICA, WITCHES, AND RESISTANCE FIGHTERS

Skye was having a hard time catching her breath in the cold morning air. Either that or it was her growing sense of excitement since they'd crossed into Transylvania. If she never rode another train in her life, she'd be happy. Armed with passports both real and fake, glamouring themselves to deflect attention, the group had actually picked up some recruits along the way. They were thirty strong now, and strong was an excellent word to describe them.

They had requisitioned some vehicles—Jamie stole them—and they would soon be at the monastery where the others were waiting for them. When last they'd spoken with Father Juan, they'd agreed to maintain radio silence until their arrival. As they got closer, the excitement over seeing her teammates, and especially Holgar, grew.

But a shadow was also growing in Skye's mind the closer they got to the monastery. There was a darkness, an evil that seemed to permeate the very air itself. She'd felt evil before, particularly in the presence of the Cursed Ones and definitely from Estefan, but nothing like this. It was as if it poisoned the very air around them.

She could tell the other witches felt it too. They were growing quieter, and when they did speak, it was in hushed tones. A sense of dread and apprehension began to fill the void.

"What is it?" Autumn, the youngest witch, finally asked. No older than ten or eleven, she rode beside Skye in the lead vehicle, an old army truck.

"I don't know," Skye said. "But I have a feeling we'll find out soon enough." The contact they had had with Father Juan had been extremely brief, and they didn't know much of what had been happening.

"Look!" Lune cried suddenly, pointing out the window.

Skye looked out each of the windows in turn. Wolves ran silently beside them. The one in the lead was jet black, and turned glowing yellow eyes toward her for just a moment.

"Werewolves," she declared.

The other witches gasped, and Skye realized that none of them had seen one before.

"Are they going to hurt us?" someone asked fearfully.

Skye stared out at them, and a peaceful feeling settled over her. She had heard stories about dolphins guiding ships into port. "I think they're our escort," she said at last, raising her hand in greeting.

That gave everyone something to talk about, and Skye was able to push the dark thoughts and feelings to the back of her mind for a while as she listened to the chatter and watched the wolves. She wondered if Holgar was out there. It was daylight out, and there would be no full moon that night. But she knew how much he'd wanted to be able to change at will.

"There it is," the driver, the English freedom fighter, said at last. Skye looked out the front window and saw the monastery perched on the mountaintop, as if it were reaching for the heavens. She sucked in her breath. If Holgar wasn't running with the pack, then he was there. She could see his face now and almost feel the warmth of his embrace. Her heart began to lift, and in that moment she felt as if she could defeat all the vampires in the world by herself.

She heard Jamie on the radio from the other vehicle, but she couldn't make out what he was saying. The next few minutes crawled by as she thought about Holgar.

"Blimey, Autumn," she murmured, and the little witch smiled at her excitedly and gave her hand a squeeze.

At last they stopped the vehicles at the base of the mountain and got out. The priests met them and drove them to the monastery on snowmobiles. Father Juan and Jenn were waiting for them at the door.

With a laugh Skye threw her arms around Jenn and hugged her tight. Then she did the same to Father Juan, who embraced her just as tightly.

"*Gracias a Dios,*" he said in Spanish. "Thanks be to God that you are safe."

"And the Goddess," Skye said pertly as the witches and resistance fighters entered the monastery behind her. She pulled away and peered around Father Juan. "Where's Holgar?"

"Skye," Jenn began, then stopped.

Skye screamed. She didn't know at first why she was screaming. She felt ripped out of her body; it was as if she stood outside it, observing. She was screaming and pushing past them. Noah came running and reached for her, but she shook him off. Somewhere a long ways off, Jamie was swearing more than usual.

And then Skye was running through the monastery. Even though she had never been there before, somehow her feet seemed to know where to go. She burst into what looked like a rudimentary hospital room. There were crosses everywhere, an enormous crucifix of wood hung on the wall, and men in brown robes knelt on stone in clusters, praying.

There.

Stretched out on a bed.

Was what was left of Holgar.

She fell to her knees beside him and felt her spirit crash back into her body.

"*Holgar!*"

He was alive; she knew he was alive. She didn't know if she felt it or if someone had told her, but she knew that much. But to look at him he seemed lifeless. He was wrapped in dressings, and the sheets were pulled up to his chin. The only part of him that she could see was his head. His face was gray, and jagged blue lines crossed his cheeks and forehead. His lips and eyelids were nearly purple.

Father Juan appeared behind her and gripped her shoulders tightly. His voice was fierce, piercing through her fog.

"We've done everything we can for him, Skye, but he was shot with a shell filled with silver pellets. We've dug out as many of them as we can. But there are a couple around his heart that we can't reach. We're afraid that if they touch his heart, he'll die."

"If they touch his heart, *I'll* die," she whispered.

"One of the monks is a doctor. He performed the surgery. He's tried everything in his power."

Skye took a deep breath. "But you haven't tried everything in my power."

She lifted her hands and placed them on Holgar's chest. She drove her energy, her senses, deep inside until she could feel the silver. Father Juan was right—the pellet was less than a hair's breadth from his heart. Anything could be enough to drive it in, even moving him, or if he breathed too deeply.

She closed her eyes and centered herself.

"Skye, no," she heard Father Juan protest. "I know what you're going to attempt. It could kill you as well."

Ignoring Father Juan—this was not his battle—she began to call the silver to her, pulling it away from Holgar's heart, out of his flesh. It didn't budge at first, so she dug deeper. Still nothing. She took a deep breath and linked her body up with Holgar's. She had done it so many times to heal other wounds, which were so small by comparison. Her body convulsed in agony as she felt what the silver poisoning was doing to him.

If it stayed in, even if it didn't move, it was going to kill him. She pulled and pushed, feeling as though the silver were ripping a path through her own chest. She screamed with the pain of it.

She could feel a warmth and healing filling the room and realized that Father Juan and her witches had joined her and were lending their energies, their healing, their prayers to the task at hand.

With them behind her, and Holgar's life in her hands, there was no way Skye could fail.

A piece of silver flew from Holgar's chest and hit the wall on the opposite side of the room, falling harmlessly to the floor. She kept going. The muscles around her own heart began to cramp and contract, causing uncontrollable spasms. She nearly lost her grip on the remaining bits of silver, which threatened to fall back to their resting place. She gritted her teeth and pushed herself harder.

She began to shake violently, and her control slipped even more. Then there was a massive shudder from Holgar's body, and she cried out in anguish. She squeezed her eyes shut against the pain, fighting to concentrate.

When she opened them again, she was staring straight into Holgar's eyes. He could see her. His lips twitched, trying to form her name.

It was all she needed. With a shout she yanked the remaining pieces of silver free.

Instantly, Holgar's body began to change. The blue veins receded; the purple lifted from his lids and mouth. Faint color rose in his cheeks. She felt the healing, far slower than she'd ever known his body to repair itself, but at least it was happening.

She collapsed with her head on his chest and sobbed in relief. After a moment she felt a hand come down on the back of her head.

"I missed you," Holgar said.

She looked up at him. He smiled faintly, and then closed his eyes and slipped into a deep, healing sleep.

After a minute Skye staggered to her feet. There were gasps, and several of the witches close to her fell back a step. She glanced down and saw that the front of her shirt was covered in blood—her own blood. As she had been doing to his body, so she had also been doing to her own body. The pain sent a wave of nausea through her, but she managed to keep her feet.

"I'll be fine," she slurred.

And that was when she realized that she hadn't broken her

connection with Holgar. Her body started healing faster than it should have without magick. She breathed in and realized it was in time with his breath. Skye knew she should break the connection, but she couldn't bring herself to do it. Not yet.

She sat down wearily on the edge of Holgar's bed. Father Juan took her hand and squeezed it. Gently she let go of him, to maintain the link with Holgar.

The crowd parted, and Jenn made her way through. She looked older and more exhausted than Skye had ever seen her. Jenn looked from her to Holgar and back again.

"Thank you," Jenn said. Beside her, Father Juan and another priest gazed down at Skye.

Skye forced a smile. "That's what teammates are for."

Jenn glanced around meaningfully. "It looks like you brought us a lot of new ones."

"Yes, I'll introduce you all later," Skye said, struggling to keep her eyes open. She gave up and let herself sink back, her head on Holgar's thigh. A moment later she, too, was asleep.

As Skye slept with her head on his thigh, Holgar gave permission for another visitor to see him. Viorica paused when she saw Skye, then smiled at Holgar.

"I heard that you were shot." She spoke in Russian, her voice soft, almost a purr. "I swear to you that I had nothing to do with it. The werewolves who tricked you were Radu's followers, trying to get back in the good graces of the vampires. They have been dealt with."

"I believe you," he murmured. He marveled at the sound of his own voice. For a while he had thought he would never speak again.

"We're ready to stand and fight Lucifer with you. I have a plan."

He listened.

Skye stirred and slowly opened her eyes. Viorica studied her a moment, then smiled again.

"Thank you for saving Holgar," she said to Skye. She gave Holgar a pointed look and left the room.

Castle Bran
Aurora, Lucifer, Dantalion, Antonio, and Heather

"I've studied his blood for hours, run so many tests. I'm telling you, there's nothing different about it," Dantalion told Lucifer, his voice tired and irritated.

"There must be something," Lucifer insisted.

Sitting out of their range of vision, Aurora just shook her head. Were they willfully ignorant? It had nothing to do with the blood and everything to do with the heart. Antonio's heart was pure, still fixed on his God and his precious Jenn. Love wasn't in the blood; it was in the heart and soul and spirit. It couldn't be measured or calculated or observed.

But it could be tested.

She rose to her feet and went to join the two men. The magnificent welcoming party she had planned would be starting soon, and she wanted to make sure that it was a success. A girl needed something to obsess about, after all. She'd been pushed out of the high-level discussions between Dantalion and Lucifer, treated like nothing more than a pretty companion, a plaything. Had Lucifer forgotten the many times she'd crossed his enemies off a very long list? The centuries maintaining her own court? Surviving the forced unmasking of the vampire race itself by that interloper, Solomon?

Yes. Yes, he had forgotten all of it.

So far it had been a very irritating, infuriating, disappointing day, and when she had discovered that the black sequined gown she had planned to wear to the festivities was missing, she'd almost risked her luck and taken it out on Flavia by ripping off her head.

But she had restrained herself, barely, and settled for nearly draining someone she'd mesmerized not to tell. It didn't make her feel any better, though. She just wished she could figure out what had happened to her dress.

Instead she was wearing a red dress, strapless, hugging her curves. True, red was her signature color, but she'd been in the mood for something darker. And Lucifer always complimented her when she wore black.

"Gentlemen, shall we?" she said as she walked up to the pair. Lucifer wore a long black robe, as had the Spanish gentlemen of their time. Dantalion had on a tuxedo, which didn't suit him at all. He still looked like the Russian peasant he'd been in life.

Dantalion swept admiring eyes over her, which irritated Aurora more than usual because Lucifer didn't.

But Lucifer gave her his arm, and together they walked to the great hall of Castle Bran, where more than two hundred of their illustrious guests were gathered. She nodded at so many she knew from her own dealings: Vampire princes, clan leaders, rulers of vast territories, powerful renegade loners — all had been summoned in anticipation of the great battle. Back home their generals were massing their armies, preparing to lay waste to humanity. Lucifer was ready too. Nothing could stop him. From the words of the master himself:

For it is written that in the Blood Times we shall walk in the light with our gods, and all shall be as has been foretold. We cast down the scourge of humanity, and inherit the earth. This is our holy calling, and our crusade.

Lucifer himself had written those words centuries before her birth. How old he was, she didn't know, nor if he had preceded other births important to humanity — generals and saviors.

Glancing at him — stately, magnificent — Aurora shivered with excitement. She'd been foolish to fear reprisals for losing Antonio. She had always been Lucifer's favorite. Together they would savor these fine moments before he took down the human race and killed that moron Solomon. Tonight he would reveal his plan of attack. He would signal the next step in his unholy crusade to establish the Vampire Kingdom on earth. Solomon had forced them to this day by stepping out of the shadows . . . but this glorious moment would have come to pass eventually. Lucifer was the anointed, and she was his beloved. At least she was at his side, if not in his war room.

When the trio entered, it was impossible not to feel like royalty, especially when everyone stopped to applaud. The great hall was festooned with black and red bunting and hundreds, if not thousands, of winter roses. Gold and black cages held sumptuous humans collected especially for the feast—elite soldiers, athletes, celebrities, fashion models. The so-called "beautiful people" of a doomed race.

The assembled vampires were even more beautiful. Black candles in gold candelabra shone down on the overlords of territories who had flown in from all over the world to stand with her sire on this momentous occasion. They were brilliant, ruthless survivors, one and all. They stood arrayed in splendid gowns, perfectly cut tuxedos, and exotic robes.

The applause was for Lucifer, of course, but she could dream that it was also for her. As Lucifer accepted the accolades, she regally inclined her head.

"Lucifer! Lucifer!" the crowd cried. Some were so moved by the night and all it meant that tears of blood dribbled down their faces. *"Lucifer!"*

Vampires came forward to embrace him, to drop to his feet. The rafters shook. Vampire after vampire kissed both of Aurora's cheeks, shook her hand, embraced her.

"Lucifer!"

They were halfway into the room when her eyes fell on a young woman she didn't recognize wearing a stunning black dress.

Aurora blinked in shock.

Wearing *her* dress.

Heather knew from the way the other Cursed Ones and the human servants were looking at her that she was breathtaking in the black gown. The reaction she was waiting for, though, was Aurora's. When the vampire came in on the arm of Lucifer and saw her, Heather was rewarded by the look of outrage on her face.

Aurora froze, and Lucifer cast a surprised and irritated glance at her.

"Why is she wearing my dress?" Aurora asked in clipped, precise syllables, sounding very Spanish, very . . . human.

Heather smiled, because she had caught Aurora completely off guard and the "queen" was showing her own weakness. And because Heather had more than one secret planned for the bitch.

Lucifer raised a hand, signaling silence. The tumult in the room faded away.

As the party guests murmured quietly with fascination, Heather stepped forward grandly. All the glowing red eyes in the room were on her . . . including Lucifer's, whose gaze swept her from head to toe. She glanced at him from underneath her lashes and was rewarded by the smile that curved his lips.

"Why are you wearing my dress?" Aurora said again.

"Because I look so much better in it than you do," Heather responded.

A hush fell over the crowd as Heather came to stand within a couple of feet of Lucifer and his lady.

Aurora's eyes narrowed. "Who are you?" she asked.

Heather dimpled. "Don't you recognize me?"

She could see the confusion in Aurora's eyes: Heather was familiar, but she couldn't place her.

Panic started creeping into Aurora's voice. "No."

"Next time you keep someone in a cage for days on end, you should bother to look at them once in a while," Heather said, lifting her chin.

Understanding slowly dawned on Aurora's face.

Heather took a step closer. "That's right. My name is Heather Leitner. My sister is Jenn Leitner. And once upon a time I prayed that she would kill you."

"And now?" Lucifer asked, amusement thick in his voice as Aurora took a step backward . . . or tried to. Lucifer held her fast.

"Now I'm ever so grateful that she didn't."

Just as Aurora started to look relieved, Heather struck. In one swift move she grabbed the stake hidden in her skirt and plunged it into Aurora's heart. "Because now *I* can," Heather hissed as Aurora turned to ash.

The crowd erupted. Heather took a step back and closed her eyes, reveling in the sensation of victory. She heard the screams and shouts around her, and waited for death. If it came, it came.

It did not come.

When she opened her eyes again, she saw that Lucifer had raised a hand to hold off the throng of vampires ready to tear her apart. She knew that if he dropped that hand, they would kill her.

She stared calmly at Lucifer. His face was inscrutable.

"You dare to kill my protégée?" he asked in an icy, contained tone. "On this night of all nights?"

"Yes, and I'd do it again gladly," Heather said, raising her chin even higher. All eyes were on her. Because she was brave. And because she was beautiful. Though she was dead, she had never felt so alive.

He cocked his head. "Why?"

"Because—especially on this night of all nights—you deserve better."

Lucifer stared at her for a long moment, as though reading her soul. She held nothing back, letting him see all of it.

He grabbed her hair with lightning speed and tilted her

head backward. She didn't flinch. She just continued to stare at him. And after an eternity had passed, he chuckled.

"I've been waiting for you a long time, my queen," he said. Then he bent and kissed her.

It was her first kiss, ever, and it was everything she had ever wanted, ever dreamed, and so much more. When Lucifer pulled away, in his eyes she saw the promise of a thousand nights by his side and a thousand days in his bed. And she laughed with the joy of it.

"And I'll be with you when you kill them all," she said.

"Perfection!" Dantalion shouted, raising his arms. On his cue the room burst into thunderous applause and cheers, and she dropped a deep curtsey, as if born to it.

The Monastery of the Brotherhood of St. Andrew
The Allied Forces

The arrival of Skye and Jamie with close to thirty others left everyone scrambling to feed them, find them places to sleep, and get organized. Jenn was happy for the distraction and willingly put herself in the thick of things. She didn't want time to think. But thoughts—fears—still crept in, and she was afraid she was going to collapse into hysterics at any moment.

It was close to dinnertime when Father Juan tracked her down in the chapel. He eased himself into the pew next to her.

"No word," he said quickly; then, "I'm surprised to see you here."

She swallowed hard. She'd hoped for news of Antonio. "It's the only quiet place here now."

"I'm afraid it's going to get busier," he said.

She waited for him to go on.

"Esther's been in contact with her resistance cell from Montana."

"And?" *Let them know something. Let them tell us where he is.*

"It seems they're heading here."

Jenn felt her eyes bug out of her head. *"Here?"*

He nodded. "And it looks like they aren't the only ones."

"How are they all finding us?" Jenn asked.

He shrugged. "Apparently the word is out. And I understand that Kent has been encouraging anyone who can to join us to fight Lucifer. It's coming. Somehow Kent knows. He's calling it the final battle."

"Final battle," she repeated. "It doesn't seem possible."

He nodded. "I know what you mean. It's been a hard, bloody war. But I have a feeling that one way or another it's about to end."

"Either we win or they do?"

"Kent says that resistance cells are trading information, making preparations," he said. "It may be *our* final battle. But perhaps the fight will go on."

Jenn closed her eyes at the waves of fear, and some kind of strange, wild eagerness rushed through her. "Some days

I'm so tired that I have to remind myself that I care which way that goes."

He patted her arm. "It's understandable, Jenn. But you must remember that you're fighting on the side of right."

"And you are not alone," an unfamiliar voice rang out. "None of us is. Not anymore."

Jenn turned to see a young Asian man standing just inside the chapel doors. He was dressed like an old-fashioned samurai, right down to the sword slung across his back. His short hair was close-cropped, and there was a ghostly familiarity to his face.

And in a rush she knew who he was.

Kenji Sakamato. Eriko's brother the Hunter.

She blinked at him in astonishment.

"How are you here?" she finally asked.

His smile was tinged with the kind of pain and sorrow that she was all too familiar with. "I heard that your team was in need of a new Hunter," he said.

Jenn stood swiftly and crossed to him. She placed her hand on his shoulder, and he didn't shy away from the contact. She looked him in the eyes. "No one can ever replace your sister. But we are honored to have you with us."

He bowed and she did likewise.

"My sword is yours," he said.

"Thank you."

"I would very much like to meet the good vampire that I have heard of," he said.

Jenn took a moment to respond.

"That will have to wait," she said finally.

Holgar had told her that Aurora had Antonio. She tried not to think about what Aurora might be doing to Antonio at that very moment.

Tried, and failed.

"When it is less difficult, I will be happy to meet him," Kenji said.

Before Jenn could explain, another figure darkened the doorway. The young woman who stood there seemed like she was from a different lifetime.

It was Tiffany, one of Heather's best friends. Jenn remembered her being at Papa Che's funeral.

Tiffany stepped forward, and Jenn was astonished at the transformation in her. Tiffany had always been slender, but now she was lean and tough-looking, with muscles and sinew twisting the length of her arms. Her once-beautiful long hair was now short, functional.

"Tiffany?" she asked, disbelieving.

Tiffany nodded.

"What are you doing here?"

Tiffany leveled intense blue eyes at her. "After what happened to Heather, I joined the resistance. And now I, we, are here to help."

Jenn turned to Father Juan. "Just who else is coming?"

He smiled. "Everyone."

CHAPTER SIXTEEN

When I was a little girl, I had so many dreams. I was going to become a princess, or the president, or an astronaut. I thought anything and everything was possible. Life was an adventure. Then the war came, and I dreamed of fighting the Cursed Ones. Then I dreamed about Antonio de la Cruz.

I stopped dreaming the first time Aurora kidnapped him.

I know that for some people, dreams can come true. I know it, but I don't really believe it.

—From the diary of Jenn Leitner,
retrieved from the ruins

THE MONASTERY OF THE BROTHERHOOD
OF ST. ANDREW
THE ALLIED FORCES

More fighters arrived every day. Feeding them and hous-
ing them was a real problem, putting increasing pressure
on Jenn to attack Lucifer. The longer they waited, the less
able she would be to take care of her people—and the more
exposed her numbers would be to Lucifer.

The full moon glinted against new-fallen snow and
made the salt circle scintillate. Standing in the precise center of the sacred space, Jenn wore a white gown made of
monastery bedsheets. Her long auburn hair was crowned
with a wreath of evergreens and Transit of Venus. In her left
hand she held a mirror, symbol of the Feminine Principle of
the Universe—giver of life and all that was beautiful and
good—and in her right a crossbow, symbol of the Goddess
as huntress, protector, destroyer.

While searching for a name for the new coven,
Gramma Esther, revered as the oldest woman in the monastery, had suggested they call it the People's Coven. The
coven dedicated to all of humanity, no matter their religion
or creed, or if they were evil or good. Under the direction
of Skye, their High Priestess, they were there to bless and
strengthen the Goddess's chosen warrior. The Warrior of
the People:

Jenn.

Esther stood in the circle, hands joined with little Autumn and Father Juan, wearing a borrowed spangled robe splotched with Estefan's blood. All those who had brought robes with them from England wore them, blood-stained or not. The monks had offered bedsheets for some of the others, but there weren't many to be spared. Father Juan wore a white hassock. More witches had arrived, from France, Germany, Russia, Spain itself, and a dozen other countries, having divined that a new coven had formed, one born of courage and strength, dedicated to saving the Lady's people. Sisters and brothers from Australia, Brazil, China, Zimbabwe, and other countries were traveling to Romania, hoping for the blessing of joining their magickal kindred in the final battle. There were at least fifty witches present, and more on the way. The coven was becoming an army—with Skye as its head, answering in turn to Jenn.

Sensing that the war was about to spill blood onto the very ground on which they stood, Skye had called for the ritual to anoint Jenn with the blessings of the Goddess and all her children—witches male and female both.

Standing beside Skye, Soleil and Lune served as her handmaidens. Soleil held a bowl of water, and Lune held aloft a sword tipped with a burning white candle. Although the wind had whipped up, the candle stayed lit.

Skye raised her athame toward the moon, and began.

In the circle
Is the Goddess
In the circle
Of the Goddess
Life, light, love.
Divine maiden, mother, crone.
You are the Mother of all goodness.
We give You our hearts, spirits, bodies,
And call You to us.
Come down, Blessed Mother,
And take Jennifer Leitner, our warrior,
In Your arms.

Skye lowered her ritual knife into the water. She beckoned Jenn to bend her head over the bowl. Jenn did so, seeing her own face reflected in ripples, candlelight. The full moon glowed behind her like a halo.

"We accept Jenn's birthright for her. We lay claim to the power of the Mother. We receive blessings from the Lady of the Moon, and the Lord, and the Spirits of the South, the North, the East, the West." Skye looked over at Father Juan. "And all the saints and apostles."

He dipped his head.

"So mote it be," the entire circle chanted.

"We accept blessings for those who are not here to accept them on their own behalf," Soleil declared.

"So mote it be," everyone replied.

Jenn swallowed hard and thought of Antonio. Skye and Father Juan had performed magickal spells on his behalf before—to cleanse him of evil and bring him back to the light. *If only Antonio were here now.*

"We accept victory in battle," Lune said next.

"So mote it be."

"All special cares and concerns, let the Mother grant them," Father Juan said.

"So mote it be."

"And please take care of my bunny until I get back," Autumn put in softly.

"So mote it be."

"Let the circle move," Skye decreed.

All the people in the circle put their arms over one another's shoulders and began to walk to the left. Somewhere a drumbeat began, and the shoes of the witches crunched in the snow to its rhythm. The circle wound around Jenn, Skye, Soleil, and Lune. Then, without any prompting, each person in the circle dropped their arms, rotated in a small circle of their own, and began to sing.

"May you be blessed in the arms of the Holy Mother."

Then they joined hands and circled Jenn and the other three again.

"Come to her. Strengthen her. Protect her," they chanted.

Jenn's spirit lifted; she felt as if she were rising toward the stars, and a woman's face glowed in front of her. The heavenly woman smiled gently at Jenn.

Arms encircled Jenn, holding her. It was Skye.

"Come back to Earth," Skye said, "and receive the blessing of each witch."

One by one, each member of the circle approached Jenn, paused, held up their left hand, and murmured a blessing on her.

"For strength in battle," Gordon said, his hand extended.

"For purity of purpose," said another.

"So she doesn't get hurt," Autumn intoned.

"For winning," Gramma Esther said.

"For the light of forgiveness," Father Juan said.

Jenn's face tingled. She still couldn't forgive her father. Or still wouldn't.

The blessings took over an hour, and when they were done, the others drifted away to give Jenn time alone with their High Priestess. Exhausted, exhilarated, Jenn gave Skye a hug.

"Thank you so much," she said.

Skye's answering smile was troubled. "The coven has given you good weapons, Jenn, but the more openhearted you are, the more powerful they will be. There are barriers between you and the blessings we want to bestow on you. You have to trust the Goddess. You have to love."

Anxious, Jenn pulled away slightly. "Isn't it enough that I'm willing to lay down my life?"

Skye sighed. "No, actually, it's not. That's why our way

is so difficult." She cupped Jenn's cheek. "But it's worth it. Please, Jenn, try."

Then Skye raised her left hand above Jenn's head and said, "So mote it be."

More people had arrived. They had told the Salamancans that word of a worldwide attack on humans was spreading, and cells of resistance fighters were trying to talk civilians into battling the vampires. But one word of dissent landed you in a camp.

"And they're horrible places," whispered a hollow-eyed man as Father Wadim dressed deep lash marks across his back. He had been freed by some brave teenage prisoners who had orchestrated an escape. "They take the strongest ones for blood, and force the rest of us to work. I had to build more cells. And dig graves."

Skye tried to put thoughts of death out of her mind as she descended the staircase into the gloomy darkness where she had helped Holgar lock himself up the night before. He had fully recovered from his injuries, but they hadn't had a real chance to talk. She hadn't yet been to sleep, and she was still keyed up from the ritual. It had been a perfect night for Drawing Down the Moon, but it also would have been a good night for them to go up against Lucifer, since Holgar would have been in wolf form and at his most powerful and least vulnerable. He was still having trouble shifting at will.

In her vision, though, he had been in human form when fighting Lucifer and his forces.

And in my vision he was killed.

She shuddered, determined to find a way to keep that from happening.

At the bottom of the stairs she pulled a key out of her pocket and unlocked the door. Holgar had told her they had been keeping Antonio in the room for a while before she and Jamie had gotten there. He had figured if it was good enough to hold a vampire, it was good enough to hold him.

She opened the door slowly, not wanting to startle him.

He was sitting up, staring at her. With a rush of relief she saw that he was wearing the sweatpants he'd had on the night before. His shirt was still crumpled up on the floor, and she couldn't help but stare at his chest and shoulders.

So strong.

"Good morning," he said.

"It will be if we get to kill Lucifer today," she drawled.

He smiled at her.

So sexy.

"I'll be ready in a minute," he said.

She should leave the room. She'd seen him shirtless dozens of times before, but it had never affected her like this. She could feel her cheeks turning pink as she stared without meaning to.

"Is there something you want to say?" he asked, his grin slowly fading.

So perceptive.

It was now or never. And given the battle ahead of them, never was a very real, very immediate possibility. She couldn't do that to either of them. She closed the door behind her, not wanting anyone to accidentally disturb them. Taking a deep breath, she walked over and sat down beside him.

She looked deep into his eyes and could feel herself shaking. It was as if she were standing on the edge of a precipice and just knew she was going to fall.

The only question was, would she crash to earth or fly toward the heavens?

"Skye," he said. He took her hand in his. Warm, comforting. "What is it?"

She cleared her throat and drew a deep breath. "I've had a lot of time to think recently."

"We've all had too much time to think," he said.

"Yeah, but it really helped me work some stuff out."

He bent his head toward her, totally engrossed in what she was saying. Nervously, she bit her lip.

"I couldn't stop thinking about you, wondering how you were, when we would see each other again," she said.

"Same here," Holgar said. "You're my partner. I was angry that I wasn't allowed to come and find you."

"It's good that you didn't. You were needed here, from everything I've heard. And it gave me a lot of time to just think."

He brushed a finger against her cheek, and she trembled. "You can tell me anything," he assured her.

She swallowed. *Why is this so difficult?*

He pulled his hand away. "But you can tell me later, if that would be better."

"No," she said, panic flooding her. There might not be a later. She dropped her eyes. "Okay," she murmured. "I love you."

"I love you too."

She looked up at Holgar and realized that he didn't understand. She could feel her heartbeat speeding up, and she shook her head. His smile began to fade.

"Not as a friend, or as a partner. Holgar, I—I love you, and I want to be with you."

His smile faded, and his eyes took on a strange look. She could feel herself beginning to panic. *He doesn't feel the same way. That's okay. At least I told him.*

"Like a mate?" he asked.

She almost started laughing. A mate was British slang for a best friend. But that's not what Holgar was likely referencing. He was a werewolf, and they called their spouses mates.

"Like a mate," she said, managing not to giggle at the unexpected language barrier.

He still looked confused and a little lost.

"For helvede," she said, using his favorite curse word. And then she leaned forward and kissed him.

She tasted surprise on his lips for just a moment, and then he wrapped his arms around her and crushed her to him. She would have to do a healing spell on her bruised ribs later, but at the moment she didn't care. All she cared about was the passion, the yearning, she felt from him.

When at last they broke apart, she whispered again, "I love you."

"I love you too," he said.

And looking into his eyes this time, she knew that they were talking about the same thing.

"So, do we want to give us a shot?" she asked, breathless.

He looked at her, confusion again returning to his eyes. "You love me, *ja*?"

"Yes, *ja*," she said.

He grinned at her. His eyes danced. "Then marry me."

Her head swam. "What?"

"Marry me, Skye," he said.

"Isn't that rushing things?" she squeaked.

"We've known each other for more than two years. What is rushed about that? We know everything we can about each other, unless we change the things we can tell each other, show each other. The way mates do."

"Blimey, Holgar. It's just—that's a huge commitment, and we've only had one kiss."

He tilted his head to the side. "It's our way."

Werewolves.

She licked her lips. "I'm a witch. We do handfasting ceremonies."

"Is it like marriage?"

"Sort of. Two people promise to stay together as long as love lasts."

A shadow seemed to pass across Holgar's face. "Werewolves mate as long as *life* lasts."

She felt like she was in free fall. "But isn't a relationship about compromise? About giving up things for the other person? So . . . we could promise to try?"

He looked at her with so much sorrow in his eyes that it nearly broke her heart.

"What?" she whispered.

"Skye, loving you, being with you, I'd already be giving up so much."

"I don't understand."

"Half of my life, the wolf half, I couldn't share with you. For a werewolf that is huge. The first ceremony, the first kiss, the first *everything* happens in wolf form. By choosing to be with you, I already give up half of what a werewolf mate expects from their partner."

"I'm so sorry," she whispered. "I didn't think."

He smiled at her. "*I* did," he said. "I've thought about this long and hard, even before you went missing. And it would be worth the sacrifice, if that mate were you."

Skye was nonplussed. "Holgar, you're asking me to marry you but telling me we can't have a relationship unless I do?"

"Ja." He gave her a firm nod. "Mated for life. Would that be so bad?"

His voice was soft, pleading. There was a part of her that responded to it. But she was so young.

But you've lived so much, struggled, seen more than most three times your age, a voice whispered inside her.

But forever?

Forever for one of you might be only a matter of hours.

But it went against all her customs, traditions.

As he will be going against his. Because he loves you.

"I have to think about it," she said.

And Holgar, wonderful, glorious Holgar, just nodded like it was the most natural thing in the world for her to say.

She stood up, heart still hammering in her chest. She turned and fled out of the room, back up the stairs. She needed fresh air. She needed to think.

Maybe it was because she had chosen so badly in the past that she didn't trust herself to make this decision. But Holgar was different. He was everything she should want in a man, and she did love him. But what if she was wrong? What if there was something deep and dark he was hiding from her?

Not everyone hides things like I do.

Still, she felt like she couldn't breathe. She wished there was someone she could talk to about it. Not Soleil or Lune. They'd be too shocked. And Jenn couldn't even handle her own guy issues; how could she help Skye with hers?

She turned a corner, wiping tears from the corner of her eyes, and nearly collided with Jenn's grandmother.

"Skye, are you okay?" Esther asked, her voice kind.

"No, I'm really not."

Holgar growled in frustration. That hadn't gone as he would have liked. It had not been his intention to declare himself for Skye so quickly or so forcefully. She had surprised him with her own admission, and he had pushed too hard.

He finished getting dressed and then headed upstairs. He wanted to find her, but he knew he should give her a little time and space. She was having a problem handling everything that was going on.

"What's wrong, wolfie?" a familiar, mocking voice asked.

"Not now, Jamie," Holgar said, his voice a low rumble even to his ears. "Leave me alone."

"Love to, but the good father has called a meeting. Looks like things are about to start getting lively around here."

Good. Holgar clenched his fists. He needed to *do* something while he was giving Skye space. So he followed Jamie through a maze of corridors until they reached a large room, dimly lit.

He had expected to find a large group there, but it was only Jenn, Noah, and Father Juan waiting for them. A minute later Skye showed up, her eyes puffy. He could still smell the salty tears on her cheeks despite the fact that she'd obviously tried to brush them dry.

He whined deep in his throat, unhappy that she was distressed. And she wasn't the only one. Jenn was also on edge, as was Father Juan. Holgar studied the priest, wondering what was happening.

Father Juan cleared his throat, and they turned to him expectantly.

"Solomon's followers are landing in the valley. As soon as they're off the planes, Jenn will meet with him to formulate our battle plan. We have to move fast. Once Lucifer realizes that Solomon is on our side, we'll lose the element of surprise. I've put out the word for everyone to come as quickly as they can."

"Jenn, *Solomon*?" Jamie said incredulously.

Jenn smiled grimly. "I'm not an idiot, Jamie. I don't trust him. If I think he's double-crossed us, all I have to do is give the word. And some of these new friends of ours will take him out."

"Earnin' their keep, then," Jamie said with satisfaction.

"The Voice of the Resistance, Kent Wallace, has been on the radio night and day sending out coded messages to freedom fighters all over the world," Father Juan said. "Urging them to action. Letting them know that things here are almost under way. Jenn will check in with Kent, too. As soon as she gives the word, we'll be moving on Lucifer." He paused, took a deep breath, and continued. "I'm nearly finished with the elixir."

Everyone stirred at that. Holgar couldn't help but think about their fallen pack mate, Eriko, who had been chosen to drink the elixir when they'd graduated from the university. That gift had bestowed upon her super speed and strength, but it had also been a curse. It had torn her body apart before she died. She had suffered agonizing pain because of it.

With their already enhanced abilities, he and Antonio stood the best chance of dealing with the side effects of the elixir. Of course, Antonio might well be dead.

He worried for the others, though, particularly Skye. She could heal herself of injuries, but he didn't know if she'd be able to stem the tide. Still, it was not his place to choose for her or for any of them. He stepped forward,

"I'll test it," Holgar said. After all, they were on a suicide mission anyway.

Skye must have been having similar thoughts, because she flinched as he spoke, fear in her eyes. He would give anything to spare her this pain, this battle, but again, it was not his place.

She had not allowed it to be.

"Bring on the mojo juice," Jamie said. He wore his two guns like an old-time gunfighter in a movie. Holgar wondered if that meant the gun that could fire wooden bullets was finished. He hoped so, and wished that they each had such a weapon. He could smell the silver bullets in the other one, and he was doing his best not to worry about it.

*   *   *

At one time Jamie would have been elated to take the elixir. But that seemed so long ago. He was tired. Tired of fighting, tired of losing, tired of being told what to do and when to do it. One way or another, though, things were ending, and he for one was happy for it.

Something was wrong with the good father, though. There was something he wasn't telling them. Jamie could see it in the dark shadows under his eyes, the pinched corners of his mouth, the look of pain and fear that mingled with something else—relief, maybe?

He wasn't sure what the trouble was, but he hoped Father Juan pulled it together. Maybe this time he'd even join them on the battlefield. That would be something. In all those years at the academy he'd never once seen Father Juan fight. Jamie wondered if he'd fought during the siege of the university, or if he'd cut and run before the punching started.

Jamie's hands slipped to his guns, and his nerves were steadied by the feel of them. Left one silver, right one wood. He had heard that some of the local werewolves had thrown in their lot with Holgar. Those wolves had better stay away from him if they knew what was good for them.

He wished for the hundredth time that Eri was there. It wasn't right that she, out of all of them, had been the one to die. Well, like as not, they'd all be joining her in heaven or wherever the hell Buddhists went. She'd never talked much about that, but he had some vague memory that had something to do with reincarnation.

Better luck this next time round, lass, if that's the way of it. Least he could do was wipe out the vampires and the werewolves and give her a fighting chance at a good, normal life if it was true. He owed her that.

"What do we need to do?" Jenn asked, finding her voice. A dose of elixir would give her strength, but she hoped it would be enough for the task at hand. Noah stood beside her, and she couldn't help but wonder at the strangeness of it. She had thought Antonio would be with her at the end.

What would happen when they were all together on the battlefield?

Would Jamie turn those guns on his teammates?

Would Noah break his promise and try to kill Antonio if they found him?

Would Antonio break all his vows and kill them?

The road had been so very, very long, but one way or another it was ending. Either the vampires would be wiped out, or they would. This hazy nightmare would be over.

Maybe if she survived, she could go back to being just Jenn.

Noah was ready. He had nothing left to lose. This fight had been coming since the day the Cursed Ones had first made their presence known. He was just grateful he'd been allowed to live to see it, to participate in it.

None of the others in the room knew what had to go into the preparation of the elixir. He knew and had agreed to help Father Juan in the end. They both understood sacrifice, and besides, none of Father Juan's team would be able to do what was required. So it fell to him, the outsider.

Wasn't that always the way for his people? Chosen, called, yet always alone, always the outsiders.

If it gave him the strength to do what had to be done, then he would embrace that.

Father Juan smiled. He never would have children in the normal sense of it, but these, and so many others like them, were his spiritual children. He had done everything he could to prepare them. As always, just as in past trials, past battles, and long-forgotten wars, he worried that it wasn't enough.

But this time he felt a new peace. God was going to let him die at last. His Lord was going to let him know the rest that had been denied him for so very long. Every time he'd closed his eyes and death had touched him, he'd been reawakened to help save the world yet again.

Yes, this time was different. He could feel it. He believed it. It was truly the end.

And he would make a great ending of it, helping his

children in the best way he could, equipping them with what they needed to prevail. In a way, Father Juan was sorry that he wouldn't get to see their victory or celebrate it with them. But this was better.

"We don't have enough of the ingredients to make separate batches of the elixir. You must all share it," he told them. "And it will be temporary."

Jamie's eyes flashed in frustration, and Juan barely suppressed a smile.

"This is a good thing," Father Juan said. "Holgar has confided in me that Eriko suffered terribly from the toll the elixir took on her body. No Hunter had ever mentioned the pain before."

"No one had lived as long, no doubt," Jamie said.

Holgar grunted.

"So the 'boost' will fade after a few weeks, and your bodies will gradually return to normal."

Father Juan could see Holgar nod almost imperceptibly. He was glad Holgar had come to him about Eriko's terrible condition. Holgar was sure that the side effects had been slowly killing Eriko.

Father Juan nodded to Noah, and he moved to join him.

"Pray, meditate, prepare yourselves. The elixir will be yours tonight," Father Juan instructed.

Jamie sank to his knees and crossed himself. Skye closed her eyes and began to chant softly. Holgar took off his shoes and shirt, preparing to be at his swiftest. Jenn just stood, looking lost, and Father Juan's heart bled for her.

But there was nothing more he could do for her.

Father Juan parted a curtain and led Noah into a small antechamber, where Esther waited for them. He had set up a small altar on which the ingredients that they had secured at such trouble waited.

"You're sure?" Esther asked him.

"I'm sure," Father Juan replied. He turned to Noah. "It's time."

CHAPTER SEVENTEEN

The end of all is come
Our hearts you will not tame
The past is gone far away
And now comes the final game
Don't think that you have won
Just because we're still
For what we cannot have
We will, most surely, kill

LOS ANGELES
SOLOMON

"Last-ditch effort," Solomon announced as he whipped out his cell phone. Katalin was seated at a new table behind him, staring into her crystal ball. Tears and sweat dripped down her face. He'd pressured her for answers, and so far all she had come up with was more predictions about his demise. "I've sent a fleet of planes to Romania loaded with vampires, monsters, and crack-shot soldiers."

She said nothing, just kept staring.

"So I figure if . . . *he* . . . will listen to reason, I can switch sides with one phone call. I mean, does he even *know* about the virus? I can be useful to him," Solomon went on.

He finished dialing, and the phone on the other end rang. A connection was made.

"Hello," a breathy woman's voice answered. It sounded familiar.

"Jennifer?" he asked, surprised. "Jennifer Leitner?"

His query was answered with a hiss.

"Solomon, I'm here," Lucifer said into the phone. Just hearing his voice made Solomon quake.

"Listen. I had a terrible lapse in judgment when I announced our existence to the human race," Solomon said. "I didn't think."

Silence.

"I should have checked in with you first," Solomon continued. "But I—I didn't know you were real."

More silence.

"So, listen, I'm sending soldiers in a show of support."

"Support," Lucifer echoed.

Katalin made a strangled sound and pushed back from the table.

"The final battle," Solomon said. "It's happening, right?"

Silence. Lucifer was making it very clear that he didn't have to interact with Solomon if he didn't feel like it. They weren't equals.

"Look, with me at your side, you've got the entire Vampire Nation at your command. I know things that could help you. You know, like about the virus?"

"Virus?" Lucifer said. "What—"

Then Katalin grabbed her crystal ball, raced across the room, and smashed it over Solomon's head. He was shocked; before he could react, she reached into the folds of her dress, pulled out a piece of the table he'd broken earlier, and rammed it into his chest. Or tried to. Her lips pulled back from her teeth in a feral roar as she threw herself against his chest again.

Solomon gave thanks for his Kevlar vest and lunged at her, fangs extended, sinking them into her neck.

His face burned as if she had lit it on fire. *Holy water.* He recoiled, taking half her neck with him. The holy water splashed into his eyes, blinding him for the moment. And suddenly he hurt *everywhere*. What was she doing to him?

"Dantalion, stop her!" Lucifer bellowed through the phone.

He was burning up. His skin was blazing away, turning black, disintegrating. He dropped the phone as the holy water melted muscle, then bone. The pain—

CASTLE BRAN
LUCIFER, DANTALION, HEATHER, AND ANTONIO

"I'm sorry, Lucifer," Dantalion said as he, Lucifer, and Heather headed for the dungeon. They wound down the circular stone staircase, Heather attired in another of Aurora's beautiful gowns. She had just found a very interesting book in Aurora's room, and she held it against her chest. "I couldn't stop the little Gypsy from killing him in time. At least now we know the new magicks work."

"I should never have agreed to let you send her to him. So far your mesmerism has caused us nothing but headaches," Lucifer said. "She wasn't even useful as a spy. He kept so much from her."

"At least he's dead," Dantalion said. "Our greatest enemy is gone."

Lucifer stopped and glared up at Dantalion. "You're much stupider than I was afraid of."

Kill Dantalion, Heather thought. *Kill him now.* Like Aurora, her predecessor, she didn't like him and trusted him less.

Lucifer glanced past Dantalion toward her, as if he could read her mind. She smiled at him.

"Don't ever answer my phone again, or I will kill you," he said to her.

"Okay, no problem," she replied, unfazed. She had

never met Solomon, and the temptation to talk to him had been too great to pass up. Of course, she had seen Solomon on TV for years, ever since he'd announced that vampires were real and he was their leader. She'd begged Jenn to take her to Spain so she could hunt the Cursed Ones too. Stupid Daddy, who had made a pact with Aurora that if he gave her Jenn, the vampire queen would leave the rest of his family alone.

My dad is stupider than Dantalion. Still she supposed she should be grateful for his treachery. She was here because of him. And Aurora was dust because of her.

Lucifer led the way into the dungeon, sweeping past Dantalion's latest batch of supersoldiers in various stages of creation.

The creatures were still decomposing at an alarming rate. Dantalion's outbuilding laboratory reeked of putrid hybrids, the stench so horrible that Dantalion had stopped using it. Dantalion was trying to slow the rate of spoilage by immersing the creatures in various chemical baths or injecting them with preservatives and vitamins. When she had asked Lucifer why they still bothered with the experiments, he'd told her that he hadn't lived so long by ignoring the future.

As the three passed, one particularly gruesome nightmare raised its head from a tank and said, "Lovely."

Heather faltered. It was her monster.

Doesn't matter. He served his purpose, she thought.

"Antonio, do you know anything about a virus?" Lucifer asked, as he opened the slot in the center of the door of Antonio de la Cruz's cell.

Antonio was manacled to the wall, sagging from his wrists. His head hung down against his chest. Dim light played on the crown of his matted hair. There was blood everywhere. His shirt was in tatters, and his jeans barely covered him. His feet were bare.

"Virus," Lucifer said, from the safe distance of the doorway. "Come on, Antonio. What do you know?"

The vampire didn't respond. Lucifer turned to Heather. "Maybe you should throw the book at him."

"Maybe I should torture him with my new magicks," Dantalion offered.

"Or I should," Heather said.

Antonio jerked. Then he slowly raised his head. His eyes blazed scarlet.

"Heather," he whispered. *"Ay, no."*

Lucifer looked from Antonio to Heather. Then he grabbed Heather and yanked her across his chest. He slipped his free hand around her neck and squeezed.

"Of course you care for her," Lucifer said. "The sister of Jenn Leitner; the vampire you were trying to save. Tell me about the virus or I'll rip off her head."

Heather was curious to see what Antonio would do. Curious, but unafraid. Lucifer was crazy about her. And if she died, she died. She had killed Aurora; she'd had her vengeance. Anything that came after was . . . a bonus.

Antonio's face was a portrait in agony, cut and burned, his expression frantic as he shook his head.

"Don't, Lucifer. The answer is simple. Solomon has a spy in Project Crusade. The black crosses let the spy think there's a virus that can wipe out our kind. But it's a lie."

"*You're* lying," Lucifer said, tightening his grip on Heather's neck. It was a good thing she didn't have to breathe. But she whimpered for Antonio's benefit, and raised up on her tiptoes.

"There was a scientist, Michael Sherman. He was working on the virus before he was converted," Antonio said.

"He's a vampire?" Lucifer said.

"*Sí*. After his conversion, the black crosses took him prisoner and locked him up. They tried to force him to resume working on it, but they finally realized he can't get it to work. They're pretending that it was successful to throw Solomon off. That's all I know," Antonio said, looking anxiously at Heather. "I swear it."

"Do you swear in the name of your God?" Lucifer asked.

"Yes, in the name of Christ, I do," Antonio said, staring at Heather as if she were drowning and he wanted to jump in to save her.

"Hmm," Lucifer said. "All right." He let go of Heather. Then he took the book from her. "Sergio's Book of Spells." He showed it to Antonio. "Did your sire share his magick use with you? I suppose he did. We've come a long way since 1942."

"We should kill him," Heather said.

"We will," Lucifer replied. "Just not right now."

As Dantalion reached the landing to the dungeon stairs, Rasputin, his Russian wolfhound, greeted him with slathering kisses. Rasputin's eyes glowed brilliant red, and his vampiric canine teeth were a sight to behold.

Dantalion gave him a few pats, then took in the sight of the gathering of Lucifer's thirteen vampiric sorcerers. They'd done a wonderful job creating the magickal potion that had burned Solomon to death. It had been a simple matter to slip it to Katalin. Solomon's organization wasn't as secure as that arrogant vampire liked to imagine.

The great hall was still decorated from the welcoming celebration, except that heavy black curtains shielded the vampires from the daylight. And the cages containing their human captives sat empty. *Eat the rich,* wasn't that what they used to say? The rich were often a bit stringy. So were the famous.

Surrounded by tall black tapers in golden candleholders, the sorcerers stood in a ring. Their robes were black, decorated with red bats, beautifully setting off their eyes, which weren't the normal glowing rubies of bloodlust but deep, shiny black. Enormous ebony leather books with maroon bindings sat on ornate golden stands before the vampires, and in the center of the room they had erected a primitive-looking stone altar. Gagged with a black silk scarf and swathed in a matching robe, a familiar-looking human girl was bound to it.

"Hey, Flavia," Lucifer's new companion, Heather Leitner, trilled, as if delighted to see someone she knew about to serve as a human sacrifice. "We should sacrifice Antonio, too," Heather said to Lucifer.

"I would still like to study him," Dantalion said.

"I'm not convinced he's told us everything he knows about this virus," Lucifer countered.

As Lucifer surveyed the circle of sorcerers, they bowed low. Black energy ticked off them like static electricity

"My lord Lucifer," said the chief sorcerer, a tall, gaunt vampire distinguished by a black diadem decorated with ruby bats.

"Have you heard about a virus created to harm us?" Lucifer asked.

The vampiric sorcerer consulted his fellows. Everyone shook their heads. "Nothing, my lord."

"Hmm." He approached the sacrifice and smiled down on her. "Heather, I hope you don't mind the loss of Aurora's maid. I thought it prudent to get rid of anyone who might still be loyal to her."

"You're so thoughtful," Heather simpered.

"We've confirmed the auguries," the head sorcerer said. "Tonight. Midnight would be auspicious."

"No," Lucifer said. "There's a time that's even more auspicious." He clapped his hands, and the wolfhound trotted over to him. He smiled at Dantalion, who smiled back. "Now, perform your ritual quickly. I have a race to wipe out."

THE MONASTERY OF THE BROTHERHOOD OF ST. ANDREW
FATHER JUAN, ESTHER, AND NOAH

Into the already fermenting elixir Father Juan added cloves and cinnamon. Next, holy water. Saint John's wort, aptly named. Shepherds' Club. Rosemary and tarragon. Oak and rowan leaves. Ginkgo biloba. Passionflower. A dozen other herbs. Then another dozen. And then the special ones: the Tears of Christ. The Transit of Venus.

He put them all in the simple wooden communion cup he had taken from the chapel. It was consecrated, holy. Into the mixture he dipped a ritual boline—a White-magick knife used for collecting herbs—then passed it through a white candle flame six times.

As he did so, he uttered the incantation that in Father Juan's tradition had to be spoken by a Catholic priest: "Greater love hath no man than that he lay his life down for his friends.'"

He said it first in Latin, for God. Then in Spanish, for himself. Then in Hebrew, for Noah. Then in English, for Esther.

Then he laid the knife across the top of the cup.

"And now for the last," he said, his voice shaky to his ears.

"Are you sure about this?" Esther asked.

He nodded. "I can't ask any of the brothers here to do it. It must be a priest, one who has set himself up as a conduit between God and man, and a priest who gives himself willingly. For generations the priests of Salamanca have been willingly making the sacrifice without the Hunter ever knowing. Father Pedro gave his life for Eriko's elixir. It is right and fitting that I should give mine for the others."

Esther looked at him with misty eyes and laid a warm hand on his arm. "We'll miss you, Padre."

"I hope so," he said, feeling a bit wistful. They could only miss him if he were well and truly dead.

He turned and began praying over the concoction. He couldn't do the deed himself, as suicide was forbidden by the Church. In the end he had been the one to kill Father Pedro.

And now Noah would kill him.

Finished, he took a deep breath. "Now," he whispered.

Noah put his hand over Father Juan's mouth and held his nose. Father Juan knew that he would fight for air. He remembered his part in the ritual: to know that his body's struggles to breathe were only birth pangs as he slid from this plane of existence into the next, fighting like a newborn for the first gasp of life. The next breath he took would be from God's mouth, in Heaven.

Still, the instinct to save himself was overwhelming, as it had been for Pedro. Death throes overtook him. He struggled, but all life was struggle.

Oh, my soul, take flight, and repair the world.

He could see the golden glow of his soul radiating out, entering the cup; he could see the elixir bubble and gleam. Through the steam he could see the room bathed in gold. See the faces of Noah and Esther, gleaming like saints.

Into Thy hands I commend my spirit.

And then he saw nothing.

Noah caught the dead priest in his arms. He gazed down with pity at the man, then carried him to a pallet made with fresh white linen. Noah laid him down.

Esther took a steadying breath. She locked eyes with Noah and nodded. Father Juan's choice of "deliverer" had been one of the two of them, and she was grateful that Noah had volunteered for the duty. She would never have been able to do it.

"Rest in peace at last, Saint John of the Cross," she said, bending down and kissing Father Juan's forehead.

On the eve of his death he had finally admitted the truth to her, though she had guessed it long before. Esther knew it had brought him some comfort, knowing that there was another who shared his secret and who would mourn for him as he really was.

Holding the cup, Esther walked back into the main room with Noah trailing behind her. The others looked up, then past them, clearly expecting Father Juan to be rejoining them.

"Where's Father Juan?" Jenn asked.

"He's gone into seclusion to pray for victory," Esther said. By agreement she and Noah weren't going to speak of his death until they could no longer stave off questions.

She handed the cup to Jenn. Jenn was the leader; it was right that she went first.

Her granddaughter took the cup with a steady hand.

"Only a small sip. There has to be enough for everybody," Esther reminded her.

Jenn nodded and raised the cup to her lips. Then she handed it to Holgar.

Before the werewolf could drink, Jenn went crashing to her knees with an anguished cry. The others jerked in alarm, but Esther put a hand on her head.

"It's all right. The pain will pass in a moment."

Jenn nodded, though she didn't say anything.

Holgar gave her one last look before taking his own swallow. He barely had time to hand the cup to Jamie before a howl was ripped from his throat. His back arched, and for a moment it was as though Esther could watch liquid fire tracing all the veins in his arms and chest.

Jamie didn't look, just turned deathly pale, swallowed, and shoved the cup at Skye, who barely had time to catch it before he, too, was on the ground screaming. Skye drank quickly as though she would back out if she gave herself time to think.

As she passed the cup to Noah, Skye's features twisted. "What else did he put in—"

Cut off by a strangled gasp she bent over, making retching sounds.

Noah held the cup for a moment, his lips moving in silent prayer. He drank and also began to scream.

Jenn staggered to her feet and grabbed the cup from his hand just as it was slipping to the floor. She glanced inside and then at Esther. "There's enough left for you," she said.

Esther smiled at her granddaughter and shook her head. "No, Father Juan meant this for the hunters of Salamanca, and I am not one."

"Then what should we do with it?" Jenn asked.

Esther produced a small vial and poured the rest of the thick, black mixture into it. She capped it tight and handed it back to Jenn. "Give it to the last Salamancan when you find him."

Jenn's eyes grew enormous, but she didn't argue. She took the vial and tucked it into a pocket in her jacket.

Esther surveyed the others as they slowly recovered. Holgar was the first to take advantage of his new abilities, crossing the room in the blink of an eye.

"It works," he said, as everyone swiveled to look at him.

"Excellent," Esther said.

"And I hear planes. They're descending," Skye said. "They must be from Solomon."

"Or Kent," Jamie said. "Still daylight out. Vampires need to stay inside. We've still got that one on the Cursers."

"Then you should go meet them," Esther said, feeling like a real freedom fighter for the first time in years. "Plan your attack."

"Are you coming, Gramma?" Jenn asked.

"In a minute," Esther replied.

Excited, eager, Holgar grabbed Skye's hand. The two flashed past Esther, and Jenn launched herself after them. After a moment's hesitation Noah and Jamie barreled out of the room, moving so fast they became blurs.

Esther braced herself, a hand against the wall, the façade she had held in place crumbling.

In her heart she felt that they were all going to die.

Her cell phone rang. The caller was blocked. Not a lot of people had her number, and there was a reason for that — they were at war, and she was off the grid. She took the call anyway.

"Esther? It's Greg."

She blinked. She'd half assumed that Noah had killed him when he'd infiltrated the lab. A rush of happiness was tempered by her instinctive caution.

"Tell me about the virus," she said as calmly as possible.

There was a pause. "I wanted to tell you, Esther, that

all those years you thought I was hunting you and Che . . ." He trailed off.

"The virus, Greg."

"I was protecting you. If I was keeping tabs on you, I knew no one else would."

Esther smiled faintly. She'd had no idea. "A fellow revolutionary?"

"I wouldn't go that far." He added, "Gotta go now."

"Why did you call me?" she asked.

The phone went dead.

Transylvania
The Allied Forces

Dozens of sheep from the nearby pasture swarmed around Jenn and Noah as they dismounted from their snowmobiles. Jenn was wearing full battle gear—a black catsuit, a vest, and her Salamanca jacket. Her boots were strapped up to her knees. Velcro pockets held crosses, holy water, garlic, and ammo. Noah wore olive-green fatigues and a vest like hers, but with the Star of David emblazoned on it. As the resistance fighters had arrived, they had brought weapons and clothing for the Salamancans. They had a well-stocked armory now.

Much later, a military transport plane taxied in the large sheep pasture; three more hovered in the air, waiting their turns. The silhouettes of choppers half a kilometer distant disgorged armed soldiers and hulking hybrids into the chilly sunshine. A few snowflakes drifted down over the scene.

Special-forces units from around the world had also arrived and put themselves under Noah's command. Mossad members mingled with what was left of American Ranger and SEAL units, most of which had gone underground when America had surrendered to the Cursed Ones.

Jamie had gone to round up his street fighters, and Skye was gathering the witches. Holgar was meeting up with Viorica and her werewolves.

Together all these "special troops" would make an amazing army.

"Solomon's Cursed Ones must be holed up inside the planes, waiting for dark," Noah said.

Jenn took a deep breath. "I hope it doesn't start to snow. The vampires in San Francisco could move in the fog."

Noah gave her hand a squeeze. "Nothing will stop us."

She squeezed back. "We're the heart of the battle, but it's going to be happening all over the world."

"When this is over, one of the things at the top of my list is to meet Kent Wallace," Noah said. "Without the Voice of the Resistance, we'd still be one group in a sea of apathy."

"Agreed," she said. "We owe him."

"Ready to review the troops?" Noah asked her.

She nodded, still unable to believe that she, Jenn Leitner, was the commander in chief of their ground forces. Noah let go of her hand, and together they began to walk toward the soldiers, who were already assembling into neat rows for her inspection. Monstrous hybrids loped up behind them.

Another plane landed with a roar.

And another.

Then Jenn spotted Jamie emerging from the trees. He held the hand of a very small girl dressed in camouflage, her hair in pigtails. Together they were leading a throng of about forty people, all brandishing Uzis and rocket launchers.

From the opposite side of the clearing at least sixty witches appeared with Skye. They wore camouflage as well, and carried weaponry. Many of them wore crowns of evergreens. Skye wore a sort of crown decorated with shards of mirrors on her head.

"I wonder what that's about," Noah said. "Something magick?"

"Yes, she told me about it," Jenn said. "They're going to cast spells so that if the vampires look into the mirrors they will get disoriented. She said she got the idea from something Estefan did."

Noah nodded appreciatively. He looked up at the sky, watching the light snowfall. "I can still see the sun very well. Remind everyone that even though the vampires can't come out of the shadows, they can still shoot weapons and use their hybrids and werewolf forces."

Then he put a hand on Jenn's forearm and pointed. "Look."

About four dozen men and women, most of them young,

marched behind an older man holding a bishop's crook. Though they were dressed like soldiers, each bore the original Crusader's cross across their chest—over a shield of white a black cross, with each of the four arms the same length. At the end of each, a smaller line lay perpendicular. They were chanting, their voices rising and falling. As they neared the throng of witches, the witches began to cheer. Then a few broke out into the same chant.

"Familiar?" Noah asked her.

Jenn shook her head. "Maybe it's some religious thing." She peered at the men. "I recognize that man. He's Bishop Diego. He is friends with Father Juan."

"It's nice that the Catholics and the witches have something in common. Shared faith," he said. Then Noah smiled at her. "My faith's in us."

She wasn't sure which "us" he was referring to, but she smiled up at him. Then his smile faded, and he put both his hands on her shoulders.

"We're going to live through this," he said. "Go tell them that."

Jenn spent the next half hour conferring with the leader of each of her armies. Though she was unused to strategizing on a large scale, she quickly determined that their assault was actually made up of a number of missions that would be conducted by each group—what she had taken to calling her "squadrons." Once she and the other leaders—her Joint Chiefs—

had decided on a plan of action, each chief took their mission back to their squadron and briefed them. It took far less time to plan the attack than she would have believed possible.

"This is worth dying for," Jenn said through the portable microphone that one of Gramma Esther's freedom fighters had brought from Montana. A dozen of them had flown in on a private plane.

Jenn was disappointed to see that Father Juan had stayed away. But he'd probably known that the priests and nuns were coming so he could devote his attention elsewhere. They were deeply religious people that Bishop Diego had met in Rome, and all of them were willing to put their lives on the line for the sake of humanity—including a half-crazy, Uzi-packing nun named Sister Toni.

About fifty of the Pamplonans Jenn and company had saved from the Cursed Ones' bullfight massacre had also arrived, and since they lacked a leader, Jenn had put Kenji Sakamoto in charge of them. Everyone was accounted for.

And everyone was ready.

"On my signal we'll march out and attack Castle Bran. We have the element of surprise and the advantage of daylight if we move fast."

She looked over at Solomon's vast army: at least two hundred strong, each wearing the symbol of the Vampire Nation—a heart clutched in the talons of a bat. Jenn wondered why she hadn't heard from him personally. Given who he was, Jenn wouldn't have been surprised if he'd been assassinated. She couldn't find it in her heart to hope he was all right—except that she wasn't sure what his troops would do if they found out their leader was gone.

They began to march; Jenn would hitch a ride in the monastery's SUV this time so she could stay at the head of the charge. Father Wadim was driving, and when she opened the door, she saw two passengers in the back seat—her mother and her father. They weren't holding hands, but they were sitting close together. And both of them looked at her with pleading expressions.

"What's *he* doing here?" Jenn asked coldly.

Father Wadim handed Jenn a note. She read it quickly.

Dear Jenn,

My coven—the People's Coven—believe we have succeeded in lifting the mesmerism from your father. We are as sure as we can be. I'm sorry to spring this on you before the big battle, but there might not be another time for him and you. It will take a miracle of good-heartedness on your part to forgive him, but we need that miracle, Jenn. Even though we have sworn to kill our enemies, my coven's magicks are still based in love. The more you can open your heart to love, the better it will be for us. Lives may be saved if you can find a way to stop hating him. Please remember that.

The Goddess protect you from all harm.

With love,

Skye, High Priestess, the People's Coven

Jenn put the letter down on the seat. Her hands shook, and she had to contain her anger. Maybe Skye wasn't trying to manipulate her into a reconciliation, but it felt that way. Her "open" heart was an icy, closed fist in her chest. She felt as though she didn't even have a pulse.

Still, she said to Father Wadim, "I'll ride in the back with them."

Her mother and father moved to give her room. She wanted to sit as far away from her father as possible, but given no choice, she sat down beside him. It took an act of will not to vomit . . . or beat him to a pulp.

"Jenn," Paul Leitner said, as Father Wadim began to drive. "There is absolutely nothing I can say in my defense."

You're right, she thought.

Jenn didn't trust herself to speak, so she remained silent. Her fury was directed at her mother, for always wanting to believe in him, wanting her to mount rescue missions for him . . . sacrifice the lives of good people for him.

"He tried to tell you to stay away from Solomon," her mother reminded her. "With his Morse code. If Solomon had realized, he would have tortured your father to death."

Too bad he didn't.

Then she thought of Skye's letter. White magick was based in love. It wasn't fair to ask her to love him. But what about the last three years—the last seven, since Solomon had appeared on TV for the first time—what had been fair in any of that?

But we make choices, she thought. *And he made bad ones. Evil ones.*

"I don't know what to say to you," she said finally, as the vehicle trundled through the forest, bouncing along in the snow.

"Oh, Jenn," he said softly. He looked over at Jenn's mom.

"It's more than he hoped for," Leslie Leitner said, looking around him at Jenn. "It's a start."

No. I don't want it to be a start. I want it to be finished, she thought. But almost as if Father Juan were sitting beside her, she heard his voice: *By your wanting it finished, it is far from over.*

She looked at her mother. "I want you to stay out of the battle," she said. "Both of you." She lowered her head so no one would see her eyes welling with tears. She was so mad at Skye for pulling that.

"We want to help," her mother said.

"You can pray." She half-turned her head toward Father Wadim. "Please stop the vehicle.

Father Wadim complied. Jenn got out and held open the door. "Get out."

Her parents slid out of the vehicle and up to their shins in snow. They looked bewildered. Jenn dug in one of her Velcro pockets and pulled out two plastic crosses, standard issue for the hunters of Salamanca.

"Start praying," Jenn said, and climbed in the front seat

with Father Wadim. "Go," she told the priest. She didn't look back as the vehicle continued to roll through the forest. Then Father Wadim murmured something under his breath, and Jenn glanced over at him.

"It's good that they're praying," he said.

In the distance the stones of Castle Bran gleamed in the sunlight.

And, with glowing red eyes and glistening fangs, dozens of vampires streamed out of it.

Charging straight for Jenn and the others.

CHAPTER EIGHTEEN

In the beginning times, we shall walk in the light, as we were intended. And then we shall know that the gods of our childhood have fallen away, and Lucifer, the Morning Star, shall lead us into our promised land. And our days shall be as long as our nights, and filled to overflowing with blood.
　　　　　—from the prophesies of Malachi del Muerto,
　　　　　　　　　　　　　　　　　　vampire mystic

CASTLE BRAN
THE ALLIES AND THEIR ENEMIES

Vampires swarmed through the daylight toward Jenn's SUV. Hybrids flanked the enemy Cursed Ones, portions of their faces and bodies bursting into flame as they hit the daylight. Humans brought up the rear, and as Jenn picked up her field radio to warn her troops, Father Wadim shouted, "Rocket launcher!"

He flung himself from the driver's side of the SUV as Jenn pushed open the passenger door and sprang out. She jumped farther than she would have expected. *The elixir,* she realized.

As she executed a forward roll, she covered her head with her hands, still clutching the radio. Behind her a deafening explosion shook the ground. Rocks, shrapnel, and massive amounts of snow from overhanging tree limbs rained down on her, covering her. She rolled over on her stomach and drew her legs up as fast as she could, to create an air pocket. She couldn't hear anything, and she thought blood might be pouring from her ears. She was enveloped in agonizing silence. She waited a second, expecting the elixir to heal her. But nothing happened.

Depressing the mic function on her radio, she said, "Cursed Ones on the move. In full daylight! Repeat, Cursed Ones on the battlefield!"

She couldn't hear a word she spoke. She thought she felt a vibration in the unit—maybe someone confirming the message—but she couldn't be sure.

I'm cut off, she thought. *I'm in command and I can't hear my people.*

Trying to catch her breath, she depressed the speech function again. "My eardrums are blown," she said. Or hoped she said. "I can't hear anything. I need a healing spell."

The ground around her shook, harder this time. Another explosion? Firmly grasping the radio, she pushed forward, then dug her elbows into the snow as she pushed. Her new-found strength saved her again as the momentum broke the crust on the dome of snow and she scrabbled to her feet. To her left, a tree promised a modicum of protection while she got her bearings. She raced over to it, then sped around it, flattening herself against the trunk

A human soldier wearing Solomon's symbol—a bat clutching a human heart—appeared at her side. She turned to him, nearly smacking into his Uzi, realizing at the same moment that she'd left her submachine gun in the SUV. So her primary weapon was gone. At least she had the elixir. As she faced him, she felt the zing of bullets coming at them both. He opened his mouth and said something, but she couldn't hear him. She grabbed him and pushed him to the ground, landing on top of him, shielding him from the gunfire. His Uzi pressed against her rib cage. At the same time, she drew a knife from her jacket and held it against his neck. She wasn't taking any chances one-on-one with Solomon's people.

He spoke again. She shook her head and pointed to her ear with her free hand. He nodded. They stayed in that position until his back arched and his eyes widened. Some-one was behind them.

Since she couldn't hear anything, she had to trust that he wasn't faking her out. She rolled onto her back and angled her knife upward. A hulking monster loomed over them, staggering forward as parts of its vampiric face burned away. Werewolf claws slashed at Jenn and Solomon's soldier as they both scooted out of direct range. The soldier grabbed his submachine gun and fired off a barrage. The creature staggered backward, then fell, hard. More pieces of it burst into flame. It began to writhe.

The soldier gestured to Jenn, then to himself. She didn't know how to read lips. Staring at him, she depressed the speaker on her radio and said, "I need a healing spell now."

The soldier took the radio and spoke into it too. Then he paused. She could tell he was listening to an answer. He handed it back to her and nodded at her. Then he pointed to himself, then to her, then up.

She stared at him, perplexed. He did it again. Pointing to . . .

"The sun," she said, though she couldn't hear the words.

He jabbed upward again.

"The sky," she said. He nodded more emphatically. "*Skye.* You'll take me to Skye."

He gave her a thumbs-up. Then he took her hand. She nodded, and she half dragged him behind her as she charged toward her squadrons. She flashed past monsters and vampires as the Allies raced up the incline, brandishing weapons.

Viorica's werewolves raced toward Jenn and her escort.

Their heads were thrown back, but she couldn't hear their howls. She didn't see Holgar among them, but smiled in grim satisfaction as two of the werewolves took down a Cursed One and flung him to the ground. The larger of the two ripped out his throat. He burst into flames and then turned into dust.

So they might be able to walk in sunlight, but they can still be killed, she thought. That was excellent news.

Then, with keen, telescoping vision, she saw the witches and the Catholics charging the castle together. The witches waved their hands and moved their lips—casting spells, Jenn guessed—while three Catholic priests took on what appeared to be two human soldiers in hand-to-hand combat. Sister Toni, the nun, was hitting one of the enemy over the head with her Uzi.

Skye broke from the center of the throng. Dodging more of Lucifer's troops—a blur of monsters and humans— Skye grabbed Jenn's hands and together they shot toward a section of the courtyard wall. The two crouched down, and Skye trailed her hands a few inches from Jenn's body in a series of downward motions. Jenn felt warmth, and thought she smelled roses.

Then Skye mouthed, *Close your eyes.* Jenn understood her, and as she did as she was told, Skye placed her hands over Jenn's ears. Jenn hadn't realized before how much they hurt, and she grunted—or thought she did. Jenn thought she heard whispering coming from inside her head, and an image of Father Juan popped into her mind. Her lids fluttered, and Skye pressed her hands more tightly over Jenn's ears.

She became dizzy, and her thighs hurt from crouching for so long. Or was that a symptom of the elixir? Still with her eyes closed, holding the radio, she gripped Skye's shoulders for balance. Anxiety coursed through her at the amount of time it was taking — and at knowing that each spell Skye cast called on her reserves. Did the elixir enhance magickal strength as well? Jenn let go of her and tried to shake her head to tell her to stop. But Skye held her fast.

"We need you, Jenn," Skye said.

"I can hear you," Jenn announced. She spoke into her radio. "Crusader One here. I'm back in the game." To Skye she said, "Thanks."

Skye leaned forward, kissed her cheek, and ran back into the battle. Jenn looked up at the castle windows, wondering where Lucifer, Dantalion, and Aurora were.

And Antonio, she thought. *Antonio, please be okay.*

Then she pushed him from her mind and got to work.

The day marched on, and Lucifer's side was steadily wearing down the good guys. Jamie wondered what would happen when the sun set. Things would get worse, of that he was certain. After the initial shock of seeing vampires out in daylight, Jamie had realized that not that many Cursed Ones had actually come out of the castle. Lucifer had to have more fighters than that. It stood to reason that not all of them could handle the sunshine, or they'd be out there now. So this was just the first wave of the enemy. There'd be more later. *And so many of us will get killed.*

Sure and he was livid with the Italians who had shown up with little Sofia, his and Eri's guide into the crumbling Venetian palazzo where they were supposed to meet up with a local resistance cell. Aurora had gotten there first, killed the freedom fighters, and left a note ordering Salamanca to give up Antonio or she'd do the same to them. Now Aurora had Antonio back, and Jamie hoped they'd be very happy together.

In hell.

Jamie had been happy to see more fighters, but to bring a little girl along was cruelty and madness. If anything happened to her, some heads were going to roll—and they weren't going to be the heads of supersoldiers and suckers.

As the special forces troops and street fighters covered them with heavy fire, Jamie and Noah stealthily crept behind an outbuilding on the castle grounds that reeked of rot and death. Their side had commenced shelling the castle, and huge chunks of wood and stone provided excellent coverage as they crept toward the main structure. The two carried a brick of C-4 plastic explosive, detonators, and timers in packs on their backs.

They worked well together, him and the Israeli. As much as Jamie detested Jenn, Noah had a fancy for her.

For that reason, and that reason only, he hoped they wound up together. On the other hand, if she died, Noah could find someone better. That shouldn't be too hard.

Except . . . Jamie had to admit that Jenn had organized the Allies pretty damn well. He should have figured she was good for something—after all, he had originally stood up for her when Father Juan put her in charge—but he had to admit, he was still impressed.

A mortar slammed into the courtyard, sending up a curtain of debris, dirt, and dust—as well as murky water from a cistern. As one, Noah and Jamie raced toward a small arched door in the castle proper. Bad location for a door on a fortress. Jamie supposed it was a modern addition.

Jamie tried the latch, yanking it from the wall. He grinned at Noah, who smiled back. The elixir was proving to be everything he'd dreamed it would be.

It was pitch-dark, and Jamie heard no approaching footfalls, no weapon fire. Grunting, he let Noah take the lead, and he was surprised at how fast the Israeli hustled through the darkness. In no time at all, Jamie's eyes adjusted too. His hand brushed past bars and loose bits of chain. They were down in the bowels of the castle dungeon. They'd discussed the castle's structure. To do the most damage they would have to go up a few floors, to dead center. Blow up its heart.

Gladly.

After a while, Noah slowed. A small light shone ahead,

and both men flattened themselves against the wall. Jamie was covered in sweat. He'd never felt so alive.

Noah muttered something that Jamie couldn't translate. Then he touched Jamie's shoulder, and they moved on.

A torch flickered in a rusty sconce. It cast a glow on a metal door. In the soft light, Noah looked at Jamie, who shrugged. If Noah thought they should check it out, fine with him.

They glided forward. Noah reached the door first and peered cautiously through the slat in the center of the door. He jerked, then moved away so Jamie could have a look.

Antonio was chained to the wall. He was covered with blood and appeared to be unconscious. If he were true dead, he'd be dust.

Jamie and Noah shared a look. Then Noah said, "I told her I wouldn't kill him. I didn't say I'd rescue him."

Jamie nodded, relieved. His thinking exactly. Liking the lad even more, he gave Noah the signal this time, and they moved on.

Jinx, one of Esther's friends from the old days, went down face-first into the mud and debris of one of the castle's exterior stairways. Esther hovered six steps above him, the vampire that had bitten him turning to dust on the end of her stake. Esther stared down at Jinx and experienced a brief flashback to the days when they were underground revolutionaries. It was 1968, the so-called Summer of Love, when Jinx had had the most magnificent Afro and Esther wore little piggy earrings, her comment on police officers. Now Jinx was bald and just too old to fight.

Bobby, another of Esther's friends from back in the day, knelt beside Jinx and turned him over. Jinx's eyes stared glassily at nothing.

Bobby closed Jinx's lids and climbed the stairs to Esther. They shared a brief hug. Esther's heart ached.

"Long live the revolution," Bobby said.

They moved on.

Kenji Sakamoto had discovered that while Japanese and Spanish shared the same pronunciation for most syllables, his troops from Pamplona had yet to realize that bellowing at him in their native tongue did no good. Still, by their pointing and shouting, he understood that something was behind him. Something bad.

So he pivoted with his *wakizashi* samurai sword at chest level, whirling around and slicing a hybrid through its leathery, fur-covered chest. The thing roared but didn't even stumble, so Kenji threw his weight on his front leg and pulled the sword back across its chest, as if he were rewinding his action. The razor-sharp blade tore through muscle, bone, and layers of cartilage as the creature's torso split in half. The upper half folded backward, and blood sprayed like a geyser.

Kenji's Pamplonans cheered, "*¡Olé! ¡Olé!*" and then got

back to the business of slaughtering everything in their path. When he'd first been put in charge of them, Kenji had been rather dismissive, assuming they were raw, untrained civilians who would get in his way. Unlike the Salamancans, the Japanese Hunter fought alone. But these men and women had grown up around bulls and bullfighting, and they quickly adapted many of those stylized moves to fighting the hybrids. Kenji's fighting style was unlike theirs; it consisted of long series of forms, or *kata*, that he employed in different combinations to achieve his end goal—slaughter.

They had planted their flag—so to speak—on the western side of the castle, and they'd been laboring for hours to take more ground. Though Kenji had seen other groups battling Cursed Ones, his team had been bombarded by hideous monsters as well as humans with wide, unfocused eyes who had been mesmerized into fighting for the enemy. Kenji killed both without mercy. His mission was clear: There were no innocent bystanders in the conflict. He felt absolutely no remorse at dealing death to those under the vampires' spell. His cause, his team, came first.

The Spaniard nearest him yelled and pointed as a hybrid leaped from a turret, falling like a bomb toward Kenji. Taking two steps back, Kenji held out his sword sharp side up, cutting the monster in two from crotch to chin.

"*¡Olé!*" his people called, and Kenji gestured for the entire group to move up one step on the stairway. One step at a time; that was how they would take the castle.

* * *

"Finally," Lucifer said. He'd put a collar around one of his hysterical vampire minions, pushed her through the black velvet curtains shielding Dantalion and his dog, Heather, and himself from the sunlight, waited ten seconds, and dragged her back in. She was intact. She hadn't been given the injection that protected their kind against the sunlight, and she hadn't burst into flames. Ergo, the sun had set.

On this night Lucifer was taking no chances.

He swept over to his bank of computers, manned by vampiric programmers, and studied the streaming images. All around the world, inspired by the so-called Voice of the Resistance, the humans were rising up and fighting the vampires. Some fought Solomon's vampires; others attacked Lucifer's "guests." In many places the humans were winning. Losses were inevitable. As long as the tide turned — and it would — he would win the war.

"What about the virus?" Heather asked anxiously.

"Oh, Heather, Heather, you have so little faith in me," he said.

Gesturing for her and Dantalion to follow him, he led them back down to the dungeon. He rapped softly on Antonio's door, then moved past it to another cell. Inside, a tall man hung from the wall in the same posture as Antonio. His eyes were swollen shut, and his jaw was broken. He was human.

"Heather, Dantalion, meet Greg Bassingwaite, the leader of Project Crusade. Which is no more," Lucifer added. "Right, Greg?"

Greg's chest rose and fell, but he remained silent.

"A team—*my* team—swept into their 'secret lab'"—Lucifer made air quotes—"and investigated. It was just as Antonio said. The virus doesn't work."

"When did you know? How?" Heather asked excitedly

"We took over the lab and spent nights analyzing it. And then we put Dr. Michael Sherman in a special vacuum chamber and opened a vial of it in there with him." Lucifer tsk-tsked. "Nothing happened to him."

Heather clapped her hands. "Good!"

Lucifer glared at Greg. "Then my entire team was exposed to it, and no one so much as sneezed." He grabbed Greg's head and smacked it against the wall. "I don't know how you fooled Solomon into thinking the virus was an actual threat, but I congratulate you."

"Huge . . . risk," Greg said through swollen gums.

"A huge risk for you? Yes. And for me, opening the genie's bottle? Yes. But as I say, we analyzed it first. Thoroughly." He gestured to Dantalion. "Of course, my own vampire scientist took part."

"There's no way it would have ever worked," Dantalion asserted. "Sherman was deluded."

"No," a voice said brokenly from a third cell.

"*Sí,*" Lucifer insisted. He steered the party out of

the human's cell and opened the door to the third. There Dr. Michael Sherman was chained, not to the wall but spread-eagled on the floor. He, too, had been horribly beaten.

"This is how we'll stake you out tomorrow," Lucifer said. "After all the humans are dead. *You* won't get the injection that lets you walk in sunlight."

"I still wish you'd let me study his blood," Dantalion said. "To see how he could do that. How he could help them. I could compare it with Antonio's blood, see if the traitors share anything in common."

"It was never about helping them," Sherman whispered.

Lucifer kicked him in the side. Then he gestured for his entourage to leave.

They swept back upstairs into the great hall, where the choicest Allied prisoners of war had been thrown into cages for the vampiric elite to dine on as they stood on the balconies of Castle Bran and watched humanity die. Some of his elegantly dressed guests were sampling American soldiers and Israeli Mossad troops. Others savored the gamey blood of a captive werewolf.

"It's time," Lucifer said to Dantalion.

With Heather at his side, Lucifer watched Dantalion walk toward the balcony where vampires in gowns, military regalia, and tuxedos were observing the battle. Uneasy smiles greeted him, and the vampires parted, making way for him. The Russian vampire's reputation preceded him.

Dantalion moved regally to the front of the balcony and placed his hands on the railing. His dog joined him. Then Dantalion leaned over.

"Do it," Lucifer murmured.

"Do what?" Heather asked curiously.

At the upper entrance to the castle, Skye was shaking. She, Lune, and Soleil had just killed a Cursed One exactly as they had murdered Estefan, by forcing the blood to stream out of his body. The vampire had screamed as he bled. Then he had exploded into dust. She hadn't expected their spell to work on a vampire. She remembered how Estefan had bent over her as if he was going to bite her — the way a vampire would. What had he become? Were there more of them inside the castle?

Something was changing in the magickal fabric around them. Not only was there less white Magick, but Skye could feel black Magick shimmer in the night sky, and she shivered. The other witches sensed it too, hesitating in battle. The male witch Gordon looked over at her, just as an enemy werewolf lunged at him, knocking him down.

"Incendio!" Skye shouted, lobbing a fireball at the werewolf. With the elixir singing through her veins, it was bigger and moved faster than she had anticipated.

It found its target, and the wolf caught fire, screeching.

The animal transformed into a man, writhing in the snow. Skye fought her impulse to heal him, instead running to Gordon. His throat was missing, and his eyes gazed at nothing. She was too late.

"Oh, Goddess, no," Skye whispered.

Another werewolf growled on the wall above her, and she leaped to her feet as other witches converged on the creature, throwing fireballs, casting lightning bolts, sending pain its way. It showed its teeth and began to spring.

"Skye!" Holgar cried, racing up behind her with a black werewolf at his side. Skye recognized Viorica, the Transylvanian female pack leader, and she was seized with fear.

"Why are so many werewolves attacking us?" she demanded.

"They're rival packs loyal to Lucifer," Holgar said. The black werewolf was growling at the werewolf on the wall. Viorica looked over at Holgar, and he gestured to Skye. "She wants to know if you can help me change with magick." He sounded desperate, humiliated.

Then an explosion rocked the earth. The werewolf on the wall lost its balance and fell backward, plummeting down the craggy mountainside. A second explosion threw Skye to the ground. She watched as Holgar flattened beside her with a roar that seemed to shake the very earth beneath her feet. And there, inches from her, he began to transform.

"It's the elixir," he said as he began to howl.

Skye gasped as she watched it happen. It was the first time she'd seen him change, and he was magnificent. When at last he was in full wolf form, she heard herself cheer. He had done it! He had shifted on his own. And the devil help all those who stood in his way.

Evil seethed like miasma around Antonio. It didn't take witchly powers to know that upstairs Lucifer was unleashing something powerful and terrible. He thought of his teammates, and of Jenn, and yanked on his chains again. The tortures inflicted by Aurora had been nothing compared to what Lucifer had done to him—with one important difference: Lucifer had not tricked him with magicks to drain humans. He was still good, still in command of himself.

He pulled and yanked, lifting his feet off the ground in order to put more stress on the manacles around his wrists. The metal cut into his flesh, and he hissed in frustration. He was a vampire, endowed with superior strength. But still the chains held him.

The evil, whatever magick it was that Lucifer was conjuring, was palpable. It seemed to rise like fog around his ankles, then his knees, then his thighs. Something was creeping up toward his mouth, and he knew that if it got inside him, he would be damned again—possibly forever. In a frenzy of horror he flailed and struggled.

And then the right manacle detached from its chain. With the handcuff still around his wrist he grabbed the chain attached to his left manacle and pulled down as hard as he could.

It, too, gave way.

Antonio was so weak that he fell to his knees. He pushed himself back up, lurching forward, then staggering to the cell door. He thought he would have to force it open, but a swift push against it and he was out.

A sense of doom wrapped around him like a shroud. He shivered, moving forward on his bare feet.

"Vampire," a voice called softly. It was the scientist Michael Sherman.

Antonio crossed to his cell door and peered through the slat. Sherman was in bad shape.

"I'm here," Antonio told him.

"It worked," Sherman said. Slowly he raised his head, and Antonio saw that they had pulled out his fangs. "My virus worked. My handler's in the next cell," he added.

Antonio moved to the third cell. A man he didn't recognize was staring at the door. He remembered the name Lucifer had spoken: Greg Bassingwaite. Was this the same Greg that Jenn had told him about?

"What's going on?" Antonio said.

"Setup," Greg slurred. "Project Crusade."

Antonio opened the door. He grabbed the man around the torso and broke first one chain, then another. Hoisting the man over his shoulder, he left the cell. Then he opened Sherman's.

"No," Sherman said weakly. "I just want it to be over." He shook his head. "It *would* work. I ran so many tests." He looked up at Antonio. "I think they planned this. Project Crusade." He jerked his head at Greg. "Why move to Romania? Why so close to this castle? So Lucifer would find us. And he would think the virus didn't work."

Antonio cocked his head. What he was saying made sense.

"I think the Allies have the virus," Sherman concluded. "And I think they're going to release it tonight. Wipe us out."

Antonio listened hard. "Why wait?"

"There are two major parts to the virus. They have to be mixed together. I made a batch, but it wasn't perfect. But I figured out the exact specifications for each part. Then we moved to Romania. Maybe they had two different people smuggle out the components and they haven't brought them together yet."

"And you think they let Lucifer break into the lab?" Antonio had thought it was weird that Noah had been able to break in. Granted, he was Mossad, but if he, Antonio, had been creating the ultimate weapon, he would have made it nearly impossible to infiltrate his base of operations.

On Antonio's back, Greg groaned. "No. Looked promising. Didn't . . . work," he said. "Noah Geller . . ."

"They convinced you of that," Sherman said to them both. "Because if you got captured, you couldn't reveal the truth. They took my research and made the virus somewhere else. I just know they did. Because I was *right*."

"Come with us. You can help," Antonio insisted.

"Help?" Sherman's eyes glowed crimson. He hissed at Antonio. "I don't want to help. I want to die."

There was a loud boom, and the castle shook around them. Pieces of wood and stone cascaded from above, and Antonio ducked back into Greg's cell to protect him.

He heard screaming. Through all the hours being locked inside his cell, he had never heard anything like it. Lucifer was escalating the battle.

The castle shook again. This time Antonio didn't wait for the aftershocks to subside. He charged out of the cell and ran for all he was worth.

"Jenn," he said. "My Jenn."

The main door to the castle was too heavily protected, so Jenn and her group made it to a door on the second level. She positioned her submachine gun and lifted her hand to tell the others to get ready to fire, when a mortar hit the castle and the stairs beneath them gave way. The others screamed as they fell; Jenn flailed for the door latch and grabbed on with both hands, as her legs swung in midair hundreds of feet above the ground. She didn't look as the members of her team fell to their deaths.

Then she discovered there was a small portion of stairway left, somehow buttressed by timbers. She found purchase with one foot, and then the other, but she held on tight to the latch.

"Jenn," said a voice behind her. It was Solomon's soldier, the one who had saved her when her eardrums had exploded. He was gripping an edge of the castle wall with his fingertips.

His arm came around her and covered her hand on the door latch. She worried about their combined weight on the precarious perch.

"Jenn," he said again, and his voice was flat and emotionless. This time Jenn hazarded a glance. He was staring at her with the eyes of a madman. They were practically spinning.

"Hey, what's going on?" she asked shrilly.

"Dantalion. He's all around you. Look," he said, gesturing with his head to the ground, far below.

Jenn wasn't going to look, but he was so insistent that she obeyed. She gasped at what she saw: Allied soldiers mowing down fellow Allied troops with Uzis, attacking with huge knives—and a werewolf flinging itself at Holgar's ally, Viorica. Blood sprayed everywhere.

"Dantalion orders you to look," said the soldier, grabbing Jenn's chin and jerking her head upward. On the balcony above her, Dantalion spread wide his arms. Beside him vampires in black robes decorated with red bats stretched their arms forward too, and a thick, black smoke streamed from their fingertips.

And what the soldier said next chilled her blood. "Hail, Dantalion. I will kill your enemy."

CHAPTER NINETEEN

The final battle is coming. I don't know if I'll live through it.

Less than a year ago, I was just Jenn. Back home I'm not even old enough to drink, but now I'm leading the fight for humanity's last stand. I'd say it's too impossible to be real, but it's too impossible that there are vampires . . . or a God in the sky who has let this happen. And yet.

I'd be lying if I wrote that I'm not afraid to die. I'm terrified. I'm even more afraid that I'll die without seeing Antonio one last time. Father Juan says we're meant to be together, but I just don't see how. Is there a life after this one? Can we be together then?

Who can answer these questions for me? Where is Father Juan? Is he off praying for us, or has he abandoned us? And if I don't believe, isn't that the same thing?

This journal was supposed to be a new Hunter's Manual, for the Hunter who comes after me. But will I be the last of the hunters of Salamanca? If the vampires win, the fight must go on. If someone does succeed me, this is what I have to say to you: There are things worth fighting for. And dying for. If you find yourself in a battle like mine, kill as many of the enemy as you can. But if you don't live in a world like this, then use your life to heal and repair the world, so that hell never comes to earth again.

I love you, Antonio de la Cruz. I will always love you.

—From the diary of Jenn Leitner,
retrieved from the ruins

Castle Bran
The Allies and Their Enemies

As Antonio set Greg down in the courtyard, he saw Jenn fall. She was a dot on a black horizon that shimmered purple and red with enemy magicks and lightning bolts that stabbed the earth and set it on fire.

But he saw her fall, arms and legs flailing. He heard her scream. It tore his heart out of his chest.

It broke his soul into pieces.

She landed on an outstretched evergreen limb that broke her fall, and he shouted so loudly his voice echoed.

And then she fell again.

"Jenn!" he roared, breaking into a run. "Jenn, land on your feet!" He willed her to live through it, praying as he ran.

Maybe she heard him. Maybe she didn't.

But she didn't land on her feet. She landed on her back, on the unyielding stone of the courtyard. And then she bounced.

"No!" he screamed. "No!"

He could see her blood pooling and running over the stones, and one leg lay crookedly beneath her. He raced to her, dying a thousand times.

Falling to his knees, he stared in disbelief. His God could not let this be real; the Blessed Mother would whisper in the ear of Her Son to perform a miracle.

Jenn lay still as death.

Antonio placed his shaking hand on her chest. Her heart was barely beating. She must have drunk the elixir; otherwise she would surely be dead. Panic surged through him.

He made the sign of the cross over her, and then over himself. *"No. Te lo ruego."* No. I beg you. Antonio pleaded with God.

"Skye! *Brujas!*" he yelled, calling for the witches to come and heal her, save her.

Jenn's heartbeat was slower still, barely beating. Only

a creature with enhanced senses would be able to tell she was still alive.

"Father, please, please," he whispered. "Please."

There was only silence.

"Look," Heather said, pointing at the courtyard from the balcony. Antonio de la Cruz was bent over someone on the ground. From where Heather stood, it looked almost as though he were feeding. "Antonio escaped!"

Lucifer grunted. "I'm not surprised. He's a magnificent vampire. What a waste." He looked at Dantalion. "Mesmerize him. Tell him to kill whoever that is."

Dantalion showed his fangs as he nodded to indicate that he'd heard. At his side his vampiric dog chuffed and whined.

"Easily done," he confirmed. Then he closed his eyes. "Antonio," he whispered, as softly as if he were murmuring in Antonio's ear. "Antonio de la Cruz."

Antonio's back stiffened. Then Heather saw who Antonio was going to kill.

"It's Jenn! My sister," she cried. She burst into peals of laughter. "I have to go watch this. I have to be there. Please, Lucifer?"

Lucifer kissed the top of her head, and then her cheek, and then her lips. She kissed him back, ardently, because she had learned very quickly that that was how to get what she wanted from him.

"We should convert Jennifer Leitner," Dantalion said. "The final irony."

"Yes!" Heather cried. She kissed Lucifer again. "Please?"

"Do it," Lucifer said to Dantalion. Go on, then," he told Heather. "But be careful. I'll watch from here."

Heather kissed Lucifer one more time and left in a blur. She didn't want to miss a moment of her sister's converoion.

She ran downstairs, leaping entire sections in her excitement. Then, when she was almost at the courtyard, she came to a halt. What was she thinking? She didn't want Jenn to become a vampire. Jenn was the older sister, the smart one, the brave one. The one who got to do everything. The one who left home to become a hunter while she, Heather, stayed at home.

She's the one who didn't save me.

Aurora held me prisoner for weeks, and Jenn didn't come. She doesn't deserve to become a vampire. But if I stop Antonio, will Lucifer be angry at me?

Another explosion from somewhere deep in the castle shook the ground, throwing her headlong down a flight of stone steps. It hurt, but it was fun, like a ride at Disneyland. She pulled herself up to her feet, glancing over the side of the staircase . . . and blinked.

Her parents were huddled together behind a pile of rubble. Her father was shielding her mother as magickal bat shapes flapped around their heads. Without another thought, Heather leaped off the stairs and landed beside them.

"Oh, my God," her father said, his hands dropping from around her mom. Heather's mother went white at the sight of her, and her knees buckled. Without realizing what she was doing, Heather caught her, and her mother's arms went around her.

Now she'll freak, Heather thought, amused and yet somehow very nervous. But there was no need to worry about what they thought of her. These people weren't "hers" anymore. They were humans. She had moved on. And besides, they had let her down very, very badly. Her father most of all.

She hated her father.

"Come, look," she said, tugging at her mother's hand as Leslie Leitner burst into sobs.

"You're all right," her mom said hoarsely.

No, I'm not, Heather thought, but then she realized that of course her mom was right. In fact she was better than all right. She was a vampire.

She tugged her mother along. Her father—to whom she hadn't spoken—ran behind, trying to catch up. Heather remembered that humans couldn't move very quickly. She didn't want to drag her mother to death—she wanted her to see the fun!—so she slowed to what felt like a snail's pace.

"You'll like this, Daddy," she said over her shoulder. "It's what you always wanted."

Castle Bran
The Survivors

In their werewolf forms, Holgar and Viorica herded Skye away from the fighting. She had lost her radio, and this had been the fastest way to reach her. Holgar could tell that Skye didn't know what they wanted, but by his yips and soft growls he tried to make her understand that it was important. Skye's crown of mirrors reflected the explosions of mortar shells against the castle wall. In the glittering squares he watched himself and Viorica transforming into their human shapes. They were wearing clothes, and Holgar smiled proudly at Skye as he completed his change.

Then his smile faded as Viorica spoke to him in Russian.

"It's time," Viorica said. "We have to do it now."

Viorica reached into the jacket of her parka and pulled out a vial containing an amber liquid. Holgar did the same, except the liquid in his vial was blue.

"Crikey, Holgar, what's going on?" Skye asked. "I thought I heard Antonio, and now you're here, and—"

"Antonio's here?" Holgar asked, stricken. His stomach clenched. Holgar was ready to do what had to be done, including knowingly causing the death of a teammate and someone he had come to love like a brother—Antonio. But it was the most difficult part of what he had pledged himself to do, and it would be all the harder if he had to watch Antonio die.

"This is the virus," Holgar said to Skye in English. "It comes in two parts. Viorica told me about it when she came to see me on my sickbed. She hid one of the vials in the monastery for me to find. She kept the other."

Viorica nodded. "Tell her that the lab your Noah infiltrated was a decoy. That I have been working for the black crosses for a long time, and they got the vials to me shortly before you were shot," she said to Holgar, again in Russian.

Holgar translated. Skye covered her mouth with both hands, then threw her arms around Holgar and kissed him hard on the lips. "You're going to save the world!" she cried.

"Help. Help me, now." Holgar heard the distant voice of Antonio de la Cruz. He *was* there. Holgar's heart sank, even in the midst of humanity's triumph.

"Skye," Holgar said. "I hear Antonio. He needs help." He squinted up at the castle. "But I don't think he's in there." He looked around and pointed toward the southern perimeter of the courtyard. "That way, I think."

Skye swallowed hard and took Holgar's hand in hers. "You mustn't hesitate, Holgar. You know Antonio wants the virus to be unleashed."

"For helvede," Holgar whispered.

Then a young girl raced up to Skye and tugged on her arm. Her face was ashen, and tears rolled down her cheeks.

"Skye, Skye!" she cried, in an English accent. "A man

named Antonio sent me to find you. Jenn is hurt. She's dying!"

"What?" Holgar cried. He swayed, and Viorica shot out a hand to steady him.

"Goddess," Skye said, looking from the girl to Holgar. "Show me."

The two took off running.

"No," Holgar said, his heart skipping beats. "Not Jenn." In his distress he began to change into wolf form.

"Easy, easy," Viorica said in Russian, grabbing the vial of blue liquid from him. "What's going on?"

He whimpered and forced his change to stop. He and Viorica had promised to remain in human form after she had handed off the vial to him. They had also agreed to stick together and back each other up. In case something happened to one of them, the other one could mix the two parts of the virus together.

"Viorica, Jenn's been wounded. She may be . . . may be dying. Wait, please. I'll be right back."

"Holgar, no!" Viorica shouted.

Running, he easily closed up the distance between Skye and the little girl, and himself. He began to change again. Then he realized what he was doing. He had a mission, and it wasn't to save Jenn. Grinding his teeth in frustration, he said to Skye, "Viorica and I will move downwind. We'll mix the compound there. It will give you time to work healing magicks on Jenn. Then Jenn and Antonio might have a few minutes before . . ." He trailed off, suddenly unable to bear what it was he must do. "But once we open the vials, the virus will spread like wildfire."

She nodded. "Thank you, Holgar." Then she raced on. Holgar quickly doubled back to Viorica.

"Gather as many witches as you can," Skye said through her tears to Autumn. But be careful, luv. I'd hate for something to happen to you."

"I won't fail you," Autumn said fervently. She let Skye run ahead as she darted toward a group of witches battling a vampire.

Then Skye rushed toward four people gathering around a prone figure. She recognized Antonio's profile, and behind him Jenn's parents and *Heather*? On high alert, Skye started to call Holgar for help, but she knew he had to stay with Viorica. Fighting down her horror, she scanned the courtyard for other familiar faces. There was fighting everywhere—humans covered in blood as vampires tore out their throats, bodies piling up. She realized that every second Holgar and Viorica delayed, human lives were being lost.

She could see the group, which was standing almost like a tableau. Antonio was bent over Jenn's throat with his eyes glowing red. Jenn's mom was screaming at Antonio.

Heather, too, was caught in bloodlust. She stood behind her mother like a cat about to pounce on a mouse—and her mother, who was focused on Antonio menacing Jenn, had no idea how much danger she was in herself. Heather's father stood behind Heather, riveted with shock.

"Antonio, no!" Skye shouted. "Antonio, stop!"

Antonio's eyes seemed redder still, and his fangs hovered mere inches from Jenn's neck.

"No!" Skye shouted. "Lady, I am your daughter. I am your High Priestess, and Jennifer Leitner has received special blessings of protection from you. I call on you. I have drawn you down and into me, and I have served you faithfully. I demand the fulfillment of your promises to my coven sister and me. Save her now. Save her from all harm."

Then, as she raced toward the Leitner family and Antonio, they froze. Still as statues, as if locked in ice, each person held their pose. Skye kept running. Above her the dark bat shapes flew and darted, attacking humans and werewolves, causing them to slump and fall to the ground. She leaped over bodies to get to Jenn and the others.

Then witches converged on the scene, acknowledging her. She reached into a pocket and pulled out a cross just as Antonio—

As Antonio—

"No!" she screamed.

As Antonio's eyes turned a deep brown, and he made the sign of the cross over Jenn.

Paul Leitner pulled a stake out of his pocket, grabbed

Heather by the shoulder, whipped her around, and plunged it through her heart.

Heather looked at him and said, "Daddy?" like a frightened little girl. "Mommy?"

"Forgive me for not saving you," Paul whispered.

Seeing what her husband had done, Jenn's mother screamed again, and fell to her knees in the dust that had been her younger daughter. Behind her Paul Leitner sobbed and collapsed—just as one of the shadow bat shapes landed on his head and dug its talons into his scalp.

"No, stop!" Leslie Leitner screamed, punching at it, trying to grab it off her husband's head. But it seemed to be made of shadow, and her fists went through it.

Skye and the other witches circled around Jenn and Antonio. Antonio looked up at her with a tear-streaked face and said, "Can you help her?" Soft, brown eyes, human tears, a man fighting mesmerism. Battling death for his beloved. And all the faith that she had ever placed in Antonio, in his goodness, and in his love for Jenn was rewarded in that moment.

Skye trembled from head to toe and wondered if Holgar and Viorica had opened the vials yet. No time for that; she joined hands with the witches and said, "Goddess, keep faith with us. Jenn is your daughter. We are your children. Do as you promised. I charge you."

"Oil, I must have oil," Antonio said in a shaky voice. "I must have it now. I am going to perform the anointing of the sick." He looked down at a dark splotch spreading from one of Jenn's Velcro pockets and opened it. Inside lay a vial of some sort, but it was broken.

"Oh, no," Skye murmured. "That was elixir. For you, Antonio."

"I don't think there's oil in it," he said, testing the texture between his thumb and forefinger.

"I have essential oil of angelica," one of the witches said, pulling it out of her pocket and handing it to Antonio. His hand was shaking so badly that Skye was afraid he was going to drop it.

Skye opened the vial for him. A sweet scent wafted into the air. She thought of the virus again, and wondered if she should tell him what was happening. She handed the vial back to him. He tipped his forefinger against it, and made the sign of the cross with the oil on Jenn's forehead. Holding her breath, Skye bit her lip and watched. She couldn't even tell if Jenn was still breathing.

"Th-through this holy anointing . . ." Antonio stopped, and cleared his throat. "May the Lord in His love and mercy help you with the grace of the Holy Spirit."

Softly, Skye chanted a spell of healing in Latin, as much for Antonio as for Jenn, so that he, too, could wield the magick of his faith. The other witches followed suit.

Then Antonio anointed Jenn's limp hands. "May the Lord who frees you from sin save you and raise you up."

* * *

I beat Dantalion, Antonio silently told Jenn. *With the help of God, I fought against his mesmerism just now. I thought of you, and how much I love you, and how I need to be a man you can love. Please,* mi amor, mi luz, *fight against death with me. Oh, my love, oh, Jenn. I can't lose you. I can never lose you again.*

In the forest in 1941 Sergio Almodóvar had changed Antonio into a vampire while Antonio had been giving a fellow freedom fighter last rites. Antonio had been unable to stop Sergio from turning him into a monster. Then something had happened, and he had been freed from committing atrocities, and from heaping sin upon sin on his head. It had been an act of grace.

Grace had descended upon him once more. He was free of the clutches of evil again, to do all he could for the soul of the woman he loved. He prayed that Skye could heal her body. He looked into the mirrors of Skye's crown, seeing Jenn's reflection but not his own. As it should be—he was a vampire. Jenn was not.

But then Skye lowered her head, and he saw she was weeping. Terror ripped through him. Tears rolled down the little witch's cheek as she looked back up at him and shook her head.

"You must have faith in your Lady," Antonio begged her. "Save her. *Please.*"

The castle was burning, but not fast enough, and Cursed Ones kept pouring out of it. There were so *many* of them that not even the elixir singing in Noah's veins could even the playing field. Noah thought of the charges he and Jamie had set. He'd been grappling with a human fighter who had suddenly turned against him — Noah suspected mesmerism — and to end the battle without killing the man, Noah had shot him in the leg. The man writhed in pain, and a strip of Velcro gave way as Noah ripped open a pocket on his own pants and pulled out the detonator.

He was about to depress it when he spotted a group of people on the ground at the southern wall of the courtyard. He squinted and made out who they were — Leslie and Paul Leitner, Skye and some of her witches, and *Antonio*. How had he gotten free? And who was that on the ground?

Jenn.

His blood ran cold. Ignoring the wounded human, Noah headed toward them. A Cursed One converged on the gathering and was just about to attack one of the women in the circle when Paul Leitner ran at the vampire with a cross extended, putting it on the defensive. The fanger turned and ran toward Noah, and he staked it with ease.

When Noah reached the circle, his worst fears were realized: Jenn lay on the ground, mortally wounded. Her face was gray, and her lips were turning blue.

"No. *No,*" he said, grief and fury coursing through him. They were losing the battle, and now *Jenn* . . .

He saw his own face reflected in the mirrors of Skye's crown. Streaked with blood and ash, grief-stricken, enraged. Noah had to fight the impulse to knock Antonio out of the way and take his place beside the woman he, too, loved.

"Noah," Skye said, choking back tears. "Holgar and Viorica have . . ." She took a breath. "They have the virus, Antonio," she said directly to the vampire. "They each have a vial, and they're going to mix them together. Once they do . . . there will be very little time."

Stunned, some of the witches stopped chanting and stared at Antonio. He absorbed the information with a single, hard swallow. Then he steadfastly nodded and continued to perform the rite. From the look on his face and the sound of his voice, Noah guessed that it was a ritual blessing for the dead.

Then Jenn's lips parted, moved. Skye cried out.

"She's alive!"

She's dying, Noah thought. He knew the signs . . . very well. He thought of Chayna, and he wanted to scream.

"What? What, Jenn?" Skye asked. "She's trying to talk," she told them. Then she leaned over and placed her ear to Jenn's lips. She was quiet for a moment, and then she sucked in her breath.

"No, Jenn," she said. Skye was quiet again, listening. "Oh, Goddess."

She reached out and grabbed Antonio's hand. "She wants you . . . she wants to be like you," she said. "So you'll have a few more moments together. She knows she's dying."

Everyone, including Antonio, reacted with revulsion. He shook his head. "I would never do that," he said hoarsely. *"Never."*

438

She bent down and listened. Pulled Antonio down beside her.

"Listen to her," Skye implored Antonio.

Jenn couldn't move or open her eyes. The pain was more than she could stand. She knew she was broken, and that she was about to die. In her mind — or somewhere else — she stared at Father Juan, who floated in the center of a blazing white light. He was crying, too.

You must make Antonio listen to you, Jenn, Father Juan said. *You must drink from him. So much depends on it.*

"Antonio, you swore . . . ," she mumbled. "Rosalita . . . never let another woman you loved . . . die . . ."

"No, Jenn, not like this," Antonio said. He kissed her ear, the side of her face. He was crying. "Let me hear your sins and absolve you. I — I will see you in heaven." He cried harder.

He doesn't believe that, Father Juan whispered. *He thinks he's going to hell.*

"Father Juan," Jenn whispered.

"He's not here. Let me anoint you, Jenn, so that you can . . . that you can die in a state of grace, and . . ." Antonio trailed off.

"Father . . . says you must," Jenn finished.

"Do you hear that, Antonio?" Skye said. "Father Juan is speaking to her."

"Oh, my God, baby," Jenn heard. It was Gramma Esther. "Dear God."

There was murmuring. Jenn couldn't make out the words, but the voices belonged to Skye, Esther, and Antonio.

"Baby, baby!" Leslie Leitner cried. "Honey, we love you! Please stay with us!"

"Father Juan," Jenn managed. "'Tonio, he's here."

"No, Jenn, you're delirious," Antonio said, but through the haze of pain Jenn heard the uncertainty in his voice.

"Wait. Father Juan is . . . don't you know who Father Juan is?" Gramma Esther was saying. "He's a *saint*. Saint John of the Cross. If he says you're supposed to do this, Antonio, *I* say it must be done."

"Antonio, the virus is coming," Skye said. "Time is running out."

"If she dies now, she dies with God," Antonio said. Jenn heard his grief, the agony. "How can you ask me to do this?"

"If you don't do it, I'll stake you before the virus gets to you," Noah said.

Then the frantic howl of two werewolves rang out. Yipping and barking . . . as if for help.

"Noah," Skye said. "It's Holgar and Viorica. They're in trouble. See if you can help them."

"I'm not leaving her," Noah insisted.

"If you don't go, I'll tear out your throat," Antonio told him.

Noah swore. Jenn faded for a few moments, staring at Father Juan. The light was so beautiful. She wanted to go to him. She wanted to be done.

Antonio, she begged Father Juan. *Let him come too.*

Then she heard a collective gasp. Though her eyes were closed, she could see them all, as if she were looking down on them.

Father Juan stood in front of Antonio, shimmering in a cloud of white light. He gazed down at Antonio and placed his hand on the crown of Antonio's head. Antonio stirred as if he felt the warmth, and the substance.

Fear not, Father Juan said. He spoke in Spanish, which Jenn miraculously understood with ease. *You are my beloved son. You and you alone have taken the blood from my veins. Trust in me. Do as I tell you.*

"*Ay, Padre, no,*" Antonio pleaded, gazing up from his knees. She saw Antonio's face, so loved, so cherished. She tried to touch him, but she was formless.

Fulfill what I have foreseen, Father Juan said. *Spirit, soul, body. There are seconds now, Antonio. Heaven watches.*

Then Jenn's world went black. She was back in her dying body.

The light pressure on her lips was Antonio's mouth. She tried to kiss him back. She wouldn't go now. She couldn't go. There was a world to save.

And a vampire to love.

Something warm and coppery dripped into her mouth. *This is my blood,* Father Juan said. *Shed for you.*

She couldn't swallow. She was too close to death. But she felt Antonio's blood trickle down her throat and diffuse into her veins.

"It won't work this way," she heard Antonio say. "I have to drain her nearly to death."

"She's already dying," Skye replied. "Don't stop."

"Who's he talking to?" Jenn's mother was saying.

Mom, Jenn thought, *I love you.*

"I don't know, " Paul Leitner replied.

And my father, Jenn thought, and her heart began to harden. Rage filled her.

You have to let it go. This hatred you feel . . . it's how Antonio has felt about himself, all these decades. If you let it go, he will be able to do it too, Father Juan said. *And then you will fulfill the runes I have cast.*

I have the right to hate him, Jenn argued.

But you have the responsibility to love him. That is the new mission of the Hunter of Salamanca, Jenn. To repair the world.

Let the new Hunter do it, then.

If you do as I say, then he will, Father Juan replied.

"It will take twenty-four hours for her to change," Antonio was saying. "We don't have time . . ."

"Trust," Jenn blurted out. In her heart she was sobbing and raging and hating her father and wishing him dead, but as the blood of St. John of the Cross spread throughout her physical body, it nourished her spirit as well.

Forgive him, Father Juan told her.

She saw her father holding her mother, both staring at her body, rocking together in mindless sorrow. Her father was coated with vampire ash.

"I'm so sorry. I would die for you. I'm so sorry," Paul Leitner said. "If I could trade places . . ."

And deep in her heart, her very soul, she knew he was telling the truth.

I forgive you, she thought.

In her mind, she saw something horrible and black rise out of her like a cloud of smoke. Then a black shape grabbed at it, squeaking as if with glee, and bore it away. She was surrounded by light.

"My love, my love," Antonio whispered desperately. *"Please."*

Jenn opened her eyes and looked into his deep brown eyes. She saw them widen. Felt his arms around her.

Then she saw Skye bending over behind Antonio, and Jenn looked into her crown of mirrors.

Noah could tell that Holgar was in trouble. Both he and Viorica were howling in fear and frustration even though they were in human form. The Allied soldiers had been mesmerized, and they were advancing on the two werewolves. More werewolves were bounding toward them, but whether friend or foe, Noah couldn't tell. He aimed his Uzi at the soldiers, cursing Dantalion's name with each round he fired. Then he stared up at the burning castle and saw figures standing on a balcony. Dantalion was mesmerizing the entire Allied forces.

He grabbed his radio out of his pocket and clicked it

on. "Crusader Kicker," he called, using Jamie's code name. "Blow it sky-high."

"Copy that, Crusader Star. See you're busy. Blowing it now, then coming to you," Jamie radioed back.

As Noah grimly mowed down more approaching soldiers, he took out a couple of the mesmerized Catholics and a witch, too. Then he braced himself for the explosions that he prayed would blow Dantalion, Lucifer, and all their vampire friends straight to hell.

He didn't have long to wait.

A huge roar threw him to the ground. Noah rolled onto his side and kept firing. He was aware of flame and smoke and huge chunks of stone and wood falling his way, but he focused on the mission, which was to protect the two werewolves.

Menaced by a man in a clerical collar and a short-haired nun with an Uzi, Holgar and Viorica dodged the gunfire by crouching as low as they could and zigzagging around the castle pieces as they fell. Smoke rolled across Noah's field of vision, and he kept shooting, his only thought to protect the virus.

Then the soldiers, the Catholics, and the witches blinked and staggered as if waking from a dream. They fell into one another's arms in shock, some collapsing; they began to tend to their wounded as they pointed up at the castle. The mesmerism was broken. Dantalion had to be dead.

We did it, we did it, Noah thought, turning his submachine gun on furious vampires as they headed in the direction of the awakened Allied troops. Exultant, he kept doing what he was made to do: kill the enemy by any means possible. He felt a rush of joy as more vampires fell.

And then a terrible pain shot through him as something picked him up. It was a nightmare ruin, one of the hybrids, soaking wet, falling apart. But it had broken something vital—maybe his back—and Noah's eyes teared with the pain.

"Lovely, lovely," the monster said. "Killed the lovely."

Noah heard something crack inside his body. Another bone broken. Sheer, blinding pain engulfed him.

Then the monster grunted, and dropped him. It fell on top of him. Noah saw the hideous face, the glazed, open eyes. It was dead.

Someone pushed it off Noah's body. As the haze of pain engulfed him, one thing became crystal clear.

"Chayna," he whispered, as she held him in her arms. His wife. His love. "Chayna, you're dead."

I'm here, she said, though he couldn't see her. He just *knew* that she was there.

"Tell me what you said," he begged, gasping through fresh pain. "When I . . . when I killed . . ."

Thank you. He felt her smile, felt her love. *I said thank you, Noah.*

He swallowed hard. He smiled against the agony.

You saved me, she said.

And then he died.

* * *

"Look," Autumn said, returning to Skye's side.

Bishop Diego, Lune, and Soleil headed their way along with other witches and Catholics. All around them vampires were choking, falling, and turning to dust.

"The virus," Skye whispered. "It's coming. It's here."

Skye reached forward and kissed Antonio on the cheek, folding her arms around him as if she could protect him from death. "I'm sorry, Antonio."

He didn't answer. He was staring down at Jenn, who lay still in his arms, gazing up at him with love, and so many hopes and regrets.

"I love you," Jenn whispered.

"Te amo," Antonio answered. "Forever."

"No, *look*," Autumn insisted, pointing at Skye's crown.

Barely able to move her eyes, Jenn followed the little witch's insistent finger. She found herself staring at her own reflection in the shards of mirror.

Then she caught her breath, and let out a laugh of pure amazement.

Because she saw Antonio's reflection there too.

Jenn laughed again. Looking confused, Skye took off the crown and studied it. Her eyes widened. She looked from it to Antonio, and back again.

"Oh, my God," Antonio murmured. "My God."

"It's a miracle!" Skye cried.

And everyone in the little group began to cheer.

CHAPTER TWENTY

As Dr. Sherman promised, the virus was carried on the air, and it infected the entire planet. Within twenty-four hours all the vampires were dead.

Antonio and I survived, because we are not vampires. I have to say it again: We are not vampires.

As far as we can tell, we're ordinary people. And we are the new Hunters of Salamanca—a pair. It's a name we're proud to carry. With all the vampires gone, we have to decide what to do, exactly, how to go about healing the world. But we have some ideas about that.

And so we'll be writing a new Hunters' Manual, together. This is the last page of my diary, recovered from the battlefield, from the ruins of the SUV that I was riding in at the beginning of the assault. I had

packed it along with all my weapons. Habit, I guess.
I've become so accustomed to having it with me.
That will change, though. It's time to start a
new book.
And a new life, with Antonio.
—from the diary of Jenn Leitner,
retrieved from the ruins

THE MONASTERY OF THE BROTHERHOOD OF ST. ANDREW
THE ALLIES

Jamie watched as witches and soldiers, street fighters and Catholics crowded into the monastery. Some camped outside. No one wanted to leave. All of them were happy to be alive, and more than a little surprised.

The effects of the elixir wore off.

The Salamancans took over the little chapel of the monastery for three funerals: Noah's, Father Juan's, and Heather's. Two coffins, one urn, a hella lot of priests, and a rabbi, for Noah. Seemed you had to have a Jew bury you if you were a Jew, or you were considered an "abandoned corpse."

Jamie wore a black sweater, jeans, and kicker boots. He dearly wished for a smoke, but he'd given it up, in honor of Noah.

Skye and the coven wore street clothes and crowns of

roses. Nobody had time for special outfits, except for His Eminence Diego Cardinal Gutiérrez, once a bishop and now promoted on the battlefield, who had flown in from Spain just before the battle with a heavenly host of old friends of Father Juan's; and Father Wadim, who was officiating; and his monks. They'd given Antonio a brown monk's robe to wear; he was serving in the capacity of a layman — a faithful member of the Catholic Church, but not a priest or someone hoping to be one. Jamie figured that had something to do with Jenn. He was working his way toward being happy about Antonio being alive.

But Jamie had more important things to do at the moment than nurse habitual vendettas. He had matters of the soul to ponder, and of saying farewell to those who had given their lives for the cause. Jamie knew the funeral Mass: knew the words, knew when to stand, kneel, and pray. Gramma Esther had shared the story of the elixir, and no one, least of all Jamie, knew what to think about Father Juan. Questions of all sorts swirled in his mind. Had Father Juan really been a living saint — the patron saint of Salamanca, St. John of the Cross? Had he, Jamie O'Leary, taken communion with one of God's own chosen? The thought made him tremble more than the Cursed Ones ever had.

Jamie looked at Holgar, whose face was somber. Everyone was pretty bloody glad to be alive, and there had been moments of heroism among them. But Holgar and Viorica had saved the world.

And that's why I didn't shoot him, Jamie thought.

Jamie had had two excellent chances to do so: The first was when Holgar and the werewolf queen had come bounding away from the fray—deserting the losing side, or so Jamie had thought at first. Then Noah had shown up, all Mossad defending them, and then Holgar and Viorica had begun pouring one cylinder of liquid into another, and the closest vamps had collapsed and burst into dust. That's when Jamie had realized what was happening. The virus, that was what. So he'd kept the gun with the silver bullets down at his side. Then, after Noah had died in his arms, so out of his head that he'd thought Jamie was his dead wife, and with the virus doing the killing for them, Jamie had had another clear shot at Holgar. But he hadn't taken it. When all was said and done, he knew that he would never take it.

Jamie had dropped the bullet marked with an *H* in Father Juan's coffin.

Now, during the Mass, Jamie thought of Skye in a werewolf's arms, and he was repulsed down to his boots. But maybe Holgar would go for the new wolf, Viorica.

You're the right bastard, O'Leary, he thought, crossing himself after His Eminence the cardinal, Father Wadim, and Antonio all crossed themselves first. *Wolfie saved the world, and Skye loves him. Leave it lie. Let it go. Be happy for them.*

Kate caught Jamie's eyes and smiled faintly. She'd made it through, and so had Skye's little Autumn, who kept tugging on Skye's hand, asking what was happening. The child had never been to a Christian funeral. All kinds of firsts she had in store, and a whole new life. Skye had adopted her. Kate was heading back to Dublin after the funerals.

He could finally go where he wanted. For years he'd dreamed of returning to Ireland to kill the werewolves who'd massacred his family and the vampires who'd let it happen. The priest who'd forced Jamie to stand on the sidelines (and by so doing had probably saved his life) had been gunned down, but Jamie had never felt any need to blame the Church entire for the destruction of his family.

Curious, that, he thought.

In the monastery the faithful were called to take communion, and Jamie found himself standing in front of Antonio, who held out a wafer to him. Jamie stubbornly set his jaw, and Antonio gazed at him steadily, the wafer extended.

It was the good father himself turned him into a real boy, he thought.

After communion Father Wadim and the cardinal sprinkled holy water on, and wafted incense around, the coffins of Heather and Father Juan. At the rabbi's nod conveying permission, they did the same to Noah's casket.

"Go in peace. The Mass is ended," Cardinal Gutiérrez, Father Juan's dearest friend, said with a melancholy tone.

Then, as had been planned, Jamie, Antonio, Holgar, Skye, Jenn, and Esther served as Noah's pallbearers. They carried his simple wooden coffin outside to the monastery graveyard, where other soldiers had dug a hole for it. As the

Salamancans looked on, Noah's coffin was lowered, and the rabbi showed them how to rend their clothes. Only seven types of relative were expected to tear their clothes to show their grief: sons, daughters, fathers, mothers, brothers, sisters, and spouses.

The Salamancans told the rabbi they were all brothers and sisters of the fallen warrior, and so they rent their garments by slicing a vertical cut in their clothing over the right side of their chests. For parents and children it was directly over the heart. But that was where Jamie's real cuts lay—in his heart. In the end he had found a kindred soul in Noah, and the bonds of battle had made them true brothers. Losing him felt like losing his little sister all over again.

Together they recited the Twenty-third Psalm: *The Lord is my shepherd . . .*

Ashes to ashes, dust to dust.

But not dust like the Cursed Ones. They were gone. Reports were coming in from all over the world. The vampires were dead, but those who had profited from helping them were putting up a fight as governments tried to seize back the power they'd lost. Through it all, Kent Wallace, the Voice of the Resistance, kept broadcasting, but he had fallen silent the night before, and the Salamancans were worried about him.

"Amen," said a very familiar voice.

Jamie looked across the grave at a dark-skinned man

who walked slowly up to the edge. He had a limp, and when he came to a stop, he stood slightly crooked.

"Kent Wallace," Jamie murmured. And after the rabbi completed the service, everyone gathered around Kent, slapping him on the back, hugging him, thanking him. Word swept through the campgrounds that the Voice of the Resistance was among them, and an impromptu celebration began to take shape. The monks brought out brandy and provisions. The werewolves brought game. Local Transylvanians arrived in droves, bringing more food and drink and inviting the overflow of fighters to stay with them in their villages.

"You kept the resistance alive," Jenn said to Kent over buoyant Gypsy music. Many were dancing in crazy circles, toasting and laughing. "Then you coordinated all our efforts."

"But I didn't know about the virus," Kent said. "That was pure black crosses."

"And Salamanca and friends," Jamie said. His smile took in Viorica, who was performing a belly dance for an appreciative audience of soldiers and werewolves in their human form. Eriko's brother, Kenji, was trying unsuccessfully to imitate her movements, to the delight of the spectators.

"What do you think will happen now?" Skye asked Kent, as she settled down beside him on a wooden bench brought outside for the festivities.

Kent stretched out his leg and rapped on it. It sounded

like plastic. "I lost my leg to a werewolf bite," he said, then smiled at Holgar as he came up behind Skye and put his arms around her. "Not that I'm faulting all werewolves. My point is, only vampires died from the virus. Just because the good guys won, doesn't mean there are no bad guys left . . . some werewolves, some human. Vampires weren't alone in subjugating the human race."

"That's true," Jenn said, as Antonio brought her something to drink. Antonio, in the sunlight. Jamie was floored. He'd never dreamed he'd see such a thing. He couldn't help his lopsided grin. It was hard to stay sour when there was so much happiness in the air.

"We have an organization now," Kent continued. "Worldwide. We can do a lot of good."

"We'll help," Antonio said, and Jenn nodded.

After a time Jamie went back down to the graves. Noah was buried. Heather's ashes, or at least someone's ashes, had been given to her parents. In two days, after more had arrived to pay their respects, Father Juan would be buried in the monastery tomb, where the monks went to their rest.

Jamie stood gazing down at Noah's grave, and thought of Eriko. Her grave was a mound of rocks at Salamanca. He'd go back and bury her proper.

Then he went into the monastery, down to the room where Sade was keeping to herself. The poor girl was so ashamed of acting the spy, even though she'd been mesmerized with no way to fight it, that she didn't want to show her face.

"Hey," Jamie said, knocking on her door. "I've come to visit."

He pushed the door open to find Jenn's parents sitting with Sade. The outcasts.

He cocked his head. "You know Jenn's forgiven you," he said to Paul Leitner.

"How can I ever forgive myself?" the stricken man asked.

"You don't need to. God handles them kind of things," Jamie replied. Then he walked over to Sade and crouched down beside her. "They don't blame you," he said. "Hell, Antonio's got more to answer for than you, and he's up there dancing a jig."

Then Jamie had an idea. "You know Kent, the Voice of the Resistance? He's here."

"Really?" Sade cried, sounding like an excited young girl for the first time.

"And truly," he replied. "Go on up." When she hesitated, he jerked his head toward the door. "He's cute," he added.

"Come with me?" she asked Jamie.

So with a nod at the Leitners, Jamie escorted Sade upstairs. Then he wandered back into the chapel, and sat in a pew. He was exhausted. And he wanted a cigarette.

"My son," said the cardinal from the back of the chapel. He had asked them to call him Father Diego, which Jamie was having a little trouble with.

His Eminence sat beside Jamie.

"*Buenos días*, Father," Jamie replied.

"You're not celebrating," the priest observed.

"I'm thinking it's too important a thing to throw a party over," Jamie replied. Then he flushed, because that sounded priggish. "But sure and I'll be drinking a pint later. Better yet a gallon."

Father Diego chuckled. He gazed at Father Juan's closed casket, candlelight flickering on the polished wood.

"Father Juan was my dearest and oldest friend."

Jamie slid the cardinal a glance. "And was he what . . . who . . . Esther says he was?"

Father Diego raised a brow. "Do you think a saint walked among you?"

"Bloody hell, Your Eminence, pardon my language, but I know a miracle when I see one." He waved a hand. "And this is all a miracle."

Father Diego nodded as if to himself. "Do you know that Father Juan was very worried about you? He was afraid all the hate you carried in your heart would harm your chances of survival. And . . . of becoming what you were meant to be."

Jamie frowned quizzically. "And what is that?"

"One of us," Father Diego replied. "A churchman."

"A *priest*?" Jamie cried. "Are you daft?" Then he back-pedaled. "Meaning no disrespect, Your Eminence. Father."

"Still, it's how he saw you," Father Diego said. "And it's how I see you."

"I'm not exactly what they look for in a priest." The idea was ridiculous, and it almost made him smile. Part of him, though, wondered what life would have been like without the Cursers and the werewolves that killed his family.

"No, but you're exactly what we need. You're a man of principles who is fiercely loyal but questions everything. You push back when others ask you to do things that don't make sense. There are tough days ahead, and we'll need priests like you."

Jamie was at a loss for words.

"I've been praying for all of you," Father Diego said. "I think you have a vocation. But listen to your heart, Jamie. It'll tell you where you belong."

Father Diego rose and left the chapel, leaving a gobsmacked Jamie in his wake.

The night of revelry continued. Tiffany, Heather's friend, told sweet stories about her that helped Jenn and her parents deal with their loss. Kenji led everyone in a medley of Eriko's songs, back when she and her two friends had sung together as the Vampire Three. The brothers of St. Andrew broke out more brandy.

The next day some of the fighters left to return home. Others couldn't bear to leave the site of humanity's victory. Gradually, thoughts turned to other matters.

Wonderful matters.

*　　*　　*

Father Diego beamed at the gathered assembly. Skye was radiant in one of the white robes with golden spangles that the witches had brought with them. Jenn had spent two hours trying to braid Skye's hair just right and lace it with flowers. It should have been simple, but it had been years since her fingers had practiced anything that wasn't related to killing, and what would have been simple for her twelve-year-old self proved maddeningly difficult. The end result was worth it, though.

Jenn stood beside Skye. Both of them held bouquets of wildflowers. It seemed so odd to be doing something so *normal*. Jenn was Skye's bridesmaid—the maid of honor, actually. Was this what real people did? Average, normal people? Was this her life now?

It seemed impossible to comprehend. There were so many things left to be done, pieces to be picked up, nations and cities to be rebuilt. Universities, too. Father Diego had confided in her that morning that the University of Salamanca was to be reconstructed. Even if the vampires were truly gone, that didn't mean there wasn't other evil to fight. Who knew when hunters would be needed again? He had offered Antonio and Jenn teaching positions there. They were the new Hunters of Salamanca, and where else should they be? Jenn, for one, couldn't think of a good reason to turn down his offer.

She'd always harbored secret fantasies about returning

home, but the California Bay Area was barely recognizable anymore, so vast was the destruction left by the Cursed Ones. The same could be said of her family. She looked at her parents, who sat a bit apart, her father still horribly ashamed by what he'd done.

She felt eyes on her and turned her head so that she could see Antonio, standing between Holgar and Jamie. She was still secretly shocked that Jamie had agreed to be a groomsman. But whatever ill will Jamie had always seemed to hold for Holgar, it had somehow vanished during the battle. Maybe he was mellowing—although she seriously doubted that. Father Diego was going to have his hands full with the likes of Jamie as a priest. Jamie had announced that he was going to enter the seminary—just as Antonio had done nearly seventy years before.

The three men looked striking in tuxedos, although where they had found them she didn't want to know. Apparently, acquiring the tuxedos had been the highlight of Holgar's bachelor party. Antonio had muttered something about "liberating them," and that was more than she'd wanted to hear. But her heart melted as she stared at him in it. His dark hair was longer, a bit rakish, and his ruby cross earring brought out the rosy glow of his once-pallid cheeks.

Next to her, Soleil and Lune also stood up as bridesmaids for Skye. They were also wearing spangled white robes. Autumn was a flower girl.

"Dearly beloved," Father Diego began. "We are here

tonight, beneath this moon, to witness the joining of this witch and this werewolf in holy matrimony."

Jenn gave Father Diego credit for being able to say that with a straight face.

Then, as Skye had instructed him, the Catholic cardinal tied their left wrists together with a golden cord. Now their hands were tied fast—they were handfasted.

"And as we see the love that they have for each other, we are reminded that love is, in the end, what truly matters. Love can move mountains," he said.

Skye had never looked so beautiful, so joyous. Holgar couldn't stop grinning.

Or shifting, for that matter.

She watched as he began to turn into a wolf and then pulled himself back time and again. She was glad that he had finally learned how to shift without the help of a full moon, but he clearly had a long way to go before he could fully control it. Every time he started to transform, Skye giggled, and her laughter was infectious.

Even Jamie was smirking. Further proof that miracles did indeed happen.

Holgar and Skye didn't exchange rings. It wasn't a tradition honored by either of their peoples. It especially made sense for Holgar, since wolfing out could be hard on a tiny piece of metal.

Jenn glanced down at the gold band on her own left hand and then over at the one Antonio was wearing, and thrilled to see it. They'd had Father Diego marry them in a private Catholic ceremony hours before. Father Wadim had offered the rings. The priest had found them in an old box of offerings the faithful had donated to the monastery.

Jenn Leitner was now Jenn de la Cruz. They hadn't wanted to steal Holgar and Skye's thunder. Besides, they both felt as if Father Juan had already performed the ritual. This had just made it official.

They'd had two witnesses — Gramma Esther and Greg Bassingwaite, whom Antonio had rescued from the castle before it had exploded. After Jenn and Antonio's wedding, Greg had asked Gramma Esther if she'd like to go out for coffee when they got back home.

And Jenn was still trying to wrap her mind around what would happen when they were alone later. They were two innocents. She figured that a lot of humor, an overflowing of love, and the patience of a saint would see them through just about anything. It was all miraculous.

"I now pronounce you a mated pair," the cardinal said, clearly pleased with himself over the phrase.

There was an expectant pause while everyone waited for the line that he'd clearly forgotten.

"Better kiss her quick, wolfie," Jamie teased gently.

Holgar swept Skye up in his arms, and she squealed with joy as they kissed.

Antonio looked at Jenn, and she saw a single, watery tear run down his cheek. Then he gave her a wink that set her blood on fire. She blushed, but she didn't look away. She was his, now and forever, just as he was hers.

He could look all he wanted. As long as soon he did more than just look. And by the gleam in his brown eyes, she could tell that was exactly what he had planned.

I love you, Antonio, she thought. *My love. My husband. My miracle.*

She said so much to him in the silence between them. The blessed silence, free of danger, full of anticipation.

Skye and Holgar were still kissing. The others were laughing and cheering. The world was a new place. Jenn couldn't wait to see what it held for Antonio and her.

Their enemies had been vanquished.

And their lives had just begun.

EPILOGUE

THE MONASTERY OF THE BROTHERHOOD OF ST. ANDREW
ST. JOHN OF THE CROSS

Silence had fallen over the little chapel, and darkness as well. Things were peaceful, calm, as they should be. Up before the altar, the wooden coffin rested, waiting for the morning when it would be sealed away in the tomb with so many other revered dead.

Suddenly a blinding light burst in the chapel interior. And inside the coffin Father Juan revived with a gasp. Panic surged through him for a moment, until he realized where he was. This wasn't heaven. He was back on earth.

"Not again," he groaned.

Then he rose.

And got to work.

Looking for another
spellbinding novel?

Don't miss
Nancy Holder and Debbie Viguié's

Witch & Curse

BARLEY MOON

☾

Fare yo well, Lord of Light
Thou wilt rule on Yuletide Night
Blackfires burn and scythe the Rows
So crieth House of Deveraux

From out thy Vessel, Lady Faire
Cahors Witches take to Aire
Blood drink of Foe and Blood of Friend
Renew the Earthe with Blood again

Mile 76 from Lee's Ferry, the Colorado River, August 1 (Lammas)

Oh, great. A storm. On top of everything else.

Ignoring for the moment the thick, hot words her parents were exchanging at the bow of the inflatable raft, Holly raised her gaze to the shard of sky between the canyon walls. Nickel and copper sunlight sheered her vision, making her eyes hurt. Clouds like decomposing gray fists rumbled, and the canyon wrens fluttered from their hiding places, cooing warnings to one another.

Behind her, the extremely buff boatman who did these rides every summer for his USC tuition money grunted and sighed. Her parents had pushed the guy beyond his "Hello, my name is Ryan and I'll be your river guide" manners, and she didn't blame him. Her mother and father were wearing everybody out—him, her, and Tina, her best friend, who had had the bad luck to be invited on this nightmare vacation. Of course, Tina got invited to everything. Being an only child had its advantages, and both Tina and Holly were onlies.

Tina's mom had dropped out at the last minute, claiming a problem with her schedule at Marin County General, but Holly wondered if the petite, dark-haired woman had known something was up. That would make sense; Barbara Davis-Chin was Holly's mom's best friend, and even grown-up best friends told their girlfriends everything.

Hey, I know the score, Holly thought. *I've seen* Sex and the City.

Five days ago, when Holly had gotten home from her horse stable job, it had been obvious something had been going on behind the closed doors of their classically San Franciscan Queen Anne Victorian row house. Her parents' shouts, cut short by the sound of Holly's key in the front lock, had practically echoed off the white plaster walls. She'd heard the rhythmic sound of a push broom as one of them swept up a mess. Above Holly's head as she stood in the foyer, taking off her jacket, the floorboards of her parents' bedroom creaked with tension.

"Hey, hi, you guys, I'm home," she'd called, but no one had answered. Then after a moment or two, her father had come downstairs, his smile reaching nowhere near his eyes as he said, "Hi, punky. Good day at the stables?"

No one had talked about what had happened. Her parents, Elise and Daniel Cathers, had joined in a conspiracy of polite silence, chilly to each other that night while packing for the trip, with the emotional frost dipping below freezing on the flight to Las Vegas. Thankfully, she'd sat with Tina in another row of the plane, and she and her best friend had had their own room in their suite at the Bellagio.

Her parents had gone out to see Cirque du Soleil, leaving Holly and Tina in their own room to talk about the upcoming senior year and their plans for college— USC for Tina, UC Santa Barbara for Holly. Then the two adults had come back, very late—and drunk, Holly hoped, because she didn't want to think that they would ever speak that way to each other when they were sober. They had flung mean words at each other like knives, words designed and honed to hurt. Holly knew it was wishful thinking that her father was not saying *bitch,* but *witch,* even though it had sounded like that through the closed doors of the suite's second bedroom. That was what Tina had heard too.

In the morning Ryan had met the four of them in the Bellagio foyer and driven them to the raft trip launch site. Mom and Dad had barely been civil to each other during the daylong safety training class.

Ryan got the raft into the water and told them where to sit. Then, as if the swirling waters of the Colorado had driven their tempers, the arguing had begun again, and during the day of white-water rafting it had grown steadily worse.

Now Holly and Tina hunched over their oars, paddling according to Ryan's directions and pointedly trying to pretend nothing weird was going on. They wore bright orange life vests and orange helmets, Tina's hanging low over her black hair, which she had dyed aquamarine in honor of the trip. Holly, her own dark hair a mass of damp, crazed ringlets, was crammed beside Tina in the center of the raft, which resembled a kind of pudgy dinghy. Cold water sluiced at them from every direction as the raft roller-coastered between slick black boulders and tree trunks. As chilly as the environment was, it was tropical compared to her parents' attitude toward each other.

"Dude, what is *wrong* with them?" Tina asked in Holly's ear. "They're going to kill each other. Or us."

"When we get home, adopt me," Holly said miserably.

"We're almost old enough to get married." Tina wagged her eyebrows suggestively. "C'mon, baby, you know you want me." She blew Holly a kiss.

Smiling faintly, Holly sighed and shook her head. "Your mom would love that."

"My mom is a bigger knee-jerk liberal than your whole family put together," Tina retorted. "She'd love to plan our commitment ceremony, *darling*."

Holly grinned and Tina grinned back. The smiles quickly faded, however, as the sound of angry voices rose once again over the rapids' roar.

"—*not* going back early," Holly's father hissed.

"You never told me." That was her mom. "You should have told me . . ."

Ay, Chihuahua, Holly thought. Tension eddied between them, and a fresh wave of anxiety washed through her. Something was basically, fundamentally wrong, and if she got really honest with herself, she knew it had been wrong for over a year.

Ever since I had that nightmare . . .

Her dad broke eye contact first and her mother

quit the field, two territorial animals both dissatisfied with the outcome of their face-off. They were both good-looking people even though they were in their forties. Dad was tall and lanky, with thick, unruly black hair and very dark brown eyes. Her mom was the odd one out, her hair so blond, it looked fake, her eyes a soft blue that reminded Holly of bridesmaid dresses. Everyone always thought they looked so good together, like TV parents. Few besides Holly knew that their conversations were more like dialogue from a horror movie.

"Okay, hang on," Ryan interrupted her thoughts—and for a split second, the arguing. "We're gonna start the Hance Rapids. Remember, stay left." He looked up at the lowering sky and muttered, "Damn."

Holly cocked her head up at him. His face was dark and durable, much too leathery for someone who was only twenty-one. *By the time he's thirty,* she thought, *he's going to look like a statue made of beef jerky.*

"Gonna be a storm, huh," she said, raising her voice to be heard over the rapids and the creaking of the raft's rubber skin.

He glanced at her. "Yeah. We'll stop early tonight." He glanced at her parents. "Tempers are getting kinda short."

"They're not usually—" she began, then shut her

mouth, nodded, and got back to paddling.

White water tumbled ahead like a kettle put on to boil, and she and Tina sat up a little straighter, getting ready for the big, exciting zoom downward. Going down rapids was officially the fun part, the reason they were there. But Holly had had enough. She wanted to go home.

The river currents rushed, threading together and then separating, curling around rocks and boulders and making eddies like potholes in a street. They skidded and slid along, the by-now familiar blend of joy and fear tightening Holly's chest and tickling her spine. "Yee-ha!" she yelled, and Tina took up the cry. They broke into laughter, bellowing "Yee-ha!" over and over in voices loud enough to echo off the canyon walls. Canyon wrens joined in and thunder rumbled overhead, and Holly felt a flash of anger that her parents were too busy being pissed off at each other to share in the fun.

The raft picked up more speed, then more; Holly's stomach lurched and Tina shrieked with fearful delight.

Then the sky rumbled once, twice, and cracked open. Rain fell immediately, huge bucketfuls of it, completely drenching them. It rushed down so hard, it slapped Holly's shoulders painfully. She flailed for her yellow raincoat wrapped around her waist, and the boat pitched and bowed as everyone lost track, startled by the downpour.

Ryan yelled, "To your oars!"

Holly's parents snapped to, guiding the boat the way Ryan had taught them. Rain came down like waterfalls; the river waters sluiced to either side of a giant boulder, and Holly remembered rather than heard Ryan's admonition to stay left of it. *Everything around here, stay left.*

The huge granite outcropping towered above them. Its face was jagged and sharp, not rounded with erosion as one would have expected.

"Wow," Tina yelled, taking a moment to gesture at it.

The rain fell even harder, pummeling them, and Holly worked frantically to pull her hood back up over her head as a bracing wind whipped it off. The torrents blinded her. She couldn't see anything.

"Jesus Christ, *duck!*" Ryan screamed.

Holly ducked, peering through the rain.

There was a millisecond where everyone froze, shocked brains registering what was happening. Then they all scrambled as if responding to an air raid in a World War II movie, grabbing their paddles and fighting the river's determination to slam them en masse against the huge piece of granite.

"No!" Tina cried as her oar was almost torn from her hands by the force of a wave. She started screaming as the raft dove down at a 45-degree angle. Foaming angry water rushed over the five passengers up to their waists. Tina screamed again and batted futilely at the water as Holly shouted, "What do we do now? What are we supposed to do?"

"Keep calm!" Ryan bellowed. "Left, left, *left!*"

Holly's oar felt entirely too fragile and slight to make any difference in the trajectory the water was flinging them into; at the same time it was too heavy and unwieldy for her to manipulate.

Then her mother shouted something and Daniel Cathers cried, *"No!"*

The river was a maelstrom now; everything was gray and cold and unforgiving and treacherous; gray stone and gray water, as the raft was propelled toward the boulder with the force of a catapult.

Holly held on to the paddle. It was useless now, but still she held it, hands frozen around it in terror. Someone, she had no idea who, was shouting her name.

Then Ryan's voice rang out. "Jump! *Now!*"

His command broke her stupefaction. As she tried to unbuckle her safety straps and jump, the river crested over the raft, completely engulfing it. Cold, unforgiving water surrounded her, cresting above her shoulders, her head; she waited for it to recede, but it just kept barreling over her. She panicked, unable to breathe, and began pushing frantically at the restraints. She couldn't remember how to undo them.

I'm going to drown. I'm going to die.

The steel waters thickened, becoming waves of blackness. She couldn't see anything, couldn't feel anything, except the terrible cold. The raft could be tumbling end over end for all she knew. Her mind seized on the image of the huge face of rock; hitting it at this speed would be like falling out of a window and splatting on the street.

Her lungs were too full; after some passage of time she could not measure, they threatened to burst; she understood that she needed to exhale and draw in more oxygen. She fumbled at the belt but she still had no clue how to get free. As her chest throbbed she batted at the water, at her lap and shoulders where the straps were, trying so hard to keep it together, so hard.

I'm gonna die. I'm gonna die.

The ability to reason vanished. She stopped thinking altogether, and instinct took over as she flapped weakly at the restraints, not recalling why she was doing it. She forgot that she had been in a raft with the three people she loved most in the world. She forgot that she was a teenager named Holly and that she had hair and eyes and hands and feet.

She was nothing but gray inside and out. The world was a flat fog color and so were her images, thoughts, and emotions. Numb and empty, she drifted in a bottomless well of nothingness, flat-lining, ceasing. She couldn't say it was a pleasant place to be. She couldn't say it was anything.

Though she didn't really know it, she finally exhaled. Eagerly she sucked in brackish river water. It filled her lungs, and her eyes rolled back in her head as her death throes began.

Struggling, wriggling like a hooked fish, her body tried to cough, to expel the suffocating fluid. It was no use; she was as good as dead. Her eyes fluttered shut.

And then, through her lids, she saw the most exquisite shade of blue. It was the color of neon tetras, though she couldn't articulate that. It shimmered like some underwater grace note at the end of a movie; she neither reached toward it nor shrank from it, because her brain didn't register it. It didn't register anything. Oxygen-starved, it was very nearly dead.

The glow glittered, then coalesced. It became a figure, and had any part of Holly's brain still been taking in and processing data, it would have reported the sight of a woman in a long-sleeved dress of gray wool and gold trimming, astonishingly beautiful, with curls of black hair mushrooming in the water. Her compassionate gaze was chestnut and ebony as she reached toward Holly.

Run. Flee, escape, don't stop to pack your belongings. Alors, she will perish if you do not go now. Maintenaint, a c'est moment la; vite, je vous en prie. . . .

Nightmare, Holly thought fuzzily. *Last year. Nightmare.* . . .

The figure raised forth her right hand; a leather glove was wrapped around her hand, and on it perched a large gray bird. She hefted the bird through the water, and it moved its wings through the rush torrent, toward Holly.

"We aren't witches!" her father shouted in her memory.

And her mother: "I know what I saw! I know what I saw in Holly's room!"

Go, take her from here; they will find her and kill her . . . je vous en prie . . . je vous en prie, Daniel de Cahors. . . .

"Je vous en prie," the man in the deer's head whispered heartbreakingly.

It was Barley Moon, the time of harvest, and the forest was warm and giving, like a woman. The man was staked to a copse of chestnut trees, his chest streaked with his own blood.

The Circle was drawn, the tallow candles set for lighting.

"I am so sorry for him, Maman," Isabeau whispered to her mother. The lady of the manor was dressed in raven silks, silver threads chasing scarlet throughout, as were the others in the Circle—there were thirteen this night, including her newly widowed mother's new husband, who was her mother's dead husband's brother, named Robert, and the sacrifice, the quaking man in the dead deer's head, who knew that he would soon die.

The Circle's beautiful familiar, the hawk Pandion, jingled her bells as she observed from her perch, which had been fashioned from bones of the de Cahorses' bitterest enemy . . . the Deveraux. She was eager for the kill; she would snatch the man's soul as it escaped his body, and daintily nibble at its edges until others caught hold of it for their own purposes.

"It is a better death," Catherine de Cahors insisted, smiling down on her child. She petted Isabeau's hair with one hand. In the other hand she held the bloody dagger. It was she who had carved the sigils into the man's chest. Her husband, Robert, had felt compelled to restrain her, reminding her that torture was not a part of tonight's rite. It was to be a good, clean execution. "His wagging tongue would have sent him to the stake eventually. He would have burned, a horrible way to die. This way . . ."

They were interrupted by a figure wearing the silver and black livery of Cahors; he raced to the edge of the Circle and dropped to his knees directly before the masked and cloaked Robert. *Robert's height must have given him away,* Isabeau thought.

"The Deveraux . . . the fire," the servant gasped. "They have managed it."

Pandion threw back her head and shrieked in lamentation. The entire Circle looked at one another in shock from behind their animal masks. Several of them sank to their knees in despair.

Isabeau was chilled, within and without. The Deveraux had been searching for the secret of the Black Fire for centuries. Now that they had it . . . what would become of the Cahors? Of anyone who stood in the way of the Deveraux?

Isabeau's mother covered her heart with her arms and cried, "*Alors,* Notre Dame! Protect us this night, our Lady Goddess!"

"This is a dark night," said one of the others. "A night rife with evil. The lowest, when it was to have been a joyous Lammas, this man's ripe death adding to the Harvest bounty. . . ."

"We are undone," a cloaked woman keened. "We are doomed."

"Damn you for your cowardice," Robert murmured in a low, dangerous voice. "We are not."

He tore off his mask, grabbed the dagger from his wife, and walked calmly to the sacrifice. Without a moment's hesitation he yanked the man's head back by the hair and cut his throat. Blood spurted, covering those nearby while others darted forward to receive the blessing. Pandion swooped down from her perch, soaring into the gushing heat, the bells on her ankles clattering with eagerness.

Isabeau's mother urged her toward the man's body. "Take the blessing," she told her daughter. "There is wild work ahead, and you must be prepared to do your part."

Isabeau stumbled forward, shutting her eyes, glancing away. Her mother took her chin and firmly turned her face toward the stream of steaming, crimson liquid.

"*Non, non,*" she protested as the blood ran into her mouth. She felt defiled, disgusted.

The gushing blood seemed to fill her vision. . . .

★ ★ ★

Holly woke up. As far as she could tell, she lay on the riverbank. The sound of rushing water filled her pounding head; she was shaking violently from head to toe and her teeth were chattering. She tried to move, but couldn't tell if she succeeded. She was completely numb.

"Mmm . . . ," she managed, struggling to call for her mother.

All she heard, all she knew, was the rushing of the river. And then . . . the flapping of a bird's wings. They sounded enormous, and in her confusion she thought it was diving for her, ready to swoop her up like a tiny, waterlogged mouse.

Her lids flickered up at the sky; a bird did hover against the moon, a startling silhouette.

Then she lost consciousness again. Her coldness faded, replaced by soothing warmth. . . .

The blood is so warm, she thought, drifting. *See how it steams in the night air. . . .*

Again, the sound of rushing water. Again the deathly chill.

The screech of a bird of prey . . .

★ ★ ★

Then once more Holly saw the hot, steaming blood—and something new: a vile, acrid odor that reeked of charnel houses and dungeon terrors. Something very evil, very wrong, very *hungry* crept toward her, unfurling slowly, like fingers of mist seeking her out, sneaking over branch and rock to find her wrist, encircle it, enclose it.

Someone—or something—whispered low and deep and seductively, *"I claim thee, Isabeau Cahors, by night and Barley Moon. Thou art mine."*

And from the darkness above the circle a massive falcon dove straight for Pandion, its talons and beak flashing and savage. . . .

"No!" Holly cried into the darkness.

A bird's wings flapped, then were still.

She was shivering with cold; and she was alive.

A brilliant yellow light struck her full force in the face. Holly whimpered as the light moved, bobbing up and down, then lowered as the figure holding it squatted and peered at her.

It was a heavyset woman dressed like a forest ranger. She said, "It's okay, honey, we're here now." Over her shoulder, she yelled, "Found a survivor!"

A ragged cheer rose up, and Holly burst into frightened, desperate tears.

Kari Hardwicke had wrapped herself in a simple, cream-colored robe of lightweight gauze that was totally see-through and that clung everywhere. In her slashed blond hair she had entwined a few wildflowers, and she had bronzed her cheeks and shoulders. Her feet were bare and she had dabbed patchouli oil in all the strategic places.

Spellcasters loved patchouli oil.

Now she curled herself around Jer Deveraux as he brooded silently before her fireplace. He had burst through her door with the storm, fierce and enraged, but he wouldn't tell her what was wrong. He had accepted the glass of cab she offered him and drawn up her leather chair before her fireplace. He sipped, and he fell silent, his dark eyes practically igniting the logs in the fireplace.

Hell hath no fury like Jeraud Deveraux when he's in a temper.

That made her want him all the more. There was something about Jer she couldn't explain. It wasn't simply his air of command, as if he could make one do his slightest bidding merely by raising one eyebrow. Nor was it his sharp wit, or his drive; the pull he had on almost everyone who knew him; the way he fascinated people, both men and women, who would fall to discussing him once he had left a room.

It was all that combined with his astonishing looks. His brown-black eyes were set deep into his face beneath dark brown eyebrows. His features were sharply defined, his cheekbones high above hollows shaded by the soft light in the room. Unlike his father and his brother, he was clean shaven; his jaw was sharp and angular, and his lips looked soft. He worked out, and it showed in his broad shoulders, covered for the moment by a black sweater. Like his family members, he wore black nearly all the time, adding to his allure of danger and sensuality.

But it's even more that that, Kari thought now. *He's . . . how does the old song go?*

A magic man.

Heavy rain rattled the dormer window of her funky student apartment; the storm matched his mood, but she was determined to shake him out of it. It was Lammastide, the witches' harvest night, and she knew he would leave in a while to go perform some kind of ritual with Eli, his brother, and Michael, his father. They were "observant," as he liked to phrase it . . . and she wanted him to take her with him tonight. She wanted to know what they did in secret. Their rites, their spells . . . all of it.

The Deveraux men are warlocks, she thought.

But use that word in front of Jer, and he would deny it.

In the early days of their relationship—a year ago, now, how it had flown!—he had been eager to bring her into the fold. Back then, he was her teaching assistant, and he, a newbie undergrad; after the first time they'd gone to bed together, he had told her he would share his "mysteries" with her. He had hinted about an ancient family Book of Spells.

She was thrilled. She was getting her PhD in folklore, a path she had chosen so that she could investigate magic and shamanism with the full resources of the university behind her. The University of Washington at Seattle treated Native American belief systems with the utmost respect; thus, her field of endeavor was encouraged, and never challenged.

But it wasn't simply Northwestern magic that interested her. She was fascinated by European magic . . . especially black magic. And though, like being a bona fide warlock he denied that his family practiced the Dark Art, she was fairly certain they spent more time in the shadows than they did in the diffuse light of Wicca. Yet she maintained the fiction that he practiced one of the Wicca traditions; it was what he had told her.

"I've dressed like the Barley Maid," she said now,

moving between him and the fireplace and stretching out her arms to him. He looked startled and—she hated to admit it—irritated by her interruption of his reverie.

Jer, you loved me once, she thought anxiously. *You were thrilled that a glamorous "older woman" graduate student wanted you, a mere freshman. What did I do wrong?*

I want you to come back to me. Not just treading water with me, but back into the deluge, the flood that was all that passion you poured into me. We made such waves . . . we drowned in such amazing ecstasy. . . .

"I've read that if we make love tonight, whatever spells we cast will be extra powerful." She smiled lustily.

"That's true," he said, giving her that much. His smile was gentle, tinged with both sadness and great wisdom. "And you've cast quite a spell on me, Kari. You're beautiful."

She let herself believe he was sincere, and he rose from his chair, scooped her up in his arms, and carried her into her bedroom.

ABOUT THE AUTHORS

NANCY HOLDER has published more than seventy-eight books, including novels and episode guide books about *Buffy the Vampire Slayer* and *Angel* for Simon Pulse. She has received five Bram Stoker awards for her supernatural fiction and is the coauthor of the *New York Times* bestselling Wicked series. She lives in San Diego with her daughter, Belle, their two cats, and their two Corgis. Visit her at nancyholder.com.

DEBBIE VIGUIÉ is the coauthor of the *New York Times* bestselling Wicked series and several additional Simon Pulse books, including the Once upon a Time novels *Violet Eyes* and *Midnight Pearls*. She lives in Florida with her husband, Scott, and their cat, Schrödinger. Visit her at debbieviguie.com.